W9-BIR-074

Praise for *Threshold*

"[Caitlín R. Kiernan is] the most singular voice to enter the genre since Neil Gaiman popped up in graphic novels and Stephen King made movies live inside books. . . . Beginning with the instant-classic *Silk* and continuing through her short fiction to this extraordinary new novel, Kiernan hasn't missed a step yet. . . . If you haven't sampled her work yet, you haven't really been reading the *future* of horror and dark fantasy, only its past."

—Lisa DuMond, SF Site, MEviews.com

Praise for *Silk*

"A debut novel of a level of accomplishment most young horror/ dark fantasy writers could not begin to approach. [Caitlín R. Kiernan's] tightly focused, unsparing, entranced gaze finds significance and beauty in the wasted landscape it surveys."   —Peter Straub

"A remarkable novel. [Caitlín Kiernan] tells a powerful and disturbing story with creepy intensity and a gift for language that borders on the scary. Deeply, wonderfully, magnificently nasty."

—Neil Gaiman

"Caitlín Kiernan writes like a Gothic cathedral on fire. If the title alone doesn't make you want to read *Silk,* the first page will do the trick. Kiernan's work is populated with the physically freaky, mentally unstable, sexually marginalized characters who have caused so much consternation in conventional circles—but Caitlín Kiernan is headed in an entirely different direction. Her unfolding of strange events evokes not horror, but a far larger sense of awe."

—Poppy Z. Brite

continued . . .

"[Kiernan] has what it takes to excite me as a reader . . . think of Poppy Z. Brite with slightly more accessible prose and characters who aren't quite so outré . . . I just loved this book and can't wait to see what she writes next."
— Charles de Lint

"I'm on safe ground wagering that Caitlín R. Kiernan's *Silk* is most certainly going to be on the short-list of finalists for 1998 . . . an observational coming-of-age novel that astutely and empathetically provides connection between characters and readers . . . an incremental triumph of texture and layering, harkening back to an earlier tradition of supernatural fiction, an era when storytelling took as much time as it needed to accrue the maximum effect. . . . Hers is a dark and mellifluous voice to which we should all listen."
— *Locus*

"Kiernan's writing is meaty, atmospheric, and evocative; her prose is well-crafted and terrifically engaging. . . . *Silk* is a strong first showing and Kiernan should have a bright future ahead of her."
— *Fangoria*

"A novel with an uncommonly rich texture . . . should establish [Kiernan] as an important writer of the future. This novel transcends the goth genre."
— *Necrofile*

"[S]pun as beautifully as the many webs within. . . . [Y]ou absolutely must read it."
— *Carpe Noctem*

"A masterful story by an extraordinary new voice in literature . . . on her way to becoming an incredibly well-known—and well-respected—talent. *Silk* is simply the extraordinary beginning of an incredible journey, both for Kiernan and her readers."
— *Alabama Forum*

THRESHOLD

A Novel of Deep Time

Caitlín R. Kiernan

A ROC BOOK

This book is best read aloud.—CRK

ROC
Published by New American Library, a division of
Penguin Putnam Inc., 375 Hudson Street, New York, New York 10014, U.S.A.
Penguin Books Ltd, 80 Strand, London WC2R ORL, England
Penguin Books Australia Ltd, Ringwood, Victoria, Australia
Penguin Books Canada Ltd, 10 Alcorn Avenue, Toronto, Ontario, Canada M4V 3B2
Penguin Books (N.Z.) Ltd, 182–190 Wairau Road, Auckland 10, New Zealand

Penguin Books Ltd, Registered Offices: Harmondsworth, Middlesex, England

First published by Roc, an imprint of New American Library,
a division of Penguin Putnam Inc.

First Printing, November 2001

1   3   5   7   9   10   8   6   4   2

Copyright © Caitlín R. Kiernan, 2001

All rights reserved

RoC REGISTERED TRADEMARK—MARCA REGISTRADA

LIBRARY OF CONGRESS CATALOGING-IN-PUBLICATION DATA:
Kiernan, Caitlín R.
Threshold / Caitlín R. Kiernan.
p. cm.
ISBN 0-451-45858-3
1. Teenage girls—Fiction.   2. Angels—Fiction.   I. Title.
PS3561.I358 T48 2001
813'.54—dc21   2001031938

Printed in the United States of America

Without limiting the rights under copyright reserved above, no part of this publication may
be reproduced, stored in or introduced into a retrieval system, or transmitted, in any form, or
by any means (electronic, mechanical, photocopying, recording, or otherwise), without the
prior written permission of both the copyright owner and the above publisher of this book.

PUBLISHER'S NOTE
This is a work of fiction. Names, characters, places, and incidents are either the product of
the author's imagination or are used fictitiously, and any resemblance to actual persons, living or dead, business establishments, events, or locales is entirely coincidental.

BOOKS ARE AVAILABLE AT QUANTITY DISCOUNTS WHEN USED TO PROMOTE PRODUCTS OR SER-
VICES. FOR INFORMATION PLEASE WRITE TO PREMIUM MARKETING DIVISION, PENGUIN PUT-
NAM INC., 375 HUDSON STREET, NEW YORK, NEW YORK 10014.

For my grandfather and grandmother,
Gordy Monroe Ramey and Mary Elizabeth Ramey,
who were the first to show me fossils
and teach me what they mean.

In Memory of Elizabeth Tillman Aldridge
(1970–1995)

AUTHOR'S NOTE

I WISH first to acknowledge Dr. Riccardo Levi-Setti's *Trilobites* (2nd Edition, 1993, University of Chicago Press) as an indispensable resource during the writing of this novel. Readers unfamiliar with the biology and evolution of the Trilobita are referred to this wonderful book. I am likewise grateful to the Birmingham Historical Society and the staff of the Southern Research Department of the Birmingham Public Library for their assistance in obtaining archival material relating to the construction of the Birmingham water works tunnel in 1888. Seamus Heaney's recent translation of *Beowulf* (Farrar, Straus & Giroux, 2000) was also particularly helpful, as was J. R. R. Tolkien's essay "The Monsters and the Critics." Readers will recognize the influence of works by Algernon Blackwood (especially "The Willows"), Lewis Carroll, and Henry Wadsworth Longfellow.

Finally, I remain indebted to the writings of Carl Jung and Joseph Campbell, William Butler Yeats and Matthew Arnold, and Charles Fort, all of which have served time and again as points of inspiration and understanding. Special thanks to Jada, Jenny, Kathryn, Scott, and my agent, Merrilee Heifetz, for getting me through this one.

"All tales may come true; and yet, at the last, redeemed, they may be as like and as unlike the forms that we give them as Man, finally redeemed, will be like and unlike the fallen that we know."

—J. R. R. TOLKIEN (1947)

In the Garden of Proserpine

THE girl named Chance is standing in the rain, plain and skinny-tall girl shivering beneath the April night sky pissing rain like icywet needles, and she can't stop giggling. She's been giggling for almost half an hour now, at least since they left Deacon's apartment where the three of them finished off a dime bag of pot, Chance and Deacon and Elise getting stoned while they listened to Billie Holiday and argued about whether or not they'd all wind up in jail if they broke into the old water works tunnel on the mountain.

"Jesus, Deke," Elise says, "will you *please* hurry the hell up? I'm freezing my ass off out here," shaky, stammered words because her teeth are chattering so bad and Chance is trying very hard to stop giggling, doesn't want to laugh at poor Elise soaked straight to the bone, drowned-rat Elise. She tries to imagine the cops pulling into the little lot at the bottom of the park, a dozen Birmingham cops with their strobing cop-car lights and blaring sirens, guns and shiny, silver handcuffs.

"Well, don't you worry about that," Deacon says, and then he drops the bolt cutter in the mud and has to bend over to look for it. "There's every reason to believe we'll all drown first."

And that's it for the scary cops and Chance is giggling again, laughing until her stomach hurts and Elise is glaring at her. She sits down in the wet grass and the sticky, red mud, sits down before she falls down, and "At least hyena girl here's having a good time," Elise mumbles between her chattering teeth.

Deacon has the bolt cutter again, fumbles around in the dark for a moment before he manages to get its razor jaws over the hasp of the rusty padlock and he slices through tempered steel like it was butter. The lock falls off the gate and lands with a loud splash in a puddle at his feet. "Oh ye of little faith," he says, pulling away the heavy chain looped through the bars to hold the wrought-iron gate closed, and Elise claps her hands, slow and sarcastic applause as the gate swings open with an ugly, grinding noise. Rust on rust creak and squeal like the hull of a ship ripping wide, violated, shearing sound, steel and ice, and Chance is lying on her back staring up at the raindrops plunging towards her, kicked out of heaven and plunging towards the soggy earth.

"'Down, down, down,'" she says, kindly quoting Lewis Carroll for the rain, "'Would the fall never come to an end? I wonder how many miles I've fallen . . .'"

"You want to just leave her out here?" Elise asks, but Deacon is already hauling Chance to her feet. She shivers and leans against him, stealing the warmth off him, and kisses his stubbly chin, the arch of his long nose. "C'mon, girlie girl," he says, "shake a leg," one arm around her tight as they step through the low, square arch leading into the tunnel. "Time to go forth and explore the Stygian bowels of the world."

Chance laughs, but there was something strange and sad about the rain that she can't quite remember and she doesn't start giggling again.

This rough, stone wall set into the side of the mountain more than a hundred years ago, blockhouse of stone and mortar and dank air to cap the north end of the tunnel, mushroom and mud and mildew air, and "All aboard," Elise says and she pulls the gate shut behind them. Dull clang of iron on stone and *She's closing us in*, Chance thinks and maybe she's just a little afraid now, the pot starting to make her paranoid, but then Deacon has his flashlight out and he plays it across the slippery walls, the punky, worm-gnawed support beams overhead. "What's *that*?" Elise asks and Deacon shines the light at the two great pipes that fill up most of the blockhouse, pipes like the mountain's steel intestines, like something from an H. R. Giger painting; neither animal nor mineral, organs trapped somewhere in between.

Deacon puts one big hand on the closest pipe and "Damn," he says. "It's cold," and Chance shivers again, opens her eyes and tries to remember having closed them. She's alone and lying on the floor of the tunnel, lying in mud and water, and Deacon's discarded flashlight isn't very far away, close enough that she can reach out and touch it. It's not shining very brightly anymore, batteries running low and when they're gone there won't be anything but this night beneath the mountain that never has a morning.

"Deacon?" she calls out and her voice booms and echoes off the tunnel walls, and no one answers anyway. Just the steady, measured drip of water, and she gets up, dizzy so she leans against one of the pipes. The ceiling low and she has to be careful not to hit her head, barely six feet, barely room to stand; Chance picks up the flashlight, something solid and radiant against the dark, against the disorientation and her head crammed too full of marijuana smoke and the cold. She points the flashlight at the tunnel wall, squints at the rock, and there's sandstone the bruised color of an overripe plum.

Ferruginous sandstone, she thinks, sober, safe geologist thought getting in or out through the dumbing fog behind her eyes. Ferruginous sandstone, so she must be at least eighty yards or more into the tunnel, past the limestone, beyond the Ordovician and into the lowermost Silurian and the thick seams of iron ore. She looks at the angle of the rocks, gentle slant of sea-floor beds lifted hundreds of millions of years ago, collision of continents to raise mountains, and "It's cold," Deacon says again. Deacon awestruck, marveling at the pipe beneath his hand, and "Yeah, well, me too," Elise says.

A noise behind Chance, then, noise like something damp and heavy, something vast and soft moving through the tunnel, and the sucking undertow squelch of water swirling down a drain; meaty, counterclockwise sound and she turns and shines the flashlight at the place she thinks it's coming from. But there's only Elise, standing a few feet away and squinting into the flashlight. She's naked, nothing against her skin but mud and tunnel slime, the chill air, and there are tears streaking her dirty face. Sloe-eyed Elise, and maybe Chance has never really noticed before how beautiful she is, even now, scared and filthy, or especially now, her perfect mouth, the fragile slant of her shoulders, and she holds one hand up, like the light hurts her eyes or she doesn't want Chance to see.

"He told me not to look, Chance," she sobs. "He told me not to look at it, but I had to see."

And then the flashlight flickers and dies and the dark rushes around them like a flood, black past black, viscous bottom of the ocean blackness that wraps itself around them and Elise screams. *No,* Chance thinks, *don't do that. Don't do that because you'll swallow and it'll get inside you,* or she's trying to talk but can't remember how to shape the words, how to put her tongue and teeth together to make sounds.

Something brushes by her in the dark, and *It's cold,* she thinks. *Yes, it* is *cold,* cold as a sky without stars, as a grave, and then the flashlight flickers dimly back to life. But Elise is gone again, and there are only the pipes leading deeper into the tunnel, deeper into the punctured, bitter heart of the mountain.

"Did you hear that?"

And Elise laughs, knows that Deacon's only trying to frighten her, but maybe Chance heard it too, starts to say so and "No," he says, shining the brilliant flashlight beam down the length of the pipes.

"Listen."

Chance opens her eyes and stares into the night sky that is only dark, into the spring rain that whispers through the trees and takes away her tears. She can hear Elise somewhere near, incoherent, crying and Deacon's trying to comfort her.

" '. . . how many miles I've fallen by this time?' " but no one hears her, so no one answers, either, and the girl named Chance closes her eyes again and lets the rain kiss her face and hide the things she never saw.

PART I

Maps and Legends

"In our dreams the ageless perils, gargoyles, trials, secret helpers, and instructive figures are nightly still encountered; and in their forms we may see reflected not only the whole picture of our present case, but also the clue to what we must do to be saved."

—JOSEPH CAMPBELL (1949)

CHAPTER ONE

Chance

Morning after the funeral, latest funeral in what seems to Chance Matthews to have become a litany of caskets and wreaths and frowning undertakers that might go on forever, if there were anyone left she cared about, anyone left to die. All night she drove the narrow back roads north of the city, countrydark roads, just her and a pint bottle of Wild Turkey, the music blaring loud from her tape deck, chasing the headlights of her old Impala, trying to escape and knowing there was no way to go that far, that fast. No gravity greater than the pull of her loss and now Chance sits on the hood of the car as the summer sun bleeds in through the trees on Red Mountain, seeps hot between dogwood and hackberry branches, and soon it will burn away the dew that sequin speckles the front yard of her dead grandparents' house. The Impala's engine pops and clicks its secret, exhausted car language as it cools after the long and restless night.

Chance squints at the rising sun, wishes she could push it back down, chase it away to the east forever and hang onto the night, the night and her drunkenness fading to hangover and shadows. Maybe no solace in the dark but at least not this hateful reminder that the world hasn't stopped turning, that it won't, no matter how much she hurts.

"What the fuck now, Grandpa?" she whispers and her voice just another thing that seems wrong, that seems improper, unseemly to be alive and breathing much less talking, but she asks again, anyway, and louder this time, "What the fuck now?"

And no answer but the birds and the traffic down on Sixteenth Avenue, the waking-up sounds, the people-going-on-about-their-business sounds, as if nothing at all has changed but the day of the week, the numbers on a calendar. Chance closes her eyes and at least then there's only the noise, only the hint of light filtered through her eyelids. And maybe that's the trick, she thinks, to *make* a night to hide inside, a night that doesn't have to stop until the emptiness inside her is gone and she can stand the thought of another sunrise, the thought of routine.

So Chance sits on the hood, green eyes closed and feeling the unwelcome July sun across her face, the gentler heat rising from the Impala's engine block through her jeans, and she imagines all the ways to fashion a night, how to sew indigo skies and not even any stars or the moon unless she wants them there, unless she cuts holes for them to shine through, obsidian skies if that's what it takes. A night to wrap around her to match the night coiled beneath her skin, eating her alive.

Stop feeling sorry for yourself, Chance, her grandfather's voice somewhere right behind her, ghostvoice from the passenger seat of the Impala, and Chance scrambles off the hood, all thoughts of retreat and nocturnal architecture gone in that instant of impossible surprise. But there's no one and nothing standing by the car but her, and Chance feels foolish and ashamed and angry all at once, meaner emotions swimming against her grief, silverbright flotsam to snag her attention for an instant before they drift away and there's nothing but the sadness again. So not her grandfather's voice at all, only her memory of her grandfather's voice, some part of herself so sick of the loss and the guilt and the deadness inside speaking in a voice that maybe she'll pay attention to, maybe, and Chance leans forward, both palms open on the stillwarm hood of the Chevy and she's crying again before she can stop the tears, can't stop what she doesn't see coming. And nothing to do but stand there, little drops of water and salt wringing themselves from her eyes to splash across the rustorange car.

◉

Her great-grandfather built this house, something fine a hundred years ago and it's not like it hasn't been kept up, not like it's been allowed to sink into ruin and neglect the way so many its age have, and this is the house where Chance has lived since she was five years old. Her great-grandfather a schoolteacher who married a schoolteacher and he built his new bride this modest shelter of gingerbread shingles and walls that have never been painted any color but the same sensible white, sandstone block and mortar chimneys and a lightning rod fixed to one high cornice where gable meets sky, pointing like a cast-iron finger towards heaven. And way up high, the window into what was the attic long before it became Chance's bedroom.

She climbs the stone steps slow, up to the big front porch that stretches halfway around the house. And there's the Boston fern and its shattered red clay pot, soil strewn across the whitewashed porch boards and the fronds already going brown. Her grandfather was carrying the fern out to the porch, a whole morning spent repotting the root-bound plant and now it marks the spot where he was standing when his heart stopped beating for the last time. No one's picked it up, swept away the dirt and broken pottery shards, but there are footprints in the dry, black soil, footprints of paramedics and policemen, and in places the dirt is ground deeply into the wood, pressed flat where Joe Matthews lay two whole hours before Chance came home and found the body already cold and stiff.

She kicks the wad of wilting fern and dirt and for a second it's airborne, then skitters and rolls across the porch, trailing rootsy bits of itself as it goes, finally coming to rest against another, unbroken pot, a huge rhododendron to shade the dying fern from the morning sun. And she doesn't feel any better, worse maybe, because the fern was something her grandfather cared about. She looks quickly away from it, one hand fast into a pocket of her jeans for her keys and in a moment the front door swings open on the foyer, the mustycool, familiar smell of the house beyond spilling out around her.

She crosses the threshold, shoescuffed strip of varnished pine to mark her reluctant steps, right foot across, left foot next, and she's passed from the indecent brightness of morning into the shadows and leftover scraps of night waiting inside; a house to anyone passing by but Chance knows that it's become something more: a dim and whispering box to hold all the memories of her life, a memorial. Frame for a thousand reminders she doesn't need because she couldn't forget if she tried, wouldn't if she could. And she just wants it to be a plain old house again.

She slowly pulls the front door shut behind her and sits on the floor, still cool and the door at her back now, whole world at her back, and she squints down the long hall running past the stairs all the way back to the kitchen and the room where her grandfather kept all his cardboard boxes and wooden crates of rocks, the cloth and plastic bags of fossils and minerals that have never been opened or cleaned or labeled. Two rooms and between them a gaudy, narrow rectangle of daylight, day sneaking in through the lead-glass window set into the back door.

And it all washes back over her again, the indisputable reality of it, truth that smells like carnations and a shovelful of red cemetery dirt—that they are *dead,* gone, *all* of them, and she's as alone at twenty-three as someone who has outlived an entire lifetime of family and friends and lovers. An old, old woman in such young skin and the truth and her mind push each other away, opposing magnetic poles, and Chance shuts her eyes again and in a moment the air has stopped smelling like funerals and there's nothing but the velvetsoft odor of dust and the ghost of her grandfather's pipe.

◉

The first funeral when her parents died in a car wreck and Chance was left alive, backseat survivor bruised black and purple and her left arm broken in two different places, but still plenty alive enough to watch their caskets being lowered into the ground, to stand between her grandparents while a minister read things she didn't understand from the Bible, things she didn't want to understand, only wanting to go home, and what she remembers most is the car ride back to her grandparents' house, listening quietly while they argued because her mother and father weren't Christians but there had been a minister anyway.

"I told them we didn't want it," her grandmother kept saying. "I told them that Henry and Carol said *they* didn't want it and you know damn well that they didn't, you know how many times they *said* they didn't."

"Mrs. Sawyer wanted it," her grandfather said, sounding as tired as Chance, and her grandmother blew her nose loud into her handkerchief, made an angry sound through her teeth, and "It wasn't Mrs. Sawyer's funeral, Joe," she said. Her grandfather didn't reply, and Chance's arm hurt but she was too tired to cry anymore, watched the houses and trees and fireplugs slipping past instead.

So she went to live with them in their big house on the mountain above the city, and six weeks later a doctor cut the plaster cast off her arm, bones healed and bruises fading and no one much seemed to notice all the *other* ways she had been hurt. In the beginning, whenever her grandmother visited her parents' graves, Chance was always with her, flowerbright bouquets and her last name carved deep in granite like a spelling lesson. Sometimes she asked questions and "Your mom and dad are asleep," her grandmother would reply, or "You'll understand when you're a little older," but never sounding as if she believed what she was saying.

Sometimes her grandmother would wander among the other tombstones, reading the other names aloud or to herself, and Chance would lie down on the green cemetery grass, her ear pressed against the earth, listening for her father's snore, the way her mother sometimes talked in her sleep. But never anything, and finally her grandmother caught her, made her promise never to do it again.

"That's disrespectful, lying on someone's grave like that," and then she was crying too hard to explain what she meant.

And one night, when Chance was six and had a cold so bad she'd already missed a week of school, she woke up and her mother was sitting in the chair beside her bedroom window, sitting very still and watching her, the January moonlight shining through her like she was made of glass. Her eyes like pearls and Chance stared back at her, fevery, and her throat too raw to say anything, wishing she had a drink of water or a Grapico but afraid her mother might disappear if she moved. She finally drifted back to sleep, and when she woke again it was morning and her mother was gone, nothing in the chair but winterpale sunlight on the cover of *McElligot's Pool* by Dr. Seuss. She told her grandmother, who said it had been a dream, only a dream because of the fever, said that people with bad fevers sometimes dreamed very strange things, but she sat up with Chance the next night, and the next, sat there in the chair where her mother had sat, every night until she was well again. Standing guard or waiting and Chance never asked which.

And then, fifteen years old when her grandmother hung herself from the lowest limb of a water oak behind the house, coarse knots tied around strong wood and her frail neck and she stood on a ladder to reach, stepped off to fall. A long night of thunder and lightning, and Chance, teenage girl caught between two storms, the one raging outside and the one trapped inside the house, laid awake listening to the raindrops shattering themselves against the roof and windows. Listening to her grandparents downstairs, up later than usual and arguing, angry, bitter words passing between them, thrown like china cups and saucers. She'd seen it coming, like the storm clouds building themselves anvil-tall across the western horizon just before dark. Always so hot in her attic room by August, nothing but an old electric desk fan, and that night Chance hadn't bothered to turn down the covers, had tried to read for an hour or so. But the storm and their voices and the sweat that dripped from her face to splotch the pages all too distracting and finally she'd given up and the secondhand paperback copy of *Dandelion Wine* folded open to Chapter Five on the floor, discarded for the night, while she tried to understand what they were fighting about. A word here, half a sentence there, muffled puzzle rising up through the floorboards.

". . . but I'm not the one trying to pretend it never even happened, now am I?"

"I don't know what you want from me, Esther."

"Just stop treating me like I'm crazy so you don't have to think about it anymore," and a door slamming very hard somewhere in the house then, before the last word, the very last word and maybe she didn't even hear that part at all, or heard it wrong; the sounds too faint, housesifted, her grandmother sobbing and one of them (Chance was never sure which, if either) said, *"Dicranurus,"* one word of Latin or Greek that meant nothing to her, repeated again and again like a litany or invocation, but not that unusual to hear Latin in the house, her grandfather still teaching geology at the university, her grandmother a retired paleontologist, so the word made strange only by circumstance, by context, that she was hearing it *then*. She found a pencil on her desk, schoolyellow No. 2 Ticonderoga nub, and scribbled a phonetic spelling inside the back cover of *Dandelion Wine* before she lay back down.

And then she fell asleep, and dreamed that the thunder was something more than simple sound, something dark and brooding far above the world and the rain fell from it in hissing, acid streaks the color of old motor oil, greasy rain to steam on the grass and trees, to clot in the rain spouts and mud holes. The sound of her grandfather's cries getting through faint at first, old man's voice basketwoven between the grayblack rain, between the deafening movements of the thing in the sky. Chance would not remember waking up, coming awake by syrupslow degrees and then she was standing in her underwear and a mostly white Smashing Pumpkins T-shirt on the back porch and this rain was cold and blacker than in her dream. Her grandfather was hanging onto a ladder, halfway up a ladder and wrestling desperately with something dangling from a limb of the big oak tree.

"Grandpa!" Chance yelled, shouting to be heard above the crash and wail of the thunderstorm. "Help me, Chance," and her grandfather not looking away from the limp thing in the tree. "Jesus Christ, help me get her *down.*" And by then Chance *could* see, her mind not yet ready to believe what she was seeing but that didn't make it any less so. The thing in the tree moved, turning in the wind or maybe from the force of her grandfather sawing at the rope with a kitchen knife. Chance stepped towards the ladder, bare feet in mud and wet grass and part of her still wandering in the nightmare, not wanting the oily rain to touch her, not wanting to look up. But the rope broke, snapped like a firecracker and her grandmother's body fell lifeless to the ground.

A few hours after her grandmother's funeral and the house filled with aunts and uncles and cousins, people Chance didn't really know and didn't want to see, at least no ministers this time but everyone bringing food like your grandmother dying made you want to fucking eat. The house stinking of casseroles and hams and butter beans, apple pies and chocolate cake, and Joe Matthews drunk in the front parlor, drinking glass after glass of Jack Daniel's whiskey like it was water, water to make him forget. Chance was hiding in the library and she could hear the women pretending to be busy in the kitchen, her Great-uncle William telling her grandfather, "That ain't gonna help, Joe. You're just gonna make yourself sick, that's all. You need to eat something. Let me have Patsy get you some coffee and something to eat."

Chance wanting to defend her grandfather, but not about to leave the library, dustysafe sanctuary of shelves and glass cases and the musty smell of all the books, the door locked from the inside against birdnervous aunts who thought maybe a few slabs of smoked ham and a spoonful of mashed potatoes would make anything better, would make anything right again. Chance was sitting at the big, walnut-burl table her grandparents had always used for looking over their topographic and geologic maps, their stratigraphic sections, big, unpolished chunks of powderwhite Sylacauga marble at each corner for paperweights, green felt glued to the bottom of the rocks so they wouldn't scratch the wood; this place for finding points of reference, orientation, place for protractors and slide-rule calculations, place for not being lost—and that's where she found the book, *Handwörterbuch der Naturwissenshaften,* 1933, and Chance's eyes moving absently down a yellowed page, detailed engravings of trilobites and they had always been her favorite fossils, her grandmother's specialty. There were hundreds or thousands of the petrified arthropods tucked away in cabinets and drawers throughout the house, most smaller than a thumbnail, but a few giants over a foot long. And so nothing out of the ordinary about this page, German and Latin, Devonian trilobites of the subfamily Miraspidinae, illustrations of fossils from Africa and Oklahoma, and way down at the bottom of the page Chance found the word, the name she'd scribbled in the back of *Dandelion Wine* three nights before, *Dicranurus,* and a circle drawn around four of the illustrations in faded, red pencil, four views of the trilobite and a red circle like a fairy charm to contain the drawings inside. *Dicranurus monstrosus,* the specimen figured from Oulmes, Morocco, coiled like a tiny gargoyle on the page; spines so long they might as well be tentacles and the twin projections that spiraled like ram's horns from its head. A chill along her arms, then the back of her neck like a gust of cold air and one finger cautiously crossing the red circle, another half second and Chance would have touched the image of the creature itself, but someone started hammering at the door. "Chance? Are you in there, honey? Chance? You should come out and eat something."

And she closed the book, slammed it shut and put it away, had long ago learned the exact position of every book in the library so it wasn't hard to find the empty place where it belonged. "I'm coming," she called to the voice behind the door. "I'll be out in a moment," and always meaning to come back to the book later, always meaning to ask her grandfather about the ugly little trilobite held within the red circle, but in time she forgot it, and forgot the dream of a night sky that leaked steaming, oilslick tears.

❁

Three months before her grandfather's heart attack, the violent last gasps of spring on the scalding heels of summer and the day she broke up with Deacon there were tornadoes, black and twisting clouds touching down all the way from Arkansas to Georgia. Civil defense sirens going off like doomsday and she gave him the news outside the cruddy, little bar where he spent so much of his time.

The place where he sat and drank himself stupid and numb so he didn't have to face the world. All the weeks it had taken her to find the nerve, the careful, padded words, to end something that was already over; Deacon listened and when she was finished he shrugged his bony shoulders, ran the fingers of one hand through his hair and looked up at the angry sky.

"Yeah," he said. "Okay, whatever," so calm, so fucking resigned, and she wanted to hit him then, all his drunkard's bullshit and even the sleeping around on her and that was the first time she'd ever wanted to hit him.

"Jesus, is that all you have to say to me? Three goddamn years and that's all you can think of to say to me?" And he just smiled a little, then, stubbly bum's smile for her and he rubbed hard at his chin.

"What do you *want* me to say, Chance? You know I'm not going to change your mind and I don't feel like arguing with you right now," and so she left him standing there, turned around and stalked quickly, determinedly, away; most of the things she'd meant to say left unspoken, the disbelief at what he'd done with Elise and the sloppy, half-assed way he'd tried to lie about it, the straw that broke the camel's back. All the soursharp anger still bottled up hot behind her eyes and she walked all the way home through the siren wail and thunder- and lightning-scented wind.

And hours later, almost dark and the thunderstorms had blown themselves away east, left the city wet and gray, and Chance was trying to concentrate on a stack of notes for her thesis, envelope of black-and-white photographs of the flat and dimpled skulls of primitive amphibians and fish with fingers, anything but Deacon Silvey and her screwed-up life, when the phone rang and it was Elise. A bad connection from the weather and that brittle, hesitant sound in her voice that said she'd been crying and might start again at the drop of a hat.

"It's my fault, isn't it?" she asked and "No," Chance said, trying hard to sound like she was absolutely certain she meant what she was saying.

"Yes it is. I *know* it is. How can you even pretend that it isn't? If I hadn't—"

"Deke's a fucking drunk and I can't deal with it anymore. That's all the reason I needed."

"You had that much reason from the start, Chance. He was a drunk when you met him."

"So I'm a slow learner. I'm a masochist. Rub it in, why don't you."

Elise sighed and "You wouldn't have ever left him over that," she said. "Not if I hadn't slept with him."

"If you say so. Fine. But I need to go now, Elise. I have work to do."

A long pause and Chance stared at her notes and photographs, listened impatiently to the static and silence as Elise scraped up the courage to finish what she'd begun.

"Chance, what happened to us in the water works tunnel that night? I've been *trying* to remember, trying to be sure that what I do remember is what really did happen . . . but it's all so blurry now, it's all so . . ." and she trailed off, then, running out of words or resolve. Chance kept her eyes on the photos, the incontestable reality of her fossils, the comfort of tangible things, and when she finally replied she used words that were just as safe, just as black and white.

"You can't remember what happened because you were stoned. Hell, Elise, I don't know. We got turned around in there somehow. We got scared and confused and lost track of the time. It was dark. But mostly we were stoned."

"That's what Deacon kept telling me," Elise said, almost whispering. "He doesn't want to talk about it, either."

"I didn't say I didn't want to talk about it."

"But you don't, do you? It frightens you just to think about it."

"Why the fuck do you bother asking me questions if you already know all the answers?"

"I know it's my fault. I *know*."

Chance glanced across the room at the clock beside her bed, the anger too close to the surface now and she knew if she didn't get off the phone very soon she'd end up telling Elise all the things she actually *did* blame her for.

"I'm sorry," she said. "I've got an important meeting with my major professor early in the morning. I'll call you tomorrow, I promise," and "Forgive me," Elise whispered and she hung up first, before Chance could say anything else.

It rained the day they buried Elise, picture-perfect funeral for a girl who swallowed a whole month's worth of Pamelor all at once, then slashed her arms from wrist to elbow, who died alone in an overflowing tub of bloodcold water in a motel that rented rooms to hookers and crack dealers, pay in cash by the hour, and Elise had paid them for a whole night.

"You take just as long as you have to," her grandfather said, one hand resting on her shoulder, gesture they both knew couldn't comfort, and he gave Chance his big, batblack umbrella before following the others back to their cars; but wrong that she should be dry and Elise in the wet ground, so she let it fall from her hand as soon as her grandfather was out of sight and the wind snatched the umbrella away, sent it bouncing and rolling off down the hill until it snagged in the lee of a towering, granite angel. And Chance sat with her while the late April rain needled Oak Hill Cemetery, persistent drizzle to scrub the old and weathered tombstones clean, to wash clayorange rivulets from the fresh wound in the grass where the workmen had just finished filling in her grave. They took away the big, green canopy and the plasticfalse squares of Astroturf, still another month before her marker would be delivered so there was only the uneven mound of mud, the gaudy flowers left to drown under the gray sky, wreaths of roses and carnations, Styrofoam and wire, baby's breath and ferns. Took away all the metal folding chairs, too, except the one Chance was sitting on and maybe they were afraid to ask for it, maybe figured it was better to come back later.

Nothing left to say, no peace to make with a corpse as dead and still as the earth piled in on top of the casket, just the ugly hole inside Chance and nothing that would ever fill that in. A place in the world where Elise had been and that place left as empty as the moment before she was born, as empty as the moment before the universe. *The price you pay for not believing in God,* she thinks.

"Is that it, Elise?" and her voice so loud, so big, in the rainhushed cemetery quiet. "Do people believe so this doesn't have to hurt so much?" and that's all she could say because she was already crying again, her tears stolen by the rain, salt absorbed and if only the storm could begin to dilute the drysocket ache trying to take her apart, if only she could crawl in after Elise and let the fucking worms have them both.

But another hour, hour and a half and night coming early, and she got up, shivering, dripping, took one rose from the grave, retrieved the umbrella, and walked away down the deadstudded hill to where Joe Matthews was waiting for her in the car. And the next day Chance turned twenty-three.

"Forgive me," Elise says and Chance is standing alone outside the building where Deacon lives, Quinlan Castle like a bad joke or the entrance to the world's shoddiest amusement park; bizarre medieval façade wrapped tight around squalid little apartments, cockroaches and one whole side of the building condemned, abandoned to the homeless people who have broken in through first-floor windows and torn up the carpet for their smoky, toxic fires.

"It wasn't your fault," she says, though she knows Elise can't hear her, says it anyway as she climbs the steps, the mustydark stairwell, and the door to Deke's third-floor apartment is painted the color of ketchup. Maybe this time she knows better than to open the door, knows better than to look inside. Maybe this time she can just turn around and what she doesn't know really *won't* hurt her, won't hurt Elise, either. But the door's already open, even though she doesn't remember reaching for the handle, doesn't even remember turning her key in the lock, and nothing's any different this time than all the times before.

"Were you raised in a barn?" Deacon asks and so Chance pulls the door closed behind her. "I can't afford to air-condition the whole goddamn building," and she *knows* the old window unit hasn't worked since last July, the apartment always so hot, never even a breeze through the open windows, but she doesn't say anything, stands perfectly still as Elise scrambles for her clothes.

"I thought maybe you really weren't coming back this time," Deke says, lifts Elise's candypink bra off the back of his sofa and hands it to her. "I thought maybe you and that shitty old car would just keep driving. Hell, I guess I should've known better."

"You shouldn't keep coming back here," Elise whispers, fastens her bra and stands there in her underwear, staring down at her bare feet. "You don't have to, you know?"

"I know that," Chance says, wishing she didn't always sound so defensive, and she sets the brown bag of groceries she's been holding down on a chair beside the door.

"You can't change what happened," and the dark blood from Elise's wrists has made a big, stickydamp stain on the carpet at her feet, and that's when Deacon always gets up to close the windows, never mind the heat because they can all hear the birds at the windows, the frightened birds trying to get in, and "You're only making it harder," Elise says.

"Time flies," and Deacon's speaking so softly now she can

hardly hear him over the racket the birds are making, and the sash rattles and the featherhard bodies batter themselves against the glass. She can already see places where their beaks have punched spiderweb cracks, the crooked hairline fractures in between, and in another minute the windowpane will break and the room will breathe them in, all the frantic, tiny bodies, all the stabbing beaks.

And this is the dream that Chance is having when she hears the telephone ring, and Elise looks up at her, glares out through hungry, blackbird eyes, crow eyes in her pale face, and "What are you waiting for, Chance? You're gonna have to go back sometime."

Chance wakes up in the house her great-grandfather built, the house where her grandparents raised her, made her something besides an orphan, and the telephone on the gossip bench down the hall is ringing; shrill, insistent bell that has pulled her out of the dream and a world where Elise was still alive. Nothing in the world now but a headache and sore muscles from sleeping all day on the hardwood floor, sore muscles and shadows, and the sense that she's lost Elise and Deacon all over again. Then Chance stumbles to her feet, bumps one elbow hard against the cast-iron coatrack and it hurts so bad she has to sit right back down. And the telephone still hasn't stopped ringing.

"I'm *coming*," like the phone can hear her, like it cares if she's banged her elbow on the damned coatrack and when she finally lifts the heavy receiver, telephone from a time before she was born, black Bakelite and a tangled cloth cord, someone's already talking on the other end.

"Chance? Is that you, Chance?"

"Yeah," and she's trying to recognize the voice, old woman voice and too much of her head still stuck in her dreams, the rolling kaleidoscope of faces and wings and bird-eyed Elise standing on the bloodstained carpet.

"I was starting to get worried about you, Chance. You didn't come by after the service, and we were getting worried."

Her Aunt Josephine, then, grandmother's sister, and Chance sits down by the phone, the little brocade and mahogany gossip bench too small for her, but squeezing in anyway, and she rubs at her elbow, tries to filter the voice through the throb at the base of her skull.

"I'm sorry, Aunt Josie," and "I just drove around for a while. I needed some time alone, to think, you know."

"Well," she says, disapproving tone and Chance doesn't have to see to know the way her aunt's frowning, the deep creases on her forehead. "We were worried, that's all. You should've called. We worry about you, Chance."

"I'm okay," and it doesn't matter whether or not that's the truth, it's what she's supposed to say, what Aunt Josephine needs to hear to let her off the telephone. But there are still more questions: "Are you eating? Have you had your dinner, Chance?" She tries to remember the last time she ate and her stomach makes a hollow, rumbling sound for an answer, rumbles so loud she's afraid Aunt Josie might have heard and so she says something quick, "I just put a pot-pie in the oven," but Chance can still hear the silent disapproval through the receiver, somehow the wrong answer but all Aunt Josie says is, "Well, you gotta take care of yourself. You have to eat. And you know that me and Walter are here if you need us. You *will* call us if you need anything, won't you, Chance?"

"Yes, but I'm okay, really," and a few more seconds, obligatory and genuine concern, Yes, I promise I'll call if I need anything at all and You know we're here, you know we love you, and then she's hanging up the phone, receiver back into its cradle, and her stomach growls again.

There's a lamp on the bench and she switches it on, squints at the 40-watt brilliance filtered through the cloth shade and it only makes her head hurt worse. Small pool of light now against the hallway gloom and Chance glances up at the grandfather clock across from the bench; a quarter before ten, so it hasn't been dark long, but she's slept the whole goddamn day propped up against the front door, sleeping off the drunk, sleeping off exhaustion, and it's a miracle she doesn't feel a lot worse than she does. Another stomach rumble, but she's a lot more interested in aspirin than food, a lot more interested in brushing her teeth, Colgate toothpaste and Listerine to get rid of the soursweet bourbon taste. Maybe then she'll think about food. One thing at a time.

Half an hour later and Chance is sitting on the floor in the study, cross-legged on the rug and her headache a little better but she's still not up to chairs and tables. She's switched on one of the Tiffany reading lamps near the back of the room, dustyellow light spilling from beneath stained-glass branches, stained-glass wisteria drooping in luminous, purple bunches. And all the shelves rising up around her like the book-lined walls of a fortress, safe in here, always safe in here from the world, guarded by books and all the secrets inside them, all the things hardly anyone else will ever care to learn.

Chance takes a bite of her cheddar cheese and mustard and tomato sandwich, chews slow as she stares at the lamp, at the books, all these things that are hers now. Her study because her grandparents are dead and that's what the will said, her house, her half acre perched on the side of Red Mountain. "So you'll always have a place to live," her grandfather had written, words put down on paper in life and sent back to her from a dead man. Chance takes a sip of root beer, the aluminum can sweatslicked with condensation, corn syrup and sassafras to wash away the sharp tastes of cheddar and mustard.

Another bite of her sandwich and *I'm an orphan again,* she thinks, if you can even be an orphan when you're twenty-three years old; something worse, perhaps, when you're twenty-three, something there isn't a specific word for, so there can't be a specific solution, either. She glances up at a tall curio cabinet, shadowy things inside, only a little light from the lamp getting in there and she wouldn't know what any of it was if she hadn't spent so much of her life hiding in this room. The lumpy, indistinct silhouettes that she knows are diamond-blade sliced and handpolished chunks of Ordovician algae, Devonian corals, Paleozoic treasures salvaged off this very mountain or from quarries and road cuts as far away as Georgia and Tennessee. Treasures from lost and ancient seas that Joe and Esther Matthews taught her how to read as plainly as the books on the library's shelves, taught her how to understand, when anyone else might only see a rock—perhaps a pretty or unusual rock if they bothered to look closely enough, but still just a rock. That cabinet is locked and Chance wonders if she can remember where her grandfather kept the key.

Chance puts the uneaten half of her sandwich down on the rug, no one left to yell at her about the crumbs now, anyway; she takes another sip of her root beer and lies down, stares up at the ceiling for a moment before she closes her eyes, then stares at the nothing behind her eyelids, tasting the pastysharp ghost of her cold supper and wishing that she could stop thinking about Elise. That she could stop thinking about the dreams of her, the loss of her, and feeling guilty because she's hardly even *cried* for her grandfather, Elise still too fresh to grieve for anyone else, any*thing* else; surely only so much hurt she can feel, can be expected to feel. And then the sudden, uninvited image of a train derailing and everything spilled out along the tracks, broken bodies in tangled, smoking wreckage and that's exactly what it feels like, to be here, alive and alone and no idea how she will be able to stand waking up tomorrow.

"Stop it," Chance says out loud, angryraw, scornful voice that she hardly recognizes. "Jesus, just fucking *stop* it," but she's crying again and her eyes burn and she's so goddamn sick of the sound, the smell and saltbland flavor of her own useless tears. She covers her face with one arm, hiding from no one but herself, making a little more dark, and in a few minutes she's asleep again.

CHAPTER TWO

Dancy

THE albino girl is reading *National Geographic,* alert, pink eyes scanning the bright and sparsely worded pages—Ethiopia, Taiwan, Cro-Magnon cave paintings in France. She's been coming here for almost two weeks now, only a few blocks from the shelter and the librarians usually leave her alone, as long as she doesn't fall asleep, as long as she doesn't forget where she is and start singing or whistling or put her feet up on the tables. They stare at her, when they think she isn't looking, scorncold faces for her dirtywhite hair and ragged clothes, the old women in their cat's-eye spectacles and the young gay men in their cheap suits meant to look expensive. But the teenagers are worse: black kids hiding from the projects one block east, all snickers and pointing fingers, mean whispers, hey freak, hey, white girl, how'd you even *get* so white? and she'd rather have the librarians' sidewise glances and dirty looks, thank you very much.

Dancy Flammarion turns another page and there's a big photograph of some place very, very far away, brooding, bruisedark clouds and foamwhite waves crashing down on a rocky beach, jagged rocks farther out to sea and a few gray gulls wheeling against the stormy sky—Ireland, Oregon, Wales—someplace she's never been and will likely never go, so it's all the same. At least she has the pictures. At least someone bothers to take pictures of faraway places so she can know that this isn't the entire world, the summer-parched streets of Birmingham, Alabama, the swamps and pine thickets of Okaloosa County, Florida, the wild and worn-out places in between—what she's been *given* of the world. And she might have been given less, she knows that, might have spent her life like her grandmother, like her mother, never going far enough from home to know that there were places without alligators and Spanish bayonets.

And then the sudden certainty that someone's watching her, that someone is very close, and she looks up and it's one of the gay boys, blonde hair and a sprinkle of freckles across the bridge of his nose, nervous hands playing with themselves. Nervous boy standing at her table so she has to look away from the stormshadowcool beach on the magazine page, squints up at him even though the fluorescents make her eyes hurt, make her wish she hadn't lost her sunglasses. The nervous gay boy looks like he wants to say something, but he's just standing there, staring at her.

"Is there something you wanted to say?" Dancy asks him, voice low so no one can shush her for talking in the library. And he looks over his shoulder, guiltyquick peek back towards the stingy corral of desks and Dancy figures he's afraid he'll get in trouble for whatever it is he's about to do, maybe just for talking to her, and for the moment that's more interesting than the magazine.

"Did I do anything wrong?"

"Oh, no," he says, reaching into a pocket and out comes a fancy leather wallet, leather the color of chocolate milk, and "I just, well," and he's opened the wallet, is fumbling around inside and she can see the ones and tens and twenty-dollar bills tucked in there, can see the credit cards, and maybe this is her lucky day. Maybe McDonald's or Taco Bell tonight instead of the shit they've been feeding her at the shelter. "I thought you might need some help, that's all," he says, "I thought maybe I might be able to help," and no money from the wallet, just a card, and she takes it anyway; plain, white card with plain, black letters that read LOVING SHEPERD CRISIS LINE, 24 HRS. A DAY, a phone number, service of the Samford Univ. Baptist Student Union, and a cross stamped in the upper left-hand corner.

"I'm Catholic," she says to the librarian and he frowns, briefest frown and then the nervous concern returns and Dancy is handing the card back to him. "And that's not how you spell *shepherd*," she says. "It has another *h* in it." Long moment then of her holding the card out to him, roles reversed now and at first she thinks he won't take it, never mind the reason but maybe he thinks he'll catch something from her, girl germs, cooties, some terrible skin disease. He looks confused and offended and unsure, and she's already thinking she should have just taken his damn card, yes, thank you so much, and left it lying there on the table for some other bum who gives a shit. But too late now and he does take it back, plucks it from her fingers but it doesn't go back into his wallet.

"I was only trying to help," he says, curt, sounding more sorry for himself than her and Dancy looks back down at the *National Geographic,* takes her eyes off him and so perhaps he'll go away and leave her alone.

"Thank you," she says and listens to his footsteps, loafers soft against the carpet, hesitant steps back to his desk and a few minutes later, when Dancy looks up from an article on jade, she catches him watching her, smiles and the librarian looks hastily down at the orderly stack of papers on his desk.

❂

Two weeks now since the bus ride, most of a night on the bus from Waycross, Greyhound winding north on dark roads, back roads where buses still stop in the middle of the night to take on passengers and Dancy tried to sleep most of the way. Something comforting in the smell of diesel and the constant rumblehum of tires against the road. A whole seat to herself when people got a good look at her, so she could stretch out and use the old duffel bag with her clothes and books and fifteen dollars hidden in a sock at the bottom for a pillow. Her grandfather's duffel, Grandpa Flammarion who came back from Germany without his left leg, and she would close her eyes and listen to the engine purr like a huge kitten, purr like a clockwork lion to lull her to sleep. But the dreams always too close, the dreams and the things she was running from, running towards, fear for what she'd done and what was left to do and finally Dancy gave up and stared out at the nightshrouded fields and woods and towns rushing past outside, squinting whenever the bus pulled into a gas station or bus stop and took on another passenger or two. She still had her sunglasses then and would slip them on against the occasional pools of sodium-arc glare, oases of light in the long, dark Southern night as the bus moved north, Georgia finally exchanged for Alabama, swamps and pine barrens for blackbelt prairies, and then, near dawn, the easy, rolling foothills of the Appalachians, and Dancy stared amazed at land the weight of the sky had not long ago crushed almost as flat as the sea.

Once or twice she noticed police cars behind the bus, following or just stuck back there on narrow state or county roads, and her heart raced, sick feeling deep in her stomach that she might have come as far as she was going to, that someone had found out after all and they would drag her back to Waycross, or Savannah, or maybe all the way back to Florida, stick her in a jail or somewhere worse. And Dancy scooted down in her seat, making herself small, until the highway patrol or sheriff passed them and once again there was only tomorrow and yesterday to be afraid of.

Just past Sylacauga and a man had sat down next to her, big, yellow teeth smiling at her, teeth that seemed to glow, and for a second she thought maybe he was one of Them and They were smarter than she'd thought, sneakier than she dared to think, that maybe one of Them had been on the bus the whole time, all the way from Waycross, just biding its time, giving her enough rope and "Hey there," the man with big teeth said. "Where you goin'?"

No answer at first, don't talk to strangers, Dancy, her mother's voice, grandmother's voice, don't *ever* talk to strangers, and the man grinned wider, showing about a thousand more teeth. "Oh, come on," he said and it was a wonder anyone could talk around all those teeth, a wonder anyone had room for a tongue in a mouth like that. "You can talk to me. I don't bite."

"What's it to you where I'm going?" she asked him and the man shrugged and shook his head, hair shaved close to the skin and ears too big for his skull. "It ain't nothin'," he said and shrugged. "I'm just tryin' to make polite conversation, that's all. Thought maybe you got a long ride ahead of you and it might help to talk some."

"Memphis," she lied. "I'm going to visit my Uncle Stewart in Memphis. My Uncle Stewart sells Elvis T-shirts at Graceland," all that spilling out of her, all-at-once deception before she could even be sure any of it made sense.

"Really?" the man replied, one eyebrow up, surprise or suspicion and Dancy couldn't tell which. "Graceland. Now that's someplace to be goin', ain't it?"

"I guess so," and she looked back at the window and maybe a police car wouldn't be such a bad thing to see, maybe a police car would scare the man with yellow teeth away.

"That's the Home of the Blues," the man said. "Memphis, I mean. W. C. Handy and Beale Street. What about you, Dancy? You listen to the blues?"

And her heart jumping, skipping a beat, because she knew she hadn't told the man her name, knew that he hadn't even asked so how could she have told him. She kept her eyes on the window, her reflection superimposed on the night, ghost of herself trapped there in the glass, trapped between him and the night outside, and "No," she said, whispered and it might be an answer or a wish.

"Well, you better start, if you're gonna be stayin' in Memphis. They take that shit pretty damn serious up there."

And then the bus was turning, air brake growl and hiss past a Denny's and a service station and a green road sign that read CHILDERSBURG.

"Well, this is where I get off," the man said and he leaned forward on the seat, spit chewing tobacco on the floor. "But you take care of yourself, way up there in Memphis. Awful big city for a little girl like you."

The bus pulled to a stop again beneath blinding bus-station lights and Dancy looked away from the window, automatic flinch, the light like needles in her eyes, and he was already gone. Just a shallow depression in the seat where he'd been, seat cushion rising slow like dough, filling in any sign he'd ever been there and her heart so loud everyone in the bus could probably hear it. *Whoosh* and *thunk* as the bus doors opened wide and she thought she glimpsed the man getting off, his silhouette indistinct against the windshield before he was gone down the stairwell and out into the garish light, bright, bright lights to shield something dark from her weak eyes.

"Jesus," she said, loud enough that someone turned around and looked at her, glared, so the rest kept to herself. *It was just a man, that's all, just a man on a bus, and you're about to pee in your pants you're so scared.* For a moment that even sounded good, good enough, anyway, and then, the smaller voice stuffed way down inside, afraid but speaking up anyhow. *So how did he know your name?* it asked, and she looked quickly back to the window, pushed her sunglasses back down on her face and watched the men unloading suitcases from the belly of the bus.

❲✦❳

Dancy's lost deep in the glossy pages of 1963, already halfway through her second heavy, librarybound volume of *National Geographic* that morning, half a year stitched between sturdy, brown covers, when she looks up, blinks, and sees the tall girl at the information counter. All skin and bones, her grandmomma would have said, Ain't nobody been feedin' you? and Dancy closes the book, closes the year, the month, story about Egyptian excavations unfinished and she watches the tall girl as she talks to the man behind the counter. The girl has set a cardboard box on the counter and keeps pointing at it. Dancy wishes that she could hear what they're saying, could see what's in the box, but the girl is whispering and too far away, besides. She has hair that isn't long but isn't short, either, stringyflat hair the color of broken walnut shells, and Dancy knows that this is *the* girl, doesn't know her name but that can wait, time for that later, sure enough that she's the same girl she's been sitting here, day in, day out, two weeks reading musty old magazines, waiting for her to come.

Dancy pushes the *National Geographic*s aside, January through June, six months smooth across varnished wood and she slides her chair back, stands up and the gay boy who tried to give her the Loving Sheperd card glances at her from his desk, then. Possessive, half-resentful glance like she's some opportunity that he's missed, gold star beside his name he'll never get because she wouldn't cooperate, because she doesn't have the good sense to know when someone's just trying to help. Dancy ignores him, picks up her duffel bag from the library floor and the brown-haired girl's still talking, still pointing at her box, Campbell's tomato soup box but anything might be in a box like that, she thinks.

She counts the steps, better than trying to figure out what the hell she's going to say when she gets there, better to think about something else, how the rough, beige carpet under her feet turns to smooth, beige linoleum halfway to the information counter. Twelve steps from her table, linoleum scuffed by shoes, scuffed by years of shoes and when she reaches twenty-seven and looks up again the girl has lifted the box, holds it under her left arm, leaning a bit to her right to compensate, to balance, and the black man behind the counter points towards the escalators, points up at the great, open atrium at the center of the library, the second or third or fourth floor, no way to know which. She can tell the box is heavy, the expression on the girl's face, the way the wirethin muscles in her arm stand out. Dancy stops, thirty-one steps and if the girl has to go to the escalator then she'll have to come right past her to get there.

"Thank you," the girl says, louder now or Dancy's close enough to hear and the man behind the counter nods his head and goes back to work, back to his computer screen. And she's right and it's only a few seconds before the girl with walnut hair is coming towards her. And of course she sees Dancy, of course she notices the girl with skin so white it's a wonder she can't see straight through her, cornsilk hair and her pink eyes with their startling, crimson pupils; dangerous to walk in the sunlight, too blind to drive, but at least she has that much going for her, hard to miss a girl like Dancy Flammarion, hard not to gawk and this one time she's glad, this one time it doesn't matter when the girl stares, maybe not meaning to but her eyes wide and then she looks quickly away. That's nice, Dancy thinks, so used to people not giving a shit, like she was in a carnival sideshow tent and they'd paid for the privilege so what business did she have being offended if they stared or laughed or pointed their piggyrude fingers at her. But now the girl's staring down at her scruffy, leather work boots as she passes, like she never even saw Dancy, so Dancy has to say something to make her stop, still no idea what she should say, so "Hi," out fast and maybe the girl will just keep walking, she thinks, maybe afraid Dancy's a beggar and wants spare change, weird albino panhandlers nailing people in the goddamn public library these days and she'll keep going until she finds a security guard to toss Dancy out on her ass.

But that isn't what she does, not this tall girl, turns around instead, turns around and her eyes are green. "Hi," she says, trying to meet Dancy's gaze and trying not to stare at the same time, have your cake and eat it too, and "Hi," Dancy says again. The girl's beginning to look confused and Dancy's trying hard to think what comes next, but she never dreamed this part, so no idea what to say to a total stranger and "Can I help you?" the girl asks, shifts the box under her arm and Dancy almost sees what's inside.

"What's in the box?" she asks, none of her business but that's the first thing that comes to mind and she takes it, probably as good a start as any since she can't tell the girl the truth and looks will only get you so far.

"Oh," the girl says, maybe the slightest hint of relief in her voice because she has an excuse to turn away for a second, a moment to look in the box like she doesn't remember what's there and "Just some old papers," she says. "Some old manuscripts. Some of my grandfather's old manuscripts that I'm giving to the library."

"He doesn't want them anymore?" Dancy asks and the girl frowns, soft frown, but Dancy knows that she's said the wrong thing even if she doesn't understand exactly why. And before she can apologize, I'm sorry or That's none of my business, is it? the girl isn't frowning anymore, is looking straight at her like she's some normal girl who's asked some perfectly normal, inconsequential question.

"He's dead," the girl says, that matter-of-fact, like she was telling Dancy it was hot outside and it was going to be hot again tomorrow. "He died last week, and I thought this stuff would be safer here."

"Oh," she says. "Oh, god. I'm sorry. I didn't mean, I mean, I shouldn't have even . . ." but the girl is shaking her head and "No, it's okay," she says. "You couldn't have known, could you?" And Dancy repeats the same question in her head, *Couldn't I have, shouldn't I have known that?* "But they're just some old papers," the girl says again. "Some things I cleaned out of his office and I'm taking them over to the archives."

"My name's Dancy. Dancy Flammarion," one hand out to shake and for a moment the girl acts like no one's ever tried to shake hands with her before. She shifts the weight of the box again and this time Dancy hears the papers shuffling inside when she does. "I'm Chance," she says back and finally takes Dancy's hand, squeezes a little too hard when she shakes it. "Chance Matthews," and Dancy smiles, trying to look friendly, trying not to look like a street crazy in her dirty clothes, her tangled hair.

"Chance," she says. "How the hell did you get a name like that?"

Chance Matthews shrugs once and not exactly a smile for her, but at least the girl isn't frowning anymore, and "Nobody ever told me," she says. "I guess they just thought it was a good idea at the time." Another glance at the Campbell's tomato soup box and "This stuff is really getting heavy," she says. "I was on my way to the elevator," and she releases Dancy's hand, then, points at two shiny brass elevator doors at the end of a short hallway past the escalators. "The archives are over in the old building, and the crosswalk's up on the third floor."

Dancy apologizes for making the girl stand there with the heavy box of papers, runs on ahead to hit the UP button, her duffel bag swinging back and forth, dangerous, canvas pendulum as she runs. A bell dings loud and the doors slide open like secret panels in the wall and Dancy holds the elevator until Chance gets there. "Third floor?" she asks, making sure, still smiling and Chance, more confused than ever and showing it, nods her head. "Thanks," she says and so Dancy presses the peppermintwhite button with a bold, black number 3 printed on it. The button glows yellow, and the elevator doors slide slowly, quietly, closed again.

◉

Two years, almost, since the first time she dreamed about Chance. Her mother was still alive then, her grandmother was still alive, and a hurricane spinning furious counterclockwise somewhere south of their cabin in the Okaloosa wilderness, big hurricane waiting somewhere offshore, sitting out there past Eglin Air Force Base and Fort Walton Beach, past the suburbs and beachfront tourist traps, crouched over gulfdeep water and just the tattered edges were almost enough to drown the swamps, to rattle the windows and bend the pines until they creaked and groaned. Her mother listening to the radio while her grandmother stared nervously at the raindark windows, oil-lamp shadows on the walls like goblins and Dancy had fallen asleep watching them, listening to the weather reports, the excited voices of men and women relaying the storm's speed and position, trying to second-guess its grayblue intentions.

Finally, too sleepy to be scared anymore, nothing she could do anyway, nothing any of them could do but hope the storm moved on south or west, anywhere but north, and "We should'a got out of here while we still could," her mother kept saying, accusing tone in her voice to blame her grandmother, blame her that they hadn't run; her grandmother accepting the blame by not saying a word in her own defense, just watching the windows, and Dancy shut her eyes, trusting the goblin shadows to keep their distance and in a moment she was asleep.

And at least the storm had the decency to stay out of her head, out of her dreams, and instead she was standing in front of a big, white house, nowhere she'd ever been before, and *You'd have to be very rich to live in a house like that,* she thought, a house with electricity and so many rooms, a house in a city. The sun hot on her exposed skin, but the grass was cool against her bare feet, bare toes, and that's when she saw the girl sitting in the window, high-up attic window looking down at her. The girl with brown hair and green eyes looking straight at her but not seeing her.

Dancy waved and the girl ignored her or didn't notice, no change in her blank, unblinking expression and Dancy turned around, hoping she might see what the girl was looking at. *I'm standing on a mountain,* she thought, staring down at treetops and rooftops and the city skyline farther out, glass and steel and stone towers, concrete highway ribbons. She'd never been on a mountain before, even a small one like this, and it made her a little dizzy, the sky closer than it should be, the world tilted at an unnatural angle and she sat down on the cool, green grass to keep from falling.

"Don't look at it," the girl in the window called down to her, "Don't look at it, Dancy," so the girl did know she was there after all, and Dancy turned to say that she'd been rude, to pretend not to see her before, and what wasn't she supposed to look at, anyway. But the girl was gone, nothing there now but an empty attic window, lacewhite curtains to flap and twist in a hot breeze that hadn't been there a second before.

And a sound then, like a freight train far away, railroad rumble as the steel begins to hum and the ballast shift, but she knew that it wasn't really a train, that this sound came from the ground beneath her, railroad or thunder trapped somewhere underground and getting louder. Something she could feel now, tremors through the palms of her hands, the tips of her fingers, and then the girl was standing over her, the brown-haired girl standing over her and one hand held out, one hand to pull Dancy back to her feet as the earth began to roll and lurch, pitch and yaw like a small boat on a rough sea. "You never should have come here," the girl said and Jesus, she looked so sad, not scared that the ground was splitting open like overripe fruit, splitting open to bleed gouts of dusty steam and a smell like something dead too long in the sun, just sad, and then they were running. Running back towards that huge white house, and rocks, boulders, were shaking themselves loose from the mountain and rolling across the yard towards them.

And she wanted to tell the girl that she'd *had* to come, because of what had happened to her mother, what had happened to her grandmother, because she had pulled the trigger, what else was she supposed to do but pull the trigger, but then she couldn't even remember what it was that had happened, nothing but a sick, lost feeling where the memories had been just a second before, and "None of it matters now," the girl said. "You did what you had to do, that's all," and the earth bellowed underfoot like a bull alligator and rose in a single wave to shatter the mountainside and the pretty, white house, wave of soil and broken stone and the squirming, living things caught inside, tumbling towards Dancy and the brown-haired girl helpless in the trough, and they held hands and waited to drown.

The doors slide open and Dancy follows Chance out of the elevator, past rows of science and computer magazines, past the children's section and a huge, cardboard cut-out of a happy, purple dinosaur, and there's the crosswalk; third-floor umbilicus of steel and glass to bridge the street below, and Chance pauses, looks back at her. It's very bright out there, two o'clock sun shining straight through smogtinted glass and the air-conditioning doesn't seem to reach beyond the building, hangs back like Dancy, lingering in the shadows. There are three antique, wooden benches in the crosswalk, discarded church pews, maybe, yellowbrown wood bolted to the carpet, left to bake beneath the sun and Chance sits down on the first one and sets the cardboard box between her feet. Now Dancy can see the papers inside and that's all they are, just old papers, notebooks, and "You're following me, aren't you?" Chance asks.

No point denying it, so she doesn't, points at the box instead. "What did your grandfather write about?" she asks, a question for an answer and maybe that'll buy her a few more minutes, stalling as long as she can because if she has to tell Chance anything like the truth she knows she'll never see her again.

"Rocks," Chance says, voice gone suddenly flat, spiritless, like she doesn't want to talk about this, but one hand into the box and she takes out a manila folder stuffed much too full of pages. "Fossils, mostly. He was a geologist. You know, someone who studies—"

"I'm not *ignorant*," Dancy snaps back, interrupting her. "I *know* what a geologist is," and already wishing she hadn't sounded so defensive, knowing Chance wasn't calling her stupid but so few years in school and so many people who assumed that being an albino had also made her retarded.

"I'm sorry," Chance says, returning the folder to the box. "You might be surprised how many people don't know."

And a few seconds' worth of silence then, silence wedged tight between them while Chance stares down at the box, at her dead grandfather's papers and Dancy squints into the merciless day separating her and the cool, dark doorway leading into the building at the other end of the crosswalk. Maybe a hundred feet across, no more than a hundred feet, surely, and there's Chance sitting in the sun like she's never heard of skin cancer, like no one's ever lectured her about melanoma, Chance and her impossible, suntanned face and arms.

"Why are there two buildings, anyway?" Dancy asks, and that seems to bring Chance back a little, back from wherever her head's gone, and she glances from one side of the street to the other and then back to Dancy.

"The one we were just in is the new library. They opened it about

'83. And that one over there," and she motions with her head towards the far side of the crosswalk, "that's the old library."

"How old?" Dancy asks and "1925, I think," Chance says. "It was built after a fire destroyed the original."

"Oh," Dancy says and steps out into the sun, cautious venture just far enough that she can see both the buildings now, the razor-sharpened, polished angles of the new library, squat and featureless façade of glass and anonymous gray stone like ugly Lego blocks, the kind of building that can seem cold even under the summer sun. And across the street, something more like a Greek temple cut from limestone, tall columns to support the upper stories, and the names of great artists and scientists, playwrights and poets, carved into a frieze around the top. "It's kind of like a time machine, you know," Chance says. "Cross the street and you cross seventy-five years, three-quarters of a century in just a few footsteps. On one side of the street you have Prohibition and it's still years till World War II, and on the other side you've got Ronald Reagan and AIDS."

Dancy looks down at her, then, and Chance is staring towards the old building; "Come over here," she says, "I want you to see something." She gets up, box of papers hefted off the floor and Dancy follows her across the street, cars honking and zipping by underneath them, the sun pricking at her skin but she's trying not to notice. "Right down there," Chance says, "Down by the sidewalk, in the tall grass there." At first Dancy doesn't see anything special, just the sandgray strip of sidewalk, the unmown grass at the edge of the old building, until Chance points and there's something the color of charcoal rising out of the grass, something that looks like a tree stump cast in dull, smoke-colored stone.

"Is it a statue?" she asks and no, Chance says, shakes her head no and Dancy stoops down for a better look.

"My grandfather found that in a coal mine up in Warrior back in the forties. It's a fossil tree stump," and now Dancy can make out roots like stone tentacles branching off the thing, snaking away into the grass. "He gave it to the library and they set it in concrete. So nobody could steal it, I guess. There used to be a little wooden sign next to it. Anyway, these days I think people just think it's a rock no one's ever bothered to move."

"Wow," Dancy whispers, glad they have something real to talk about. "How old is it?"

"About two hundred and ten, maybe two hundred and twenty million years or so. They're really not that hard to find out in the coalfields," and Chance looks back down at the soup box then, like she's forgotten it for a moment, just remembering and "You want to see the old library?" she asks.

Dancy nods, "Yeah, thank you. That would be nice," but all the time she's thinking how 1925 isn't old at all, how 1925 is just last week compared to that lump of gray rock sitting down there by the sidewalk.

"Well, come on then," Chance Matthews says. "This box isn't getting any lighter," and she leads Dancy out of the hateful sun and into kindly shadows, and *Maybe this* will *be okay,* she thinks. *Maybe she will listen, when it's time to tell,* and the limestone blocks stacked and mortared one to the other since her grandmother was her age close protectively around them.

An hour later and Chance has left her box of papers in the library basement, handed them all over to a jowly, pink-faced woman who smiled and gave her a yellow receipt that she stuffed thoughtlessly into a front pocket of her blue jeans. And then she led Dancy back up to the first floor, and this time the elevator is wood paneled and its gears and cables clank, shudder like an old man trying to wake up and wanting to go back to sleep. But hauling them up anyway, slow, to the huge ground-floor gallery for Southern History, all the books arranged alphabetically by state and two whole wings set aside for the Civil War and genealogy.

But the most amazing thing, a mural wrapped around these four high walls, figures drawn from history and myth, literature and legend and painted there, oil-paint parade of heroes and heroines, and Chance and Dancy sit together at a long reading table, brass lamps with glassgreen shades and the sunlight filtered through tall windows instead of the antiseptic, stark fluorescence from the newer building across the street. This library the opposite of almost everything across the street and how has she spent two weeks over there, not even suspecting this existed?

Chance points to a figure labeled SIGURD, eighteen feet tall above the books, Sigurd and beautiful Brynhild watching him from her seat on a bench carved with the image of a fanged and slinking dragon.

"Isn't that cool?" Chance asks and Dancy nods her head. "It was painted in the twenties, by an artist named Ezra Winter. He did it in his studio in New York City and it was shipped all the way down here and hung on the bare walls with white lead.

"I loved this place when I was a kid. I *still* love it, but when I was a kid I'd take the bus down here and spend all day long reading in this room."

And she stops, maybe something she didn't really mean to say, to Dancy or anyone else, and Dancy points quickly to another towering figure on the wall, another dragon and white blossoms on a tree, Confucius, and she smiles for Chance, smiles against whatever melancholy lies coiled like a canebrake rattler inside this girl. And that was one of her grandmother's words, melancholy instead of just plain old sad and suddenly Dancy feels homesick for the first time in weeks.

Then Chance is looking at her wristwatch and "Damn," she whispers, librarywhisper but urgent and "I have to go," she says. And Dancy almost says no, please stay just a little longer, Chance noticing the time like a demon called up by her homesickness, something to make it worse. But that's not the way it goes, she reminds herself, not yet, too afraid of pushing and ruining everything after she's come this far. So, "I'm sorry," and that will have to do instead of the things she really feels, really wants to say to Chance.

"I have some errands," Chance says. "Stupid shit, but it has to be done," standing up, pushing her chair back from the table. And then she's looking down at Dancy, expression like she's just noticed her all over again. But this time Dancy knows it's not her white skin and pinkred eyes, this time it's her shabby clothes, her filthy hair, and "You have someplace to go, right? I mean, a place to stay?"

"I've got some friends," she says, simple enough answer to forestall anything else Chance might ask, ashamed of the way she looks, the way she smells; Chance takes a twenty-dollar bill from her back pocket and Dancy shakes her head, doesn't want to accept the money, more embarrassed now, but god it's twenty dollars and part of her hopes Chance *won't* change her mind. Which she doesn't, shakes her head and "Call it a loan," she says, "If that's what you want it to be. I needed someone to talk to today, really."

So Dancy crumples the bill in one palm and shakes Chance's hand again, less awkward shake this time and she doesn't squeeze quite so hard.

"Thanks," she says, and then almost, *Will I see you again?* but that might be too much, something she could take the wrong way, and no matter how nice she's been it's never too late to scare someone away, never too late to make a bad impression. Chance looks at her watch again. "I really gotta run," she says. "But it was good to meet you, Dancy Flammarion," and she smiles, the first real smile she's seen from her and the tall girl wears it well.

And then she's gone, dashing back towards the elevator and Dancy watches her go, watches until the doors slide closed, and she opens her palm and examines the twenty. Lays it on the table in front of her and smooths it out flat, tries to iron out the paperwrinkles, the creases, and then she slips the money inside her duffel bag.

"See you soon, Chance Matthews," she whispers, knows that it's true, one way or another, and then Dancy looks back up at the mute and colorful pantheon watching over her.

CHAPTER THREE

Deacon

LATE afternoon and one impertinent shaft of sunlight slipping between the drapes of the bar, drapes drawn against the summer heat and shine, respect for the aching eyes of daytime customers, and the sunlight stabbing its cruel or thoughtless way through drifting cigarette smoke and dust and the thick and sour smell of old beer. THE PLAZA, except someone hung the sign upside down so it reads ⱯZⱯ⅂Ԁ ƎHⱢ, but that was a long time ago, a long story everyone's tired of repeating, or a short story simply not worth repeating again. The Plaza and Deacon sitting alone at the bar, lanky, stoop-shouldered Deacon Silvey nursing his third PBR of the day and dreading seven o'clock and the beginning of his Friday night shift at the Highland Wash-N-Fold, five immeasurable hours of rumbling dryers and washing machines like the strangling lungs of drowning men. If he didn't still have a hangover from the night before, that would be enough to give him one, just thinking about all those goddamn washers and dryers chugging half the night.

And this asshole parked on the stool next to him, talking, talking like he's just invented The Mouth and it needs a test drive; Deacon turns and stares at him, stares hard at the very fat man with greasylong hair and a black T-shirt that reads KILL ALL THE MOTHERFUCKERS, happy clown face and KILL ALL THE MOTHERFUCKERS in drippy, red letters. The fat man has a zit at the left corner of his mouth as big as a peanut and skin the cheesewhite color of something washed up on a beach. The fat man slurps at his beer and is talking again before he's even swallowed.

"Now, don't *think* they're gonna stop with the faggots and nig-gers," the fat man says. "All this AIDS shit, that's just a smoke screen, you know, what you might call a red herring to get us all lookin' off the other way while they get the *big* guns in place, while they get FEMA and the fuckin' EPA and the fuckin' FBI all workin' *together....*"

And every single word from the man's mouth like a threepenny nail hammered between Deacon's eyeballs and he glances over to Sheryl, railthin girl mopping lazily at the bar with a gray rag and she's not even pretending to listen to the fat man anymore so you'd think the asshole would get a clue and shut the hell up.

"Oh man, you don't even want to get me started on AIDS," the fat man says and the happy clown face jiggles like cottonblack Jell-O. "You get me started on AIDS and I'll be here until Gabriel blows his horn, I fuckin' swear. You wanna know how much money, how much of *our* tax dollars, goes into so-called AIDS research? You wanna hear how we've had the goddamn vaccine since 1975?"

Deacon lifts his mug, pisscheap beer gone lukewarm but he has to pace himself, better to spend the whole afternoon sipping flat, lukewarm beer than run out of cash with half the day left to go. He swallows, wipes the scabbed knuckles of one hand across his chin, stubble there like sandpaper to remind him he's forgotten to shave again.

"Are you as tired of listening to this guy as I am?" he asks Sheryl. She stops mopping the bar and glances at Deacon, cautious glance that says Maybe it's better just to listen until the asshole gets tired and goes away, better because she knows Deacon and Jesus, her shift's over in another thirty minutes and she'd rather make it until three without a fight. All that in her tired, green eyes like dusty emeralds and Deacon nods, sets his mug down; Sheryl sighs, loud, resigned sigh and goes back to her gray bar rag and the countertop like maybe nothing will happen if she isn't watching. Deacon turns to the fat man, jabs one thumb back towards Sheryl.

"The lady's getting tired of listening to you, buddy," he says and immediately, "I did *not* say that, Deke, you son of a bitch," Sheryl sounding more annoyed than worried and Deacon Silvey's glad it's the fat man he's telling to shut up instead of the bartender.

But the fat man has stopped talking, stares wide-eyed at Deacon like he's some exotic species of fungus sprouting from the bar stool. "What d'you say to me?" he says and his tongue flicks past chapped lips, licks nervously at the huge zit.

"Of course, *she's* way too polite to tell you to shut the fuck up. But that's what she's thinking. Ordinarily I'd just sit here, drink my beer, and mind my own goddamn business. Figure, hey, you know, if the girl's gonna work in a dive like this she has to expect to listen to creeps like you. Am I right?"

Not a peep from the fat man now, just his doughy face changing color, turning the shade of funeral-parlor carnations, and Sheryl tosses her rag somewhere beneath the edge of the bar, snakehiss between her teeth that might have been a word or only anger looking for a way out.

"I swear to God, Deke, you start a fight with this guy on *my* shift and *I'm* gonna call the cops," sounding like she means it, already reaching for the telephone beside the register and the fat man still hasn't said anything else.

"So we're cool then?" and Deacon almost manages half a grimace, his head hurting way too much to smile, but one eyebrow cocked like a pistol. "You're gonna save the rest of your cut-rate, anti-Semite, conspiracy-theory bullshit for somebody that cares, okay?"

"You're some kinda faggot, ain't you," the fat man says, not asking, telling, and now his face is almost the exact color of strawberry preserves.

"Hey buddy, seriously," Deacon says, pointing a finger at the guy's forehead. "If you don't calm down I think you're gonna blow a corpuscle or something—"

"I'm picking up the phone, Deke. Do you *see* me picking up the motherfucking telephone?" and "Yeah," he says, "I see, and I know you mean it, Sheryl," enough calm in his voice to keep her from dialing the police for at least another fifteen or twenty seconds, so she just stands there, holding the receiver, glaring at him and chewing at the stainless steel ring in her lower lip.

"But we're not gonna *need* the cops, are we, buddy?" Deacon asks the fat man and now everyone else in the bar is watching, all those booze-and-smoke bleary eyes squinting from the shadows, all those faces waiting to see how much more interesting this is going to get.

"You're gonna need a meat wagon, you say one more word to me, you crazy, Jew fairy," the fat man growls. "I don't have to sit here, in a public place, and get myself verbally assaulted 'cause you believe everything *they* want you to believe. Jesus, I oughta have my fuckin' head examined, even comin' in a place like this."

And Deacon's up and moving then, hands faster than the eye, too fast for the fat man to do anything much but make a small, squeaking sound, stepped-on mouse sort of sound, and then Deacon's left fist is tangled deep in the man's long hair, right hand holding tight to the seat of his baggy jeans. Almost like the fat man's suspended on piano wires no one else can see, dangling weightless, half an inch off the dirty tile as Deacon shoves him towards the door. The fat man hasn't turned loose of his beer mug and he's trying to use it as a weapon, cut-glass cudgel flailing side to side and beer splashing the walls, splashing Deacon until the man manages to hit himself in the head with the mug and yelps.

Six, maybe seven feet left before the closed door and there's already blood streaming down the man's face, blood in his eyes, and Deacon is beginning to wonder in a sluggish, drunken way if he's strong enough, or the man's heavy enough, if there's enough velocity, enough momentum, to break through the redpainted glass. But a skinny kid in a yellow Curious George shirt opens the door, quick sidestep as the fat man sails out of The Plaza and into the brilliant July afternoon, trips on the sidewalk and lands on his ass in the middle of the street.

Deacon quickly pulls the door closed again, turns the dead bolt fast and for a moment they can all hear the man cursing, bellowing out there in the heat about papists and homos and fucking space aliens before the screech of tires drowns him out, car-horn blat like an exclamation point; Deke thanks the skinny guy who opened the door, stares a second at his banana-colored shirt, and then heads slowly back to his stool at the bar.

"You're crazy," Sheryl grumbles, still holding the telephone receiver. "One day you're gonna pull that shit with the wrong guy and get your sorry punk ass kicked to hell and back. You know that, don't you?"

And yeah, he says, yeah, sure, whatever you say, boss lady, but she's setting the receiver back in its cradle, anger traded for disgust, pouring him another beer even though he hasn't asked for it and there's still at least three inches of the waterthin draft left in his mug.

"On the house, you crazy fuckin' drunk," she says, frowning, and Deacon Silvey finishes off the warm beer before he lets himself start on the cold.

◉

Ask Deacon Silvey where and when his life first landed in the shitter, how it got there and never really climbed out again, and every time he'll point to an October afternoon and the ratmaze-neat Atlanta suburb where he grew up, October 1970, when he was eight years old and his mother lost her car keys. Had promised to take him to the movies, and he can never remember which movie, never mind, it doesn't matter, but she'd promised and then she couldn't find the car keys. His father out back raking leaves and his mother searching the house, annoyed, probing under sofa cushions and then down on her knees to peer beneath the recliner, beneath the china cabinet, Deacon watching the clock and pretty soon it wouldn't matter, another ten minutes and it would be too late to make the matinee anyway.

So Deacon going to her purse on the coffee table, then, because that's where the keys *should* have been, that's all, opening the metal catch and the pungent smell of new patent leather before he began to feel sick, suddensharp pain at his temples, stomach rolling, and when Deacon opened his eyes he was lying on the carpet staring up at his mother bending over him, the pinched look on her face that said she was scared to death, and "Deke, oh god, honey, are you okay? What happened?" and he told her that the car keys were in the pocket of her coat. Long and silent second as her expression changed from worry to confusion, finally helping him up off the floor and Deacon's legs unsteady, helping him to the sofa, and "They're in there, Momma. Really," he said. And they were, right where she'd left them the night before. "How'd you know that, Deke?" but it didn't matter because his head hurt too much to go to the movies, hurt so bad that he spent the rest of the afternoon in his bedroom with the curtains pulled closed and didn't even come out for supper.

A trip to the doctor after that, several trips, several doctors, specialists, and after the tests each of them assuring his parents that their son wasn't epileptic and, no, he didn't have a brain tumor, either, and neither his mother nor father mentioning the car keys. Like that wasn't really a part of the story, just the blackout and the headache afterwards. His father complaining about the bills the doctors sent when there was nothing even wrong with the kid, but no one asking Deacon about the keys again, and a month, two months, and the whole thing forgotten by Christmas.

But that was the beginning, that's where it started, not nearly as dramatic as the story about Davey Barber's beagle puppy, nothing grisly or sad about lost car keys and later everyone would always point back to the dead dog, never the sunny afternoon and the lost car keys.

Five minutes left until Sheryl's shift is over before anyone remembers that Deacon locked the door, convenient amnesia and then a fist pounding hard on the glass, *bang, bang, bang,* and Deacon thinks maybe it's the fat guy come back with the cops and so maybe he won't have to go to work at the laundromat tonight after all. Sheryl glaring at the door and cursing Deacon, glancing up at the Budweiser clock over the bar and cursing because Bunky Tolbert is late again. She steps out from behind the counter and Deacon swivels on his stool, turns to face the door just in case it really is The Second Coming of the Fat Guy.

"You locked the fucking door, Deke," Sheryl says, then she yells at whoever it is outside to please stop banging on the glass, give her one second for Christ's sake.

"You ain't heard nobody complaining," Deacon says coolly.

"You're gonna get me fired, you asshole," she snaps back, door open now and it's not the fat guy after all. Just Sadie in black polyester and the eyeliner she never bothers to wash off, easier just to put more on so she always looks a little like an anemic raccoon. Sadie Jasper, with her silver purse shaped like a coffin and Deacon smiles for her, easy drunken smile, only a little disappointed that it isn't Mr. Kill-All-The-Motherfuckers and he still has to go to work.

"Hey babe," he says and Sadie sits down on the stool next to him, kisses Deacon on the cheek and she smells like clove cigarettes and vanilla oil, comfortable, safe smells, and "You didn't happen to see a really fat son of a bitch dead in the street out there, did you?" he asks her. Sadie stares at him with those eyes that still give him the willies every now and then, heavy-lidded and her pale, blue irises surrounded by all that smudged eyeliner and her coalblack hair.

"No," she replies. "But I wasn't paying all that much attention," deadpan solemn but enough of a smile that Deke can tell she knows he's joking, and "More's the pity," he says and kisses her back, tastes her waxy, black lipstick and he can think of so many things he'd rather spend the night doing than watching Highland Avenue yuppies separate their whites from their colors.

"You want anything, Sadie?" Sheryl asks, talking to Sadie but looking at the clock and she should have been out of here five minutes ago. Sadie scowls at her reflection in the mirror behind the bar, squints hard at the long row of bottles lined up back there, all concentration like she ever orders anything different, and "I think I'll have a White Russian, please," she says, finally, and Deacon would bet ten dollars she's never had anything else, that somewhere, sometime, a White Russian was Sadie's first taste of alcohol and she's never seen any point in trying anything different.

Sadie opens her shiny coffin purse and digs out a wrinkled five, lays it on the counter while Sheryl adds vodka to ice cubes and half-and-half. "And give dumb-ass here another glass of that cow piss," she says and grins at the bartender.

"Jesus, it must be my goddamn birthday," Deke says. "Two free beers in one afternoon," and he finishes his PBR, sets the mug down and slides it towards Sheryl as she puts Sadie's White Russian on a cocktail napkin with a flaming eight ball printed on one side.

"No, just guilt money from home," Sadie says and takes a mint-green slip of paper from her purse, a check with her father's name printed neatly across the top and enough zeros that at least they won't have to worry about paying the rent for another month. "As long as my mother's new therapist keeps telling her it really *is* all her fault that I turned out this way, I figure we can expect a steady trickle," and Sadie takes a sip of her drink before she puts the check safely back inside her purse and snaps the little coffin shut again.

"Well, it's reassuring to know that at least one of us isn't burdened with a conscience," Deacon says and Sadie punches him in the arm, not hard but he groans like she's broken a bone, groans until she leans over and kisses his shoulder.

"Jesus, you guys are making me sick," Sheryl mutters. "You know how long it's been since I even had a *date*?" and Sadie sticks her tongue out at the bartender, tongue the color of milkstained bubble gum and then turns back to Deacon.

"I saw your friend Chance at the post office today," she says and Deacon sips at his fresh beer, and "How's she holding up?" he asks; Sadie shrugs and stirs at her drink with a red, plastic swizzle stick.

"Beats me. She was buying stamps. You know she doesn't like talking to me."

"I don't think Chance much likes talking to anybody these days, baby. I wouldn't take it personally."

"No, I'm pretty sure she thinks weird rubs off," Sadie says and lays the swizzle stick on her napkin, stares at Deke with those unreal blue eyes like something in a taxidermist's shop window, eyes like glass and "She's a very *detached* young lady."

"Yeah?" and Deacon watches her in the mirror, watches her between the liquor bottles. "Well, I expect you'd be pretty detached too, Little Miss Pickled Sunshine, if you'd been through all the shit Chance has been through lately." And she doesn't say a word, no response but another shrug, Sadie's eternal answer to a whole messy world of things she'd rather not think about.

Deacon runs his fingers through his short, mousebrown hair, not quite pissed at Sadie yet and hoping he didn't sound that way because now she's pouting, stirring aimlessly at her drink and her lower lip looks like something a yellow jacket stung. But sometimes her callous goth-girl shtick is hard to stomach, sometimes like now, and suddenly Deacon feels very old and very tired, all the hell he's caught and he honestly can't imagine how Chance Matthews is alive, still walking and talking. Someone like that almost enough to make you believe in bad luck or karma, the fucking sins of the father, someone like that enough to keep things in perspective.

"You didn't have to *yell* at me," Sadie says, almost whispers, and "I didn't yell at you, Sadie," Deacon says and now they're talking to each other through the mirror, too bad his parents never figured out this trick. It might have saved a lot of broken dishes.

"It's not my fault she doesn't like me," and that's enough to light the short and ragged fuse that's never far beneath Deke's skin, enough to get him up off the bar stool and moving towards the door. Forget the beer, forget Sadie, because he really doesn't want to be anywhere near her or anyone else when the bomb in his head goes off.

But she's already calling after him, still hasn't learned when to let him go, when to shut up and sit it out until the shit blows over. "What the fuck did I say, Deacon?" she asks, raising her voice and Sheryl's watching them both now, starting to look a lot more worried than she did about the fat man. Her smokedusty eyes doing all the talking and Just keep walking, Deke, she's trying to say without opening her mouth, Just keep on going and she'll get over it and you'll get over it and nobody gets hurt this time. But Deke stops halfway to the red door and "Every goddamn thing isn't about you, Sadie. *This* isn't about you."

"I never said it was," and god he hates the way she can flinch without moving a muscle, flinch with words like she's afraid he's going to hit her when he's never laid a hand on her. "All I was saying—"

"All you were *saying,* Sadie, is that you're just too goddamned simple or shallow or selfish or *whatever* to figure out why someone who's lost everything, everyone she ever loved or gave two shits for, why someone like that can't stop being miserable for five minutes to smile and make you feel like the sparkling center of the goddamn universe."

Not even looking at Sadie in the mirror now, that much a coward, that much a jerk, but everything he needs to see right there in Sheryl's green eyes, like just exactly how unnecessary that was, like how someone who spends every day hiding in the hooch because he can't deal with his own life has a hell of a nerve telling anyone else to get a clue.

"Whatever," Deacon Silvey says. And he turns away from Sheryl and Sadie and the cold beer he's hardly touched, stalks past the cigarette machine and out of The Plaza's crimson door, out of the mustycool shadows and into the merciless heat and sundrowned day he deserves.

◉

Deacon had just turned nine and the beagle had been missing for three weeks, three stickyhot weeks in the middle of August, too hot to be outside but him and Davey Barber and some other boys playing football behind Davey's house anyway. Someone passed Deacon the ball and he lost his balance, fell and tumbled crash into the puppy's doghouse. Boys laughing and Deacon disoriented, his right ankle hurting but he was about to get up and run for the garden hose stretched across the grass for a goal line when he smelled oranges, something like orange peels or raw fish and he'd never even noticed how the two smelled so much alike.

"Hey, you okay, Deke?" and more laughter, then, Greg Musgrove calling him a pussy, and "Yeah, sure," he said, "I'm fine. Just got my feet tangled up," but that orangeandfish smell so strong, strong enough it was making him nauseous, making him gag, and he leaned back against the abandoned doghouse, eyes watering and trying not to puke.

And "Jesus, man, what's the matter with you?" Davey asked him, but Deacon's head hurt too much to answer, too much to even think, and if he opened his mouth he knew he'd puke for sure. The football rolling from his hands, bump to the ground, bouncing away, and by then all the boys standing around him while the smell dragged Deacon Silvey down and down, falling like something in a fairy story his mother read to him once, falling and going nowhere fast and he saw the puppy, the older kids that took it away one night when everyone in Davey's house was asleep and "Oh," he said, "Oh shit," seeing the rest, seeing it all, but nothing else out of his mouth before he was vomiting, his lunch sprayed all over the nearest pair of sneakers and someone was running for Davey's mother, shouting, scared, and the world folded up like a crumpled paper cup and Deacon tumbled into the black space left behind.

Straight to the hospital in an ambulance that time, paramedics and a stretcher and everything; not that he remembered the ride, the sirens blaring, or the emergency room, nothing but black and dreamless sleep until he opened his eyes in a white room that smelled like medicine and Pine-Sol and his mother was crying.

"They killed it," he said, words all croaky because his throat was so dry and sore, but needing to talk before he forgot and his father turning away from the window, then, his father looking angry, inconvenienced, embarrassed, something Deacon knew was inappropriate but his father looking that way regardless. His mother crying louder, and "Davey's dog," Deacon said. "They killed it. It's in the field."

His father took one step closer to the bed, and "Son," he said, "if you're doing this just to get attention, you better tell us right this minute. Right now. Before it gets any more out of hand than it already has," and the dazzling sun, sun setting like a fireball behind his father, too bright to look at, so he looked at his mother instead.

"They killed it," he said again, speaking to her because she only seemed frightened, not angry, not ready to blame him for whatever was happening, and she shook her head, not understanding, either.

"Killed what, Deke? We don't know what you're talking about." And neither did he, not really, but telling her anyway while his father turned away, turned back to the window. Deacon telling her how the boys had stolen the puppy and beat it to death with a hammer, beat it until all its bones were broken and then they'd nailed it to a tree in the field behind the high school and left it there. Telling her as fast as he could talk, before he forgot all their names, boys he didn't know, and he could see she thought he was crazy, crazy or lying or both, maybe.

"You hit your head," she said, talking to him like he was five years old or seventy-five, talking the way she talked to his grandmother at the nursing home. "You were playing football at Davey's house and you hit your head. Don't you remember playing football, Deke?"

"I didn't hit my head, Mom. I just twisted my ankle. I didn't hit my head, I swear," and his father turning around again, angry father framed in fire and his mother was already uncovering his bare feet and "His ankle's swollen, Marty," she said, mothervoice like something thin and brittle, like something strained.

"That doesn't mean he isn't lying. That doesn't mean he didn't hit his head," and then his father staring at him, just staring at him and bitter secrets behind Martin Silvey's eyes that Deke could see but wouldn't even begin to understand for years, old secrets dressed up like resentment or disappointment.

"You keep talking this way, Deacon, and they're gonna start thinking you're crazy. Do you know what that means, if they think you're crazy?"

"You're scaring him. Jesus, what's the point of scaring him when he's already lying here in a hospital bed and we don't even know what's wrong with him."

But his father not hearing her or not listening, leaning close now, faint smell of whiskey on his breath and whatever Deacon had seen in his eyes before was gone, nothing left but a strange and serious concern.

"I'm not *trying* to scare you, Deke. You don't know what these people, what these doctors, will believe, and sometimes it's better if we keep the things we *think* we know to ourselves. It won't fix anything, telling them about the dog. It won't *change* things so that those boys never killed it. They might even get the idea *you* had something to do with it."

His mother crying again, covering his swollen ankle and she stepped out of the room, left him alone with his father, and Deacon knew he was going to cry, cry like his mother, cry like a girl, and he didn't want his father to see. Wanted to go back to the black place that wasn't a place, the place where nothing hurt and he didn't have to think about why anyone would beat a puppy to death with a hammer or why his father was telling him he should pretend he hit his head or the doctors would think he was crazy.

"The puppy will still be dead, Deke," his father said. "I just want you to realize you can't change that. I want you to think about that," and Deacon rolled over, pushed his face deep into his pillow to hide the tears, muffle the sobs he couldn't swallow, and in a few more minutes his father followed his mother out into the hallway and left him alone in the white room.

Another week in the hospital, almost time for school to start again when they finally let him go home, a week of puzzled frowns from men and women in lab coats and still no explanation for his "seizure," no matter how much blood they took from his arms or how many pictures they made of the inside of his head. And Deacon never told them about Davey Barber's beagle.

But the week after he started fourth grade, he pedaled his bicycle out past the high school, past the football stadium and the older kids at band practice, all the way to the field; tall grass and pollen-yellow stalks of goldenrod, Queen Anne's lace and a scatter of oaks just far enough away that he couldn't see anything from the road. Only an hour or so left until dark, but Deacon hid his bike in the grass and walked towards the trees, picked his way slow across the weedthick field, watching for copperheads and rattlesnakes. Standing finally in the long, uneasy shadows gathering below the limbs, and the puppy was right where he knew it would be, what was left of it after a month, anyway, a month of the summer sun and rain, crows and maggots working at its body. Deacon used a pair of pliers to pull the nail out of its skull and then he buried the body in a sandy, barren place beneath the trees. No tears this time, just a sick and final feeling in his belly because he could never tell anyone, could never even tell Davey what had happened to his dog and no way to know when it might happen all over again, no way to know what not to touch.

On the other side of the field, one hundred yards and five years away, past chain-link fence to hold in the safer world of teenagers, illusions of a safer world perched on the slippery edge of growing up, the marching band began to play "Aura Lee," trumpets and clarinets, flutes and snare drum cadence, and Deacon Silvey followed the music back the way he'd come.

❁

Deacon is sitting alone on a candyblue plastic milk crate outside The Plaza, drawing circles in the dirt with a stick, circles within circles, and a little while ago Sadie left the bar, the door easing itself shut behind her and she headed off towards Five Points without even looking at him. That quick, determined way she has of walking, eyes fixed on the ground straight ahead of her, dead ahead, and he probably couldn't have gotten her attention if he wanted to; Sadie wrapped up snug and fretting in her sulky, black cocoon until she's ready to come out again. Deacon draws another circle, seventh from the outer rim and this exercise he taught himself a long time ago, trapping the fury in smaller and smaller circles, concentric restraint, putting it all away where it can't hurt anyone but him and he usually has it coming.

He tilts the crate back, all his weight resting against the wall of The Plaza, semicircle of glazed bricks the soft color of butter, odd semicircle of a building jutting out from under a shopping center: a florist and an Indian restaurant up there, Western Supermarket and a video rental place, and The Plaza tucked neatly beneath. Not as hot now as when he first left the bar, a few clouds and maybe a thunderstorm on the way, car exhaust, hot asphalt and a spicy hint of curry in the air.

The Plaza door opens again and this time it's Sheryl, still wearing her beer-stained bar apron, lighting a cigarette as she walks towards him. She squats down in the gravel and dirt next to his crate and exhales a cloud of smoke, takes another drag off her Marlboro before she says anything. Bunky Tolbert hasn't shown up and Deacon wonders who's watching the bar.

"I asked Jess to watch after things for me while I took a break," she says, reply to his unspoken question like a sideshow mind reader's trick and then Sheryl offers him a cigarette and Deacon says no, but thanks, and she shrugs, have-it-your-way shrug and slips the pack back into her apron pocket. "What's that supposed to be?" she asks, pointing at Deacon's circles with the smoldering tip of her cigarette.

A quick, embarrassed swipe from one of his boots and Deacon erases them all, nothing there now but bits of limestone and sand again, and "Just doodling," he replies. "It wasn't anything." Sheryl nods and puffs her cigarette.

"Look, I know you're a smart guy, Deke," she says, taps gray ash to the ground and looks up at him, squints at him through her own smoke. "So I'm not going to bother telling you what an asshole you can be. I figure you already know that part." And Deacon nods once, tosses away his stick and leans forward on the blue milk crate, all four corners back down to earth again.

"Then what *are* you gonna say, Sheryl?" he asks, not in the mood for guessing games, not really in the mood to listen to her or anyone else, for that matter.

"That she's just a kid, that's all, Deke. And I know she can be a freaky little pain in the ass sometimes, but if I were you and wanted her to hang around, well . . . I'd take it just a little easier on her, cowboy."

Deacon kicks at the dirt, kicks away the smooth place his boot made of the circles, and "It'll work itself out, Sheryl. It always does." And Sheryl nods, thoughtful, sure, whatever-you-say sort of nod, one more drag off her cigarette and she crushes the butt out beneath the toe of a sneaker.

"I just keep wondering if you're pissed off at Sadie, or if you're pissed off at Elise and it's just a lot easier to hurt someone who isn't dead."

Deacon swallows, wishing he had another beer or a bottle of gin, bottle of vodka, almost anything to wash away the dry. "That's a hell of a shitty thing to say," he mumbles and Sheryl nods her head.

"All I'm sayin' is be careful, man," and she gets up, glances at the darkening sky, the powdergray undersides of the thunderheads beginning to stack up above the city. "I gotta get back inside before Jessie decides to start handing out free martinis. If you see Bunky, kick his lazy ass for me," and then she's gone and Deacon Silvey is alone and there's a sound like thunder off towards Red Mountain.

CHAPTER FOUR

Sadie

SADIE Jasper stalks down the steep hill leading away from The Plaza, away from Deacon, her pointy black boots clock-clock-clocking loud on the asphalt and never mind the sidewalk, half-overgrown with kudzu, anyway, so she's walking down the middle of the road; if anyone runs her down that's their problem, a dent in their fender, their cracked windshield, an explanation they'll have to come up with for the police. She imagines her body lying limp and broken beside the road, bloody rag doll held inside chalkwhite lines, imagines little hairy bits of her scalp caught beneath the wiper blades of some asshole's Saab or BMW and that almost makes her smile. She kicks at an empty, plastic bottle that once held brake fluid and it bounces on ahead of her, finally comes to rest against the curb.

No good pretending that Deacon would really give a shit. *Hey, buddy, someone just ran over your girlfriend and now she's dead. Man, now she's fucking road pizza*, and Sadie knows precisely the way he'd rub at his eyes for a moment or two, the dull and calculated squint towards the ceiling of that shitty little bar, before he'd shake his head and order a shot of whiskey. Something almost expensive, in her memory. One alcoholic tear for poor, crumpled Sadie, if she was lucky, and so she glances around for something else to kick, something else that can't kick back.

The steep road intersecting with Twenty-first Street and she turns right, turns north towards home, the tiny apartment she shares with Deacon, and Sadie spots an old diet Coke can in the gutter. She starts to kick it, then pictures Chance Matthews' face printed across the red-and-white aluminum and stomps it hard instead. Much more satisfying to feel the soft metal fold and flatten out beneath the heel of her boot, delicious, ruined, scrunchy sound as she grinds it back and forth against the blacktop. And then a car rushes past, shinyblack blur and tires squealing, horn like a fucking banshee on crack, and some guy yelling at her to get out of the middle of the goddamn road, *Get out of the middle of the road you fucking freak;* sudden swoosh of air and exhaust fumes and Sadie watches the car speed away, then stares down at the squashed diet Coke can and it doesn't really look anything like Chance Matthews anymore.

"Fucker," she whispers and kicks it, sends it skittering and skipping away after the car that almost ran her down, and Sadie Jasper decides that maybe the sidewalk isn't such a bad idea after all.

Another block to the bank where she usually manages to keep just enough in checking that they don't cancel her account or charge her fees for letting it sit empty. The teller smiles politely, requisite, insincere smile, and takes away the candygreen slip of paper with her mother's signature, the deposit slip scarred by her own sprawling, unsteady handwriting, and gives her back a hundred and fifty in cash; the rest tucked away safe for now, and Sadie counts the money twice before stuffing it into her Bad Badtz-Maru billfold. "Thank you, Miss Jasper. You have a nice day now," the teller says, but Sadie knows she doesn't mean it any more than she means the plastic smile, that she's probably only thinking about all the customers standing impatiently behind Sadie, or wondering how anyone could walk around in public dressed like a refugee from *The Addams Family*; Sadie takes an extra few seconds to return her billfold to her purse, another second to snap the purse shut again, and then she glares at the woman behind the counter, not a smile but the distressed sort of face she might make if someone told her that she'd stepped in dog shit, maybe, and "You're welcome," she says.

She leaves the bank, leaves the air-conditioning and carpetsmelling air, crosses Twentieth Street to the dusty, secondhand bookshop squeezed between a hardware store and a place that repairs bicycles. Cowbell jingle when she opens the door and no air conditioner here, just a couple of huge ceiling fans that must have been around at least since Eisenhower was president, rusty steel blades to move the stale, bookscented heat around and around and the old man behind the counter smiles at her. But this is a genuine smile, his white beard that always makes Sadie think of the grandfathers she never knew, white eyebrows and "Good afternoon, Sadie," the old man says.

"Good afternoon, Jerome," she says, returning the smile in her hard, uneasy way, and "I think I might have something for you today," he says, reaches beneath the counter and his hand comes back with a book, clothbound cover the color of antique ivory, title and author stamped in faded gold and art deco letters. *Best Ghost Stories* by Algernon Blackwood and she lifts it carefully off the countertop, picks it up the way someone else might lift a diamond necklace or a sick kitten and opens the book to the frontispiece and title page, black-and-white photo of the author in a dapper suit, sadkind eyes and his bow tie just a little crooked.

"It's an ex–library copy, I'm afraid," Jerome says, and Sadie's eyes drift from the author's portrait to the word DISCARD stamped crimson and blockylarge just below the title, and PROPERTY OF NEWBURGH PUBLIC LIBRARY, NEWBURGH, NEW YORK, stamped underneath that in ink the color of blackberry juice. She sighs loud, frowns, something almost violent about marking a book that way, disrespectful and indelible inkbruises on paper gone yellowbrown around the edges.

"I know," Jerome says. "But it *is* the 1938 edition."

"You just *saw* me leaving the bank, didn't you?" she asks the old man. He shrugs a guilty, unrepentant shrug while she flips carefully through the pages, past "The Willows" and "The Wendigo" and "Accessory Before the Fact," thinks about the cheap, dog-eared Dover paperback she's had for years, a rubber band around it so the loose pages don't get lost.

"Twelve fifty," Jerome says. "Because it's a discard, and because I know you'll give it a good home."

Sadie closes the book and lays it gently on the counter, already nodding her head, no point pretending she's going to leave the shop without the Blackwood and she doesn't have the heart to haggle with Jerome when she knows he's hardly making enough these days to keep the power bill paid; all his business swallowed up years ago by strip-mall megastores and now people buying their books off the Internet, so she smiles for him again and Jerome says he'll hold onto it if she wants to browse around a while. And that's all she ever intended to do, of course, browse the shelves for an hour or two until she stopped feeling so pissed at Deke, crisp money in her purse but she knows how to be a good girl and Jerome never fusses if she hangs around without buying anything.

"How's Deke these days?" Jerome asks. "Haven't seen him

around in weeks," putting the book into a small, brown paper bag, now, folding the bag neatly closed.

"Maybe you better ask me that again a little later," she says, smile fading and Sadie slips away into the history section, past towering, overcrowded Civil War shelves, shelves for ancient Rome and Greece, shortest cut to the one narrow shelf labeled "Spiritualism and The Occult," stuck way off by itself in the very back of the shop. Nothing too heavy or too spooky, a few beat-up, spinebroken copies of Aleister Crowley and Eden Gray, Edgar Cayce and the prognostications of Nostradamus, various, interchangeable manuals for the Tarot and I Ching; she's halfway through Yeats' *A Vision,* hoping that no one buys it before she's finished. Her place marked with a movie ticket stub from her purse, and Sadie finds a wobbly stool, one leg an inch too short, finds Yeats still waiting where she left him tucked safe and secret behind a copy of *The Book of Mormon.* There's a tin of Altoids in her purse because Jerome won't let her smoke in the shop, and she digs it out, puts one of the powderwhite peppermints under her tongue, slides a coverless, water-damaged *Witchcraft in Old and New England* under the crippled stool, and in a moment she's lost in the soothing flow of words, concentration and focus to let her forget the argument with Deacon for a while.

Almost three months since the first night that Sadie Jasper slept with Deacon Silvey, and the first time that's all it was. She slept in his bed, lay very still and listened to his uneven breathing, the desperate sounds that people lost in nightmares make. Smelled his sweat and watched the restless flutter of his eyelids, wishing she could see, could know the images rolling wild through his head. She held him because that's all he asked her to do, Hold me, Sadie, just fucking *hold* me tonight, okay? and somewhere near dawn he awoke suddenly, sat up straight, gulping air like a junky with a syringe full of adrenaline pouring into his heart, gasping like a drowned man coming back to life. Sadie groggy, confused, trying to force herself awake, and What's wrong, Deke? What's wrong? but he was already out of bed, already across the room and the bathroom door squeaking open. Deacon? and no answer but the water gurgling from the faucet into the ruststained sink, staccato lampcord click and then a white, white light like rubbing alcohol in her eyes.

Stumbling across the bedroom, stubborn shadows and her eyes

trying to adjust to the light spilling out of the bathroom and she stubbed a toe against the edge of his chest of drawers. And then she was standing beside him, his face in the medicine cabinet mirror above the sink, face so pale, sickpale, scaredpale, cold water dripping from his chin and the end of his nose, dripping from his hair. No idea what to say to a face like that, what would comfort or console and so she didn't say anything at all. Stood silent beside him and waited while he stared into his own frightened eyes, his own green eyes gone mad, madman's intensity in that stare, and "Fuck," he whispered. "Fuck me, fuck me," and when she touched his arm he flinched.

"It's just *me*, Deke," but no sign that he understood, that he'd even heard her and he turned away from the mirror, turned and stared at the big, cast-iron bathtub, stared *into* the tub and by then Sadie was staring, too, straining to see whatever could drain the last, stingy bit of color from Deacon's face, bitterhard Deacon Silvey who never showed anything he didn't want you to see. A sound from his lips a lost child might make and he sank to his knees beside the tub and began to cry.

"It's Elise, isn't it?" she whispered, fearful, tentative whisper, and for an answer he slammed both fists into the side of the tub, furious blows that should have shattered his knuckles, but only left his hands bruised and bleeding.

"Get away from me, Sadie," he growled. "Get the hell away from me right this goddamned minute," and she shook her head no, reached instead for his injured hands and turned her back on the bathtub. Whatever it was he saw in there nothing meant for her, probably nothing meant for anyone anymore. His skin so cold, dead man's hands and she rubbed them, friction to bring him back, kicking and screaming if that's the way it had to be.

"Was it a dream, Deke? Did you have a dream about Elise or . . ." and pausing then because she knew how dangerous the words would be, how thin the ice beneath them, between them, was becoming.

"Was it a dream, or is she *here*?"

And his face like crystalperfect condemnation for a moment, crazy, burning face like a holy man confronted with some blasphemy too terrible to forgive and there could be only punishment. *He's going to kill me,* she thought, no other way she could imagine an end to that expression, release from that rage, and then he closed his eyes and squeezed her hands tight, squeezed so hard it hurt and he was shaking his head, the fire gone from his face as quickly as it had come. But she knew that he had let nothing go, had only pulled it all back inside himself somehow.

And before the moment was gone, before he'd smothered the last sparking embers, she asked the question again, the fury on his face all the proof she needed that it had been the *right* question; a hiss through Deacon's clenched teeth like steam, then, demon breath to scald, and he slowly opened his eyes, fresh tears escaping and rolling down his stubbled cheeks.

"You really think there's any goddamned difference?" he asked. "You really think that matters?"

"No," she said, pulling him closer to her, arms around him now, circle of her arms to bind him and keep him safe. "I don't think there's really any difference at all."

For almost two months Sadie has been trying to write a novel; not a very good novel, she knows that much, of that much she's absolutely certain, but something inside her that wants out. No matter that it's nothing anyone will ever want to read, that when she finally finds the place where the story ends, all the pages will go into a box and the box will go under her bed or onto the top shelf of a closet because she has no intention of ever letting anyone read it, no delusions of agents or publishers, no fantasies of an audience.

This makes it *her* book, and if she's deluded herself about anything it's that this fact somehow makes the writing of it more pure, more genuine, unsullied by the things that other people might want to read, or might not want to read.

Pecking it all out on a temperamental old Macintosh SE II that she found in a Dumpster behind an accounting firm on Morris Avenue, actually found the thing; no mouse in the Dumpster but it wasn't that hard to shoplift one. So she sits in the cold, whitegray light of the computer screen and pecks with two fingers, left and right index fingers because she never learned to type, and the Mac hums and sometimes it makes angryrude R2D2 noises for no apparent reason. Plugged into an outlet in one corner of Deke's bedroom, sitting on the floor between the bed and a stack of the science fiction novels he reads; and that's where she writes, legs crossed, slouched like a vulture over the keyboard and Deacon keeps telling her she's going to wind up with a pinched nerve or carpal tunnel syndrome, some office monkey yuppie shit like that if she doesn't move the Mac to the kitchen table and sit in a chair while she writes. But Deacon's kitchen smells too much like his refrigerator, like the ancient gas stove, so she's content with her nappy patch of carpet.

No printer, of course, so every single word stored on the hard drive and one blue back-up diskette that Deke made her buy at Kinko's. "Just in case," he said, because the building's wiring has seen better days and how much can you trust a computer you found in a garbage Dumpster, anyway? She makes herself write at least two whole pages every night, four or five on a really good night, writes while Deke lies on the bed reading Ben Bova or Robert Heinlein, sipping his cheap gin or Thunderbird, and the sound of her two fingers dancing slowly, uncertainly, over the plastic alphabet keys. Making a story from the messy thoughts and half-thoughts in her head, building a world and lives and taking them apart again, fitting the pieces together another way until it feels right, as right as she can make it feel.

"When you gonna let me read it?" Deacon asks her once a week, the question like clockwork, and sometimes she shrugs and sometimes it makes her angry and she tells him he can read it when there's an ice rink in Hell. Always the same mock hurt from Deke, the same pretend affront or indignity, and she likes the way he looks when he isn't really sulking.

"Well, you can at least tell me what it's about," and she tells him that's even worse than asking if he can read it. An insult, the assumption that what she's doing can be reduced to a convenient synopsis. "That's what's wrong with you," she says, "you're a goddamn reductionist."

"Whoa, girl. Who's been teaching you all these big fucking words?" and she flings a copy of *Dune* or *Again, Dangerous Visions* at him, something thick with some weight, with some gravity. She rarely ever actually hits him; there's a jumbled pile of paperbacks on her side of the bed, books that have missed Deke's head by inches.

"That's okay," he says, or "Whatever," smiles and takes a sip from his jelly glass of liquor, bottle of wine the color of an eggplant or nothing at all. "It's probably just some of that trashy Lovecraft shit you read. 'The Moldering Big Toe of Dagon' or 'The Whisperer from Behind the Laundry Hamper,' something like that," and so she has to throw another book at him.

"You haven't even ever read Lovecraft, dumb-ass," and he always rolls his eyes and mutters something condescending, "When you were still watching goddamn *Sesame Street*, kiddo, when you were still into Mr. Rogers and King Friday, Mr. fucking Greenjeans, kiddo."

"You know, I always thought Mr. Moose was especially creepy, didn't you?" and "Now you're trying to change the subject," he says. Never exactly like that, but never very different, either. Comfortable little ritual, something almost approaching domestic, as close as they'll probably ever get to domestic. And maybe she *will* let him read it one day, when she's done. When she's finished the last sentence, transferred the last muddy thought from her head to the screen, and it's all there to speak for itself.

Maybe that would prove that she loves him, that it's not just the sex or a weakness for irredeemable losers, the romance of a life of poverty with an alcoholic of questionable sanity and dubious hygiene. Not just that they saw a ghost together one night a long time ago, saw something in a warehouse once that might have been a ghost, or that they both like Charlie Parker and Joy Division. That would be showing him a part of her soul, a part of her mind, that she's never risked showing anyone. The raw and squirming part that indifferent high-school counselors were always prying at, the part therapists tried to trick her into showing them for free, the part her parents hated her for. The light and the darkness behind her eyes, the soft places.

But it would also mean admitting how much of what she's writing is *about* him, the patchwork bits and pieces she's learned about him, about Elise's suicide and why he can't ever stop loving Chance Matthews. It would mean confessing her own resentment in words more honest than she's ever had the nerve to say to his face.

And then there are her own bad dreams, the dreams about the mountain, the secret places below the mountain, and perhaps that would be the worst of all.

◉

"It's starting to rain," Jerome says and Sadie glances up from the Yeats, and the old man's pointing towards the high and shadowy ceiling of the book shop. "Just thought you might want to know, since I ain't never seen you carrying an umbrella."

"Thanks," she says, her head still lost in Yeats' cyclical theories of history, marking her place with the ticket stub and returning the volume to its hiding place behind *The Book of Mormon.*

"I got an extra one you can borrow, though, if you want it," Jerome says, and Sadie glances at her Sanrio wristwatch, trying to figure out how it got so late so fast.

"Sure," she says. "Thanks."

She follows him back to the register, pays the twelve fifty, plus tax, for the book of ghost stories and he's wrapped it in a second bag, plastic grocery bag from the Piggly Wiggly, so it won't get wet, hands her the umbrella and she thanks him again. Big umbrella the color of overripe bananas, the color of a banana Popsicle, but at least it'll keep her dry. The door jingles shut behind her and she stands for a moment beneath the raggedy bookshop awning, green-and-white canvas stripes, looking out at the stormslick street, up at the sky gone dark as silt and ashes, and the falling rain makes an incongruous sound, like eggs frying in a skillet. Sadie opens the umbrella and sighs when she sees that there's a giant smiley face printed on the underside, smirking, happy cartoon face to leer down at her while she splashes through the puddles.

"Yeah, well fuck you too," she says to the smiley face and glances over her shoulder. Jerome's watching her from his chair behind the counter; he nods his head once, waves good-bye and she waves back, tucks the twice-wrapped book beneath one arm and crosses Twentieth Street.

Back home, the dank and mildewstinking halls of Quinlan Castle, and she pauses on the concrete front steps to shake the rain off Jerome's happy yellow umbrella, flaps it open and closed, open and closed, making a furious noise like the death throes of a giant bat or a pterodactyl, spraying a thousand droplets across the steps and the sidewalk. The storm has almost passed, just a sickly drizzle now and the thunder fading away, distant, muffled cacophony done with Birmingham and taking its wrath elsewhere.

On the way upstairs, she passes Mrs. Schmidt who lives across the hall, elderly Mrs. Schmidt who hears voices if she forgets to take her medication, who has an ugly little dog of no discernible breed named Tinkle and once she brought Sadie and Deke a plate of hot oatmeal cookies that tasted faintly of fish. Sadie smiles at her, says hello and the old woman smiles back, her no-denture smile, healthy pink gums but no teeth, and she lightly touches Sadie's arm and "I told her to come back when you or Deacon were at home," she says.

"Who?" Sadie asks, groaning inside because this is probably just something Mrs. Schmidt got into her head halfway through *General Hospital*, something crazy and Sadie doesn't have the patience for it today.

"The albino girl," Mrs. Schmidt replies, her trembling fingers still resting on Sadie's forearm, age spots and skin like wrinkled silk, and "Oh, her eyes were so pink, just like a white Easter rabbit's."

"There was an albino girl looking for us?"

"Yes," Mrs. Schmidt says, leaning closer now, and she smells like menthol and violets. "She was sitting in front of your door eating a bag of gumdrops and when I asked her what she was doing there she said waiting. Just waiting. And I told her that she should come back when you were home."

"Did you remember to take your pills this morning, Mrs. Schmidt?" Sadie asks, trying not to sound annoyed or patronizing. "The green ones?" Puzzled squint from the old woman for a second and then she blinks and smiles again. "Yes, dear," she says, laughs softly and "She wasn't *that* sort of a girl at all."

"Well, I just wanted to be sure. You know, just in case," Sadie says, still not certain whether to believe Mrs. Schmidt or not. "It isn't good for you to miss your pills."

"Thank you, dear. It's very nice of you to worry about me. But she said that she would find you," and then the old woman says good-bye and is toddling unsteadily away towards the row of mailboxes by the front door. Sadie watches her go, and she's pretty sure she doesn't believe that there was an albino sitting at their front door eating gumdrops.

She takes the stairs two or three at a time, out of breath and her heart racing when she reaches the third floor and the musty smell is worse up here because the landlords refuse to fix a seeping, rotten patch of ceiling at the far end of the hallway. The plaster like soft and molded cheese down there, a couple of places where it's fallen away completely and you can see the lathe, can look straight up into the attic darkness showing between the timegray wood slats. So, the perpetual stench of rotten ceiling, and if it rains long enough, small, pinkwhite mushrooms sprout from the carpet below the hole. The mushrooms seem to make Deacon nervous, though she's never asked him why, and he doesn't ever walk down to that end of the hall alone.

Digging through her purse for the door key, the ring with a toothy, rubber vampire bat on it and keys to places she hasn't lived for years, keys to her parents' house, keys to a car she wrecked last summer, and of course it's hiding at the bottom under all the other purse junk. As usual, the lock sticks and she's wrestling with it when she notices the mound of black gumdrops on the threshold, neat and sugared pile of discarded candy, and so the troublesome door forgotten for the moment, the rubber bat left dangling from the lock, as she bends down for a closer look. Black gumdrops, eight of them, and Sadie picks one up and looks at it like she's never seen one before, glances across the hall to Mrs. Schmidt's door. Certainly not impossible that the old woman put them there herself, like the time she drew big X's and O's in blue chalk on every door in the building; Sadie sets the gumdrop back on top of the pile and opens the door, thinking that she'll just leave them there and let Deke figure out what to do about it, probably best to forget the whole thing anyway, and that's when she sees the folded sheet of paper that someone's slid under the door.

◈

The first bad dream about a week after she moved in with Deke, right before she found the computer in the Dumpster, and if Sadie told him that he might start talking about synchronicity and meaningful coincidence. But she hasn't told him. Hasn't told anyone, admitting the nightmares to nobody but herself and the Mac, confidence kept between her and the squat box of microchips and cybergreen circuit board. The black and waterdripping dreams, wandering someplace beneath the city and she's never alone but never quite sure who's with her, their voices always indistinct, their faces lost in the darkness. A strangling smell like stagnant water and something dead, something drowned, and the moldy hallway stench magnified a thousandfold. Walking and listening to the voices up ahead, wondering if she should call out, if she's lost, if they're all lost and searching for a way out, but she's never said a word. Hugs herself against the damp and cold, against the deadwetdecay smells, and the rocks beneath her feet are slick with slime and mud, with whatever can grow untouched by the sun.

And at first these strange dreams like déjà vu, maddeningly familiar but a fleeting, intangible sort of familiarity, always fading with her first cup of coffee, her first cigarette of the morning. Then one night she was bored and channel-surfing on Deke's crappy, Salvation Army television and she flipped past a PBS documentary, *Nova* or *Nature,* something about bats or caves, and suddenly the pieces fit together, dot-to-dot revelation, and Sadie remembered when she was ten years old and she had other dreams of being lost underground, nightmares that lasted for a whole month after her parents took her to Kentucky to see Mammoth Cave.

The trip a present for her tenth birthday and the three of them following a guide who explained about stalagmites and stalactites as he led them deeper and deeper underground, farther from the light, farther from the day. Travertine flowstone formations like monsters hulking in the shadows, waiting until no one was looking so they could reach out and drag her screaming into the forever night of the caverns. They passed bottomless reflecting pools where pale, eyeless salamanders and crayfish lived, lingered before fantastic gardens of calcite and quartz. And at some point all the lights were turned out, sixty blindperfect seconds so that everyone would know how dark the cave *really* was, how absolute and complete that blackness, and she held desperately onto her mother, feeling dank and insubstantial teeth sink straight through her skin, all the way to her bones.

And these new nightmares stitching now to then, these dreams to those, and sometimes the two bleed together and she's ten again, lost under Birmingham and trying to find her parents or the way back to the world above, trying to catch up with the mumbling voices ahead of her. So close she should be able to reach out and touch whoever it is that's talking, but if she holds her hands out there's only the chilly underground air and the dark between her fingertips. Except for once, and most of the time she'd rather pretend that isn't actually part of the dreams; a figment of her imagination's daystarved imagination, a dream's insane dream, and in that subterranean place she did *not* reach out with urgent, imploring fingers and brush the shoulder of a dead girl. Did not feel that skin like ice, but Sadie Jasper's never been a very good liar, even when she's only lying to herself, and in that one dream the lights finally did come back on, and she saw that the grand cathedral theater of Mammoth Cave had become a narrow tunnel, purposeful mine shaft sort of tunnel, so maybe she'd wandered away from her parents, away from the guide. Maybe all she had to do was stop and retrace her steps. But the dead girl turned around, instead, and Sadie knew that face, even though the hungry worms and beetles had been at it for days and days, even though she never met Elise Alden, no eyes left but she knew *that* face and she saw the blackred gashes that ran from the girl's wrists to the bends of her elbows. And the girl smiled for her like a polar night sky where every star has died.

A single white sheet of paper, folded twice, and her name and Deacon's scribbled across the front in pencil, scribbled like someone in a hurry or maybe just someone with shitty handwriting, ugly cursive, and Sadie carries the note to the couch and sits down. The door left wide open, and she sets her purse, the book and the yellow umbrella down on the floor at her feet. Unfolds the sheet of paper and there's more of the same tight scrawl, all the words tilting sharply to the left and *You do not know me yet,* it says at the very top. *You do not know me yet, but there is not much time left. I waited all day long and now the woman with the dog says I should go and I am afraid she'll call the police so I am writing you this note instead.*

"Instead of *what,*" Sadie whispers, frowning at the piece of paper, the sticky, gumdrop fingerprints at the edges, and the handwriting is getting worse as it goes along and she has to hold the note closer to her face and squint.

I will tell you why I am and then something that's been scratched out, violentsudden graphite scratches to obliterate a mistake, three or four words written down and then taken back, thought better of, and *I need to talk to you both very soon. You know a girl named Chance who lives in a big house on the mountain and I have already talked to her. I have not told her why, but when I do she will not believe me but I know that you both will. I am sorry I had to leave a note like this. I am not a bad person,* and then printed much more legibly below the last line, *Dancy Flammarion.*

"Your door is open," and Sadie looks up from the note and there's Mrs. Schmidt standing in the doorway, clutching a fat wad of junk mail in her left hand. She's stepped on the little pile of gumdrops, one of her blue bedroom slippers squashing them flat. "You really shouldn't leave your door standing open like that, Sadie. It's not a good neighborhood anymore."

"I know," Sadie says and then she glances back down at the note, that last line before the signature.

I am not a bad person.

"There are all sorts of people wandering about that don't belong here. Let me close the door for you, Sadie," and Sadie looks up at the old woman, the deep worry lines on Mrs. Schmidt's creased face even deeper than usual.

"Thank you, Mrs. Schmidt," Sadie says and when the door is shut and she's alone again, she reads the note over from the beginning.

CHAPTER FIVE

The Dead and the Moonstruck

ALICE Sprinkle has hands like a bricklayer, sturdylong fingers and calluses and muscle, all the white and inconsequential scars that come from twenty years spent climbing around in limestone quarries, shale quarries, road cuts. Scars and the damage the sun does to a woman's skin, the fine wrinkles and her nails thick and nubby, a fresh Band-Aid wrapped around her left index finger; Chance smiles politely at her across the cluttered kitchen table and pours Alice another cup of coffee.

"I just can't see any reason for it, Chance," Alice says and sighs, lifts her grayblue china cup and blows hard on the steaming, black liquid inside. Breath to send tiny ripples across the dark surface and "It's a goddamned, stupid waste," she says.

"You really don't have to keep saying that," Chance says quietly, trying to sound confident, trying to sound like she doesn't know she's losing this argument again, and she drinks her own coffee, scaldingquick mouthful and a glance out the kitchen window at the summer night filling up the backyard. July night full of crickets and the metronome cicada thrum, a little cooler now because of the thunderstorms this afternoon and the grass out there will still be wet, the soil underfoot still damp.

"Maybe I wouldn't, if you'd listen to reason," Alice says, setting her cup down too hard and a few drops of coffee slosh over the brim, run down the side of the cup to stain the tablecloth. "What do you think Joe would say if he knew what you were doing? You think he wouldn't be telling you the same things I am?"

"Joe's dead," Chance says, looks away from the backyard, back to her cup, and "Yeah, well, and you know what? You're *not*," Alice Sprinkle says, leaning towards Chance now. Not exactly anger on her face, but something more angry than simple concern.

"I just need some time to get my head together, Alice. That's not stupid. My grandfather just died, okay? It's not stupid if I can't deal with school right now."

"But that's not what you *said*. You said you didn't think you'd be coming back. You said you didn't see the point."

Chance closes her eyes for a moment, and that *is* what she said, more or less, two days since she talked to Alice on the phone, Dr. Alice K. Sprinkle from her thesis committee and she should've known better, should have simply dropped out of sight and let everyone figure it out for themselves. But all the responsible parts of her mind refusing to shut down along with the parts that gave a shit about fossils and grade-point averages and where she was going to do her doctoral work, all the parts that drove her through six years of college in less than five. The parts that got her published in the *Journal of Paleontology* and *Palaios* when she was still an undergrad. She should have vanished and let them wonder. Instead she called Alice, *I don't think I'll be coming back,* nothing but cold silence from the other end of the phone as she stuttered out her practiced apologies and suggested someone who might be good to take over her Tuesday/ Thursday freshman ES 102 lab. "I'll be by in a few days to clean out my office," she said and Alice said nothing but "We'll talk about this later, Chance." So now here they are, later, talking about it in her dead grandfather's kitchen, talking about it since six o'clock this evening, arguing in smaller and smaller circles and Chance always wrong, always the one who isn't making sense.

"I think you know very well what your career meant to Joe," Alice says and lights a cigarette, even though she knows how much it bothers Chance, that Chance doesn't like people smoking in the house. She taps a Winston from a half-empty pack and lights it, blows a single, ghostperfect smoke ring towards the light above the table, dim bulb in a frosted, antique globe.

"This work you're doing in the Parkwood and Pottsville with those new fish and tetrapods, and the trackways, Dr. Bierce keeps telling me how important this stuff is. How your work on Middle Carboniferous vertebrates is gonna raise some eyebrows," and Alice takes another drag off the Winston, doesn't take her eyes off Chance. "Do you have any idea how proud of you Joe was? He never would've pushed you to go into paleo', but you know how happy he was when that's what you wanted."

"Look, I don't need this fucking guilt trip," the words tumbling out of Chance's mouth in a growl, never mind that she knows this is exactly what Alice Sprinkle wants, trying to provoke, digging for a flintstrike spark of passion and here it is and maybe if she digs just a little deeper she can build a fire.

Alice still talking, like she didn't hear the resentment in Chance's voice, like she doesn't care, and "So it's not just what Joe wanted, it's what *you* want, Chance. Goddamn, you're fucking brilliant. You know that. I *know* you know that. And you love—"

"Don't try to tell me what I love, Dr. Sprinkle," she says, hard and formal words to build a wall between them, titles and last names because she knows the familiarity is only working against her.

"Call it whatever you want. I don't care what you call it. But it's rarer than brains," and Alice taps her temple hard with her bandaged index finger for emphasis. "I see smarts every goddamn day of the week. Smart is cheap stuff, kiddo. You're smart, but you do *this* because you'll never be whole without it, and you're so goddamn lucky that your grandparents were there to back you up. You know what *my* mother did when I told her what I wanted to do with my life? First she asked what the hell a 'paleontologist' was, and then, when I told her, she cried. My dad, he just wanted to know if it meant I was a lesbian."

"I'm sorry," Chance says and her stomach hurts from all the black coffee and no supper, her head from all the talk, and the clock on the wall above the oven says it's almost nine.

"Yeah, well, whatever. I did it anyway, didn't I? But if just once they had encouraged me, had even tried to understand. If just once they had *pretended* to be proud of me. That's why I'm in your face like this, Chance. This is what you want, and Joe was so proud of you."

"You're not being fair," and immediately Chance knows she shouldn't have said that, a weakness she shouldn't have shown, and Alice rocks back in her chair and smokes her Winston and watches Chance silently.

"I just can't *think* right now," Chance says, no growl left in her, almost a whisper; shaky, whispered words and in another minute or two she'll be crying again; last thing in the world she wants, to start bawling in front of this implacable, determined woman. "Can't you *see* that? I can't act like everything's normal, like nothing's changed."

Not precisely silence then, but no one saying anything else, either; brittlelong moments filled up with all the outside insect noises getting in and finally Alice exhales, loud, cigarette-smoky exhalation and she stubs the Winston out in the unused saucer meant for her coffee cup. Chance not looking at her, staring at the yellow sunflowers on the tablecloth, yellow flowers with black eyes, and "I can show myself out," Alice says. "Thanks for the coffee."

"I just need some time, that's all. Just a little time," Chance says.

"Yeah," Alice Sprinkle replies. "Maybe you do. But I'm taking over your Tuesday/Thursday, just until you get your head together. We'll talk again next week, Chance." And the woman leaves her alone in the kitchen with the dirty china cups and the smell of coffee and cigarette smoke.

Going through the motions, everyday chores to keep both her feet on the ground, dustdry eyes, and Chance cleans the kitchen, empties Alice's cigarette ash from the china saucer, rinses the old percolator, rearranges the clutter on the table so it's the same mess disorganized another way. She carries out half a bag of trash and leaves it on the curb for the rumbling, green garbage truck to haul off in the middle of the night. Brief and meaningless things that take away some of the time and require no thought, as little thought as possible. And then her stomach growls, emptysick feeling now to remind Chance that she hasn't eaten since breakfast, her belly as hollow as everything else, so she opens some Chef Boyardee ravioli and eats it cold from the can, sits on the floor in front of the television, flipping channels and not tasting the tomato sauce and whatever it is that's supposed to be meat. A documentary on The Learning Channel about coral reefs off the coast of Australia, but that only makes her think about school, her unfinished thesis, so she keeps flipping, finally settles on a Humphrey Bogart film she can't remember the name of, Humphrey Bogart as a Devil's Island convict, and she turns the volume up loud enough that she doesn't have to listen to the summer night sounds outside the living room windows.

Running alone through the water works tunnel, through the dimly lit hallways of the apartment building where Elise lived, where she *lives* because she isn't dead yet, because this time Chance isn't at home, isn't sitting in her room with her head stuck in her work while Elise is dying behind one of these doors. Doors painted the color of dried blood and vomit and there are no numbers on them, nothing to distinguish one from another and no doorknobs, gaping rustrimmed holes where the doorknobs should be, corrosion the same flaking color as blood, and white light spills from the rooms through the holes.

"How the fuck are people supposed to know where anyone lives," Deacon says, Deacon somewhere close behind her and she tells him to shut up. She doesn't want him here, all his fault anyway and he knows it. Selfish but not that stupid, Elise dying because of him, and Chance follows the spiraldown halls that tilt and lead them around and around, dizzying whorl inside a snail's cast-off shell, floors warped and walls buckled.

No, not apartments, Chance thinks, *Elise didn't die at home, did she?* and then Deacon's ahead of her, no memory of him passing her, but there he is anyway, standing in front of one of the doors. The painwhite light from the doorknob hole eating at the legs of his jeans, his raggedy, black tennis shoes, and he puts his fingers through the hole, slides them into the light, into the room behind the door and there's an ugly, tearing sound like raw meat and waxed paper, and Chance looks away. *Coward,* she thinks, but the light suddenly so bright, bright past blinding, and she can feel it scorching her bare skin, searing Hiroshima flash to swallow her whole, and that means that Deacon's opened the door, that means he's found her.

And a hot wind is filling the motel hallway then, and he's shouting but the wind steals all the words, nothing left but the familiar shell of his voice. Chance is on her knees, screaming his name, and she can feel the light getting inside her, getting into her bones.

"You learn things over here," Elise says, and now Chance is sitting on the toilet in a bathroom with dirtywhite ceramic tile on the walls while Elise Alden bleeds to death in the tub. "Oh, not as much as you might think, but more than is really necessary, I suspect. More than I wanted to know."

"Deacon opened the door," Chance says, trying not to look at the bathwater like cherry Kool-Aid.

"That's one of the things he does."

No idea what Elise means, and Chance can't remember what it is that she's supposed to be doing, something urgent that doesn't seem to matter anymore. Hard to think because the room smells like blood, and "Aren't you cold?" she asks the dead girl.

"They tell me things," Elise says, like an answer.

"I don't understand," Chance replies, "I don't know what you're talking about," because she doesn't and Elise smiles, not a pretty smile, a crooked smile to hide something worse, and "You're not supposed to," she says. "Not yet. But I think you will."

Elise bends forward a little, pulls a chain to let the water out of the bathtub.

"Deacon opened the door," she says. "That's one of the things he can do."

"Fuck him," and Chance is getting nauseous from the commingled smell of Elise's blood and bathroom cleansers, disinfectant and the crimson water swirling down the drain. Tired of sitting in a dirty motel bathroom, talking about Deacon Silvey, smelling blood and Lysol. "He put you here. He doesn't give a shit about anyone in the world but himself."

"I'm supposed to show you something, Chance."

And there's an impatient flutter from the other side of the tiny window above the bathtub, abrupt flutter like a flock of starlings all taking off at once, flutter like a hundred frantic, feathered wings, and Chance didn't even notice the window before. Perfect rectangle of smudgy glass and there's a bright light shining in.

"No, I'm not supposed to tell you anything," Elise says and she sounds frightened, sounds confused.

"You don't have to tell me anything, Elise. I haven't asked you to tell me anything."

"You wouldn't even know to ask," the dead girl says. "You never ask anyone anything," and that fluttering again, closer this time, twice as loud, and the light outside the window seems to swell and pulse like a toothache.

"I won't let it hurt you again," Chance says, watching the window and now there are spiderweb cracks in the glass, the shadow of something outside, something big moving around between the light and the window.

"Is that what you think?" Elise asks. "Is that how you think this works?"

A sucking, squelching sound from the tub, then, the last of the water and Elise down the drain, but barely audible over the noise from the window. The pane pops loud and cracks all the way across, shudders in its rotten, wooden frame. And Chance remembers the hallway and Deacon's fingers through the hole where there wasn't a doorknob, remembers why she's here, that Elise isn't dead, dying but she isn't dead yet, and if there's a telephone in the room she can still call an ambulance and maybe this time everything will be different. This time it will end in a hospital room and Elise crying because she knows she didn't really want to die, Chance telling her not to cry. Or cry if she needs to, but everything will be right again anyway, wait and see, everything will be just fine.

Chance gets up off the toilet seat and now the condensation on the bathroom window is rising in wispy tendrils of steam, steam like little tentacles, and she can feel the heat from the light on her face.

"I'm not supposed to show you anything," Elise whispers, small and scared childwhisper, and Chance looks away from the light, the devouring light and the restless feather shadows, and she sees what's lying in the empty bathtub.

◉

Waking up on the floor, waking up on the floor a lot these days, dreamsweat chill and the gooeysharp aftertaste of Chef Boyardee in her mouth, and for a little while Chance just lies there staring at the television screen. Familiar images to drive away the bad things in her head, John Wayne and Henry Fonda, black-and-white phosphor security blanket when there's no one alive she can call out to, no one to turn on a light and tell her it was only a nightmare and it's over now, no one to hold her or mumble something irrelevant and reassuring. Her left arm's gone to sleep, jabbing pins and needles when she rolls over onto her back to stare at the ceiling, the light and dark watercolor patterns the TV screen makes on the high ceiling.

Gunfire and startled shouts from the television and Chance realizes that she's going to throw up, tries a trick that Deacon taught her, counting backwards from one hundred—ninety-nine, ninety-eight, ninety-seven—but it's too late for that and at least she manages to reach the downstairs bathroom before she pukes up all the half-digested ravioli. Heaving into the toilet bowl until her stomach's empty again, wondering if it's food poisoning, if maybe she caught a bug, and then she flushes and leans back against the tub, the tile floor cool against her skin. Chance wipes at her mouth with a wad of toilet paper, tosses it away and closes her eyes, heart beating slower now, and she feels better already, the sickness fading almost as quickly as it came.

Not thinking about the bathroom because it would only remind her of the dream, trying not to think about anything but *The Man Who Shot Liberty Valence* playing loud in the living room. John Wayne hiding in the alleyway so that Jimmy Stewart thinks he's the one that killed Lee Marvin, that he's the hero and so he'll get the girl in the end. One of her grandfather's favorite movies, almost anything with John Wayne one of his favorites, and there are hot tears running down her face before she can think of something else. No thought safe anymore, no memory or thought that hasn't been ruined for her, that isn't waiting to cut, waiting to bite, and then the phone starts ringing.

"Leave me the fuck alone," she yells at it, but yelling makes her stomach roll again so she stops.

Fourth ring and then the answering machine clicks on, Joe Matthews' voice and Jesus Christ, she hasn't even changed the message on the fucking answering machine and her grandfather's rambling on about leaving your name and number, the date and time, her grandfather talking from the grave. His voice trapped and rattling from the tinny answering-machine speaker and Chance manages to get to her feet, stands up to walk the ten or fifteen steps to the gossip bench in the hall when the machine beeps and her stomach feels so bad she sits quickly back down on the edge of the tub. A pause before Deacon Silvey clears his throat and "Chance?" he asks, like he knows she's sitting there, like he *could* know, and "Pick up if you're listening," and then a longer pause.

The very last person in the world she wants to talk to, so maybe this is still the nightmare, maybe if she pinches herself really hard she'll wake up.

"Yeah. Okay," he says and the skeptical tone in his voice that says, *I know you're there, I know you just don't want to speak to me.* "Look. There's something we have to talk about and it's entirely too goddamn weird to go into over the phone."

"Right," Chance mumbles and looks back at the toilet bowl, the wad of tissue she used to wipe the vomit from her mouth floating around in there and her stomach cramps at the sight of it.

"I know you don't want to talk to me. I wouldn't have called, but—"

"You're an asshole," Chance mumbles.

"But there's this girl and she says she talked to you at the downtown library a few days ago. She says you'll remember her, that you gave her twenty bucks. Look, Chance. This is just too strange for me to try and explain over the telephone, so call me back. Call me back tonight, okay?"

Dull click when he hangs up and then the phone beeps again, beeps like it's pissed off, pissed at Chance for sitting there and making Deke leave a message. For making it speak to Deacon with a dead man's voice; Chance flushes the toilet again and turns off the bathroom light behind her. When she gets to the gossip bench in the hall she jabs the eject button hard with one finger and the answering machine spits out the miniature cassette tape. She holds it tightly in her palm for a minute, squeezes the plastic and there's hardly any weight at all, when something that hurt so much to hear should weigh a ton. Chance thinks about smashing the tape against the wall or hurling it to the floor, stomping it to translucent shards and a tangled mess of black, magnetic ribbon. Pretends for a moment she could ever do a thing like that, could ever be that decided, that resolute, the sort of thing that Alice Sprinkle would do, surely, but Chance can only open her palm and stare at it, Memorex and the two tiny spools that seem so innocent, so mute, and she sets it on the edge of the bench next to the telephone book. Which is what Chance Matthews would do, she thinks, *exactly* what Chance Matthews would do.

Her shadow in the colorless television glow from the living room, the noise of John Wayne burning down his own house because he's drunk and alone and he probably wants to burn down a lot of other things, too, but the ranch house will have to do. Chance stares at the phone a few more minutes and then she picks up the receiver and dials Deacon's number.

Over an hour before there's finally a knock at the front door. Chance is sitting on the sofa in the living room eating Saltine crackers, trying to settle her stomach, has half the lights downstairs burning now and the television turned off. Thinking about the argument with Deacon when he wouldn't tell her what was going on over the phone, and the second one when he wanted her to come all the way over to his place at one o'clock in the morning to find out. She jumps at the sound of his knuckles against wood, *blam blam blam* like he wants to break the door down and she drops a half-eaten Saltine.

"Just one goddamn minute!" Yelling loud but he starts knocking again anyway; *blam blam blam blam;* Chance stoops to retrieve the Saltine, brushes cracker crumbs from her blue jeans to the floor, and "I'm *coming*!" she yells at the front door. Ten bucks from her back pocket for Deke to pay the taxi, the only way she could talk him into coming to her, promising to pay the carfare so she didn't have to smell the must and decay of Quinlan Castle, the smell like mold and nests of fat cockroaches, almost enough to get her puking again, just thinking about the place.

Chance opens the door and there's Deacon in a once-black Velvet Underground T-shirt that's been washed so many times it's almost gray, black turning the dingygray of mouse fur or mockingbird feathers, and he's squinting, blinking at the light from the front porch, from the foyer. He has a big, armygreen duffel bag in one hand and she thinks maybe he isn't drunk, thinks maybe he's actually sober, and then she notices Sadie Jasper standing there beside him and the albino girl holding her hand like a weird twin sister, Sadie's paler shadow, and Chance shoves the ten-dollar bill into Deke's hand before he can ask for it.

"Here," she says. "And hurry." Deacon blinks at the ten once or twice and then he's on his way back down to the driveway, back down to the old Ford station wagon trying to pass for a taxi, one headlight and its motor purring like a huge, impatient cat. *A cat with really bad sinuses,* Chance thinks and then Sadie smiles her waxyblack smile and tries to look happy to be there, points at the albino girl and "This is Dancy," she says. "I think you two have met already."

"Yeah," Chance says, talking to Sadie, but still watching Deacon as he hands the guy in the station wagon the ten and waits for change. "At the library," she says.

"Your grandfather was a geologist," Dancy says, not smiling but there's something gentle in her voice, a soothing voice when Chance's nerves are humming like electric guitar strings, humming like the cicadas in the humidwarm night.

"Yeah," Chance says, "he was," and then Deke is on his way back up to the house, the station wagon turning around behind him, rear wheels flinging a little gravel and the driver's probably ticked off because Deacon stiffed him on the tip, Chance thinks, thinks Deke probably pocketed the change and now he's hoping she won't think to ask if there was any.

"Well, come on," she says to Sadie and the albino girl and they follow her inside and Chance leaves the door open for Deacon.

All of them in Chance's living room, Chance at one end of the long sofa and Sadie at the other, Deke in a gingham armchair near the silent television, and Dancy Flammarion sitting on a footstool in the middle of the room, facing Chance, the duffel bag Deacon was carrying at her feet now, and "I can see monsters," she says again.

Chance stops staring at her and looks across the room at Deacon. He shrugs a small, apprehensive sort of shrug and rubs hard at his eyes like they hurt, like the light's too bright, covers them with his right hand.

"Monsters," Chance says, repeating the word carefully just in case there are secrets hidden somewhere between the two syllables, something that she's missing, secret code or the punch line to a joke that she isn't getting. But Dancy only nods her head, the same quiet grace in that movement as in her voice, and an earnest intensity in her pink eyes that makes it hard for Chance to look directly at her for very long.

"Deacon," Chance says, his name spoken quiet like a warning, but he still has his hand over his eyes.

"It's okay," Dancy says. "I already know that you can't see them. I know you don't believe in monsters."

"I'm sorry, Dancy. I don't think I even understand what you're trying to say, or why you're saying it to me," and Sadie glances at Chance, quick and scowling glance from Sadie Jasper's iceblue eyes, eyes almost as strange as Dancy's. *Maybe that's it,* Chance thinks. *Maybe she sees the monsters too,* and she has to bite down hard on the inside of her lower lip to stifle a nervous laugh; everything way too weird and getting weirder, but still not sure if this is a joke and she suspects it might be rude to laugh.

"The Children of Cain," Dancy says earnestly and Chance can taste blood in her mouth, only a trace, but salty and warm, real enough to keep her in line. She's trying to remember the day in the library, all the details, but nothing she can recall that made her doubt the girl's sanity, and sure, Deke's a jerk but this isn't his style, too bizarre and sure as hell too much trouble for Deacon Silvey to stage anything half this twisted.

"Slow down," Sadie says to the albino girl. "You're going too fast. It's coming out all wrong."

"I'm sorry," Dancy says, smiles softly, looks almost embarrassed and she scoots her footstool a few inches closer to Chance. "I'm tired. I didn't sleep very much last night."

"Jesus," Deacon hisses from his chair. "Just fucking spit it the hell out and let's get this over with. Please," and Chance knows from the fraying tone in his voice that this isn't a joke, now she's sure it's not some sick prank to make her look like an ass, whatever else it might be.

"Dancy can see monsters," Sadie says and the way she says it, as if she might actually believe it was true, makes the fine hairs on the back of Chance's neck prickle, goose bumps on her arms. "And she has been sent by an angel to kill them. Show her what you showed us, Dancy."

"But she doesn't believe me," Dancy whispers and she's still watching Chance, but her smile's gone, a sad and wary sort of face instead, all the calm drained from her voice. "She isn't ever going to believe me."

"Yes she will," Sadie says, coaxing patience like a teacher with a difficult student, a mother with a frightened child. "You just got ahead of yourself, that's all. Show her, Dancy."

Dancy bends over then, opens the duffel bag and begins digging around inside it, burrowing through the grimy-looking tangle of shirts and jeans; a sock that might have been white a long time ago tumbles out and Chance tries to pretend she hasn't noticed it. When Dancy sits back up she's holding a handful of yellowed newspaper clippings and a small jar, baby food jar, Chance thinks, Gerber's strained peas or carrots or something like that, but the label's missing.

"I kept this from the first one. My grandmomma told me to keep it, so I wouldn't forget," and the lid on the jar makes a sharp, metallic *pop* when she unscrews it. Dancy shakes the jar once and hands it to Chance.

"Don't freak out, okay," Sadie says and Deacon makes a noise that isn't a cough and isn't a laugh, an anxious, weary noise and Chance accepts the jar from the albino girl.

"She was afraid I would forget," Dancy says, and Chance is staring at the bruisedark finger curled like a fat, rotten grub in the bottom of the baby food jar—not a whole finger, just the second joint down to a short, cracked nail the unhealthy color of an infection, the color of pus. Chance's stomach lurches, ready to be sick all over again whether there's a toilet handy or not, whether or not there's anything left in her to puke up; she gives the jar back to Dancy, swallows hard and almost gags on the acidsour bile taste rising hot from the back of her mouth.

"They all have claws," Dancy says. "At least the ones I've seen so far."

Chance looks across the room at Deacon, looking for any sort of explanation on his face, anything to make sense of this, but he's watching the floor between his feet, rubbing his big hands together, grinding his teeth.

"I've never had to ask anyone to help me before," Dancy says and she sounds ashamed, sounds like she's admitting to something a whole lot worse than carrying a severed human finger around in her duffel bag.

"I don't want to *hear* any more of this," Chance says and she stands up, wipes her hands back and forth on the legs of her jeans, trying to wipe away the memory of the thing in the jar. Sadie reaches to pull her back down onto the sofa, but Chance is already too far away, stepping quickly past Dancy and "I want her out of my house, Deke," she says. "I want you to get her out of my house right this minute."

"Not yet," Deacon says, and now he does look at her, turns his head slow and there's nothing like sense in his green eyes, nothing like explanation. The same sadness as the day she told him it was over between them, and "I'm sorry, Chance," he says.

"Here," and the albino girl is gently shoving the brittle wad of newspaper clippings into Chance's hands, some of them crumbling at the edges, dry and butterscotch flakes falling to the floor at her feet, ancient newsprint and cracker crumbs littering the floor between Chance and Dancy Flammarion.

"I didn't *want* to ask," Dancy whispers and she still sounds ashamed. "I swear, I didn't ever want to ask you or anybody else to help me."

Chance glances down at the headlines clutched reluctantly in her hands—"Water Works Marks 80th Anniversary" and "Wilfred Gillette McConnel, builder of water works, dies"—bold and blocky words almost half a century old. "Where did you even get these?" Chance asks and Dancy shakes her head.

"I know I shouldn't have taken them out of the library," she says, speaking so low that Chance can barely hear her. "I *know* that's stealing. But I had to. I didn't have any money and they wanted ten cents a page for the copier."

And towards the bottom of the pile there are two smaller clippings, one of them gone only the faintest yellow and the other could be new, could have been cut from the morning paper, the morning obituary column. The name on the first is Chance's grandmother's, and the name on the second is Elise Alden.

"What in the hell were you thinking?" Chance asks Deke and he doesn't answer, turns away from her for a moment, instead, back towards the living room where Sadie and Dancy are sitting together on the sofa, watching television. "Do you actually think I *need* this sort of crazy horseshit, that my life isn't fucked-up enough already? Or maybe you think I need to be *reminded* what an asshole you are."

Chance is sitting halfway up the staircase leading to the second story of the house, her back pressed to the wall and both feet braced against the banisters, chewing at a thumbnail and not looking at Deacon. He's standing two steps below her, slouching in the shadows like a scarecrow that's lost the poles or planks that hold it upright and at any moment he might tumble over.

"The girl is *not* well," Chance says. "And Jesus, where the hell do you think she got that finger?"

"She says she cut it off the first monster that she killed," Deacon replies, talking quiet, either more concerned than Chance about Dancy overhearing them or he just doesn't feel like speaking up, feels like mumbling so she has to strain to hear, has to pay more attention to him.

"It's a *human* finger, Deke," and Chance stops chewing her thumb long enough to wiggle her right index finger up and down at him.

"Yeah," he mumbles. "I kinda noticed that myself."

"Well, that's because you're such a goddamn brainy son of a bitch, Deacon. Now, why don't you cut the crap and take your girlfriend and her creepy little playmate and get out of my house."

Deacon sighs through his teeth, disappointed or impatient sigh, as if he expected more from Chance, as if this is exactly what he expected, and it makes her want to get up and slap him.

"How'd she know about Elise?" he asks her, the temerity to ask her a question like that and she looks away from him again. "Answer me that one, Chance, and I'll go and take her with me."

"Fuck you," she mutters around her ragged thumbnail.

"No, I'm serious. Come on. You're good at explaining away whatever you don't feel like dealing with, whatever's too illogical or inconvenient. You're a pro."

"And you're an asshole."

Deacon leans closer, lowers his voice even more and now he's almost whispering, urgent whisper like he's afraid, desperate for her to understand and maybe this will be his last chance to get the point across.

"Perhaps you should've listened to her story, Chance. Just stop and *think* about it a second. The clippings about the water works and Elise's obit. She knows about the night in the tunnel."

And those last five words, that last word alone, enough to get her up and moving again, climbing the few steps to the top in two long strides and she stops then, turns around and glares furiously down at him from the landing, knows she would glare holes through his shabby soul if she could. So much fury so fast that she's dizzy with it and he isn't even looking at her, is gazing off towards the living room again.

"*That's* what this is all about, isn't it? This whole thing, it's some bogus tale you've cobbled together to try and get me to believe that you didn't have anything to do with what happened to her. That you're not responsible. Christ, I honestly didn't think you had it in you, Deke."

"You're wrong," he whispers, but her head buzzing with hate and adrenaline, a head full of wasps and hornets and "That's the only way she *could* know," she says. "If *you* told her about the tunnel. How much are you paying Dancy to say this shit?"

"I didn't tell her a goddamn thing," and Deacon's raising his voice now, punching out the words, takes one step towards her and Chance takes a step back from the edge of the stairs; actual displays of anger as foreign to Deacon Silvey as sobriety and she's not so pissed off that it doesn't frighten her.

"This girl, she shows up at my apartment, and starts telling me and Sadie some bullshit story about a monster under the mountain," and Deacon points down, points at his feet, the stairs, at the ground beneath the house. "Then she tells us she's spent the last two months riding around on a Greyhound bus killing off monsters because an angel told her to, and just in case we don't happen to believe her, she pulls out that goddamn finger to prove it."

Deacon takes another step forward and she can see his eyes, those two bottomless, siltgreen pools always so indifferent, always so flat and still, and now they're as jagged as the edge in his voice.

"Hell, at first, I thought maybe Sadie had set the whole thing up, maybe she'd found this kid and was getting back at me because we had a fight this afternoon. But then Miss Dancy Flammarion down there tells me that she's certain I'll believe her, and that I'll help convince you, because she knows what I saw in the fucking tunnel."

"This is crazy, Deacon," Chance says, barely muttering, not wanting to hear any more and why can't he understand that and leave her alone? "You *know* that this is crazy."

"Yeah, it is, Chance. It's absolutely fucking psychotic, and if you ask me, I think the girl's a few fries short of a Happy Meal, but that doesn't answer my question. How the hell does she know about Elise, and how could she possibly know about the night we were in the tunnel?"

Chance's eyes hot and wet and she realizes that she's crying, hot tears streaking her cheeks and it's almost enough to get her angry again, almost enough to push back the fear coiling itself up cold and hard inside her belly; this whole fucked-up night and now she has to start crying in front of Deacon Silvey.

"Listen to me, Chance. I know you've heard the stories about me and the cops in Atlanta, about what I did for them before I came to Birmingham."

"You know I never believed any of that shit," she says, sobbing and hating the way she sounds, hating that she can't be stronger. Looking down at the floor now so he can't see her face, and "I know," Deacon replies. "I think that's one of the reasons we got along. I never had to try and explain it all to you.

"But I touched that finger, to see if it was real, to be sure it wasn't made of rubber or something—"

And then Dancy Flammarion interrupts him, the albino girl watching them from the gloom at the bottom of the stairs. "Please don't cry, Chance," she says. "There's no reason to cry. I can show you I'm not lying."

"*Please* get her out of here, Deacon," and she turns away, turns towards the narrow stairs that lead up to the attic, putting all these impossible things behind her and then Dancy says something else, something that makes Chance stop. She stands very still, doesn't dare look back at the girl or Deacon, stares through the blur of her tears at a faded Currier and Ives print hanging on the wall.

"What did you say?" Chance whispers and Dancy repeats the word, louder this time.

"*Dicranurus*," she says again, and Chance closes her eyes, shuts them tight and lets gravity and nausea and the certainty that none of this is happening pull her to the floor.

CHAPTER SIX

Touched

"YOU want to tell me what the hell that was all about?" Sadie asks him and Deacon doesn't stop staring at the ceiling over Joe Matthews' bed, the raised, fault-line crack beneath the paint where the sheetrock has begun to flake and buckle; doesn't look at her because he still can't get Chance's face out of his head, the cranberry smear of blood across her lips after she fainted, after she fell and struck her chin hard on the floor, bit the tip of her tongue and he thinks it's a wonder that she didn't bite it off.

"I'm not sure I can, baby," he says and closes his eyes against the lamp light. The room smells like dust and cough drops, reminds him of being a little boy and visiting old people, his grandparents, an aunt, Sunday afternoon smell to remind him how long it's been since he had a drink. Lying here with Sadie beside him, wishing he had a glass of bourbon or rye or just a goddamn beer, anything would be better than this dusty place inside his mouth.

"You mean you're not sure you want to," Sadie says, making no attempt to hide her jealousy, the suspicious edge in her voice and he doesn't bother opening his eyes, shrugs and "Yeah, that too," he says.

"You know, you're not supposed to just let someone go to sleep after they hit their head like that," Sadie whispers. "She might have a concussion or something. She could go into a coma."

"And I'm sure that would break your heart," then quick, before she can pinch him or tell him that he's being a dick, "Anyway, she didn't hit her head. I don't think anyone's ever gotten a concussion because they bit their tongue."

Deacon opens his eyes and the crack in the ceiling's still there, waiting for him, almost reminding him of something he probably doesn't want to remember. "Turn out the lamp now. I'm sleepy," and that's a lie, but at least if it's dark he won't have to look at the ceiling anymore.

"I don't think I want to. I think this house is giving me the creeps. It's too big and empty, and it makes sounds."

"It's an old house," he says. "Old houses make sounds." He rolls over onto his side, puts his back to the wall, and stares at her: Sadie lying on top of the white chenille bedspread in nothing but her panties, her small nipples the color of a burn, and she's staring up at the ceiling, too.

"What *was* that word?" she asks again, like she hasn't asked him the same question two or three times already, and "I told you I don't know," Deacon says.

"Whatever." She rolls her eyes and starts chewing at her lower lip, gnaws away a small patch of her black lipstick and probably some skin in the bargain.

"Christ, Sadie, why don't you get up, go down the hall and ask Dancy what the hell she said? And why don't you ask her what it's supposed to mean, while you're at it?"

"I did. I asked her while you were up there in the attic with Chance," and she frowns and points at the ceiling, the crack in the ceiling. "She said she didn't know. She said Chance knew."

"Then just turn out the light and in the morning you can ask Chance what it means."

And for a moment he thinks that maybe she's actually had enough for one night, enough unanswered questions, enough weird shit even for Sadie, that maybe she'll finally turn off the lamp and he can get some sleep. Plenty of time in the morning to think about what happened on the stairs, to think about Dancy and Chance, Elise and the tunnel; plenty of time then to tell her what he does and doesn't know, later, when the sun is shining and the sky is harmless and blue and far away. But then Sadie rolls over and he can see exactly how mistaken he is, that she's a very long way from sleepy, a long way from resigned. Those eyes too bright, too full, too hungry for secrets. Afraid of the sounds an old house makes at night, but she's starving to learn something *really* terrible.

"What's happening here, Deke?" she asks him and there's not the slightest trace of sarcasm left in her voice, no room for anything now but reckless curiosity. "And don't tell me you don't know, because I *know* that you know something. I *saw* the look on your face when you touched that thing in the jar. I know what that look means."

"You don't know half as much as you like to pretend," and he brushes back the tangled, black hair from her eyes, small and intimate gesture that might distract her, if he's lucky. But he isn't, and she pushes his hand away, holds it locked up tight in hers so he can't try that again, can't do anything but answer her questions or tell her to fuck off.

"At least I don't pretend I don't know what you did for the cops when you lived in Atlanta, and I'm not going to pretend you don't have some idea why Dancy needs to talk to Chance so badly, or where that goddamned finger came from. I know better, Deke."

And he thinks about pulling his hand away, then, shoving Sadie roughly out of the bed, thump to the cold hardwood floor and she can get pissed off if she wants, can find somewhere else to sleep, somewhere else to lie awake till dawn, eating her lipstick and looking for whatever profound and appalling revelations she thinks he's holding back, all the truths he's holding hostage. *It would feel too good,* he thinks, taking his stingy measure of satisfaction from the thought alone and wishing that it made him feel just a little bit guilty, just a little ashamed down deep inside. *You're an asshole, Deke,* and that's Chance's voice in his head, Chance who only wanted them to leave her alone, to go away, and now it's too late.

Deacon pries Sadie's fingers from around his hand. "Go to sleep," he says, not sounding angry but no room for an argument there, either, and he turns to face the wall and all the things waiting for him when he shuts his eyes.

After he left college, dropping out of Emory halfway through an undergraduate degree in philosophy, Deacon Silvey was swallowed alive by Atlanta like Jonah by the great fish and, in the end, there was very little left to spit back out. Kant and Sartre and Kierkegaard traded in for convenience store jobs, liquor store jobs, anything to pay the rent and enough left over to stay drunk whenever he needed to stay drunk. Weak enough orbit to begin with, downward enough spiral, falling into the sun sooner or later, a lot sooner if he hadn't met an APD homicide detective named Vincent Hammond.

The way it all began almost funny, almost, if he looks back at it the right way, the wrong way, if he pretends to be a much sicker fuck than he really is, and that summer, 1988 and he was working graveyard shift at an all-night liquor store on Edgewood, all-night target for every nickel-and-dime holdup right there in the grit and grimy heart of downtown. The robberies about as regular as his paychecks, the long parade of pistols and shotguns, never more than $100 in the register at a time but word never got out or no one cared, the gangbangers and crackheads that indiscriminate, that desperate. And Deke always playing the obedient, cooperative clerk, always eager to please any customer shoving a gun in his face. Sometimes the cops caught the robbers and sometimes they didn't and Deacon honestly never really gave a shit either way.

Then one muggy July night, Deacon rereading a tattered paper-back copy of *Watership Down,* Fiver and Hazel, and the bald white dude built like a steroid case, like a pro wrestler, coming in and not buying anything, just hanging around the back of the store half an hour, pretending to browse, picking up bottles and reading the labels, putting them down again, casting an occasional nervous glance towards the front of the store. Deacon already thinking *Let's just get it over with, okay, just please get this the hell over with,* when the guy screwed the cap off a pint bottle of Bacardi 151 and emptied it over his head. Deacon knew he ought to keep his fucking mouth shut, look the other way, but the whole thing getting way too strange and "Hey!" he shouted at the guy. "Hey, what the hell are you doing?"

Another bottle of rum over the bald guy's head and "It ain't none of your business," he sputtered at Deke through the Bacardi getting up his nose and into his mouth. "It ain't none of your business, man, so don't get in my way." Another bottle and whatever was happening, it wasn't exactly a stick-up and Deacon was still trying to decide whether to call the cops or just wait for the guy to soak up his fill and leave, when he fished a shiny Zippo lighter from a shirt pocket and flipped open the lid, thumb on the strike wheel, and "Jesus," Deke said, loud enough that the guy looked up at him, paused long enough for Deacon to make it around the counter.

"Don't try to fuckin' stop me, man. I can't keep doin' it anymore, I swear to God, I just can't keep doin' it."

"Yeah," Deacon said. "Yeah, that's cool, but look, let's just talk about this a second, okay?" and maybe that's what people said on TV, maybe that's how television heroes talked suicides off ledges and hostage-takers into setting children free, but the bald guy just smiled at him, sad and exhausted smile, and went up like a bonfire. Sudden comic book *fwump* of an explosion and the store was filling with greasy smoke and the porkstink of burning human skin before Deke could even get the dinky fire extinguisher off the wall and figure out which end to point at the crazy son of a bitch. The bottles on the shelves already popping from the heat, sudden staccato bursts of rum and whiskey, more fuel for the fire, for the hungry, bluewhite flames racing across the floor, bluewhite tentacles spreading towards Deacon as the man flailed around and screamed, screamed about how much it hurt, his voice barely a ragged murmur above the roar.

What the hell did you expect, asshole?, Deacon's head full of half-delirious, unreal thoughts as he aimed the extinguisher at the man and tried not to breathe in the smoke stinging his eyes and lungs. Nothing he could do about the inferno already writhing along the walls and licking at the ceiling, no way to even slow it down, but somehow he managed to put the guy out and then Deacon was dragging him from the store, his hands sinking deep into fire-retardant foam and the stickysoft soles of melted shoes. Dragging him over broken bottles and rough cement, finally over asphalt, and if the guy had a single square inch of skin left on his back it was a miracle. Deacon stopped halfway across the parking lot, choking on the smoke, the world swimming in and out of focus, the bald man black as a burnt marshmallow and still screaming that he wanted to die.

The windows of the liquor store exploded then, released a searing, crackling blast of heat that knocked Deacon off his feet and would leave his skin pink and tender for days, fat blisters on his face and arms, the backs of his hands, and the shattered glass fell around him in a jagged, noisy shower. One last thing before he passed out, the bald guy so burned he ought to be dead already, ought to be dead as fucking roadkill, but he rolled over and grabbed Deacon's hand, squeezed it hard, and suddenly there was no more smoke to smell, nothing but the sweetsick rush of oranges and raw fish clogging his nostrils, nothing but the knives at his temples, at his eyes, and Deacon saw the bodies stacked like rotting cords of wood, stacked somewhere dark and cool, before he couldn't see anything at all.

The next morning, groggy from pain pills and bad dreams, Deacon lay in his hospital bed at Grady Memorial and watched cartoons until the two detectives finally showed up. Officer Vincent Hammond and another guy whose name he forgot almost immediately, but Hammond not someone you forget easily; big, hollow-cheeked man always needing to lose a few pounds of belly and no chance he ever would, nicotine teeth and brooding, restless eyes that seemed incapable of lingering on any one spot for more than a few seconds at a time. And fuck all the things Deke's father had said to him seventeen years before, the threatful, stern warnings, the secrecy and denial, because there was no way he was keeping what he'd seen when the dying man touched him to himself. They could lock him up, throw away the key, feed him antipsychotics for the rest of his goddamn life, and how much worse could that really be than the liquor stores, anyway? So he told Hammond the whole story, told it straight and fast and didn't really care whether it made sense or not, if the detective thought he was nuts, just as long as he didn't have to carry the images of those dead and decomposing bodies around inside his head all his life without anyone else ever knowing, without ever knowing the truth himself.

And maybe Hammond hadn't believed him, but someone searched the basement of the bald guy's house and found the ten girls heaped neatly together in a corner, another five buried out in the backyard, resolutions to missing persons cases dating back six years or more. Their killer was dead before the week was out, too far gone to bring back, too much of him eaten away in the blaze, and so the investigation turned on Deacon for a while, long weeks of questions he had no answers for, at least no answers that Hammond wanted to believe. But only the most circumstantial evidence linking Deacon to the killer, the simple fact the fucker had walked into that particular liquor store to set himself on fire, that and what Deacon had known afterwards. Not nearly enough for a warrant, but Hammond showing up at his apartment one night with a dirty sweatshirt in his hand, child's sweatshirt with something cute and colorful across the front and "Okay, Deacon," he said. "You want me to buy all this psychic bullshit and leave you the hell alone? Yeah? Then I want you to tell me about this shirt."

The child missing since 1979, and her name had been Regina, Regina Sparks, and when Deacon Silvey sat down at the table in his dingy kitchenette, enough empty beer cans and gin bottles on the floor and countertops to start his own recycling plant, when he sat down and reluctantly took the shirt from the detective there was nothing at first. The trail gone cold, but not *too* cold, and finally the smells, the citrus and fish and the pain in his head, and five minutes later he told Hammond that the girl had been stabbed to death by her stepfather and the body dumped in a flooded rock quarry in Cobb County.

"She's still there," Deacon said. "Go and see for yourself." And she was, or at least enough of her dredged from the murky, moss-green water to make a believer out of Vince Hammond.

That first time, the second if he counted the bald guy, Hammond came back to his apartment and sat staring at him for a long time, half an hour just staring and chain-smoking Kools, like maybe there was some hidden way to make sense of this, some prosaic explanation overlooked, anything short of *believing,* and finally he shook his head, stubbed out his cigarette, and "We'll talk about this later," he said.

"You said you'd leave me alone . . ." Deacon began, but no need to finish once he saw Hammond's face, the intent and settled expression there.

"Sorry, bubba," the detective said. "I guess I shouldn't go around making promises I can't keep."

"I saw the look on your face," Sadie says, making the words sound like an accusation, like a judgment, before the water closes over her again, still and tea-colored water stained by everything that's lived and died in the swamps; he watches, silent, uncertain, as she sinks slow to the bottom of the pool and lies there staring up at him from the sand and the rotting, shit-colored leaves. The tapering stream of air bubbles from her nostrils and her open mouth, bleeding out her life, bleeding the swamp in, impossible, primordial transfusion and when it's finally done her skeleton is as smooth and clean as the silver-white scales of the fish that picked the last stringy shreds of meat from her skull. A fat turtle with scarlet spots behind its eyes nestles in her empty ribcage, and a drop of Deacon's sweat slips off the end of his nose and now it's part of the swamp, too.

The sun so high, so bright, all alone up there in the bottomless sky, baking the world from its high and lonely place; Deacon moves through simmering air that smells like pine sap and sand, snakes and magnolia blossoms, pushing his way through the air as thick as the underbrush, as alive, and he walks a long time before he comes to the dirt road that leads down to the cabin. There are footprints on the road, but something wrong about the lazy splay of those toes, the wide and crooked heel, and he tries not to look at them or hear the dry, distrustful whispers from the trees.

"Aren't you getting thirsty?" Chance asks him. "Aren't you getting scared?" And she passes him a bottle of something clear that tastes like pears but burns his throat like whiskey or gasoline, sets his belly on fire, and he gives her the bottle back, not quite that thirsty yet and not quite that scared either.

"What do you think you're gonna find at the end of this road, Deacon?" she asks and he shakes his head, spits to get the syrupy taste of Chance's liquor out of his mouth, and he keeps following the tracks like he doesn't already know where they lead and the answer to her question, like he hasn't already seen this once before. Holding the severed finger cupped in his hands because it might have been fake, might have meant nothing at all, and "What difference did it make to you?" Chance murmurs.

"Stop asking me questions," he says, barks loud like a dog, sun dog following the trail of ugly footprints down the red dirt road and something moves at the blurry edges of his vision, a shadow's shadow beneath the summer sky. He doesn't turn to look because he doesn't really want to see, because it wouldn't still be there anyway.

"We both know what really happened that night," Chance says, sounding bitter, sounding hurt. "This doesn't change a thing."

The road ends and he's watching the albino girl, or he is the albino girl this time, one or the other or both, Dancy Flammarion alone on the front porch of the cabin. *Barely a shack,* Deacon thinks, these four pine-log walls and a corrugated tin roof, walls studded with sunbleached antlers, a hundred or a thousand pairs of deer antlers nailed up so it bristles like a giant porcupine against the canebrake and rustling saw grass, against whatever she sees watching her from the woods. Whatever it is that draws her squinting out into the noonday sun with both barrels of the old shotgun loaded and frightens her so much that she doesn't dare look away.

"You *still* think I won't shoot you?" she shouts at the trees, at all the places where the dusty clearing turns back into trees and tangled blackberry briars, aims the shotgun like she knows what she's doing, pretending she's someone who's lived her whole life behind the Winchester when she hardly even knows how to cock the goddamned thing.

The hot breeze dies and the trees stand tall and still, waiting for this to end, the sky holding its breath, even though it was all over a long time ago; *This has already happened,* he thinks, or Dancy thinks it for him, and nothing he sees will change a thing, nothing he tells Chance will ever make her stop hating him.

"Come on back inside, child," the old woman says from the cabin door and that's what she wants, all she wants, to turn around and go back inside where the sun can't get at her, where she doesn't have to look at the way the gray thing at the edge of the swamp is smiling; spikewhite teeth in that mouth stretching wider and wider because it can taste how afraid she is of what comes next.

"No, Grandmomma," she says. "Shut the door," and Deacon turns his head, closes his eyes, and the roar of the shotgun is the sky breaking apart and tumbling down in bloody chunks to bury them all.

Deacon lies thirsty and sweating on the bed in Chance's grandfather's room, Sadie curled up next to him and snoring softly, and he stares at a gun rack on the wall across from them, the shotgun like it's followed him back from the dream; waiting for his heart to stop racing, until the dream seems enough like a dream and he remembers what he's doing in Chance's house, exactly how he got there. And then he tries to get out of bed without waking Sadie, but she stops snoring and blinks at him, half-awake grumble, and "It's okay," he tells her. "Go back to sleep. I just gotta take a piss," and he slips past her, over the side of the bed to the nightcool floorboards. She makes a fretful sound he doesn't understand, words or something simpler, then curls herself up tighter than before, rumpled, fetal lump of girl, and Deacon stands in the dark room watching her for a moment.

"I shouldn't have ever let you come here," he mutters, like he really thinks he could have stopped her, but he might have tried a little harder, if he hadn't been so nervous about facing Chance alone. *None of this has anything to do with you,* and then he wishes he knew for certain whether that's true or just something he wants to believe.

Sadie frowns in her sleep, presses her face deep into her pillowcase, and that makes him think of the dream sun hot against his skin, reminds him how dry his throat is, mouth like dust and ashes, and "I'll be right back," he says. Deacon walks as quietly as he can to the bedroom door and shuts it softly behind him.

Down the long and creaky stairs and he looks in the kitchen first, checks the refrigerator and rummages through all the cabinets, underneath the sink, and his hands have started to shake, the sour beads of drunksweat standing out on his forehead, as if he needs a reminder. He finds half a bottle of Robitussin-DM sitting beside the sink and hangs onto it, just in case, hates the taste of the stuff but it might have to be better than nothing at all, might have to hold him until morning. He carries it down the hall to the dining room, from the dining room to the living room because he remembers that Joe Matthews always kept a bottle or two tucked away inside the antique secretary and that would be fine, that would be wonderful. *But what if it's locked,* he thinks. *What if Chance keeps it locked and I can't find the fucking key,* and that's when he sees Dancy sitting alone in the window seat.

She turns and looks at him, might have smiled but it's hard to tell in the dark.

"I wasn't sleepy," she says, answer before he can think to ask the question, and Deacon glances anxiously towards the old secretary sitting by itself in one corner of the room.

"Yeah, I know what you mean," and he sets the bottle of cough syrup down on the coffee table, sits himself down on the sofa in front of it, and Dancy nods and turns back to stare out the window.

"Someone should stay awake," she says.

"Why? Are we expecting company?" Deacon asks her and he rubs at his cheeks with both hands, wonders how many days it's been since the last time he shaved, how many days since the last time Sadie bitched about his beard scratching her when they kissed, chased him into the bathroom and handed him his razor.

"I think you're making fun of me now," and Dancy doesn't turn away from the window to face him, might be speaking to the night or the whole world outside. "I'm used to that," she says, not sounding very hurt or disappointed and somehow that only makes it worse. A long second or two for him to remember what he said that she could have possibly taken as an insult, trying to think clearly through his thirst and the all-too-familiar certainty that he's said or done exactly the wrong thing without even trying.

"No, I'm not." But he knows how much it sounds like a lie, the words hardly out of his mouth and he doesn't quite believe them himself; Dancy shrugs and nods her head.

"I never had to try to make anyone believe me before," she says. "It hasn't ever mattered until now. It's always been a secret."

Deacon steals another glance at the secretary and now it almost seems to be mocking him from its corner, smirking with drawers and cabinet doors, its polished, walnut silence, and he looks reluctantly back down at the bottle of Robitussin sitting on the coffee table.

"You're asking an awful lot," he says and picks up the bottle, squints at the label, but there's not enough light to read the small print. "You *know* that, don't you?"

Nothing for a moment, just Dancy staring out the window like she's waiting for something, like she's sure it's only a matter of time, and then, "You saw what's in the jar," she says. "I showed you."

"You showed me a severed finger, Dancy. That's all. I don't think we see the same thing when we look into that little jar of yours."

"You only see what you *want* to see," she whispers from the window seat, and just the faintest trace of anger at the edges of her voice, but enough that he hears it whether she wants him to or not. Anger and something else, something righteous, indignant, a Puritan's offense at doubt, and Deacon sets the bottle of cough syrup back down with a careless, loud thunk.

"That's bullshit and you know it," and now there's anger blooming in his voice as well, his turn for indignation, uglyblack flowers opening up between his words, and Deacon doesn't try to hide it from her. "You wouldn't even be here tonight if you thought that was true. Jesus, I fucking *wish* it was. I'd give my left nut to *make* it true."

"Then you saw more than a finger in the jar and you just won't admit it. You're scared to admit it."

"I saw you cut it off a dead man's hand with a kitchen knife. A dead *man,* okay? Not a monster, a man."

"That's not all you saw, Deacon Silvey," sounding smug, suddenly very, very sure of herself and the anger already receding, its designing purpose served and she's putting it all away until the next time she needs it. *You little freak,* he thinks, understanding the game too late, seeing the strings after the fact. *You messed-up, creepy little fuck,* and he wants to cross the room and slap her, wants to shake her until her pink eyes rattle like marbles in her head.

"Why are you a drunkard?" Dancy asks, finally turning away

from the window, swiveling around to face him, "Because you don't like hearing what the angels say, what they show you?"

"There are no goddamn angels!"

"It doesn't matter *what* you call them," she says, so calm, so confident. "My momma said they usually don't care."

And Deacon gets up and walks quickly over to the secretary, yanks hard at the top drawer and it's unlocked, stuffed full of paper and nothing else as far as he can tell. He slams it shut again and begins searching other drawers, opening the cabinet doors and there's nothing but dusty stacks of papers, bundles of envelopes tied together with string, old power and water bills, like no one in this house has ever thrown anything away. A Blue Plate mayonnaise jar half filled with pennies and nickels, an unopened box of lead for a mechanical pencil.

"Well, that's what my momma tried to do, too," Dancy says from somewhere behind him, somewhere closer than her seat at the window. "She ran off to Pensacola when she was fifteen and tried to stay drunk until the angels would shut up and leave her alone."

Deacon comes to the last door on the secretary, pulls too hard and the brass handle comes off in his hand, this door locked against him, and he has to start all over again. Praying there's a key hidden somewhere and he didn't see it the first time through, a key missed in the clutter and his sloppy, headlong inspection.

"It didn't work, of course," Dancy Flammarion says and he tells her to shut up, please shut the fuck up, but if she hears him she doesn't care. "So she tried to drown herself in the Gulf of Mexico. Walked right out into the water until her feet didn't touch bottom anymore and then she just started swimming."

And there it is at last, a tarnished and silvergray key masking-taped to the underside of one of the drawers; it slides smoothly into the keyhole on the cabinet door, perfect fit, slides in and there's an audible *click* when he turns it and the tumblers roll.

"She swallowed a lot of water, but a fishing boat found her and brought her back. She said she saw bad things in the sea while she was drowning, bad things that were glad she was trying to die."

The cabinet door swings open and there's another stack of yellowed envelopes and a little strongbox, and in the very back, two unopened bottles of scotch whiskey.

"When the fishermen were hauling her into their boat, all the bad things in the sea tried to hold onto her soul and keep her from getting away. They promised her she'd never have to hear angels ever again, told her how deep and quiet the sea was."

Deacon sits on the floor beside the secretary, leans against the wall, and he breaks the paper seal on one of the dustskinned bottles of Johnnie Walker Black; the bottle to his trembling lips, but Dancy is there, standing over him, watching, no expression on her porcelain face or her expression hidden by the shadows, by the night.

"I *know* what you saw when you held the finger, Deacon," she says. "And I know what it feels like to be afraid of the things that you see. I'm almost always scared." She walks away, then, walks back to her place at the window seat, keeping watch for angels or monsters or whoever the hell comes looking for crazy albino girls who save rotting fingers in baby food jars. Deacon raises the bottle of scotch and lets its amber fire fill his mouth and throat, merciful liquid to burn through his guts and his mind, until the warm and whiskeystinking darkness closes hard around him, and the night slips away, forgotten, like a drowning woman's last view of the sky.

CHAPTER SEVEN

Uroboros

THE morning sun is hot and bright across Chance's face, shining straight through her eyelids, and the angry, uneasy dreams finally let her go, reluctantly send her dazed and blinking back to the waking world. July sun through the open window and the sugarsoft smell of dandelions and daisy fleabane from the yard below, the room filled with the smell of summer flowers and rich, black coffee and "You're awake," the girl says. *Am I?* Chance thinks, trying to remember the strange girl's name. *Am I really awake?*

"What time is it?" Chance asks, straining to read the clock beside the bed but still too groggy to make out its blocky, digital numbers, red numbers that all look like eights or zeros, and *Dancy,* she remembers, the girl from the library, the albino girl and then Chance also remembers the finger in the jar, the newspaper clippings, and worse things, and she closes her eyes again.

"Ten thirty-four," the albino girl says.

"I fainted," murky glimmer of surprise or wonder in her sleepy voice, nothing she ever expected to hear herself say. *I fainted.*

"I brought you some coffee, if you want it."

"You didn't have to do that," and Chance has started thinking about the flowery smell instead of the night before, better to worry about the grass that will need cutting soon, pulling up weeds, setting traps for moles, anything but what it means that Dancy Flammarion wasn't only a part of the dreams.

"I don't mind," Dancy says. "I had to make some for Deacon

anyway. He's sick," and Chance rubs at her eyes and sits up in bed, sees that she's still wearing her clothes from the day before, the same pair of blue jeans and T-shirt, same socks, and she puts the pillows between her back and the headboard. Dancy hands her the coffee cup—the cup and the matching saucer, her grandmother's good china—not the cups she uses for breakfast but Dancy couldn't have known that. The cup is trimmed in gold and there are primroses painted on it, pink primroses on the saucer, too.

"Sick? What's wrong with him?" and Dancy looks out the window like she's said too much already; Chance takes a sip of the steaming, black coffee. "You mean Deacon has a hangover," she says and Dancy nods her head once.

"He's an alcoholic," Chance says and she takes another sip of the strong coffee, bitter and so hot that she has to be careful not to scald the roof of her mouth, her throat; she usually takes lots of milk, milk or half-and-half, but Dancy wouldn't have known that either. "Deacon has hangovers the way most people have toast and jelly. It's what he does in the morning."

"I think this one is worse," Dancy says and frowns. "And besides, Sadie keeps yelling at him."

"Yeah, well, they deserve each other. Fuck, my tongue hurts," and she sticks out her tongue and carefully touches the tip end of it with an index finger.

"Deacon said you bit it pretty hard when you fell," Dancy says, and yeah, she remembers that, too, salty mouthful of blood like seawater and old pennies, then Deke wiping at her face with a wet washcloth, Deke cleaning her face and putting her to bed in her clothes.

Chance puts her tongue back in her mouth and looks at her finger like she expects to see more blood, but there's only a drop of coffee-stained spittle. And for a little while neither of them says anything else. Chance drinks her black coffee and tries not to think about anything but the hopeful way the morning smells, and Dancy watches the window, the ivory curtains stirring in the light breeze, the leafygreen branches of the oaks and pecan trees in the front yard. *Maybe if this could just go on forever,* Chance thinks, *or just for a while longer,* because it isn't so bad, really, isn't even so strange if she doesn't think about what it *means,* what it all signifies—this rumpled albino girl bringing her coffee, the morning half over and Chance still in bed, Deacon puking downstairs, Deacon in her house again.

But then the gold and primrose cup is empty, and she's staring at the grounds stranded at the bottom, and Chance sighs, probably a louder sigh than she intended and Dancy turns towards her. "Does your tongue still hurt?" she asks and Chance shrugs. "Yeah, but I think the coffee helped a little bit," and that makes Dancy smile.

"We have to talk, don't we?" Chance asks her and Dancy nods again, her pink eyes like the secret insides of conch shells, like the hearts of roses, and they don't make Chance uneasy, they actually frighten her.

"I thought so."

"I didn't mean to upset you last night," Dancy says very softly, apology that's almost a whisper, regretful, nervous whisper, and "I knew I shouldn't say that . . . that word, but I had to say something that would make you believe me."

"I haven't said that I believe you, Dancy. I'm not even sure what it is you want me to believe," and that makes Dancy look away again, makes her frown again and she chews fretfully at one of her stubby fingernails.

"You don't even believe in God," Dancy says. "I don't know where I'm supposed to start."

Chance takes a deep breath, fills her lungs with all the brightness getting in through the window, filling herself with that sane and ordinary air, with what she *knows* is real, reality to make her brave.

"Do you even know what a *Dicranurus* is?" Chance asks her.

Dancy shakes her head slow, stops chewing her nail and Chance can see that her cuticle has started bleeding, that there are fresh drops of blood like red berries against her white, white skin.

"No, but *you* do, Chance. I know you do and I need you to tell me what it means."

"And what about the water works tunnel, and Elise, all the stuff in those old newspaper clippings?"

"All those things fit together some way," Dancy says. "It's all supposed to fit together in my dreams, but—"

"So you're saying that you have dreams about the tunnel and Elise? That you dream about my grandmother?" And Chance is sitting closer to Dancy now, watching the albino girl, keeping tabs on her nervous, apologetic eyes.

"That's why I'm here, Chance," she says. "This time I can't see how all the pieces fit together. That's never happened to me before."

Chance gives the coffee cup and saucer back to Dancy, pushes away the tangle of sheets, and climbs out of bed. She stands next to the chair where Dancy is sitting and rubs at her chin, the sore spot just beneath her chin, and there's probably already a bruise there.

"You need me to answer your questions so that you can find someone you think is a monster," she says, and now she isn't looking at Dancy, hard enough to say these things aloud without having to look at her, too. "So you can find them and kill them. Like the person you took that finger from."

"Chance, just tell me what killed Elise and your grandmother," Dancy asks and her voice has changed somehow, grown suddenly older, an old woman's knowing, weary voice from Dancy's lips. "Tell me what you and Deacon and Elise saw in the tunnel."

"They killed *themselves*," Chance replies and Dancy's standing beside her, takes her hand and somewhere downstairs Sadie's started yelling at Deacon again. "That's *all*, Dancy. They both killed themselves."

"That's only what it wants you to think," Dancy says.

For almost a minute Chance stands staring silently at Dancy Flammarion, almost a minute because now she can read the clock radio on the table by the bed. But there's nothing left she can think to say, nothing this girl doesn't have another crazy answer for, so what's the point. Dancy's still holding her hand, holding it the way she was holding Sadie's on the porch, the way a shy child holds its mother's hand.

"Well, let's go downstairs," Chance says. "I certainly don't want that bitch killing him in my house."

Cold cereal and more coffee, Sadie and Chance sharing the last of a box of stale Cheerios, Dancy eating straight from a box of Nabisco shredded wheat, dipping the fibrous little biscuits into her coffee so they make a soggy sort of crunch when she bites into them; Deacon still too sick to come to the kitchen table, sitting on the floor in the hall bathroom, nursing his fourth or fifth cup of Red Diamond, because puking up coffee is better than dry heaves, he says.

"You're absolutely sure you don't want some milk with those things?" Sadie asks Dancy for the third time and Dancy shakes her head before her hand disappears back into the box of shredded wheat.

There are two crows in the backyard pecking at something in the grass, something that Chance can't quite see from her chair by the window. One of the crows spreads its wings very wide; hops backwards and for a moment Chance sees or thinks she sees a dark shape writhing in the grass, dark coils, a small snake or a very big worm, stickywet skin or glinting scales the color of licorice, and then both the crows are on top of it again.

"We owe you an apology," Sadie says, hesitant, uncertain, and Chance looks away from the window. "You know, about Deacon finding those bottles last night and getting pissed in your house. I know how you feel about that—"

"Sadie, if Deacon really wants to say he's sorry, let him do it for himself," and Chance gets up from the table, walks past Dancy to the sink and pours her Cheerio-stained milk down the drain. She turns on the faucet and rinses her bowl with lukewarm water.

"Yeah. I know that. But this whole thing has him pretty goddamn freaked out. I mean, Jesus, I swear I haven't seen him that drunk in a long time," Sadie says. And Chance sets her bowl down in the sink, starts to tell Sadie Jasper she doesn't want to hear it, too much of her own life spent making excuses for Deacon, but now Sadie's rummaging noisily through her purse, her ridiculous, silver purse shaped like a fucking casket and a red velvet cross glued on the lid, gaudy silver or chrome flashing in the morning sun; Sadie digs out a bubblegumpink plastic mirror, something plastic from a little girl's dimestore vanity set, the mirror and a black eyeliner pencil.

"I'm finished," Dancy says and then she carefully folds the lid of the cereal box closed and sets it near the center of the table, near the Dresden-blue sugar bowl and a half-gallon carton of Barber's milk, a pair of souvenir salt and pepper shakers from Niagara Falls. "Thank you," she says to Chance and wipes her mouth on the back of her hand.

"You're welcome," Chance says, glad for an excuse to think of anything besides Deacon and Sadie and her morbid, death-rocker affectations. "Did you eat enough?"

"Yeah," Dancy says and then she's dusting shredded wheat crumbs off her hand onto the faded, sunflower-print oilcloth that covers the tabletop. Sadie pauses, looks towards Dancy and absently taps one end of her eyeliner against her front teeth. "How old are you, anyway?" and Dancy looks back at her; *Wary,* Chance thinks, catching the apprehension that washes so quick across the albino girl's face, across her carnation eyes, that it might never have been there at all.

"Seventeen," Dancy says. "Well, I'll be seventeen come September."

"Damn," Sadie says and goes back to her mirror, back to painting her eyes like an oil spill. "You're not even legal, girl. Are you a runaway or what?"

That apprehension on Dancy's face again and this time Chance is sure that she sees it in the guarded, sidelong glance towards Sadie, and "No," she says firmly. "I'm not running from anything anymore."

"Hey, kiddo, *everybody's* running from something. It ain't nothing to be ashamed of," and Sadie looks at Chance over the top of her mirror. "Ain't that right, Chance?"

"I lived with my mother and my grandmomma. But my mother died," Dancy says, and she's speaking in the old woman voice from upstairs again and it gives Chance the creeps, gooseflesh prickling her forearms, too much time locked up in a voice like that for sixteen years. "Then my grandmomma died and I didn't want to live there all by myself. There wasn't anything left for me to run away from."

"Christ, I'm sorry," and at least Sadie sounds like she means it, sounds ashamed, embarrassed, and Chance takes the box of shredded wheat off the table and returns it to one of the cabinets.

"It's not your fault," Dancy says, staring at the brown scatter of crumbs in front of her, and she's the nervous girl from the library again, sixteen instead of seventy-five. "I don't think it's anybody's fault."

Sadie puts the mirror and eyeliner back into her purse, takes out an unopened pack of Camels and a disposable lighter and she glances up at Chance, who shrugs, annoyed but determined not to let it show. "Thanks," Sadie says and she begins to peel the cellophane wrapper from the cigarettes.

"I just wish I still had my sunglasses," Dancy says, wincing at the brilliant backyard sunlight through the windows, and Sadie stops, an unlit Camel dangling between her black lips and she pulls a pair of bug-eyed, orchidpurple shades from her purse and hands them to Dancy.

Dancy looks at Chance, like she's asking for permission, and "C'mon," Sadie mumbles around the filter of the Camel. "I always carry a spare. Here. Take 'em."

"Thanks," and Dancy smiles a shy and grateful smile and reaches for the purple sunglasses, her alabaster fingers closing around them when the crow crashes into one of the windows and Sadie jumps. The sunglasses slip from Dancy's hand, clatter to the kitchen floor, and the bird hits the glass again; this time Chance can see a dull smear of blood and bird shit streaking the window, a few feathers stuck in the mess. The crow is perched on the sill, pecks weakly at the glass once, and "Don't *look* at it," Dancy says urgently, growls at them in the impossible old woman voice, just before the crow folds its broken wings and topples, lifeless, into the holly bushes beneath the window.

"Jesus H. Christ," Sadie whispers, one hand to her chest like she's having a heart attack, someone scared halfway to death and back again, and she takes the unlit cigarette from her mouth and lays it on the table. "What the fuck was that?"

"A crow," Chance says, "Just a crow," but she can hear the doubt in her own voice, the adrenaline-hot confusion, and "I think I saw it out in the yard a few minutes ago," she says.

"Jesus," Sadie says again and takes a cautious, slow step towards the gore-smeared windowpane. "So what the hell was it *doing*?"

"No," Dancy growls, "not yet," the old woman growling with Dancy's throat, and she makes an abrupt and breathless noise, strangling noise, her mouth open too wide and both hands gripping desperately for the edges of the table as her white rabbit eyes roll back in her head. "I know you," she says. "I've *always* known you," gravel and glass words ground flat between her teeth, and now there's foam flecking her lips, foam like a mad dog or the edge of the sea.

"Oh god, Chance, I think she's choking," Sadie says, reaching for Dancy, moving too fast, too careless, knocking her purse off the corner of the table and everything spills out of it onto the kitchen floor. A rubber eyeball bounces clear of the jumble of cosmetics and spare change, the broken pink mirror and scraps of paper, bounces towards Chance, who's still staring at the birdstained window. Not as if she doesn't know what's happening at the table, not like she can't hear Dancy, but something about the crow too familiar, too real . . .

I'm not supposed to show you anything.

You don't have to tell me anything, Elise. I haven't asked you to tell me anything.

You wouldn't even know to ask . . .

"Don't you *look* at it," Dancy Flammarion snarls, angry old woman or rabid animal snarl that finally makes her look away from the window. Sadie is standing directly behind Dancy's chair now, both her arms tight around the girl's skinny shoulders, her thumbs pressed together, pressed to the soft place where ribs meet sternum, Heimlich pressure point below the girl's ribcage; *What's that called?* Chance thinks. *That little piece of bone right there,* orderly classroom game to bring her back to earth again.

The xiphoid process, she answers herself. *That little piece of bone is called the xiphoid process.*

"No, Sadie," she says, reaching into the sink. "She isn't choking. She couldn't talk if she was choking," and Chance finds what she's looking for, the spoon hiding beneath her cereal bowl.

"Then what the fuck's wrong with her?" Sadie snaps back, not so very far from hysterical now, her wolfblue eyes gazing bright from their twin bruise pools of smudged eyeliner.

"I think it's a seizure," Chance says, pushing Sadie away, not meaning to be rough but knowing it will seem that way to Sadie later, and Dancy's body shudders on cue. Violent, living tremor like her muscles want off her bones and her head jerks back, slams itself hard against the chair's wooden headrest.

"Try to hold her still," Chance says. "She's going to hurt herself. She's going to swallow her tongue."

And this time Sadie doesn't argue, holds both sides of Dancy's pale face while Chance slips the spoon between her lips. Her teeth click castanet loud against the silver handle and her eyelids flutter and dance, tears from her eyes, a dark trickle of blood from one corner of her mouth.

"Don't you die," Sadie whispers, desperateloud whisper that's almost a hiss. "Don't you *dare* fuckin' die on us," and Chance realizes that Sadie's started crying. Behind her there's a wild sound at the window, crowblack feathers against the glass, wings battering weakly, wanting in or only wanting Chance to turn around and see. *Look, Chance. Look quick,* but she keeps her eyes on Dancy and in another moment or two the sound is gone, if it was ever really there, and Dancy's body stops shaking, rattles down to sweatsoaked calm, and she opens her pink eyes wide.

"Jesus," Sadie says. "Jesus Christ," but now she sounds more relieved than scared, and Chance slides the spoon slowly from Dancy's mouth. The metal drips blood and saliva, blood and spit running down Dancy's chin and Chance wipes it away with her hand.

"Can you hear me?" Chance asks and Dancy nods her head slowly, but her eyes are still far away, focused somewhere beyond the kitchen, beyond the walls of the old house.

"I'm sorry," she says, coughs once or twice, swallows, and this time Dancy wipes her own mouth. "It's too late, isn't it? I didn't get here soon enough."

"You got here as soon as you could," Sadie says, crying harder now, brushing colorless strands of hair from Dancy's face and sobbing the grateful way a mother cries because her child hasn't drowned after all, because it isn't lost in the woods anymore. "God, kiddo. You scared the shit out of us, you know that?"

"I'm sorry," Dancy says again and then she turns in her chair and looks towards the kitchen door, towards the hall and the front of the house, blinks and wipes at her watering eyes; Chance looks, too, and Deacon's standing there, leaning sickly, unsteadily, against the door frame, watching them.

"No more bullshit, Chance," he says hoarsely and glances down at the floor, at his big, bare feet.

"I don't know what you're—" but he holds one hand out like a traffic cop, cutting her off. "Okay," Chance says, wanting to take back the words before they're even out of her mouth. "No more bullshit," and Deacon turns around and walks slowly away into the shadowy heart of her house.

Almost half an hour later, almost noon, and Dancy is resting quietly on the living room sofa. Chance wanted to call an ambulance, had even picked up the telephone, but "She hasn't got any money," Sadie said. "She hasn't got any money and she sure as hell hasn't got any insurance." Then when Chance offered to pay the bills herself, Dancy frowned and shook her head. "No. I'll be all right now," she said, and then Sadie covered her up snug with a caramel-colored afghan that Chance's Aunt Josie gave her grandfather last Christmas. So no one has said anything else about ambulances or doctors or hospitals; Dancy lies on the big sofa with her eyes half opened or half closed behind her new purple sunglasses, and Sadie sits on the floor beside her, holding her hand, keeping watch.

She isn't your daughter, Chance wants to say. *She isn't your little sister,* but she doesn't, because maybe Sadie has never had anyone to care for, to watch over, and maybe that's what Dancy needs more than anything else right now.

"No more bullshit," Dancy says and turns her head towards Deacon, who's standing alone on the other side of the room, staring out a window at the sunwashed gravel driveway like he's waiting for someone.

"So where do we start?" he asks, asks no one in particular, and he doesn't look away from the window.

"What's a *Dicranurus*?" Dancy replies, turning away from Deacon and now she's looking up at Chance through her bug-eyed purple sunglasses. "I *know* it means something. I know you know what it means, Chance."

"It's just a trilobite," she says. "A kind of Devonian trilobite, that's all," and Dancy and Sadie are looking at her like she's suddenly started speaking in tongues.

"Hold on a minute. It's probably easier if I show you," and so she leaves them in the living room, glad for an excuse to get away from Dancy's questions and Deacon's sullen, hungover resignation, even if it's only for a few minutes; she follows the hall to the door of her grandparents' study, door she hasn't opened since the day after Joe Matthews' funeral, day that seems years and years ago already when it's hardly been two weeks. She closes it behind her and nothing has changed in here, only a little more dust and the faintest beginnings of that shuttered, shut-away room smell. Chance pulls a brass cord on one of the Tiffany lamps, releases gentle, stained-glass light to chase away the shadows. It doesn't take her long to find what she's looking for, eight years since she closed the heavy German monograph and slid it back into its assigned place on the crowded shelves, but she remembers. Chance takes it down and pauses for a moment before she pulls the lamp cord again, before she gives the room back to the shadows and cobwebs and dust, thinking about what Alice Sprinkle said the night before and how weird things have gotten, how fast they've gotten that way.

"Well, so what the hell would *you* do, Alice?" she says, and the sound of the lamp switching off seems very loud in the small, still room.

Back in the living room she finds Dancy sitting up, the cushions arranged neatly behind her back and Aunt Josie's caramel afghan still covering her legs. Sadie's sitting on the sofa next to her now, one arm around Dancy's shoulders, and Deacon hasn't moved from his spot at the window. Stands there like his head isn't killing him and his stomach doesn't feel like shit, like he doesn't need a drink when she knows perfectly well he's hurting. But she's glad he's trying not to let it show and *At least that's something*, Chance thinks.

"Okay. *Dicranurus*," she says, sitting down on the edge of the coffee table in front of Dancy and Sadie as she opens the book, turns the old pages carefully until she finds the right one. She's trying not to think about the last time she looked at this book, the fact that she never bothered to ask her grandfather about it because she forgot or she really didn't want to know, trying not to notice the chill bumps prickling her arms, her legs underneath her jeans. And here it is, four views of *Dicranurus monstrosus*: dorsal, anterior, left lateral view, and a meticulously drafted close-up of the thorny head, the cephalon, and the sloppy, pencil-red circle enclosing all four illustrations. She turns the book around so that Dancy can see the pictures.

The albino girl leans forward a few inches and squints at the yellowed page through her sunglasses, reaches one hand out and touches the paper with the tip of an index finger. "It's like a horseshoe crab, isn't it?" she asks, and Chance shrugs.

"Well, horseshoe crabs are actually more closely related to spiders than to trilobites, but yeah, I suppose there's a resemblance. They're both arthropods."

"It's sure an ugly little bastard," Sadie says and Dancy glances at her and then back to the book.

"Sometimes I used to find horseshoe crabs in the swamps back home," she says. "They were *huge*."

"This bug here wasn't more than two or three inches long," and Chance holds up her right hand, thumb and index finger a couple of inches apart for Dancy to see what she means. "Ugly, I guess, but not very big."

"Why's there a red circle drawn around it?" Dancy asks, focused on nothing now but the four drawings of the grotesque creature. She stares up at Chance, her face expectant, expecting an answer, and Chance can only shake her head and shrug.

"I'm not sure. I think my grandmother might have been studying these trilobites when she died."

"When she *killed* herself," Deacon says coldly from his place at the window, doesn't turn around, and "Yeah," Chance says, glares over her right shoulder at Deacon. "When she killed herself."

"She drew the circle?" Dancy asks, tracing its sloppy, uneven diameter with her finger.

"As far as I know, but I can't say for sure."

"These are *all* dead," and that's not really a question but it makes Chance less nervous to talk and so she answers it anyway. "Yeah, they are. Trilobites died out at the end of the Permian Period, about two hundred and fifty million years ago. A *lot* of things went extinct at the end of the Permian. It's one of what paleontologists call the 'big five,' the five major extinction events. The fourth one got the dinosaurs."

"You're lecturing," Deacon says, takes a step closer to the window, and he lights a cigarette.

"She wanted to know, Deke. She asked and I'm telling her. What the hell do you *want* me to do?"

"It's okay," Dancy says and smiles faintly, looks past Chance to Deacon. "I need to know," and then she goes back to tracing the red circle with her finger. "Circles hold things inside, circles protect," she says and there's a dry hint of the old woman voice again, just a hint but enough to give Chance a fresh attack of goose bumps.

"They keep things in or they keep things out," Dancy says, almost whispering, almost singsong, and leaning closer to the book now, the weak smile already faded, and she cocks her head to one side like a cat, curious, considering, her eyes far away, and "So, you can find these around here?" she asks Chance.

"No. Well, not exactly. This species, *monstrosus,* is from Africa, but I think there's another kind of *Dicranurus* from the Devonian of Oklahoma. I don't know of any from Alabama, but I suppose it's possible. Africa and Alabama were still connected then, the way the continental plates were arranged—"

"*Monstrosus,*" Dancy says softly, interrupting, excited and talking to herself if she's talking to anyone at all; she stands up, pulling free of Sadie and the afghan slides off her lap to the floor. Chance doesn't move, sits with the book open on her knees, no idea what she's supposed to do next, but she's pretty sure that Dancy shouldn't be getting this worked up after the scene in the kitchen.

"This is where it began," Dancy whispers, hushed whisper like revelation or epiphany. "And this is where it ends," and she's pointing down at the book, at the drawings on the page and the red circle. "Right here, Chance."

"What? This is where *what* started?" but Dancy is already past Chance and the coffee table and on her way out of the living room, heading for the hallway.

"Where the fuck's she going now?" Deacon growls, finally turning away from the window and "Just how the hell should I know?" Chance growls right back at him and she closes the book and sets it carefully down on the table beside her.

"Well, I think maybe we should follow her and find out," Sadie says. "Unless either of you has a better idea." Chance doesn't look at Sadie Jasper, too close to telling her to shut up and go home, too close to telling them all to get the hell out of her house. She runs her fingers through her brown hair and sighs, a loud and weary sigh and she looks over her shoulder at Deacon again.

"Is this what you meant by 'no more bullshit'?" she asks, not caring if she sounds sarcastic, if she's starting to sound angry again.

"Maybe it's a start," he replies and then the three of them follow Dancy, Sadie first, and Chance last of all.

This small, blue room at the back of the house that has never been anything but a storage place for cardboard boxes and wooden crates, at least not as far back as Chance can remember. Bright and sunlit walls lined with sagging plywood and metal shelves, and some of the boxes are labeled but more of them aren't. Tidy and not-so-tidy boxes and crates packed past overflowing with canvas and plastic collection bags; picks and shovels filling in the corners, a hoe with a broken handle, screen-wire sieves for sifting through broken shale and the orangered clay of weathered limestone. Piles of camping equipment and a ragtag assortment of gardening tools, a rusty wheelbarrow, an oil-encrusted lawn mower missing most of its engine, and the dust as thick and fine as a gray, velvet drop cloth over everything.

This room the perfect, disordered antithesis of the study and Dancy Flammarion picks her way through the clutter like she's been here a hundred times before. Chance follows her as far as the lawn mower, halfway to the far side of the room, and stops by a box marked "Monteagle, Tuscumbia, and Bangor Lms.—Summer '59." Deacon and Sadie are waiting together at the door, lingering in the doorway like they're both afraid to cross the threshold.

"What are you looking for?" Chance asks and Dancy doesn't answer her, but she stops abruptly in front of one of the tall, crooked shelves, aluminum utility shelf almost twice as tall as her and Chance imagines it tumbling over and crushing the girl underneath its load of cardboard and stone. Dancy uses her palm to wipe away the dust from the ends of the boxes, pausing long enough to read the ones that are labeled, peering briefly inside the ones that aren't.

"Be careful, Dancy. Some of these shelves aren't so sturdy anymore." Chance steps over the box from 1959 and she's almost close enough to reach out and touch Dancy now, wants to pull her back out into the hall, lock the door to this room because she doesn't like the urgency on Dancy's face, the grim determination as if she knows exactly what she's looking for, as if she's been looking for it a long, long time.

"What the hell's she after, anyway?" Deacon asks, and Chance shakes her head, keeping her eyes on Dancy, who's standing on her tiptoes now, straining to get a better look at a crate on a shelf above her head. There's nothing written on the box, nothing Chance can see, just one of the many pine ammo crates that Joe Matthews bought from the army surplus store, and she can see that it's been nailed shut.

"That one," Dancy says, pointing at the crate and she taps it hard with one finger. The shelf wobbles precariously, lists a little more to the right, and Dancy taps it again like she didn't notice. "I need to see what's inside that crate, Chance."

"It's just a bunch of rocks," Chance tells her, exasperated, and she looks back at Deacon for help, but he's already stepping over and around the confusion of boxes; Sadie standing alone in the doorway now, and in a moment Deacon's lifting the ammo crate off the wobbly shelf, all the scrawnytaut muscles standing out in his arms as he sets it on the floor at Dancy's feet.

"It's nailed shut," he says, stating the obvious, staring down at the pine lid and the heads of a dozen threepenny nails sunk deep into the strawyellow wood. There's nothing written on the top of the crate, either, and Chance tries hard to pretend that it doesn't make her nervous, just one more box that her grandfather or grandmother never got around to unpacking. More junk they picked up in a quarry or a strip mine somewhere, and then she spots a pry bar leaning against the wall a few feet from where Deacon and Dancy are standing.

"That ought to do the job," she says, pointing out the pry bar to Deacon, deciding it's better to get this nonsense over with and maybe when Dancy sees that there's nothing in the crate, nothing at all but a bunch of rocks, maybe then she'll be satisfied, maybe then Chance can get them all out of her house and this will finally be over.

The nails make an ugly noise that isn't exactly a squeak or a scrunch, a bit of both at once, something in between, as they bend and twist and pull free of the wood, the flat end of the pry bar forced in between the lid and the upper edge of the crate and Deacon works it back and forth, up and down, until the lid gives one last squeakyscrunchy protest and pops completely loose. He picks it up, examining the underside of boards studded with nails still as sharp as the day they were driven into the crate, nails like cold, steel teeth. Dancy is on her knees, kneeling beside the open crate, digging through cotton and excelsior and Chance takes another hesitant step towards her.

"What is it? What's in there?" Sadie asks from the doorway, but no one answers her.

"Your grandmother understood about the monsters," Dancy says. "She knew about the Children of Cain, about the nightwalkers," and there's still that excitement in her voice but an excitement weighted at the corners now by some solemn purpose, by the gravity of whatever she thinks is waiting for them beneath all that packing material. *You really are crazy,* Chance thinks, *crazy as a loon,* almost says it aloud, and then Dancy pulls something from the crate, a thick ledger and she looks at it a moment and passes it to Chance.

"This was my grandmother's," Chance says, hearing the distant flatness in her voice, maybe a shred of surprise, too, as she reads the first page, reads it to herself because it wouldn't mean anything to Deacon or Dancy or Sadie, anyway. "Notes on Trilobita of the Red Mountain Fm., L. and M. Silurian, Alexandrian-Lockportian, Alabama Valley and Ridge Province," and a date, March 1991, all scribbled down in her grandmother's tight and almost indecipherable cursive.

"This is what she was working on when she died," Chance says, flipping through the pages, perhaps the first hundred or so filled up with Esther Matthews' handwriting and a few hurried sketches of various species of trilobites, some familiar and some a mystery, and then the rest devoted to what look like geometry problems. "But what the hell's it doing hidden away in here?"

On the floor, Dancy has pulled something else from the crate and holds it up for Chance to see. A large piece of purplered rock, rock the color of dried blood, and Chance knows right away that it's iron ore, a fist-sized chunk of sandstone and hematite from the mountain. *"Dicranurus,"* Dancy says and she's smiling, some of the solemnity that was there only a moment ago vanished; she looks proud of herself.

Chance takes the rock from her and there are indeed five or six trilobites exposed on one side, the largest no more than an inch and a half across, shinydark exoskeletons preserved on the granular sandstone, a concentric ring of scrape marks surrounding the fossils where her grandmother must have used small chisels and picks to clean away the hard matrix. No mistaking the identity of these trilobites, the bizarre ornamentation, the coiling occipital ring spines like slender ram's horns. "Goddamn," she whispers, realizing these rocks are too old, this rock tens of millions of years older than any published records of *Dicranurus,* realizing how important these fossils must have been to her grandmother, a new species at the very least and "Now, Chance, turn it over," Dancy says.

For a moment Chance can't take her eyes off the amazing little animals on the maroon chunk of ore, knows that whatever Dancy wants her to see can't be half this incredible. But "Please," Dancy says, "it's important," so Chance turns the rock over, only expecting to find more of the trilobites.

"That's why your grandfather hid these things," Dancy says. "That's why your grandmother died."

And as far as Chance can tell it's just another fossil, not a trilobite but something she's never seen before and she holds the rock closer to her face, turns so she isn't blocking the noonday light through the windows. A perfect starshaped impression in the stone, no bigger than a quarter, and at its center a sort of polyhedron, upraised polyhedric structure that she thinks has seven sides, but there might be more, and its smooth surface glints iridescent in the light.

"What are *you*?" she asks the rock, as if it might answer, and then Dancy is holding up something else, forcing her to look away from the strange fossil; a small bottle, old-fashioned apothecary bottle, Chance thinks, ground glass stopper shoved in tight and there's an inch or two of tea-colored liquid inside. Chance sets her grandmother's journal down on a big cardboard box that originally held cans of Green Giant creamed corn, "Fort Payne Chert, Happy Hollow, '65" scrawled on one side in her grandfather's hand, and she takes the bottle from Dancy.

"This is where it all begins," the albino girl says. "The teeth of the dragon."

Chance ignores her, stares into the small bottle, the murky liquid inside and there's something else, something like a fat slug, curled up dead and floating on its side. And then she sees the segments, the armored segments of its wormlike body, and the fine and bristling hairs growing between the plates.

"The dragon has a hundred thousand children," Dancy says, "And it was old when the angels fell from Heaven."

"What is it, Chance?" Deacon asks. "What the hell's she talking about?" and Chance turns towards him, turns slow and holds the bottle out for him to see.

"You tell me, Deke," and Chance sits down on the floor beside Dancy to see what else has been waiting out the last eight years inside the ammo crate.

◉

Midafternoon before Chance is finally alone in the big house, sits alone in the kitchen and stares at the wooden crate where Deacon left it sitting on the table, where she asked him to put it before she apologized and herded all three of them towards the front door. "I have to have some time to myself," she said. "To think."

And an expression on Dancy's face then that was almost panic, the joy or relief at her discovery replaced abruptly by alarm and "No, Chance. There isn't time," she said and grabbed hold of Chance's shirtsleeve. "They'll know that you found it, that you've begun to see what's going on. It's not safe to be alone."

Chance glanced at Deacon and Sadie, beseeching glance, and "We'll come back tomorrow," Sadie said, reassuring words and a hand on Dancy's shoulder, something meant to comfort her, but no room for comfort in that face, those pink eyes tinted magenta by the purple sunglasses.

"Tomorrow will be too *late*," she said, and then to Chance, "We haven't even talked about the tunnel. We have to talk about the tunnel and we have to go there, *today*, while there's still time."

"That tunnel's been there for more than a hundred years, Dancy. It'll still be there in the morning," and Chance very gently pried Dancy's fingers from the sleeve of her T-shirt. "I have to read the things my grandmother wrote in this ledger," she said. "There's a lot I have to think about."

"It's not *safe*," and Dancy was getting hysterical, close to tears, close to something Chance didn't want to hear or see, maybe another of the seizures or she was about to start talking in the creepy old woman voice again. And "You won't be safe here all by yourself, not when they come," Dancy pleaded. "*None* of us will be safe when they find out what we know." She brushed Sadie's hand off her shoulder then, wiped it roughly, quickly, away like a dangerous insect or the uninvited touch of an unclean person, a beggar or a leper, but her eyes still on Chance.

"Goddamn it, there isn't anything *left* to understand and you don't need to understand. That's what they *want* you to do, to try to make sense of what's been happening, to try and understand what there's no *way* to understand. They want you to think about it, because then you'll start doubting everything and that buys them *time*."

"Dancy," Chance said, trying hard to sound calm, hiding the anger blooming hot and violent inside her.

"I've seen all of this before," Dancy said and there were tears leaking from behind her sunglasses, tears starting to roll down her pale cheeks. "I know *exactly* what's coming."

"Chance, maybe we *should* listen to her," Sadie said. "She knew about the box, didn't she, so how can you be so sure . . ." But the look on Chance's face enough to cut her short, the look that showed her anger and the brittle end of her patience even if she didn't say it out loud.

"*Tomorrow*, Sadie," she said, firm, no room left for debate.

"Yeah," Deacon replied, careful to keep his eyes down so that Chance couldn't see them, so he couldn't see her, either. "Tomorrow. I gotta be at work in a few hours, anyway, or old lady Taylor's gonna bust a gut. I've already been late twice this month."

And Chance called a taxi and followed them to the door, Deacon hauling Dancy's duffel bag, severed finger and all, and Dancy crying harder, begging Chance to let them stay. Sadie was trying to console her, promising her that everything would be fine, that Chance could take care of herself and nothing was going to happen to any of them.

Five more minutes before the taxi pulled up out front, a bright green Pontiac sedan this time instead of a station wagon. "You'll see," Dancy said, hard to make out what she was saying through the tears and the snot, the breathless, hitching sobs. "I can't protect you if I'm not here."

And then Chance reached into a front pocket of her jeans and pulled out her big Swiss Army knife, five sharp blades folded up snug in the apple-red plastic casing, a corkscrew, tweezers, and a bottle opener, and she put it in Dancy's hand. The taxi driver honked and Dancy stared down at the knife, confused. "My grandfather gave me this for my tenth birthday, Dancy, and I want you to hold onto it for me, just until tomorrow morning. It means more to me than almost anything else I own and if I wasn't absolutely *sure* I'd be seeing you again real soon, there's no way I'd let you keep it for me."

"C'mon. We gotta go," Deacon said and Dancy looked up at her, no sign of comfort in her face, no sign she believed a single word that Chance had said, but she nodded once and squeezed the Swiss Army knife tight in her hand. Then Sadie and Deacon led her to the Pontiac and in a moment the driver was turning right, back towards Five Points, leaving Chance alone in her driveway.

And now she sits in the kitchen, 2:37 by the clock on the wall above the stove, and she's holding the chunk of ore and sandstone from the crate, turning it over and over in her hand, examining the trilobites and the odd, star-shaped impression on the other side of the rock, glancing occasionally at the dried blood on the window where the crow crashed into the glass that morning, or at the stoppered bottle of alcohol and the dark, segmented thing floating inside. Like the pieces of a puzzle, or some of them are the pieces of a puzzle and the real trick is figuring out which ones are and which ones aren't. Not used to feeling stupid, but that's the way she feels and maybe if sensible Alice Sprinkle were here, or her grandfather, maybe they could show her something perfectly obvious, something right in front of her nose to make sense of all this, to tie it all together: the stuff from the crate and the suicidal bird, Dancy Flammarion and the night that she and Deacon and Elise got stoned and decided to break into the old water works tunnel.

Five more minutes, ten, and she packs the fossils and the dead thing in the jar back into the crate (and there are other things in there, as well, things she hasn't had the nerve to look too closely at yet), leaves the ledger lying on the table and carries the rest out to her car, sets it carefully on the Impala's backseat. Saturday afternoon, so maybe nobody will be at the lab, maybe she'll have it to herself for a few hours if she's lucky. Chance goes back up the front porch steps to lock the door, checks it twice, and she's turning towards the car again when she notices the dead crow lying at the edge of the porch, ebony wings spread wide and the crimsondark cavity in its breast like a bullet hole.

Chance uses the toe of her boot to scoot the bird off the porch and into the grass, leaves a bloody smear on the wood but that'll just have to wait until later. And she tries not to think about Dancy or the crows, tries not to think about anything in particular, as she walks quickly back to the car.

CHAPTER EIGHT

At the Round Earth's Imagined Corners

AFTER Deacon has gone to the laundromat, Dancy sits in the kitchen by herself and stares out the window over the stove, watches the bright patch of sky visible between the curtains, sun-faded chintz the color of buttermilk and decorated with smiling baby-blue cats. There's a can of Coke open and getting warm, going flat on the table in front of her, the can that Sadie opened for her, Coke and some stale Oreos like she was a five-year-old. Chance Matthews' fancy pocketknife is lying beside the Coke can and every now and then Dancy looks away from the patch of sky and stares at the knife for a few minutes instead, those two things, the knife and the summer sky, and she listens to Sadie in the bedroom, typing slow at her computer.

There's no clock in the kitchen but she knows it must be almost four by now, a few more hours until dark, *only* a few more hours until dark, and there's nothing left for her to say that will make them listen.

"He doesn't like the light," her mother says. "He'll wait until dark," and when Dancy turns away from the window, turns towards the corner where she heard her mother's voice, she almost expects to see her, her sharp blue eyes and chestnut hair, so disappointment when there's nothing but the peeling wallpaper and a couple of dead roaches. Disappointment and it makes her mad, makes her glare at the dead bugs like they're to blame somehow that her mother isn't there.

"But it *was* daytime, wasn't it, Momma?" she asks the cockroaches, savoring the bitterness, the tiny, black flakes of fury hiding somewhere deep down inside her. "It was broad daylight and he just came on ahead anyway."

And it got him killed, didn't it? her mother says, but this time Dancy knows the voice is only in her head and she stops glaring at the bugs, looks back at the knife. Chance's pretty, red knife. Dancy has a knife of her own, her grandmother's big carving knife hidden at the bottom of her duffel bag and maybe it doesn't fold up all nice and neat, doesn't have five blades and a screwdriver, but it always gets the job done. She touches the silver cross stamped into the red plastic, silver cross inside a sort of shield, five-sided emblem, and Dancy doesn't know what it's supposed to mean, and maybe it doesn't mean anything.

You gotta be strong now, Dancy, her mother says. *Strong for all of us,* and for just a moment it's that last terrible day in the swamp again, and she can smell the heat and gunpowder smoke, can smell blood and she closes her eyes, wants to tell her dead mother's voice to leave her alone, please just leave her alone now because she's *been* strong for a long, long time and it hasn't made any difference at all. So much fear and guilt, all the things she's done that she'll never be sure if they were right or wrong, and it might go on this way the rest of her life and it still wouldn't make any difference.

It don't make you crazy just because nobody else can see what's true, her mother says, but now her voice seems farther away, hushed and far away as the sky, almost, fading like Deacon's ugly curtains, and Dancy doesn't want to hear any more, squeezes her eyes shut as tightly as she can and shakes her head. "I'm *not* strong," she says. "I'm tired. I'm tired and I want to stop now." Almost says, *I just want to go home,* but she's the one that built the fire when it was over, watched from the pines and brambles while the cabin burned down around her mother and her grandmother and the smoke turned the Florida twilight sky as dark as midnight.

Dancy opens her eyes then, sudden, certain impression that she isn't alone and there *might* have been a quick and cindergray blur at the window, something staring into the kitchen with eyes like poisonous, black berries, there one instant and gone the next. And then there's only the bright and empty sky again and her right hand hurts. She looks down at it and sees she's holding Chance's knife, the largest blade folded out and a gash in her palm from the base of her thumb all the way to her middle finger; a big pool of her blood collecting in the space between the stale Oreos and the can of Coca-Cola, blood flowing down and around her wrist like a liquid bracelet before it drips to the tabletop.

I know exactly what's coming.

Dancy drops the knife, stares at all that wasted blood for a minute and then she gets up and goes to the sink, careful to keep her eyes away from the window, whatever may or may not be out there, while she runs cold and stinging tap water over the cut. She finds an orange-and-white striped dish towel that looks almost clean and wraps it around her hand, finds another hidden behind half a loaf of moldy bread and a jar of peanut butter and she uses it to wipe up the pool of blood on the kitchen table. When she's done, she rinses the bloody towel and hangs it over the faucet to dry, her hand really starting to hurt now, starting to ache all the way to the bone, and she sits back down at the table, cradles her hand to her chest and listens to Sadie still pecking slowly away at her keyboard.

The Swiss Army knife is lying on the table where she dropped it, her blood already beginning to crust on the shiny, stainless steel blade, and Dancy takes a sip of the lukewarm Coke, holds it in her mouth a moment before she swallows.

And there are no voices now, not her dead mother's, or her grandmother, or the angel with his eyes like furnace embers and his wings like a bluegray flock of herons before a hurricane. All of them forsaking her, finally, abandoning her and maybe that's the price for having admitted that she's tired, that she's too scared to go down to the dragon alone.

"This is where it starts," she whispers, picking up Chance's red knife in her left hand, knife red as her blood, and "This is where it ends," she says.

Dancy wipes the blade on her jeans, then folds it shut again and slips it into a back pocket. She doesn't take anything else but her duffel bag, stands at the front door for a moment because there's something comforting in the clack-clack-clack sound of Sadie Jasper's fingers moving over the plastic keys, Sadie making words. And then Dancy steps out into the musty hallway and pulls the door very quietly shut behind her.

◊

Today Chance isn't lucky and when she pulls up outside the lab Alice's old Toyota pickup's parked out front under the negligible shade of a crooked sycamore tree and all the louvered windows are cranked open just in case there's a breeze. Chance curses, glances at the crate in the backseat, and she almost turns around and drives straight home again; not up to Alice and certainly not up to trying to explain to Alice what she doesn't half understand herself, so almost five whole minutes spent sitting in the hot afternoon sun, sweating and listening to the unhappy rumble of the idling motor and an old Nirvana song playing loud on the radio, before she sighs and pulls the Impala up next to the truck.

This tiny building, stingy rectangle of autumnred and shitbrown bricks, concrete blocks and peeling, white paint, stranded on a neglected island of grass and gravel in the middle of a faculty parking lot on the shabby north edge of campus. Browngreen island in a baking, black asphalt sea, and almost fifteen years ago one of Esther Matthews' students carefully printed PALEONTOLOGY LAB on one of the doors, one heavy metal door at each end of the building. But no other indication that this is anything but an eyesore, maybe someplace to store files or janitorial supplies, and "Welcome to the endlessly rewarding and glamorous limbo of pure science," Alice Sprinkle says whenever she brings a new student to the lab for the first time.

The door's already unlocked, already open, and Chance finds Alice at a big table in the front room, this end of the building mostly set aside for collection storage, so there are dozens of squat, steel Lane cabinets, all the same battleship gray, stacked two high along the walls and another double row down the center of the room; but this one table near the door where Alice sits beneath a cloud of cigarette smoke and she's staring through the lens of a fluorescent magnifying lamp at a plastic tray of shale fragments, fine shale shards the color of charcoal and she stirs intently at the bits of rock with a pair of tweezers.

"Well, hello there, stranger," she says, not looking up from the tray, from the lamp. "Didn't expect to see you this afternoon, certainly not after what you said yesterday."

Chance sets the heavy crate down on the bare concrete floor before she replies. "Well, I didn't exactly expect to be here, either," she says, keeping her eyes on the crate.

"So what's in the box?" Alice asks and Chance shrugs and shakes her head. "That's a good question," and then, before Alice can say anything else, "Do you know what my grandmother was working on when she died?" and she raises her head, risks a glimpse at the older woman.

And now Alice does look up, lays her tweezers on the table and stares thoughtfully at Chance over the dull glare from the lamp. She's wearing her glasses and the thick, bifocal lenses make her eyes look huge and fish-like.

"That was a pretty long time ago, Chance."

"Yeah, but do you remember?" and then she looks back down at the crate.

"Not offhand. I think she was collecting again. She'd just finished a report for the Geological Survey, so she was probably out in the field. She always liked being in the field more than sitting around this shithole."

"Do you know *what* she was collecting, Alice?" and Chance hates sounding anxious, sounding impatient, wishes that Alice Sprinkle could have been anywhere but here this afternoon, anywhere else and then they wouldn't even be having this conversation.

"Well, if I had to bet cash money on it, I'd say trilobites. Esther was usually looking for trilobites. But I'm not telling you anything that you don't already know, Chance."

"No," Chance says. "You're not," and Alice points at the ammo crate, raises both her eyebrows above the wire rims of her glasses so that her eyes look even larger. "I don't have to be a terribly clever lady to guess this has something to do with whatever's in that box there."

"Some stuff my grandfather must have packed up after she died. I found it this afternoon."

Alice lights a cigarette and blows smoke towards the low ceiling. "And? Are you gonna tell me what it is or is that none of my business?"

Chance shrugs again but she doesn't answer, stoops and picks the crate up off the floor instead, carries it over to the table while Alice hastily clears off a space big enough for her to put it down, shoves aside a stack of books, several thick volumes of the *Treatise on Invertebrate Paleontology* and a few old journals.

"I don't want you to tell anyone else about this stuff," Chance says, setting the crate in the small, uncluttered spot Alice has made on the table. "Maybe later, but not now, okay? I want you to *promise* me that you'll keep this to yourself."

"Scout's honor and hope to die," Alice says, "etcetera, etcetera," and then she crosses her heart, takes another drag off her cigarette and "Shit, we can take a blood oath if you think it's necessary."

Chance reaches down through the top layer of excelsior and

pulls out the stoppered bottle. She hands it to Alice, who puts her cigarette between her lips so both hands are free, holds the bottle a few inches from her face, and stares through her bifocals at the dark thing floating inside, no particular expression now, only silent contemplation, maybe the faintest flicker of surprise. She slowly tilts the bottle on its side and shakes it gently, causing the thing inside to bob and roll over.

"Well, it beats the hell out of me," she says, mumbling around the filter of her cigarette. "I've never seen anything like it. But whatever it is, I don't think Esther found it. Not originally, anyway." She taps hard at the yellowed label about the size of a large postage stamp that's pasted onto one side of the bottle. "Did you happen to notice this?"

"Yeah," Chance says, "I did," and Alice holds the bottle a little closer to her face, squints to make out the spidery, sepia-colored handwriting on the label, antique ink faded to an almost illegible scrawl. "Birmingham Water Works tunnel, Red Mountain, Alabama," and she pauses for a moment, squints harder to read the second line. "October 1888. Or 1886. I'm not sure which."

"'88," Chance says. "They didn't dig the tunnel until '88, so it can't be '86."

"Damn, this is one peculiar bug. Do you have any idea what Esther was doing with it?"

Chance glances at the crate again. "There's a letter in there from someone at the Geological Survey. Apparently she wrote to them about the tunnel, asking if they had anything important from the site, I guess. They sent her this."

"I doubt it's what she had in mind," Alice says and turns the bottle for a different view of the thing inside. "What was it doing at the Survey?"

"The letter says that a foreman at the water works excavation sent it to them that October. He wanted to know what it was. I assume he found it when they were digging the tunnel."

Alice smiles, small, approving smile for Chance, and "As usual, our girl's done her homework," she says. "I think we should have a closer look at this little bastard, don't you?"

"There's more," Chance says, "a lot more," and she's reaching back into the crate, already has her hand around the chunk of iron ore, but "No," Alice says firmly. "Let's take this one thing at a time."

◊

Dancy knows where the tunnel is, remembers everything important from all the stolen newspaper clippings and a library book on the industrial history of Birmingham, and after she leaves the castle, after she takes a deep breath and steps from mildewcool shadows into the firestorm brilliance of the summer afternoon, she heads southwest towards the mountain. As straight a line as possible with so many buildings and chain-link fences in her way, razor wire and concrete obstructions, and it doesn't matter that the sun has begun its painful, slow descent, westward slide from a bluewhite and blindscorched Heaven but still hours until dark and the air sizzles against her white skin, light to sear its way through the purple sunglasses that Sadie gave her and set her brain on fire. Who needs a dragon when the whole sky's ablaze, when every breath fills her lungs with gasoline and smoke and the smell of streets that have begun to melt and flow like sticky, coalblack, brimstone rivers?

The day on Their side and if the night ever comes They own that as well, own that *twice* as much, both light and darkness set against her, and Dancy tries not to think about that, lugs her heavy duffel across Twentieth Street while the asphalt sucks wetly at the soles of her shoes; wanting to suck her all the way down to the grindstone belly of the World—and then she's on the sidewalk again, concrete-narrow sanctuary but she can hear the sniggering laughter leaking from beneath the street, taunting, gravel-throated laughter for this crazy girl who thinks she's going to do anything but die. Anything but burn forever between gnashing teeth like red-hot pokers, and she wipes at her forehead, wipes away the sweatsalt that stings her eyes and blurs her vision. Dancy turns her back on the laughing things below the street and here's an alley in front of her, a mean rind of halfshadow clinging to one side of the alley and she squeezes herself into this niggardly shade, presses herself scrapbook rosepetal flat against the old bricks and mortar as far as the wall runs.

And another parking lot then, this one as wide as the whole Gulf of Mexico, as wide as a dead sea gone all the colors of coal and blackbirds, but a shimmering glimpse of cool, green trees on the other side, trees and grass and a sprinkler spraying endless crystal drops. Dancy sets her duffel down behind a pink garbage Dumpster with a hippopotamus stenciled on it, another stingy pool of shadow here and she huddles in it, in the soursweet reek of roasting garbage and the buzzing flies trying to ruin this air that's only stifling.

"What happened to your hand, Dancy?"

She looks up and there's a tall, thin man standing a few feet away, standing right out there in the sun, sunk up to his tubesock ankles in the blacktop but he doesn't seem to notice or he simply doesn't care.

"I *know* you," she says, and she does, the jug-eared man from the bus, the man with all those yellow teeth crammed into his wide, wide mouth and he smiles for her now, showing her all those teeth at once.

"You're a long way from Memphis, aren't you?" the man asks. "A long, long way from Graceland."

The man looks up at the sky, narrows his eyes against the day and wipes his forehead with a red-and-white checkered handkerchief.

"Are you lost, Dancy?" he asks, honey and rattlesnake voice, and "Do you need someone to show you the way? I can do that, you know. I know *all* the roads—"

"I don't want anything from you," she says, her throat too dry to sound brave, to sound tough, barely enough spit left to make words at all and she swallows a thick mouthful of nothing but the parking-lot hot air. "So you may as well crawl right back where you came from and leave me alone."

The tall man stops smiling and folds his sweatstained handkerchief neatly before he stuffs it back into a front pocket of his gray trousers. The asphalt is all the way up to his knees now, pulling him down into the bubbling goo and he holds a hand out to Dancy, and for a moment she thinks how wonderful and dark it would be beneath the ground, how cool down there where the sun's never been.

"You weren't made for this world," the man says. "But there are roads I could show you, night roads that wind forever between milkwhite trees and the starlight would kiss your skin like ice. There are roads where nothing ever burns and the sun is only a fairy tale to frighten pale children to bed."

Dancy looks down at her duffel bag, and there are things hidden in there that might frighten the tall and toothy man away, that might send him howling and slithering back to all the Others, but the canvas bag seems so far away and his twiglong fingers are so close. All she'd have to do is reach out and take his hand, let those skeletal fingers carry her off to the dark and soothing cold.

"That's a girl," the man says, his breath falling about her like a shroud of spring water and night. "That's a good, good girl. You know, none of this was ever really about you, Dancy. You shouldn't have to suffer this way. Your mother should have told you the truth, the *whole* truth and none of this would have been necessary."

And then Dancy's fingertips brush the edge of something vast and sharp and raw, something made of lies and flesh sewn from lies, something that's never been anything but hungry. A devouring hunger that goes on and on until the very end of time, end of the world starvation in that icing touch, and she pulls her injured, dishragswaddled hand back, makes a fist and drives her short nails through the cloth and into the flesh of her palm, squeezes hard until she knows her hand is bleeding again, until the pain is wiping the toothy man's smile from his face, his voice from her mind. She can hear the buzzing, garbagebloated flies again, can feel the indifferent July heat on her cheeks, only the sun eating away at her now and there's no sign the man was ever there. Just the choking smells of tar and trash, car exhaust, and Dancy picks up her duffel bag, which seems at least twice as heavy now, steps out from behind the pink Dumpster. She fixes her eyes on the faraway sprinkler, tiny shower sweeping back and forth across the lush, green lawn of what might be a church, great, graywhite building of stone and confidence, imagines the water falling against her blistering skin, and Dancy steps out of the shadow and into the parking lot.

◉

"Well, my first guess would have been an amphineuran of some sort," Alice Sprinkle says, looking away from the black rubber eyepieces of the stereomicroscope. The thing from the jar is lying in a small glass dish, with a little of the tea-colored alcohol to keep it from drying out. "But it's not a chiton," she says, leans back in her chair and reaches for her pack of Winstons on the tabletop. "It has the right sort of gills and those *look* like calcareous spicules there between the plates, but the plates themselves are all wrong. For one thing, chitons only have one overlapping row of dorsal plates. This thing here has a dorsal *and* a ventral set, almost completely encircling the body with no room for a functional foot. So it isn't an amphineuran. I don't think it's a mollusk at all."

Alice takes a cigarette from the pack and lights it, careful to blow the smoke away from Chance who's sitting next to her, staring at the thing in the dish. "And it's not a worm," Chance says vacantly, the idea that it could possibly be a worm discarded half an hour ago.

"Nope," Alice says, "it's not a worm." She sets her cigarette in an ashtray made from a huge fossil oyster shell and looks through the microscope again.

"There's no sign of a cerebral ganglion or any visible sensory organs, unless that's what all those little hairs along the midline are for. But this bastard's got a mouth on him, I'll tell you that much," and Alice picks up a probe and pokes gently at the front end of the thing, pushes the first set of plates apart and Chance leans closer, watches over her shoulder. "There's a radula, attached to the floor of what must be the digestive canal," Alice says, "almost like a snail, so I'm guessing it's some sort of a predator. And look at this," and now Alice is using the probe to point at the rear of the animal.

"The mantle tissue here's been torn and this last set of plates is broken along the back edges, like this thing was bitten in two or cut in half, so whatever it is, we don't even have a whole specimen. Which just fucking figures," and she takes her eyes away from the microscope again and rubs at them, pushes her chair back from the table. "Have a look for yourself," she says.

Chance leans over the scope and there's nothing through the eyepieces but a dusky, drawn-out blur, so she plays with the fine adjustment a moment, rotates the knobs up and down until the blur resolves, solidifies, and she's looking at the thing from the stoppered jar, magnified ten times and if it was ugly before, now it's something from a monster movie.

"I know you've spent the last couple of years fooling around with your little fishies and salamanders and shit," Alice says, faintest and insincere hint of derision in her voice because she once tried to steer Chance towards studying invertebrate fossils instead. "So I don't know if you quite appreciate exactly how utterly full-tilt weird this thing here is."

"I think I'm beginning to get an idea," and Chance rotates the microscope's nosepiece to the next highest setting, refocuses at 40x, and she's looking at the armored head, uses a pair of forceps to get a better view of the sharp and horny radula, pinkwhite tongue like a minute, rasping file, tongue made for boring through the hard shells of other animals.

"Then you know that we need to show this to someone over in biology, someone with a little more experience with *recent* animals," Alice says, but Chance shakes her head no, and "You already promised," she says.

"Yeah," Alice replies, sullen, defeated, and starting to sound more than a little annoyed with Chance, not someone who's exactly in the habit of hiding her feelings. "I promised," she sighs.

"Now, have a look at this," Chance says, changing the subject, trying to ignore the disgruntled tone in Alice's voice, plenty enough time for that later, and she turns away from the microscope, reaches into the crate again and this time she takes out the chunk of hematite and sandstone. "You're pretty good with trilobites, right?"

"Well, I'm not your grandmother, if that's what you mean," she says and Chance passes the purplered rock to Alice Sprinkle; a long moment of silence while she examines the cluster of spiny trilobites through her bifocals, and she grins, any sign of irritation melting quickly from her face. "You and that box, girl, you're getting to be like some kind of goddamn magic act, you know that? 'Hey Rocky. Watch me pull a rabbit outta my hat,' " and then Alice glances at her wristwatch and frowns, hands the rock back to Chance.

"Jesus, I was supposed to be over at Campbell Hall ten minutes ago."

"They're *Dicranurus,* aren't they?" Chance asks while Alice gathers up a stack of files and her pack of Winstons from the confusion on the table. "I know this rock's a lot older than any record for the genus, but I think that's what they are anyway."

"Yeah, well, I think you're probably right," Alice says, talking fast now and another glance at her watch, another frown. "We've got some stuff from the Haragan Formation of Oklahoma around here somewhere. It should be in the computer and I'm pretty sure there are a few *Dicranurus.* Oh, and have a look at *Ceratonurus* while you're at it, just to be sure."

"Yeah," Chance says. "Well, thanks," and Alice rushes past her towards the open door, trailing a cloud of cigarette smoke and agitation; she stops in the doorway, framed in the fading late afternoon sunlight. "So, does this mean that you're back among the living?" she asks. Chance shrugs and "We'll see," she says. "Let's take this one thing at a time."

"Call me tonight," Alice says, smiling again, and then she's gone and Chance is standing alone, looking down at the trilobites and thinking about Dancy Flammarion and magic tricks.

In her dream, this is the day after the night that something crawled out of the woods and took her mother away, and Dancy's sitting on her bed pretending to read, sitting on the threadbare quilt her mother made before she was born, crazy quilt of leftover reds and browns and daisy yellows, and her grandmomma is still watching the cabin door. Sits at the table with the double-barreled Winchester across her lap and she doesn't take her eyes off the door or the big, broken window next to it. The Bible and a box of shotgun shells on the table, a glass of water and the bloodstone onyx and silver rosary that Dancy's grandfather brought back with him from Germany; every now and then she picks up the rosary and fingers the vivid green beads specked with red, red and green like drops of blood on moss, whispers her prayers and sometimes Dancy whispers along with her, matching word for word, breath for breath, and other times she stares at the pages of her book of Henry Wadsworth Longfellow, one of her mother's books from when she went off to Pensacola and the pages are turning like autumn leaves.

There are things of which I may not speak, all these poems she knows by heart, all these words, knows them with her eyes shut. She only has six books, besides her grandmother's Bible, and she stares at the yellowbrittle pages but she's listening to the cicadas in the trees, every noise from the scalding day beyond the cabin's walls, and if a twig snaps or a single blade of grass bends she'll hear it. The day a hushed tangle of sound, the droning rise and fall of insect voices and an alligator bellowing off towards Wampee Creek, and Dancy looks back down at her book of poems.

There are dreams that cannot die . . .

Flutter of wings then, like the day she surprised a flock of vultures picking at the carcass of a wild pig and they all took off at once, loud and unexpected rustle of carrion feathers against air, but that sound trapped within the close, pine walls of the cabin now. Her grandmother hasn't heard, hasn't moved, but the angel is standing on the other side of the room, watching Dancy with its flaming, holocaust eyes. "You let her die," Dancy says. "You let them both die," because she remembers that in a few minutes she'll look up, past the table and through the shattered window and he'll be standing right there at the edge of the trees, watching them like he wasn't afraid of the sun or shotguns or angels or anything. Smiling at them, all ripping teeth and skin the color of soot and blacksnakes, and Julia Flammarion's blood still drying in his matted hair.

There are thoughts that make the strong heart weak . . .

"They have seen two such huge walkers in the wasteland," the angel says, angeltongue to make the sun seem cold, to make the sun a cinder, and "I won't listen anymore," Dancy whispers, resentful, everything she's lost and everything she'll lose wrapped up like Christmas for the angel to hear. "I'm not your fucking butcher anymore."

Fire drips from the angel's lips to scorch the floor, drip, drip, drip like molten lead, and now Dancy can hear rain beginning to fall on the tar-paper roof of the cabin. Fat summer raindrops and it's the sweetest sound, almost, sweet as the end of a fever, as ripe, red apples.

"They know of no father," the angel roars and murmurs and wails, all those things at once, because it hasn't noticed the rain or it just doesn't care, "whether in earlier times any was begotten for them among the dark spirits."

The cool rain against the roof and Dancy closes her eyes, so good to finally close her eyes and hear nothing now but the rain, falling harder and harder and she doesn't care that the angel won't shut up or that this isn't the way it happened. This is the way it's happening *this* time and that's good enough for her.

"You can't sleep here," her grandmother says, old woman with her rosary beads and shotgun bending close, old woman that smells like dust and wintergreen candy.

"Now once again is the cure in you," the angel says, and the angel smells like nothing real.

"Wake up. You can't sleep here, miss," and Dancy doesn't want to wake up ever again, wants the rain to melt her like sugar and sand, wash her away bit by bit until there's nothing left but a sticky place on the bed, but the old woman is shaking her, and when she opens her eyes it isn't her grandmother, some other old woman getting wet from the sprinkler, shaking Dancy awake on the lawn of the church.

"You can't sleep here," the old woman says again indignantly and Dancy stares up at her, the wet, consoling grass pressed into her cheek, her clothes soaked straight through, and now that she's awake the old woman retreats to the sidewalk where the sprinkler can't reach her. "Please don't make me call the police, miss," she says. "I don't want to have to call the police."

Dancy sits up and wipes sprinkler water from her eyes; her skin has turned the hot color of pink carnations, no telling how long she's been lying in front of the church, the sun burning her skin and never mind the heat, she's shivering, and her mother told her all the things that can happen if she ever gets a bad sunburn. Dancy reaches for her duffel bag lying a few feet away from her on the lawn and she almost remembers how she got here, dim recollections of the long and stumbling walk across the parking lot, sinking to her knees in the wet grass.

"We can't have people sleeping on the grass," the old woman says, and now she sounds as bewildered as she sounds indignant. "This is a house of God. We can't have people sleeping on the grass."

"I'm sorry," Dancy says and the sprinkler sweeps back over her, a few seconds of rain and then it's gone again. "I didn't mean to fall asleep."

"Well, okay," the old woman mumbles. "Okay, I guess, but you understand that we can't have people sleeping here," so Dancy gets to her feet, picks up the duffel bag, every inch of exposed skin like she's fallen into a bed of fire ants but she keeps moving anyway, doesn't even wait for the traffic light to turn green, walks across the street and she stands for a moment in the shade of an elm tree growing in front of a post office. The old woman's still watching her like she's afraid Dancy will come sneaking back the moment she turns away; Dancy smiles at her, but the old woman only glares suspiciously from her dry spot on the sidewalk.

Dancy notices that the dishrag bandage has come off her hand, lies bloody and discarded on the lawn in front of the church. The cut has gone an angry, violated red at the edges, stiff and starting to swell, and it hurts too much to make a fist. She takes a deep breath of air so hot that her hair and clothes have already begun to dry, and looks over her shoulder at the steep road that leads past the post office and a health-food store, steep road leading up the mountain and towards the water works tunnel; *I know exactly what's coming,* she thinks, because she does, and Dancy starts walking again.

❋

After Alice left, Chance switched on the antique electric fan sitting on top of one of the cabinets, something to stir the stagnant, smoky air, a token gesture against the heat. A quick search of the lab's computer catalog turned up one whole drawer of fossils collected from the Haragan Formation of Coal County, Oklahoma, all of them tucked away in Cabinet 25, Drawer 4; ancient shells and calcite exoskeletons exposed on marly limestone or weathered completely free of the rock, stored in cardboard trays and glass vials, hand-printed labels for hundreds of brachiopods and net-like bryozoans, horn corals and trilobites, and each one filled out in her grandmother's handwriting. Exquisitely preserved trilobites with poetic and tongue-twisting names like *Leonaspis williamsi* and *Huntonia lingulifer,* and towards the back of the metal drawer, one small *Ceratonurus* and several large examples of the subspecies *Dicranurus hamatus elegans.*

Chance pulls a stool over to the cabinet, retrieves the chunk of Red Mountain iron ore and spends almost half an hour comparing it to the Oklahoma fossils. Invertebrates not her strong point, more used to puzzling over crushed scraps of fish and tetrapod skulls, but she can see that the trilobites from the crate are virtually identical to the specimens of *Dicranurus* from the Haragan, the Oklahoma fossils perhaps fifty million years younger and not so well preserved, but the same genus, if not the same species.

"And that means *what,* exactly?" Chance asks, her voice low but seeming very loud in the empty lab. Her head too full of questions and most of them have nothing at all to do with trilobites. *No, that would be simple,* she thinks. *That would be easy,* better than the ghosts dredged up by this box of oddities, better than trying to re-call exactly what it was she did and did not hear the stormy night her grandmother hung herself. What she does and does not know about her grandfather, trying to imagine why he would have hidden any of these things, buried Esther Matthews' last, hard work in-stead of finishing it himself. Obvious now that they must have been arguing about these fossils the night she died, these fossils and maybe the thing in the jar, as well, but why? The trilobites almost certainly a new and undescribed species, and a Silurian record of the genus *Dicranurus* would be a small but important addition to the long story of trilobite evolution, evidence that one lineage of the group was far older than previously suspected, but still a common enough sort of discovery, the sort of problem her grandmother spent her life solving.

Chance slides the drawer full of Haragan fossils back into the gray steel cabinet, closes the door and locks it. Questions for a dead man, and maybe she's better off not asking them. Perhaps there's nothing left to do but follow Alice's advice and pass the things from the crate along to the people best suited to solve whatever mysteries they pose, whatever scientific mysteries, and leave the rest alone. Se-crets between her grandparents that she might be happier not knowing, their secrets, their problems, and neither of them burdened with them any longer. So she sits on the stool in front of Cabinet 25, listening to the whir of the fan across the room, and stares blankly down at the fossils embedded in the piece of ore.

So what about Dancy, and what about Elise? What about Deacon? and she suspects these are only more questions better left unanswered; too many unlikely or impossible connections drawn for the wrong reasons, string art for loss and hurt and insanity, too little that she can hold in her hands, that she can see; Chance turns the rock over and there's the star-shaped fossil on the bottom, not much bigger than a silver dollar and the smaller polygon centered within the stellate impression. She'd completely forgotten about it, and *I'll have to remember to show you to Alice,* she thinks. No doubt it's only some echinoderm she's never seen before, a poorly preserved crinoid or an eocrinoid, possibly something rarer, a very early true starfish, perhaps, and wouldn't that make this chunk of rock something special?

The sunlight through the windows is getting dim, already fading away towards twilight, towards the merciful end of this long, weird day, and Chance squints to get a better view of the fossil. She counts the sides of the polygon and there are seven, not an unusual number for the plates of some pelmatozoans, so it's probably only a crinoid after all. She tilts the rock a little to one side and the flat surface of the plate glimmers beneath the stark row of florescents overhead, an almost oily sheen off the septagon.

Unpleasant light, Chance thinks. *Unclean, slippery sort of light,* and scolds herself for letting all the weirdness get to her, letting it freak her out like children telling spooky stories. But then the rock seems to wink at her again, briefest flash of greasy light, and there's something else, the realization that it's difficult to look directly at the septagonal plate for very long, that it seems to force her eyes away after only a few seconds.

She carries the piece of iron ore back across the room to the table with the microscope. There's a wooden case somewhere in all the clutter, polished wooden case with a pair of digital calipers inside, and that's what she needs right now, the mundane certainty of measurements to clear her head. She sets the rock aside and begins searching under computer printouts and pages torn from notebooks, Alice's tray of broken shale, and she doesn't find the calipers, but there's a protractor, black lines and numbers printed on translucent green plastic. And that's even better, really, following the vertical and horizontal axes to find the specific angles of the septagon, simple and everyday exercise to bring her back down to earth.

Chance reaches for the rock again, hears something outside and she pauses, thinks she hears footsteps at the gravel edge of the parking lot; probably Alice finished with her meeting and dropping back by to see if Chance is still working, hoping that she is and wanting to talk, or it's just someone taking a shortcut. Chance glances towards the lab door standing wide open, the last of the day in sunset reds and oranges bleeding away outside, and then the footsteps stop somewhere near one corner of the building, corner closest to her and closest to the door. And immediately there's another sound, a snuffling, animal sound that makes Chance think of pigs and dogs and her skin prickles with the sudden urge to shut the door, to run and shut it quickly, but she makes herself stand still and listen.

The snuffling is getting louder, right up against the wall now, maybe less than five feet between her and whatever's making the noise, five feet and a brick wall. Chance puts the protractor down again and she keeps her eyes on the open door.

It's just a dog, just a hungry, stray dog sniffing about for something to eat, and she tries to picture the ribsythin mongrel in her head, the skittish kind of stray that always looks as if it expects you to kick it, that flinches if you so much as look at it hard.

The snuffling stops as abruptly as it began but another sound to take its place, like a very big dog panting, breathless, wet pant from mottled, canine lips, and under that, much softer, hardly as loud as Chance's heartbeat, a noise no dog could make. A wheezing, satisfied sigh and then a laugh that isn't anything like a laugh, a thin and labored sound trying to pass itself off for a laugh. And a long shadow falling across the crumbling square of concrete set in front of the door, falling across the threshold and into the lab itself, crooked, laughing shadow like the sun shining past the mockery of a dog made from sticks and baling wire.

And Chance turns and runs, no more room left inside for explanations, no room for deciding what can and cannot be with that shadow slipping towards her, dragging its maker close behind. She follows the long, dark hall that divides the lab straight down the middle, doesn't bother fumbling about for the light switch because it can't be more than fifty yards to the door at the other end, fifty yards of pitch darkness and the only light is back the way she came. She can hear it behind her now, the uneven click and scrape of claws on the cement floor, the panting noise, and then Chance runs into the door, hits it so hard she almost falls, sees stars or only pinprick holes in the gloom, and there's a long and terrible moment when she can't find the doorknob, another when it's locked and she has to search for the dead bolt. Certain that she isn't alone in the hallway now, that the snuffling, laughing thing is striding though the darkness on its long, stilt legs, broomstick, mophandle legs, and then the dead bolt turns and the door swings open, and Chance tumbles out into daylight. Almost falls again, and she runs at least another hundred feet across the gravel and asphalt before she stops and looks behind her, and there's nothing back there but the lab door standing open and the taunting blackness coiled inside.

⟨●⟩

Dancy knows perfectly well where the entrance to the water works tunnel is, spent enough hours, enough days at the library studying the maps and diagrams of Red Mountain in a book called *Birmingham Bound,* finally snuck the book into a restroom and carefully ripped out the relevant pages, has been keeping them folded at the bottom of her duffel bag in case she forgot. But she hasn't forgotten, doesn't need to open up the wet duffel and find the maps because she remembers: follow Nineteenth Street South, all the way to the place where it dead ends at Valley View Park. More like the *streets* have forgotten where they're supposed to lead and she keeps turning when she means to go straight, has walked the same circle around Ramsey High School three times now, almost like her ninth birthday when she and her mother took the bus into Milligan to see a carnival. A big, noisy carnival on the edge of town and she got lost in the hall of mirrors. Almost like that, walking three times around the same block, reading lies on street signs, passing corners that aren't there until she looks over her shoulder.

The sun has begun to set, too low now to make her sunburn worse and the air's cooler, but there's precious little comfort there, not when her skin's already gone the color of a boiled crawfish; fat blisters on the backs of her hands, on her sweatsmooth cheeks, enough aches and chills that she's sure she's running a fever, and pretty soon it'll be dark and They won't have to bother playing games with street corners anymore.

Dancy looks up, stops walking and counting the cracks in the sidewalk, counting off her steps, and sees that she's standing in front of the high school again. The cut on her hand is bleeding, fresh drops of blood spattering the cement at her feet, and her other arm's gone numb from carrying the duffel. She lets the heavy bag slide off her shoulder, thump to the ground, and stares up at the high and cloudless sky, knows that it would be so easy to just sit down and wait for this to end, caught in their clever mirrorstreet trap, going round and round until night comes crashing down on top of her and then the nightwalkers can take their time. Then they can do all the things they've always promised they would do, sooner or later, worse things even than what they did to her mother before she finally died.

"All this crazy shit and now you're just gonna give up?" and Dancy turns to see who said that, already knows but turning anyway, and the smiling, rawboned man from the bus is sitting near the bottom of the stairs that lead up to the whitewashed front doors of the high school. The man from the parking lot, and his face has grown almost as long and hairy as a wolf's, no need for masks with twilight so close.

"Hell, you might as well have stayed on the bus, girl, done like you said and rode it all the way to Graceland."

A rustyblue Volkswagen bug rattles by and the man on the steps smiles and waves to the driver and the driver smiles and waves back. Dancy wonders exactly what the woman in the car saw, and then the chills are back and she's shivering too hard to care. Her head feels light, head like a rubber helium balloon, and she puts her bleeding hand around her throat to keep it from floating away.

"Ain't you never even heard of umbrellas?"

"I'm sick," she says to the man and he blinks his eyes like swollen red-wasp stings, eyes like blind things inside his skull wanting out, and "No," he says. "You're dying. I think you've been dying all along."

Maybe it wouldn't be so bad to let go, Dancy thinks. *Maybe it would be good,* and she can see her head rising up and up above the trees and the rooftops, sailing away into the summer sky and then she wouldn't have to listen to men with wolf faces and running-sore eyes.

"Frankly, I'm a little disappointed. I thought you'd put up more of a fight," the man says. "We were all impressed, the way you handled things back there in Florida. I thought, 'Look at this one here. This one's gonna teach us all a thing or two.'"

"He killed my mother," Dancy whispers, and she's disappointed, too, has turned loose of her throat but her head's still on her shoulders, just a sticky smear at her throat from her bleeding hand, sticky handprint smear on the collar of her T-shirt. "He killed my mother and then he killed my grandmother."

"That's right," the man says and runs a long, pinkred tongue around his muzzle, maybe the sight of her blood making him hungry, and he leans towards her and sniffs at the air. "He did. But you fixed his little red wagon, didn't you? You even waited around until his momma came looking for him and you put some holes in her, too, didn't you? Damn, you were gonna send us *all* to Hell. Isn't that what you said?"

"No. That's what the angel said," and Dancy doesn't think she can stand up much longer, wants to sit down on the sidewalk beside her duffel bag if the smiling man intends to talk her to death.

"There ain't no angels, girl. I thought you would've figured that out by now."

"Can I sit down please? I think this will all make more sense if I sit down," but the smiling man laughs and shakes his head. He holds out a hand to Dancy, opens his long fingers and there's a fat, silkwhite roll of twine lying in his hairy palm.

"Not just yet," he says firmly. "You've done us harm, child, and we expect a little more sport for our trouble," but when she reaches for the twine it rolls out of his hand and bounces down the steps towards her. Dancy stoops to pick it up, moves slow because she's very dizzy, and when she looks back at the place the man was sitting he's gone.

This is what they want me to do, isn't it? she thinks, *They want me to find the tunnel;* it doesn't make sense, but she's pretty sure that doesn't matter anymore, all of it gone beyond making sense, and Dancy ties one end of the smiling man's twine around the trunk of a small dogwood tree growing in front of the high school. A strong square knot and she tugs at it with what's left of her strength until she's sure it's strong enough, sure that it won't slip loose. Then she crosses the street, leaves a careful, straight line of string on the blacktop, and when she's on the other side, loops it twice around the post of a bright yellow school-zone sign before turning left and trailing it along the ground behind her half a block to the corner of Thirteenth Avenue and Nineteenth Street.

Another loop around another silver post and this time she turns right, turns south, and when she looks back the school is already growing small and distant and she knows she's found her way out of the maze, that he's *shown* her the way out. Dancy unwinds the twine as she walks, lets it fall to the ground to mark the way she's come, Hansel and Gretel bread-crumb trick, something she'll recognize if she starts going around in circles again.

She's almost all the way to the corner of Fourteenth and Nineteenth before she realizes that she left her duffel bag back at the high school, everything she owns in there: the few small things she saved from the cabin before it burned, photographs of her mother and grandmother and grandfather, her grandmother's rosary, the big carving knife. But she doesn't have the strength to walk all the way back and retrieve it, not if she's going to reach the park, if she's ever going to reach the tunnel at the end of this road.

Dancy tries not to think about the duffel bag, crosses the street, is busy wrapping the twine tight around one leg of a mailbox when she hears the sound and looks up. Sharp and wooden sound like someone tapping a broomstick hard against the pavement, sound like tapping broomsticks and rustling straw. She's heard that sound once before, tap-tapping along a midnight alley in Savannah, and she tries to stop shivering for a minute, long enough to listen, tries not to think about how bad she hurts.

But there's only the scoldingharsh squawk of a mockingbird somewhere close by, and the constant city sound of traffic; Dancy stands up, so dizzy and hot and she only wants to lie down on the cooling sidewalk. The eastern sky turning indigo and violet while the west burns alive and there's a cold, crescent moon hanging in between; the heavens like a velvet lullaby for her, an apology for what the sun has done to her skin and what the night gives shelter. *Lie down, Dancy. Lie down and close your eyes,* but the memory of what she saw that night in Savannah enough to get her moving again, unwinding more of this ball of string that isn't getting any smaller and she knows she could walk all the way back to Florida and it never would.

This unhealing cleft in the side of the mountain, deep furrow between park-tended grass and trees that have already turned the dusk beneath their branches into night; steep, red earth on either side and rough, gray boulders, and Dancy walks up to the gates of the water works tunnel. Hundreds of miles, a thousand, to bring her finally to this spot, to stand before this grim and mosscrusted façade of limestone blocks and mortar, the entrance with its rusty, iron gate and a small window set high on either side. No bars across the windows but they're both so small and so high that it doesn't matter because no one's going in or coming out that way.

This is the ravenous stone face that Dancy's dreamt of so many times, the same yawning, toothless mouth and those vacant, hollow eyes. Face of the thing that killed her mother and the vengeful, ebony thing that came to take its body back into the swamp, the face of the smiling man from the Greyhound bus and the auburn-haired woman in Waycross with stubby, writhing tentacles where her breasts should have been, the pretty boy in Savannah who showed her a corked, amber bottle that held three thousand ways to suffer, three thousand ways to hurt, before she killed him. All of them dead because that's what the angel said, and she's standing here holding tight to these iron bars so she doesn't fall, too weak to stand and the mountain looming above her, because this is where the angel said she had to go.

This entrance to all the nowhere places where their gods sleep, where they've slept since the first day, the first scorching sunrise, and Chance Matthews should be here beside her, Chance and Deacon, and she should have her duffel bag and all the things inside. All this way and now she knows that this is as far as she goes, that she can only stand and stare between the bars into the blackness beyond this gate sealed with loops of chain like serpent coils and a shiny new padlock, can only glimpse the elbow bends of enormous water pipes, the corroded valves slick with mold.

Dancy's started shaking so badly that her teeth clack loud as a pocketful of pennies, loud as jumping railroad steel under locomotive wheels, and she shuts her eyes, sits down with her back against the gate, her back to the abyss and its mushroom-damp exhalations. Doesn't move again until her head has stopped swimming enough that she can tell up from down, right from left, and she reaches into her jeans pocket and takes out Chance's red knife.

She opens the largest blade and uses it to sever the twine, and then Dancy drops the rest and the ball of string rolls away into the shadows, rolling all the way back to the smiling man, for all she knows or cares. She ties the free end to one of the iron bars, ties it tight, a knot to match the one around the dogwood's trunk, and there are sounds coming from the trees now, from the dark beneath the trees and the spindly things crouched there, broomstick legs and the huffing breath of thirsty dogs.

"What the hell are you waiting for?" she asks the soulless, red eyes watching her, not wanting to cry, wanting to be brave at the end, and Dancy crosses herself and waits for them to come.

PART II

The Dragon

"*Chaos and muck and filth—the indeterminable and the unrecordable and the unknowable—and all men are liars—and yet—*"

—CHARLES FORT (1919)

CHAPTER NINE

The Other Word for Catchfly

SADIE at the window, the florescent-bright inside of the laundromat window, and she's watching the street, the sidewalk streetlight pools and the less certain spaces in between, the big pine trees and oaks at the edge of Rushton Park all blending together in the dark. Deacon's still on the phone, still trying to find someone willing to drop whatever they're doing and come in on a Saturday night, someone with nothing better to do, nothing worse, but no luck so far. His reflection is superimposed over her view of Highland Avenue, so Sadie can see him watching her from his stool behind the counter without taking her eyes off the street or the park or the trees. Looking ahead of herself and behind at the same time, and Deacon frowns and shakes his head, because he knows she can see him, eyes in the back of her head, and she nods.

"Look, man, yeah, I *know* it's Saturday night, all right?" he says and he's starting to sound the way her stomach feels. "So why don't you just say no and get it the hell over with so I can call somebody else?"

A pickup truck full of teenagers cruises slowly past the laundromat and Sadie can feel the *whump whump whump* of its stereo through the plateglass; shitty rap and a truckload of drunken white boys all looking for a cop to pull them over, a couple of nights in the Birmingham jail and maybe that would rub a little bit of the suburbia off their dumb asses. She closes her eyes and doesn't open them again until she can't hear the pounding music anymore, until there's nothing but the night outside, and *That's right*, she thinks. *Nothing at all but the night.*

"Jesus, didn't I say to just forget about it, Soda," Deacon growls and hangs up the phone, rubs hard at his eyes, and Sadie turns around, sits down in one of the hard, plastic chairs lined up in front of the window.

"Why don't you call Peggy? Maybe if you tell her it's an emergency," but Deacon coughs up a dry scrap of a laugh and squints at the wall clock hanging above the vending machine that sells little boxes of soap powder and fabric softener.

"You know she's already looking for an excuse to tell me to hit the road. Making her come all the way down here on a Saturday night would probably be the last straw."

"But if you told her it's an *emergency*," Sadie says again. "Deke, she couldn't fire you if it was an emergency," trying hard not to sound impatient, but she's looking at the clock too and it's almost an hour now since she left the apartment, longer than that since she realized that Dancy was gone.

"Is that what this is? An emergency?"

"What's that supposed to mean?" And the quick, accusing edge in her voice unintended, unanticipated, but it feels good regardless; better than sitting here like she isn't scared, playing calm because she doesn't want Deacon to see what's going on inside her head.

"It means maybe we should let her go. She isn't your responsibility and she *sure* as hell isn't mine."

Deacon licks at his thin, dry lips and Sadie can tell how badly he wants a drink, probably the only thing in the world he wants more than for her to shut up and leave him alone, a beer and a shot of cheap, bar-brand whiskey, maybe a dark corner where he can get drunk in peace.

"We can't save her, Sadie," he says and she glances down at the dirty linoleum floor, her bare feet against the scuffed red and dirty-white squares like a chessboard; *Your move now, babycakes,* small and mocking whisper wedged in somewhere behind her eyes, wedged beneath her skin, voice to speak from the weary part of herself that wishes Dancy Flammarion had picked someone else's life to screw around with. But it's only a very small voice and in a moment she looks back up at Deacon.

"You know, it's one thing to be a drunk. I've never judged you for being a drunk. But it's something else to be a coward."

"I never figured there was a whole hell of a lot of difference," he says, and then there's a long and leadheavy silence between them, nothing to mark the time but the monotonous slosh and throb from one of the washing machines. Silence to let Sadie's anger get almost as big as her fear, time enough that she knows he's seen it in her eyes. And she doesn't pretend that she can't see the contempt in his, as well, that she doesn't know just how far she's pushed him and any moment now he'll tell her to go fuck herself. Fuck herself *and* all the creepy, little albino lunatics she can find, while she's at it, and then Deacon sighs loud and looks down at the telephone and his list of names and numbers; after he starts dialing again, Sadie turns back to the window and the wide night full of shadows still waiting for her.

The long nub end of the afternoon spent at her keyboard, her hands moving so much slower than her racing mind. The frustrating lag between her thoughts and the hunt and peck; a hot flood of ideas where there had been months of trickling, uncertain sentences and Sadie trying to keep up with herself, wishing she'd taken typing in high school, scared that this inspiration would soon grow restless, impatient with her, and slink back to whatever hole it crawled out of. Listening to the same Brian Eno album over and over on her headphones and smoking too much, as if that would help. Finishing a stale pack of Lucky Strikes left from the last time Deacon quit instead of her Djarum cloves, and it was dark by the time she finally began to run out of steam.

Ten new pages on the Mac's hard drive, ten and half, really, when she'd never done better than seven before; she fished the last of the Luckys from the pack and lit it with a wooden kitchen match, squinted through smoke at the softly glowing screen. Her words, her jumbled, mad thoughts tamed or simply broken, made language, and she took another drag off the Lucky, exhaled, and read the last sentence aloud.

"'I can't get it off,' Val said and she held out her red hands for Wendy to see."

This scene, and the girls named Wendy and Val were hiding in the rusted shell of an old caboose, a wide and desolate place just across the tracks from Morris Avenue where dozens of box cars and engines lay abandoned, and, in the story, something like meat started falling from the cloudless sky. A hailstorm of blood and marbled flakes of something that *wanted* to be meat, and the girls huddled together in the dark listening to the sticky, spattering sounds the stuff made as it struck the steel roof of the caboose. Red smears down the one window that wasn't broken, Val afraid to even look outside, and then Sadie knew that it was time to stop for the day, because the words were coming *too* easily, too fast, and that usually meant that she was getting tired and wasn't thinking hard enough anymore. She saved the file to her back-up diskette, switched off the computer, and leaned back against the edge of the bed to finish her cigarette.

And that's when she remembered Dancy. A glance at the alarm clock beside the bed, 8:07 P.M., so almost five whole hours sitting here on the floor, hunched over the keyboard and it was no wonder her typing fingers were numb and her back ached, no wonder she needed to piss, and Dancy was probably asleep out on the couch. Was probably exhausted after the weird shit at Chance Matthews' house and grateful for a quiet place to rest for a while. Sadie stubbed out the butt of the Lucky Strike in the saucer she was using for an ashtray, looked at the dark computer screen one more time, some part of her reluctant to walk away, uncomfortable with the thought of leaving Val and Wendy trapped inside the caboose while the sky hemorrhaged above them.

She walked quietly from the bed, her bare feet almost silent on the carpet, and stood for a moment in the doorway staring at the ratty sofa where Dancy wasn't sleeping. Only the final, unreliable dregs of dusk to illuminate the room, murky sunset light the color of raisins, and a gauzy haze of cigarette smoke drifting a few feet above the floor. No sign of Dancy anywhere, here or in the kitchen, so Sadie called her name once, "Dancy?" but no one answered and she didn't like the way her voice sounded in the empty apartment, the way it bounced back at her from the gray walls and grayer corners. Not quite an echo, but still the impression that someone was taunting her, throwing her words in her face and smiling at her unease.

Sadie kept both eyes on the room as she fumbled for the switch plate on the wall, and in another moment the darkness was gone, washed away by warmsafe incandescent bulbs, and she could see that Dancy was gone, as well. An empty spot where her duffel bag had been, no one left in the apartment but Sadie, and she looked at the front door, half expecting to find it standing open, but it wasn't. She walked across the room to the kitchen, and there were the Coke and the uneaten Oreos waiting for her on the table.

The next five minutes spent walking through the apartment

again, turning on all the lights as she went; maybe just a game, Dancy Flammarion's idea of hide-and-go-seek, but there were only so many places to hide in Deacon's apartment: the bathtub, underneath the bed, behind the sofa, and five minutes was more than time enough to check them all twice. So Sadie searched the hallway, too, one end to the other, from the damp spot where the ceiling leaked to the top of the stairs, walked downstairs to the front door, and then back up to the apartment. And finally, when there was no more denying that Dancy was gone, Sadie sat down on the sofa and stared at the floor between her feet, the carpet the color of vomit, her black toenails; half an hour before and her head had been so full, reeling from all the things that Deacon and Chance wouldn't explain to her, the stranger things that Dancy had only ever hinted at, the unexpected outpouring of words. And now she felt as tired, as empty, as the moment before she found the pile of black gumdrops on the threshold. Maybe just some crazy girl, after all, and gullible Sadie wanting to believe as badly as Deacon and Chance wanted to deny, needing the same way they needed, and in the end the crazy girl had gotten bored with them all or moved on to the next delusion, had walked out on her and in a few weeks Deacon would tell her how silly they'd all been and there must be a hundred rational explanations.

Or . . .

We haven't even talked about the tunnel, and Sadie looked up quickly, knew that she was still alone and only remembering something Dancy said while they waited for the taxi to take them away from Chance's house. Something else exciting and nonsensical, but Sadie stared at the closed door, the doorknob and her heart beating too fast.

We have to talk about the tunnel, and we have to go there, today, *while there's still time.*

The urgency in Dancy's voice more immediate than mere memory could ever be and there was a noise from the bedroom or the bathroom, a bumping, clumsy sort of a noise, and Sadie stood up very slowly. Watching the doorway to the bedroom, swallowing the tin-foil adrenaline taste at the back of her throat, and "Dancy!" she called out, shouting loud enough that everyone on the third floor probably got an earful. "This isn't funny anymore, goddamnit!"

But it wasn't Dancy that answered her, not really an answer at all, a laugh, maybe. A dry and perfectly humorless sound that was *meant* to be a laugh. A sound to make Sadie think of dead leaves and cold wind, of dark streets and the forsaken places where men left the skeletons of trains to decay beneath impossible rains of meat and blood.

It's not safe, and whatever was making the sound that wasn't laughter must have been remembering all the things that Dancy said, too, because it snorted once and there was the shattering sound of the bathroom mirror breaking, shards of glass falling into the sink, bouncing off the porcelain and smashing against the tile floor.

"Run, Sadie. *Now,*" and it didn't matter if it was her voice she was hearing, or Dancy's she was remembering, and Sadie didn't stop and look back until she was outside Quinlan Castle and standing in the dark on the other side of Twenty-first Street.

And if she'd been braver, she might have gone to the entrance to the tunnel in Valley View Park instead of going to Deacon. If she'd been half the person she'd always hoped she could be, because that's what Dancy had said, wasn't it? "We have to talk about the tunnel, and we have to *go* there, today," and so she knew that was where Dancy had gone. And Sadie also knew that she'd gone there alone, that it hadn't mattered if Chance believed her or Deacon believed her, not in the end, because Dancy believed, and finally there had been no other option.

Sadie stood beneath a street lamp and stared up at the castle silhouetted against the last fiery rind of the day, absurd edifice of rough sandstone blocks and corner towers lost in a wilderness of office buildings, watched the windows of her and Deacon's apartment; all the lights burning and she couldn't even remember if she'd shut the door behind her. There she was standing on the street, barefoot and afraid of something she might have heard or something she might only have imagined after five hours alone with her own bizarre thoughts.

Scaring myself half to fucking death, that's what I'm doing, she thought, *that's all I'm doing,* and the noises she heard had probably come from the apartment next door, if they'd come from anywhere at all. The guys next door and their PlayStation, all hours of the day and night, fighting zombies and wrecking cars, the volume cranked up so loud the windows rattled. Either video games or one of the kung-fu movies they were always watching over there, and Sadie stepped off the curb, first uncertain step back towards the castle, when a shadow moved slow across the bedroom curtains. A flowing, liquid shadow that almost seemed a thing unto itself, shadow of nothing but itself, and she stopped, one foot in the street, and watched as it moved across the window. As indistinct and undeniable as the edges of an eclipse and in another moment it was gone and she was standing on the curb again.

"C'mon, baby," she whispered to herself, trying to salvage the meanest scrap of calm, to sound the way that Deacon would sound—scared, because anyone sane would be scared, but together. Much too easy to let the fear shut her down and so she turned her eyes away from the third-floor bedroom window and towards the north flank of the lightspeckled mountain, the darker ridge raised against the indigo sky and the dim form of Vulcan outlined against the coming night, the great iron statue standing like the city's pagan, patron saint of steel and fire, rusting guardian towering high above Southside.

That's where she is, isn't it? Sadie thought. *Right up there,* and she pictured Dancy standing alone outside the padlocked gate to the water works tunnel, peering between the corroded bars into the damp, black core of the mountain. If Dancy looked up through the trees she would be able see the statue, too, looming huge from his pedestal a few hundred feet farther up the slope from her and almost directly above the park.

Sadie crossed the street, careful not to look at the castle as she passed by it, trying hard not to think about anything but Dancy alone in the darkness at Vulcan's feet, alone because they were all three too busy or frightened or stubborn to go with her. *If I don't have the courage, maybe shame will do. Maybe shame is enough to keep me moving,* and she followed the asphalt and chain-link margin of a parking lot towards the welcoming noise and traffic of Twentieth Street. Later, secure in the whitestark light of the laundry, she would tell herself the thing that hobbled out of a row of bushes ahead of her was only a dog, a big, hungry stray with legs long and thin as rails, its ribs and spine showing straight through its mangy fur. She would tell herself that, and she wouldn't let herself think too much about the sounds it was making, or where she'd heard them before.

Sadie stood very still, not believing and knowing that her belief was irrelevant, while it sniffed at the concrete a moment before raising its wobbly head and turning towards her. It moved as slowly as the shadow she'd seen at the bedroom window; slow but this movement as jerky as a marionette, wooden blocks dangling on puppet strings and eyes like hateful buttons of bluegreen fire. And when it sat back on its narrow haunches, turned its head to one side, and stretched its black lips back in a wide, wide smile, she forgot about courage and shame and she ran.

"No, Pooh, I swear, you're a goddamn lifesaver," Deacon says and the girl with the chemistry textbook, whose real name is Winnie, pretends to smile. He gives her a twenty and she stares at it a moment like the bribe might be counterfeit before she folds it once and stuffs the bill into the bib pocket of her overalls.

"Yeah, thanks," Sadie says and Pooh shrugs and glances down at Sadie's dirty feet.

"Jesus, Deke. You really ought to buy your girlfriend some shoes," and she turns away, drops her textbook loudly onto the mint-green Formica countertop; Sadie starts to tell her to fuck off, never fucking mind, they can find somebody else, but Deacon jabs her hard with his elbow and he's talking again before Sadie can even open her mouth.

"Well, like I said, I'm gonna *try* and make it back by midnight, but I can't promise anything. I don't really know how this will turn out."

"Yeah," Pooh says. "Whatever. I'm here now. I might as well work," and she opens her book, flips aimlessly through the glossy pages, and Deacon takes Sadie's arm and leads her out of the laundromat into the warm summer night.

"They ought to call her Eeyore," Sadie grumbles and Deacon nods his head, keeps a firm grip on her right arm like he's afraid she's going to turn around, go right back inside the Wash-N-Fold and pick a fight with Pooh. But that's just fine with Sadie. It's good to have him close, good to feel him there beside her. "So, what now, Miss Jasper?" he asks and Sadie points southwest, in the direction of the little park and the tunnel entrance. A mile or more between here and there and it'll take them at least another twenty or twenty-five minutes to walk that far.

"Now we have to find her. We have to make sure that she's okay," and without another word, Sadie leads him around the corner.

Less than a block from the park and Sadie steps on a chunk of broken bottle, viciousgreen 7UP shard hiding in the grass and dandelions at the edge of the sidewalk, overgrown edge of someone's yard, and it leaves an inch-long gash in the heel of her right foot.

"Jesus, we're almost *there*," she says. "We can't stop now," and she's trying to act like it doesn't hurt like hell, like she hasn't noticed all the blood on the concrete. But Deacon makes her sit down anyway, and he squints grimly at the cut by the dim, yellow light from a nearby porch.

"It's pretty deep," he says, scowling at the bottom of her foot. "I think you're gonna need stitches."

"Well, I can fucking need stitches later," and Sadie starts to get up, but he makes her sit back down again.

"I can't let you walk on that, baby. I wasn't kidding when I said it was deep," and now he's hastily unlacing one of his sneakers, takes it off and pulls his sock off as well. Sadie hardly even notices what he's doing, stares anxiously towards the park, her eyes following the row of sodium-arc fireflies and lamplit windows bracketing the street, electric fairy trail that ends in Dancy and the hole in Red Mountain. She can see the edge of the park from where she's sitting, and there aren't any lights at all back there. Just the night curled in on itself, pressed black against the earth. "It's trying to stop me, Deacon," she says, her voice gone as brittle as a handful of old newspaper clippings, so close to tears now and she doesn't care. "It's trying to keep me from getting to her."

"What are you talking about, Sadie? *What's* trying to stop you?" Deacon slips the white tube sock on over Sadie's injured foot and she flinches, grimaces and closes her eyes; she can feel the hot tears leaking down her cheeks, tears that have a lot more to do with anger than any pain, more to do with the bottomless conviction that she's failed Dancy than her fear of laughing shadows or scrawny, grinning dog monsters.

"Why won't you tell me what happened at the apartment? What did you see back there?" and she looks up at him, then, no time or patience for this, every second they sit here talking a second lost, a second wasted, and "Why won't *you* tell me about the tunnel, Deke?" she asks him, hoping she sounds every bit as resentful as she feels. "*You* haven't told me a goddamn thing since this began. Like it's all some holy fucking secret between you and Chance, like I'm just too stupid to understand or it's none of my business. Like I'm too big a flake to deal with it. Well, fine. Wonderful. It doesn't matter anymore. Right now all that matters is that you find Dancy before something happens, because there's no one else to help her."

Deacon watches her silently for a moment, the surprised, uncertain expression on his face that says maybe he's seeing her for the first time, that perhaps he's never seen more than a pale ghost of this angry, bleeding girl, and "Yeah," he says finally. "But you're staying here, Sadie. Promise me you'll wait right here for me to come back."

"Cross my heart," and she does, draws a big X across her left breast, then glances down at Deacon's ridiculous, white sock stuck on her foot. Cottonwhite sock turning scarlet, and "Be careful," she says. "I don't *know* what I saw, if I even saw anything at all, but . . ." and she pauses, hunting words that aren't there. "It was something wrong, Deacon."

Part of her hoping that he'll laugh at her, tell her she's full of shit, but Deacon only rubs at his stubbly cheeks and puts his tennis shoe back on his bare foot. "Everything's gonna be okay," he says, and Sadie can tell how much he wants her to believe him, even if he doesn't believe himself. So she smiles and Deacon leans forward and kisses her, a quick kiss that leaves her lips tingling, the faint, musky taste of him on her mouth, and she tries to stop crying. He stands up and points at the porch behind her.

"Stay close to the lights, okay? If you hear anything, I want you to head straight for that house there. Or if I'm not back here in ten minutes. Don't think about it, Sadie, just do it. Tell them to call the cops."

"I love you," she says, but Deacon has turned away and he doesn't seem to hear her, too busy staring up the street at the darker place where the park begins.

"Everything's gonna be okay," he says again and then he's moving away from her, his long strides carrying him quickly off into the gloom and she's alone with the ache in her foot and the air smells like kudzu and her blood drying on the sidewalk.

Deacon Silvey never saw the park or the entrance to the water works tunnel before he met Chance Matthews. She brought him here the first time, a few weeks after they began seeing each other. Someplace different to get drunk and hang out, someplace to talk, and she showed him the old blockhouse at the entrance to the tunnel, and they shared a bottle of Jack Daniel's, listened to Nick Cave on Chance's boombox, while she pointed out fossils in the limestone boulders scattered near the tunnel. Hard rock the dingygray color of lead, weather-rounded clumps of ancient reefs pressed flat by unimaginable pressures and the weight of ages.

They sat together in the grass while she talked, teaching him how to tell the difference between sponges and algae, bryozoans and corals, that there was a trilobite, *Acaste birminghamensis*, named after the city, and then telling the story of the men who'd carved the hole through the mountain more than a hundred years before. This tunnel one link in a system designed to bring fresh water all the way from the Cahaba River five miles south of the city, rough shaft dug more than two thousand feet straight through the limestone and chert and iron-ore bones of the mountain, and "My grandmother did some collecting in there sometime back in the early nineties," she said.

"So *that's* why you're such a big ol' geek," and he grinned and scratched at his chin. "It's all your grandmomma's fault."

Chance smiled back at him, and "Well, can *you* think of anything else I could do with my life that could ever possibly be half this splendid, half this important? I'm learning to *read,* Deke, and not just the handful of things men have been around long enough to write down. The history of the whole damned *planet* is written in rocks, just lying there waiting for us to learn how to read the words.

"How to read *time,*" she said and he kissed her, then, tasting the bourbon on her tongue and wishing he could share even the smallest part of her passion, loving her for that if nothing else, that she was still *alive.* That she had not lost herself, had not lost her heart or wonder, and perhaps she was strong enough that she never would.

But tonight that afternoon seems as far away and unredeemable as a time when the mountain was still silt, still mud, and living, oceanwarm waters blanketed the world, and Deacon pauses where the street dead-ends. Where the blacktop turns abruptly to well-tended park lawn and a winding trail leads between and through the trees to a picnic table near the blockhouse, and he looks back over his shoulder. He can't see Sadie from here, just the soft glow of porch lights and all the cars lined up neatly along both sides of the narrow, sloping street.

And he's suddenly so terribly afraid for her, this last thing keeping him together, tether for his shabby soul, and he wants to run back to Sadie and take her away from here, let Dancy fight her own demons and he'll forget about Chance once and for all, forget the rainy night in April when he and Chance and Elise Alden came here with a pair of bolt cutters, and that's where all this crazy shit started, isn't it? Everything that's gone wrong and keeps going wronger, whatever the hell happened here that none of them ever talked about and now Elise is dead. Forget that and forget the ghosts he's spent his whole life seeing, the horrors he left Atlanta to escape. Walk away right now and finally he'll just be plain old

Deke; if he can't get it from Sadie or a good bottle of whiskey then who needs it anyway. Who needs their whole goddamn life turned into a bad episode of the *Twilight Zone* and Deacon takes one step away from the nightshrouded park.

"Don't you think maybe you've come just a little too far for that?" and the steelhard and silk and burning voice is both inside him and hiding somewhere just out of sight, somewhere on the trail leading to the tunnel, and he knows it's his own voice just as surely as he knows that it's Elise's, as surely as it's Dancy Flammarion's. All these things at once like all the fraying lines of a wasted, coward's life that have brought him here and won't let him walk away, and Deacon turns to face the darkness waiting beneath the trees.

And that's when he sees the string looped tight around the trunk of a small dogwood growing beside the trail, white twine like lost kite string leading from the street to the tree and then on to the next tree after that. Deacon reaches out and gently brushes the taut cord with the tips of his fingers, the fingers of his left hand, like he shouldn't have known better, and all the smells of the muggy, July evening are immediately swept aside by the sweetraw stench of putrefying fish and oranges. His knees suddenly gone weak as kittens and he has to hold onto the tree to keep from sinking to the ground, the pain at his temples, migraine throb between and behind his eyes, and "No," he snarls. "Not now," as if he has some say in the matter, as if there's any way to intimidate or bargain with the hole tearing itself wide around him, tattered hole in time or his sanity, and Deacon can only lean against the little tree and watch.

The iridescent eyes beneath writhing, seeping trees with fat leaves as soft and white as cheese, the lupine faces roughly woven from straw and hair and feathers, and "They hold to the secret land," Dancy says. Dancy slumped against the iron gate, the tunnel at her back and she holds something out in front of her, something small and sharp and silver that catches the faint glint of starlight through the sick and ashen trees.

". . . the wolf-slopes . . ."

And Deacon's lost his hold on the tree now, the ground as insubstantial beneath his hands and knees as the sky overhead, the jealous sky clotted with angelflesh and deceit, and he claws at the dirt, anything to keep him from sliding any closer to the gaping, iron-toothed mouth in the side of the mountain.

". . . the paths where the mountain stream goes down under the darkness of the hills, the flood under the earth."

He understands that she's calling them down, calling them out, opens his mouth to tell her to please shut the hell up and now he can hear the *snick snick snick* of claws and stolen teeth.

"Dancy . . ." he croaks, hoarse, pathetic whisper from his lips as dry as sand, but she hears him and looks up, like the shades creeping towards her matter less, or matter hardly at all, and her skin shimmers faintly in the night. Dark and blisterbright shimmer instead of the powdery luster of her alabaster complexion, and *She's sunburned,* he thinks. He can't see her eyes but he can *feel* them, everything locked there inside her pink eyes, and in another moment they'll be on top of her. "You know this is already over, Deacon," she says, sounding sad and brave and grateful in a single breath, chiding him and thanking him at the same time.

"Try to change what *hasn't* happened yet," and Deacon recognizes the knife in her hand, Chance's Swiss Army knife, before he can't see her anymore, one of the twiggy, scarecrow nightmares closing the space between them.

And the earth rolls like a broken carnival ride, seasick Tilt-A-Whirl lurch and loll as the sky cracks apart and tumbles down in ebon splinters, and he opens his eyes. Opens his watering, corporeal eyes, closing those other, secret eyes, those inward eyes that will take him to pieces one day, and the world falls back in place, the world and the night and the only smells are dirt and grass. No telling how long since he touched the string wrapped around the dogwood tree.

Deacon rolls over on his back, breathless, his head like a throbbing, open wound; he blinks up at the low branches, canopy of limbs and leaves between him and infinity, but nothing strong enough to hold if he could let go and fall that one last time.

"Deacon? Fuck . . ." and then the stars are blotted out by Sadie, her thin, sweaty face hanging somewhere above his own, her cheeks flushed and sweating like she's been running. "I heard you," she says. "I heard you scream."

And he can't remember screaming, but he can remember Dancy Flammarion brandishing a pocketknife against the things that slunk out of the parkquiet night, Dancy sitting with her back against the locked and rusty gates of the water works tunnel, her skin shining like blistered pearls.

He can remember all the things she said.

"Dancy," he whispers, and Sadie shakes her head slow, bending close now and she looks scared, looks worried.

"She's not here, Deke."

"No," he says. "She *was* here." He tries to sit and feels like he's going to puke, the vise at his temples tightening until it's surely only a matter of minutes, a matter of seconds, before his eyes pop out of his skull. "She was here," he says again and lies down and shuts his eyes.

"Well, she's not here now," Sadie says. "There's no one here now but us," and that makes him want to laugh, and he thinks that maybe the trees *are* laughing, maybe the tunnel is cackling through its wrought-iron teeth, because *they* know better. Deacon opens his eyes again, eyes full of tears, and he sees that he's only a few yards from the blockhouse.

"How did I get here, Sadie?" but she only shakes her head again and looks more concerned.

"Don't you remember?"

"No, I don't," and then he sees the twine lying on the ground and he reaches for it, never mind the hurt, the hurt will be there anyway, until it gets bored with him and goes looking for someone else to torment. "What is it, Deke?" Sadie asks, whispers, but he doesn't answer her because he doesn't know, doesn't know anything more than she can see for herself. A white piece of twine and he tugs at it and the string goes tight in his hand.

"It's tied to the gate," Sadie says and she gets up, leaves him lying in the dirt and follows the line to the place where it's knotted around one of the bars.

"She was here, Deke," she says and Deacon props himself up on one elbow, blinks and squints through the pain and nausea, forcing his blurry vision into focus, a sloppy surrogate for focus, until he can make out the dim form of Sadie crouched at the tunnel entrance. Sadie reaches down and picks something up, holds it out for Deacon to see. The blade of the Swiss Army knife twinkles dull and cold, hardly any light left here for steel to catch and shine back, so little light that isn't swallowed by the hungry tunnel.

"What's happened to her?" Sadie asks him. "Where the hell is she, Deke?" And he doesn't answer her, because he doesn't know, lies down and shuts his eyes and Deacon listens to the crickets and Sadie crying while he waits for the pain to end.

Sometime later, an hour, two hours, and Deacon and Sadie are standing on Chance's big front porch again. Deacon's knocked three times already and no one's come to the door, not a sound from inside even though Chance's car is parked in the driveway and it seems like every light in the house is on.

Sadie's sitting alone in the porch swing, rocking slowly back and forth, the remains of Dancy's duffel bag draped across her lap. All they found after Deacon could walk and they followed the wandering trail of twine for three blocks, Sadie limping along as it led them from tree to telephone pole to sign post, dot to dot to dot, all the way from the tunnel to the marble steps of Ramsey High School. The duffel was lying beneath some oleander bushes near the sidewalk, two or three long slashes through the olivegreen canvas like somebody had been at it with a straight razor and Dancy's ragged belongings were scattered up and down Thirteenth Street. Deacon said to leave them, just leave it all, Sadie, and come on, but she gathered up what she could find, a few dirty T-shirts and a pair of dirtier underwear, some books and an old Folger's coffee can with a plastic lid, and stuffed the things back into the bag.

Deacon knocks again, knocks harder than before, and this time he hears footsteps; "Just a minute," Chance calls out and a second later, "Who is it?" Her voice seems nervous and faraway, muffled, muted by the door.

"It's me," Deacon says, talking loud and he puts his mouth near the wood so she can hear him on the other side. "Just me and Sadie."

The metal-against-metal sound of locks being turned, rolling tumblers and dullsharp dead-bolt click, the hesitant rattle of a safety chain, and when Chance finally opens the door, the glare from the hallway leaves Deacon half-blind after so much night, drives two fresh and searing spikes straight through his pupils and all the way to the back of his skull. Chance doesn't say a word, stares at him, and Deacon covers his eyes with one hand and squints back at her, strains to see through the light and the pain.

"Yeah, I know I should have called first," he says, but then he catches the furious swirl of emotions trapped inside her green eyes, the wild and emerald storm brewing there, something he's interrupted, and he forgets whatever he was going to say next.

"What do you *want*, Deacon?"

"Sadie's hurt. She cut her foot," and Chance takes an impatient breath, glances past him towards the porch swing. "And I think that Dancy might be dead," he says.

"You don't *know* that," Sadie snarls. "You don't know that at all. There wasn't a body. There wasn't even any blood, so don't fucking act like you know that, Deacon."

Chance looks back to Deacon and there's something else in her eyes now, something new moving through the storm behind her eyes, and "What the hell are the two of you talking about?" she asks him.

"Dancy went to the tunnel alone," and there's nothing else he can think of to say that will make sense of this, certainly no way he can tell her what he really saw in the park, not yet, anyway. So he reaches into the front pocket of his jeans instead, takes out Chance's Swiss Army knife and holds it out to her in the palm of his hand. She stares at it, handful of time and no sound but the still, cicadawhisper night and the rhythmic porch-swing creak. And then she takes the knife from Deacon and "You'd both better come inside," she says.

"No, I haven't been back. Not yet," Chance says and she stares at the half inch of whiskey in her glass, doesn't look at Deacon or Sadie as she talks. "I finally made myself call Alice about an hour after I got home, and she called the cops. I was on the phone with her again when you guys showed up."

Deacon pours himself another drink from the pint bottle on the kitchen table, his third since they sat down and his head is beginning to clear enough that he can think around the thorny edges of the headache. Amber fire to drive away the agony and that's no exaggeration; agony the best or only word for the crippling headaches that almost always follow his visions, his episodes, the seizures, whatever the fuck happens when he touches the wrong thing. And alcohol the quickest fix he's ever found. He takes a large swallow from his glass and watches Chance across the table. The old ledger from the crate is lying in front of her and she's resting her right hand on the cover like someone taking an oath.

"Alice met campus security at the lab and they did a walk-through with her."

"And? What'd they find?" Deacon asks and spits an ice cube back into his glass.

Chance shrugs her sagging, boybroad shoulders and "Nothing. They didn't find anything at all," she replies. "Except that the crate was missing, and everything we'd taken out of the crate was gone. This is all that's left." She taps the cover of the ledger twice with the middle finger of her right hand, smiles a cold and weary smile. "I left it here when I took the crate to the lab this afternoon."

"I don't know why *we* haven't called the police," Sadie says. Her hands are still shaking so badly that Deacon can hear the ice cubes in her glass clinking against each other. She hasn't taken a single sip of her whiskey, has asked three times if Chance has a cigarette even though Sadie knows that she's never smoked. "We *have* to call the police."

"What would we tell them, Sadie?" Chance asks her, and Deacon can see how hard she's trying to say the right thing, say it exactly the right way, Chance's voice the strained calm of the profoundly uneasy trying to comfort the hysterical. Or maybe the chronically rational facing the undeniably weird, he thinks, and takes another drink of bourbon. And Jesus, none of them has even said anything yet, not really, so maybe that's the scariest part. What happens when they find the guts to start talking, filling in the gaping holes in their respective stories, and he decides it's probably best not to think about that until after he's had at least another glass or two of whiskey.

"What do you mean? We tell them she's missing," and there's just enough shrillness creeping into Sadie's voice that it's starting to get on Deacon's nerves. "We tell them she might be in trouble."

"But we don't know that," Chance says. "Right now we don't know anything except that she left your apartment without saying good-bye, lost her duffel bag, and dropped my pocketknife in the park."

Sadie makes a bewildered, breathless noise in her throat and stares at Chance, confusion and rage competing silently for control of her face and finally settling on a grudging compromise, something that isn't exactly one or the other, the worst of both. She slams her glass down and most of the ice and bourbon sloshes out onto the sunflowered oilcloth. "Christ, you don't *care* what happens to her, do you?" and she's almost shouting now. "Why the hell did we even come back here, anyhow?"

"She's right, Sadie," Deacon says, rubs his eyes and stares at his empty glass. "I mean, you don't honestly think the cops give a shit if we've misplaced some homeless girl? And that's *all* she is to them, one more goddamn transient that they'd just as soon not even know about."

"She's just a *kid*," Sadie hisses and Deacon sighs and reaches for the bottle of Jim Beam, but she grabs it, stands up and steps quickly away from the table.

"Now what the fuck did you do that for?"

"'Cause I'm not gonna sit here and watch you get shit-faced, Deke, and watch *her* pretend that nothing's happening."

"Then what are you going to do, Sadie?" Chance asks, and now she sounds a lot less interested in coddling Sadie, or anyone else for that matter, a lot less interested in keeping the peace. "Why don't you stop yelling at us for a minute and tell us what precisely it is you intend to do?"

But Sadie only shakes her head and stares pitifully down at the mutilated duffel bag dangling from her right hand, sets the whiskey bottle back on the table. There's an orange and green striped T-shirt poking out through one of the slashes in the canvas and "She's just a kid," she says again.

"Yeah," Deacon whispers, wishing he knew anything at all to say that might help, and then he notices the blood seeping out of the tube sock he put on Sadie's right foot, crimsonwide pool spreading across the floor of Chance's kitchen.

"Jesus, baby, you're bleeding again," and she looks down at the mess and starts crying, apologizes to Chance and sits back down, hugs the duffel bag to her chest, hides her face in the folds of ruined fabric.

"No, it's okay, Sadie. There's hydrogen peroxide and gauze in the medicine cabinet. I'll be right back," and Chance gets up from the table, takes the ledger with her, and "Thank you," Sadie sobs as Deacon screws the cap off the bottle of Jim Beam and pours himself another shot.

The headache dwindled to an almost bearable pang lost somewhere between his ears and the whiskey tastes sweet and hot and more forgiving than the night outside the kitchen windows. Something that Dancy said at the tunnel, something familiar, and he mumbles it out loud. "The paths where the mountain stream goes down under the darkness of the hills," he says and Sadie looks up from the duffel bag and she blinks at him through a runny mask of smeared mascara.

"What? What did you say?" she asks and "Nothing," he replies. "No, it's probably nothing at all."

After Chance has finished doctoring Sadie's foot, has carefully washed the cut and wrapped it in clean, white gauze up to the ankle, and after Sadie has hobbled silently back out onto the porch alone, Chance and Deacon sit on opposite ends of the sofa. The front door is open and Deacon can hear Sadie in the noisy, old swing, back and forth lament of rusted chains and weathertired boards and the occasional thump or thud of Sadie's good foot against the porch as she kicks off again, keeping the swing in motion, keeping herself moving without ever going anywhere at all.

"She needs stitches," Chance says, and Deacon nods his head once.

"Try telling her that," he replies. "Try telling her anything at all."

And then nothing else for a minute or two, just the porch-swing pendulum squeak and groan and the mute house and the murmuring summer night outside. Sounds that aren't sounds or only things that Deacon imagines he hears because there's too much quiet. He sighs and leans forward, his shadow stretching out across the coffee table and the floor, and rests his forearms on his legs.

"What's happening, Deke?" and it's a very quick and urgent whisper as if she's afraid or maybe she just doesn't want Sadie to hear her. "I mean, I can still tell when you know more than you're saying. I remember that look you get."

Deacon picks up his drink from the table and finishes the whiskey, fills the glass to the rim again. He's drunk enough now that the headache is almost inconsequential, drunk enough that he smiles at Chance instead of getting angry.

"And what look would that be, exactly?" he asks, the thinnest, wry edge to his voice, the softest slur, and he sips at his drink. She's rubbing her hands together now like they're cold, like she needs to pee. Her grandmother's ledger is lying in her lap, and he's pretty sure she's afraid to let it out of her sight.

"I need you to give me a break, please," and she turns towards him, raises her voice just enough that there's no danger that she'll have to repeat herself. "I'm in the dark here, okay? I don't think I've ever been this kind of scared before."

"Well, then. By all means, welcome to the club," and he smiles again and raises his glass in her direction, gestures in a mock toast and takes a long drink.

"*Please,* Deacon. I mean it."

"I'm sorry. That was just a little too goddamned ironic, you know?"

"But I'm right, aren't I? You saw something at the water works tunnel that you're not telling Sadie. You know what happened to Dancy."

Deacon leans slowly forward again and sets his glass back down on the coffee table, stares at the condensation on the dark wood, the overlapping rings of water to leave pale scars on the wax.

"Isn't it a little late to start believing in shit like this, Chance? I mean, you've made it this far just fine without the Easter Bunny or Jesus or fucking Santa Claus. Are you absolutely sure you want to blow it now and succumb to the irrational after all these years of faithful disbelief? Hell, what would Joe think?"

Deacon thinks that he can feel her glare, if looks could kill glare, and "Next time you're lying awake," she says, "trying to figure out why I left you, why I couldn't take any more, try to remember what you just said to me, Deacon."

"*Touché,*" and he turns to face her, then, wipes his wet lips with the back of one hand. And Chance isn't even looking at him, glassy, nowhere stare of a junky or a taxidermied deer instead of what he expected, eyes fixed on nothing and no one in the world. An expression so lost, so turned back upon itself, that it makes the little hairs on the back of his neck prickle and stand up, and he reaches for his whiskey.

"You're a son of a bitch," she says and runs her fingers over the cover of the ledger, not seeing it now instead of not seeing him.

"Yeah, right," Deacon says. He swallows a soothing mouthful of Jim Beam and rubs at his face, trying to rub away the familiar regret, that he can't take back words that are already history, that have found their mark and already done their damage.

"What did you see at the tunnel, Deke?" she asks again. "What happened to her?"

"I don't *know* what happened to her, all right? And if I *told* you what I saw out there, I don't care what sort of revelation or epiphany you've had, Chance, you wouldn't fucking believe me. Right now, I don't think I believe me."

"It has something to do with Elise," Chance says, and she's chewing at her lower lip so hard that Deacon thinks it's going to start bleeding. "It has something to do with why Elise died, and that night we broke into the tunnel. And it has something to do with why my grandmother killed herself."

"Maybe," Deacon says quietly, staring intently at the lumps of bourbonstained ice melting in his glass because he doesn't want to see that ugly, nowhere look on Chance's face anymore. "I don't know. I honestly don't know."

"That would be—" and she pauses, searching for just the right word, and Deacon keeps his eyes on his glass. "That would be elegant, wouldn't it? No, that would be *sublime.*"

"Or schizophrenic," Deacon grumbles and now he turns to pour himself another drink.

"If all these things, all these awful things, if they're all connected somehow—"

"Yeah, that would be very convenient, wouldn't it?"

Out on the porch, Sadie has stopped swinging and for a moment there's only the wet sounds of whiskey being poured, the tinkle of ice against glass.

"I'm not joking," she says and begins rubbing at the cover of the ledger again.

"And I'm not making fun of you, Chance. But I don't want you to go getting paranoid on me and start seeing connections that aren't there. I don't want you to start believing in shit just because you *need* to believe in something. Not now."

"Do you think I'm going crazy?" and she looks up from the book in her lap, looks directly *at* Deacon this time instead of through him or past him, and at least some of the emptiness is gone from her eyes. *She wants me to say yes,* he thinks. *That would be the kindest thing I could say to her, the most comforting thing.*

"You know that isn't what I meant, Chance."

"Then do you think that was really a dog at the lab today?" she asks. "And whatever it was Sadie saw tonight, do you think that was a dog, too?"

Deacon licks his lips, his mouth suddenly dry as dust and old bones, but he sets the fresh whiskey back on the coffee table untouched. "No," he says. "No, I don't." And she nods and reaches out and takes his hand, so long since he's felt that touch that he can't even fucking remember the last time and now she's squeezing his hand so hard it hurts.

"I want you and Sadie to stay here with me tonight," Chance says. "I'll drive you over to your place if there's anything you need, but I think we should stick together."

"Sure, okay," Deacon says, feeling drunk and stupid, and Chance sighs a long and ragged sigh, relieved rush of air across her teeth, and she lets go of his hand and turns back to the ledger. And that's almost as bad as anything he saw or only thought he saw at the tunnel, the sudden absence of her touch after that brief, unexpected contact almost as terrible as the scarecrow things that weren't dogs and the sorrow and resolve in Dancy Flammarion's pink eyes.

CHAPTER TEN

Life Before Man

L ATE Sunday morning and Chance cooked breakfast for Deacon and Sadie before she left the house—bacon and runny scrambled eggs, steaming black coffee, toast and Bama apple jelly—and no one said anything during the meal. Not a word about Dancy or the water works, menacing phantom dogs or what they should do next, and when they were finished she drove away to school alone, to the unavoidable meeting with Alice. Because the crate was still missing, everything in the crate and everything that came out of the crate still missing, as well—the chunk of hematite, the trilobites, the ugly, pickled thing and the old jar of alcohol that had held it for more than a century, all the specimens that Chance hadn't even unpacked yet—all of it simply gone.

And now Chance is sitting in an uncomfortable molded plastic chair in Alice Sprinkle's office, modular chair the color of yellow Play-Doh in the middle of this cramped and disorderly broom-closet excuse for an office. She tries to sit still, rubs at her eyes and tries hard to look like she isn't thinking about a dozen things that seem more important than what Alice is saying to her.

"Girl, I *promise* if it was anybody else, I'd be asking for your keys right now," and Alice glares at Chance from the safe, other side of her papercluttered desk, other side of her thick bifocals, and Chance knows she's telling the truth. Knows that Alice is so protective of the shoddy little building and the treasures inside that she'd probably have done a lot worse than take back a set of keys if it had been someone else who ran off and left both doors standing wide open for two hours. Part of Chance wants to feel grateful, and part of her still suspects she should be ashamed of herself, jumping at shadows like a child, like a silly girl, letting her imagination take the place of common sense, but after the last two days she isn't much of either.

"I'm sorry," she says again, whether she actually means it or not; she's already lost track of how many times she's apologized in the twenty minutes since she walked into the office.

"Yeah, that's what you keep *saying*," and Alice takes another stick of Juicy Fruit from the pack lying in front of her, slowly peels the silver foil away from the chewing gum without ever taking her eyes off Chance. "But I still haven't heard you sound like you actually *mean* it."

"Of course I mean it," Chance says. "That was my grandmother's work and it was important. I don't know what else you expect from me, Alice. I don't know what you want me to *say*."

Alice stares at her silently for a moment, the cold, familiar scrutiny in her eyes like Chance is just another one of her fossilized bugs beneath a microscope, something to be classified and cataloged, something to be labeled and filed sensibly away, and "Maybe if you tried a little bit harder to help me understand," she says finally.

"How? I've told you what happened. I've told you three times what happened."

"Right. A stray dog came into the lab and it chased you," Alice says, making no attempt to hide the skepticism in her voice. "It scared you so badly you went home and didn't even think to call anyone about it for nearly two hours. That's what you said."

Chance sighs and glances anxiously down at her backpack sitting on the floor between her boots. Her grandmother's ledger is in there and she was up half the night reading the damned thing, understanding less and less with every page she turned. Meticulous notes that eventually disintegrated into undated, rambling speculation and strings of numbers, lengthy linear and quadratic equations and geometrical diagrams. The book frightens her, but right now it's better than facing the doubt on Alice Sprinkle's face, the doubt that might as well be an accusation, and she wishes Alice would tell her that she imagined the whole thing or that she's lying and be done with it.

"It just doesn't make any goddamn sense," Alice mutters, almost whispering now, talking to herself, and she inspects the puttygray stick of Juicy Fruit before she folds it double and puts it in her mouth. "Why would someone want the stuff from that crate and, in fact, *only* the stuff from that crate? As far as I can tell, they didn't so much as touch the computers or the scopes or any of the cabinets, all the things they might have been able to sell . . ." and she trails off, chews her gum and stares intently down at the confusion of reprints and ungraded papers littering her desk, picks up a pencil and begins tapping the eraser end against the coffee-stained cover of a stratigraphy textbook.

"What I'm about to ask you next," Alice says and she leans a little ways towards Chance, but she's still looking at the desktop, still tapping the pencil against the textbook. "I wouldn't even ask you something like this, except I figure that the cops are probably gonna do it and I'd rather you heard it from me first."

"Ask me what, Alice?"

Alice lays the pencil down and looks up at Chance; there's something reluctant in her eyes, something more than hesitant and out of place on her face that's always so damned sure of itself, always so entirely confident.

"Yesterday you were pretty adamant about keeping the contents of that crate a secret. So I was wondering, is it possible, after I left, that you had second thoughts. Decided maybe you shouldn't have shown it to me, that maybe you shouldn't have brought it down to the lab at all—?"

"Oh, *please*," Chance moans and she stands up, indignant and angrytired sigh to sum up almost everything she feels and she reaches for her backpack, just wanting to be anywhere else in the world right now, wanting to get away fast.

"No, Chance. Wait," Alice says. "You have to understand, I'm only trying to make some kind of sense out of this."

"I did not fucking *lie* to you. Why the hell do you think it makes sense that I would have lied to you? I've *never* lied to you."

"I'm sorry, but it makes more sense than a thief who steals nothing but that one crate. You *have* to see that, Chance. You have to try to look at this from my position."

"Yeah? And how do I know that *you* didn't take the crate, Alice? I mean, shit, that makes sense, too, doesn't it? You were the one that wanted to start showing that stuff all over campus—"

"Hey, hey, okay," and now Alice is standing up, too, the paper-strewn bulwark of the desk still safe between them, but the impatience and anger coming off Alice Sprinkle no less immediate for that barrier. "Just calm down, all right? If you say you didn't take it, then you didn't take it. Fine. I have no reason in the world not to believe you."

Chance's heart is racing, heart like a scared rabbit, heart like something hunted, something cornered, and she leans against the edge of the desk because her legs feel too weak to support her as the adrenaline drains away, quickly as it came, and leaves her feeling nauseous and dizzy.

"Then why the hell did you ask me that? I didn't take it," she says, her voice as unsteady as her legs. "It was mine already and if I'd changed my mind, I would have told you and then I would have carried it back home. That's all. I certainly wouldn't have needed to concoct this sort of crazy, bullshit story."

"Okay," Alice says and she sits back down. "That's cool. I believe you, Chance," and she takes another stick of Juicy Fruit from the pack on her desk.

Chance slides her arm through one of the canvas straps of the backpack and nods her head. "Yeah. Look, I've got to *do* something. Get some work done, anything to take my mind off this for a while. I'll be at the lab."

"That sounds like a good idea," and Alice rolls the gum wrapper into a tiny, silver ball, tosses it in the general direction of a wastepaper basket and misses. "You see why I didn't go into basketball."

"I'll be at the lab if you need me," Chance says and then she leaves Alice in her messy office with her suspicions and unanswered questions, and closes the door behind her.

Moments of discovery, conspiracies of the unlikely and the inevitable, the dustdim glint of a rock from a quarry wall, a hammer's careless blow—one instant at the shining end of a billion billion coincidences, and the course of a life is decided.

It's been almost three years since the day that Chance found her first tetrapod fossil in the scabby, bulldozer wastes of a Carbon Hill strip mine. Still only an undergraduate then, but she was already teaching the laboratory course and field trips for Introduction to Historical Geology and one rainy March morning she drove a vanload of freshmen fifty miles to give them a firsthand look at the Walker County coalfields. They listened or pretended to listen while Chance explained the cycle of transgressive and regressive marine sedimentation that had created these rocks, as she guided them through the autumn-colored beds of sandstone and shale, the silt-stones and conglomerates of the Pottsville Formation, all the count-less earth-tone shades of red and orange and brown, tawny yellows and pale violetgrays, and here and there a preciousthin seam of an-thracite coal like pure and crystallized midnight. The miners had scraped away the pine woods and topsoil to reveal the stratified re-mains of peat bogs and vast river deltas, lowland forests and barrier islands that had long ago lined the shores of a shallow, western sea at the edge of a great floodplain. A time when all the world's land masses were being driven together into the great Pangean super-continent, almost a hundred million years before the first dinosaurs appeared.

It was late afternoon when she finally finished with her lecture and turned the students loose to clamber over the towering spoil piles in search of fossil seed ferns, sandstone casts of *Calamites* trunks and the garskin bark of extinct scale trees. Earlier in the day, Chance had found a thick layer of shale studded with rustbrown siderite concretions and she retraced her steps to that spot, picked out a reasonably comfortable place in the rubble to sit, and began breaking the hard nodules open with her crack hammer. If she was lucky she might find the imprint of an insect inside one of them, or perhaps a jellyfish or a primitive shrimp-like crustacean, something uncommon and delicate from the steamy Carboniferous rivers and brackish lagoons. Most of the concretions were empty, of course, but still more interesting than ferns and she had almost an hour to kill before it was time to load up the van and head back to Bir-mingham.

Chance had split sixty or seventy of the rounded and oblong concretions, and nothing to show for her trouble but a couple of pyritized snails and a few tonguebroad leaves of *Neuropteris* and *Asterotheca,* that and the heap of broken stone scattered about her feet. Bored and discouraged, she looked at her watch, was thinking of calling everyone in fifteen minutes early, and then she noticed a nodule the size of a softball embedded firmly in the quarry wall. She popped it free with a chisel and the stone split cleanly in two on the very first blow, cleaved easily along the bedding plane created by the dead thing inside, and Chance stared amazed at the extraordinary, fan-shaped fossil she'd exposed.

Something that was no longer a fish's fin, but not yet precisely a foot either, eight tiny "fingers" formed from the arrangement of hourglass carpals and metacarpals, and each petrified bone in perfect articulation with the next; a less tidy confusion of wrist bones towards the center of the rock, the upper end of the "fingers," before the stocky radius and ulna, and finally the short, squarish humerus, and she realized that she was holding the forelimb of an animal that had never been found in that part of the country, much less the state, some new species from the wide, gray territory between fish and amphibian. Half an hour later, Chance was still sitting on the ground, still gawking at the fossil, when one of her students finally wandered over and asked if they shouldn't be heading back to town soon.

After that, two months of field work at the strip mine and a nearby railroad cut turned up seven more specimens, mostly limb material and a few vertebrae, but Chance also discovered a toothy lower jaw and a few bits of a broad, froglike skull in another concretion. And that October she attended the annual meeting of the Society of Vertebrate Paleontology at the Field Museum in Chicago where she presented a preliminary report on the Carbon Hill tetrapod, and the following summer a formal description of the fossils was published in the *Journal of Paleontology*—"A new temnospondyl amphibian from Alabama"—in which she christened the creature *Walkerpeton carbonhillensis.*

Her grandfather had always wanted Chance to begin her graduate work somewhere besides Birmingham, someplace with a vertebrate paleo' program or at least a geology department with money for research and an interest in science beyond the purely pragmatic, economic aspects. And though he did manage to talk her into applying to a few southeastern schools, North Carolina State and the University of Florida, Duke and Louisiana State, and even though she was eagerly accepted by every one of them, Chance didn't want to leave him alone. One heart attack already and he was all the family she had left in the world, so she stayed at UAB and took her place among the teaching assistants, mostly practical-minded microfossil geeks headed for high-paying jobs with oil companies and private consulting firms.

Content with her decision, or at least resigned to it, Chance continued to prowl the mines and quarries, patiently uncovering new remains of *Walkerpeton,* and by the time her thesis topic was approved, she'd attracted the attention and respect of researchers from as far away as London and Munich. This girl from an undistinguished college in the boonies, and she'd also discovered another new tetrapod and at least four new species of actinistian and rhipidistian fish, and her days were filled with the mysteries and revelations of their ancient, alien skeletons. But never mysteries whose understandings lay any farther away from her than the familiar confines of the rational, the empirical, and never revelations that left her with anything other than a deeper respect for the methods of science and a deeper faith in the constant, foreseeable patterns of nature.

◉

The lab almost exactly the way she left it the day before, exactly the same except for the missing crate, and Chance stands just inside the front doorsill, staring at the vacant place on the table where the crate *should* be. The place where she left it, and standing there in the solitude while Sunday morning turns quickly into Sunday afternoon, surrounded by silent specimen cabinets and whitewashed walls, it's a lot more difficult to discount the things she thought she saw and heard, to pretend she wasn't and isn't still afraid. So maybe this wasn't such a good idea after all. Maybe she'd be better off spending the day at home, and she thinks about grabbing a handful of files and a couple of fossils from her desk; not entirely comfortable leaving Deacon and Sadie alone anyway and if she tells them not to bother her, just leave me alone for a few hours, a couple of hours, please, then her bedroom or her grandparents' study is as good a place to work as the lab, a better place, really.

Exactly who the hell are you trying to kid this time? as if she'd ever actually intended to work on her thesis today, as if she could possibly think about cladograms and morphometrics, anything half so sane and comprehensible, with the riddles of her grandmother's journal still unanswered. And Chance glances back over her shoulder, the heat and brilliant, midday slant of sunlight through the open door, the wide asphalt desolation of the parking lot beyond and she feels a little dizzy, the subtlest disorientation as if the world outside were moving slowly away from her.

It's not safe, she thinks, one of the last things that Dancy said to her. *You won't be safe here all by yourself, not when they come,* and remembering the lost look on her face when she said that, the urgent and emphatic cast of her eyes, sends a sudden rash of chill bumps up and down Chance's arms despite the stuffy warmth of the lab.

"C'mon. Get a goddamned grip," she whispers, aloud and to herself, even though she hasn't felt like she's had a grip on much of anything since Friday night, not since Dancy called out the name of a trilobite from the foot of the staircase, not since the newspaper clippings and the rotting finger in the old baby food jar. These small and impossible things to take her mind apart, incremental drift from sanity towards this moment when anything seems as probable, as reasonable, as anything else.

Chance swallows hard and pulls the lab door slowly closed behind her; it clicks shut, metal-loud click in the quiet, and she takes a deep breath, exhales, and walks past the table where she left the vanished crate and its contents, slips her pack off her shoulder and follows the dark and narrow hallway back to the office that she shares with two other geology grad students.

But an office only in the loosest possible sense of the word, three graffiti-scarred, wooden school desks that were probably antiques when her mother and father were children, a reversible chalkboard and a few nubs of colored chalk. One squeaky, rusted file cabinet that might have been painted industrial gray a long time ago rubbing shoulders with a pressboard bookshelf crammed way beyond capacity and all its shelves have started to sag. There's an untidy assortment of field gear on the walls—screens and bundles of nylon rope, shovels and Marsh picks hung on nails and hooks—because the "office" serves double duty as a toolshed. One of the other students, a short and excitable guy named Winston, has taped a poster up above the file cabinet, color photograph of a rugged, misty seashore, Oregon or northern California, maybe, and THINGS TAKE TIME printed in bold, white letters across the bottom.

Chance's desk is neater than the others, but that's not saying much, and she sets her pack on a fat bundle of last week's pop quizzes that she hasn't gotten around to grading yet. Sits down in the swivel chair she bought for five dollars and fifty cents at a Salvation Army thrift store a year ago, torn leatherette the muddy color of red clay and there's a spring broken in the base so she always has to be careful not to lean too far back or the chair flips over and dumps her on the hard, concrete floor. She undoes the frayed canvas straps and opens the backpack, pulls out her grandmother's ledger and stares at the cover; there's nothing she's ever felt before to match the incongruous mix of dread and excitement she feels every time she looks at the book, the jangling, bitter alloy of fear and something almost pleasurable, a sickening sort of thrill, and she thinks that maybe this is the way that people who like to ride roller coasters must feel. Chance begins reading the words written on the cover aloud, the unremarkable words written in Esther Matthews' unremarkable hand.

"Notes on Trilobita of the Red Mountain Formation, Lower and Middle Silurian . . ." and she trails off, then, knows it all by heart now anyway, the long title and the date scribbled underneath. She opens the book to the place she's marked with a Hershey bar wrapper, the page where her grandmother's notes on trilobites and biostratigraphy end and the obsessive attempt to solve an elusive geometry problem begins. #134 stamped in navy blue ink at the upper-left-hand corner, and under that the last lines of an entry from July 28th, 1991, a comparison of the compound eyes of two closely related trilobites, *Cryptolithus* and *Onnia,* and a hopeful comment that she might have access to a scanning electron microscope soon; a few lines left blank and then, halfway down the page, there's a seven-sided polygon drawn neatly in pencil.

The angle of each intersection and the length of each side noted in handwriting almost too small to read, but each side longer or shorter than the one before and after, each angle a little more or less obtuse. Chance has never been a whiz at math, but she knows the impossibility of ever constructing a regular heptagon, a polygon with seven sides of equal length and equal angles. One of those nasty quirks of the universe, like pi or Schrödinger's cat, a seemingly simple and ultimately insoluble equation or paradox. She flips past page #134, past dozens more heptagons drawn as carefully as the first, all the sums of their sides and angles duly noted, scrawled proofs and endless streams of numbers that mean about as much to Chance as Sanskrit or Japanese. But it's easy enough to see what her grandmother was trying to do, plain as day, page after page after page of figures and she was merely wrestling with the impossible, merely attempting to construct the unconstructable.

No, Chance thinks, *That's not it at all. She was trying to* reproduce *the impossible.* Trying to draw something on paper that she'd seen, or something that she was looking at even as she measured and calculated, even as she filled these pages with her drawings and numbers.

Alone in her room the night before, the last hour or two before dawn, Deacon and Sadie asleep downstairs, and that's when Chance first made the connection between these futile calculations and the strange fossil on the chunk of iron ore from the crate. One side dotted with the perfect *Dicranurus* exuviae and the other marked only by a single, enigmatic impression, the odd fossil she thought might be a starfish, or some other echinoderm. And the seven-sided polyhedron inside that star, the thing that caught the late afternoon sunlight through the lab windows and flashed it back some way that made her uneasy, that made it difficult to keep her eyes focused on the stone.

Directly below the first heptagon her grandmother has written the closest thing to an explanation that Chance has found anywhere in the ledger, and she reads it again, strains and frets at the words like a madwoman trying to force reality back into focus one last time. Knows already that it won't make any difference, that it can't, that these words are more damning than all the rest of it combined— the night in the tunnel, Elise's suicide, the things that Deacon sees, Dancy and her fairy-tale cosmos of angels and monsters—but she reads it anyway, because it's all she has, because she doesn't have the strength or will to close the book and put it away forever.

Ink that dried ten long years ago, and when she's finished reading Chance gets up and walks the short distance to the chalkboard, the ledger still open in her left hand, and she takes a stubby, green piece of Crayola chalk from a plastic bowl on top of the file cabinet. Chalk the sweetsoft color of mint candy, and she searches impatiently through the pages until she finds the detailed diagram Esther Matthews made of the thing on the rock, all that's left of it now. Chance copies the star-shaped outer structure first, draws each line as straight as she can manage without a ruler or a yardstick, and then she adds the upraised, inner heptagon, and stares at what she's drawn there. But there's nothing startling or strange in this geometry, no answer to anything in the convergence of these green lines against black paint, and Chance rubs at her forehead with her right hand. The first, faint twinges of a headache kicking in somewhere towards the front of her skull, even though she hardly ever gets headaches, and she closes her eyes. *It was only a fossil,* she thinks. *It was only a fossil and my grandmother was only a crazy old lady. I don't understand because there's nothing here to understand.*

And then a sudden realization so obvious it seems almost silly, something she should have seen at the start, something that her grandmother had to have seen at some point, and Chance opens her eyes again and the imperfect polygon is still waiting for her snug inside its star.

"Imperfect, because it's only a plane figure, right?" talking loud and it doesn't matter because there's no one to hear her, no one to answer or wonder. "The fossil was *three*-dimensional," and Chance places the rough tip of the chalk at the lowermost point of the heptagon and this time she draws curved lines to connect the intersections.

"Curve the fucking lines," she says, "*then* all the sides and angles could be congruent," just like the thing in the hematite, close enough, maybe, and Chance traces over her seven curved lines again, pressing down so hard that the chalk begins to crumble and mintgreen bits of it fall to the floor and speckle the tops of her boots.

She pauses, trying to remember the moment the day before when she placed the protractor against the stone, the moment before she thought she heard something moving around outside the lab.

But the edges weren't *curved, were they? The edges of the fossil were straight.*

And there's a noise then from somewhere close behind her, wet and ripping noise like a head of lettuce being torn slowly apart, torn in half, a rending that's almost as much a feeling as a sound. Chance doesn't turn to see, doesn't want to move, but the pain in her head has doubled, trebled, hot tears streaming down her cheeks from the force of it now and she shuts her eyes again so she won't have to look at what she's drawn on the blackboard. As if simply closing her eyes might make the pain and the terrible sound go away, and "I'm not afraid anymore," she whispers angrily between clenched teeth.

What could have been a second or an hour, an indefinite interval when the sound behind her might have changed somehow, might have climbed the slightest octave or been joined by yet another voice, another sensation, and Chance smells something that makes her think of dark places that are never dry, that will never see the sun.

"I will not be afraid," she says again. "Whatever the hell is happening to me, I *won't* be afraid."

"No one's trying to scare you, Chance," but she screams when it touches her, and the lifeless voice that can't be Elise Alden's seems to drip like blood and honey from a wound in the shredding heart of the sound.

Her head has stopped hurting, but the fetidwet smell grown so strong, sour night and tiny, white mushrooms, and it's almost thick enough to suffocate, thick enough that Chance reaches instinctively to wipe it from her nostrils and mouth. She gags and wherever she is now, it isn't the lab. Rough stone at her back, moss-slicked wall of rock and frigid rivulets of water tracing their way crookedly down from somewhere overhead. And she's blind or there's no trace of light here, one or the other or both, and when she takes a hesitant step forward her boots squelch loud in the mud.

"I'm not supposed to show you anything," Elise says softly from someplace nearby, her voice unmistakable, but changed, too, withered, a blighted garden of a voice, and "I think they're losing patience with both of us," she says.

"Elise? *Fuck.*" Chance is groping frantically about in the darkness, her fingers for ten surrogate eyes. "Let me see you! If it's really you, then let me *see,* goddamn it!"

"It's nothing you can ever even imagine, Chance. It's nothing you can *know,* and when you've opened your eyes down *here,* it's nothing you'll ever be able to doubt again."

Chance swings her right arm in a wild and clumsy arc, striking out in the direction she thinks the voice is coming from, the withered voice that can't be Elise no matter who it sounds like or who wants her to think it is, and she touches something damp and cold, like dangling strips of raw liver, a trembling curtain of flesh, and her hand comes away sticky and chilled.

"There will be nonsense in it," the voice whispers, sweet and bittersad whisper before it laughs at her and a wind begins to blow. Lukewarm wind to stir the blackness and the Antarctic cold, and Chance wipes her hand on her jeans, trying to scrub away the stain and the memory of what she's touched. There are new smells on the wind, the healthy scent of green and growing things, the way a summer day can smell, or a greenhouse, sugarsmooth aroma of budding trees and water flowing free across coarse and sparkling sand. Everything this boundless darkness isn't, and Chance turns away from the voice, away from the raw and quivering mass that's stolen Elise's voice for its own.

And she's standing on the sloping, pebblestrewn bank of a broad river, crystal-green waters that slip gently past on their way to the sea, that ripple and eddy beneath the high tropical sun. A river like this to put the Mississippi to shame, a river even the Amazon could only envy, restless depths to divide a forest of strange trees, giant club mosses and the towering, evergreen *Lepidodendron* that stand as tall and straight as redwoods, their ancient branches spread out above a billowing carpet of ferns. No sound here but the river lapping hungry at the edge of the forest, the sigh of the wind in the leaves and the rasping drone of insects. The Paleozoic sunlight falls in cathedral-brilliant shafts across a million shades of green, and Chance knows that she has already walked the broken sedimentary memory of this world, the shale and sandstone ruin of it. Has spent so many years struggling to read its stingy, carbonized remains and here it is laid out before her, made whole again, restored, and suddenly she's crying, tears as warm as the sun and the wind.

"My god," and something else that she's already forgotten, thoughts silenced on her tongue because there are no words she knows to express what she feels, the utter joy and terror of these sights, this Eden stretching wide beneath the gemblue sky.

"We did not think you *believed* in gods."

She turns around and Elise is standing where the ferns end and the beach begins, standing there in the shifting, dappled shadow of the trees and she squints painfully through the light at Chance. Elise, but not Elise's eyes, eyes that have been consumed by their own pupils, collapsed into the infinite gravity of their own visions. She's wet and naked and her wrists are bleeding.

"I don't believe any of *this,*" Chance says, the salt from her tears getting into her mouth. "I *can't.*"

"Neither did your grandmother," Elise says and she smiles, flashes perfect and piranha-sharp teeth. "And she knew more than you. She had almost begun to understand."

"Is that why she's dead? Because she'd started to understand? Is that what happened to Dancy, too?"

"I'm not here to answer questions. I'm not supposed to tell you anything—"

And before the girl can say another word Chance rushes forward, strikes her hard across the face, hard enough to send her stumbling backwards into a deadfall tangle of unearthed roots and logs. She grabs for a branch and misses, lands hard on her ass, and glares up at Chance with those brutal eyes. The smile around her razor teeth grown even wider than before; wicked, leering smile so wide that her face doesn't look quite so much like Elise's anymore, something about as far from human as possible, a mask stretched too tight over its skull, and the sound coming from its throat isn't laughter, but Chance knows it means almost the same thing as laughter.

"*Shut up,*" she screams and it nods its head obediently and stops making the not-laughing noise, raises a pale and blood-encrusted hand and points at Chance.

"I should see the garden *far* better," it says, speaking in that purling, ice water and acid mockery of Elise's voice, "if I could get to the top of *that* hill: and here's a path that leads straight to it."

"I *told* you to shut up, fucker," and Chance reaches for a big piece of driftwood, means to bash its head in, smear whatever it has for brains into the loamy soil. But the thing dissolves in a violent burst of purplish light, light like a bruise that swells and swarms fiercely around her, bloated, aubergine fireflies, and in less than an instant the forest breaks apart and is gone, swallowed as the light becomes a night as bottomless as a sky without stars. A night that wraps itself tight about Chance, light that could crush her bones to jelly if it wanted.

"Close your eyes," and this time the voice isn't Elise, this time the voice is Dancy Flammarion. "Don't see what it wants you to see. Don't listen—"

But there's not even time to shut her eyes before the smothering night releases her, drains away and Chance is left on her knees, shivering and her clothes soaked through with the water and slime that leaks from the close, rough walls of the tunnel.

The tunnel. I'm in the water works tunnel.

She can see by the sickly, greenyellow glow of phosphorescent fungi, chartreuse clumps of the stuff sprouting all around her like tumors, can tell that the tunnel ends only a few more yards ahead. Ten or twelve feet and the narrow rock walls open abruptly into some sort of cavern, something that the workmen must have broken through to a hundred years ago, and the great cast-iron pipes turn downwards and disappear from view.

So cold now that her hands are numb and her bones ache, her teeth ache, but Chance gets to her feet, leans against the slippery walls of the tunnel until her head stops spinning. There should be ice, all this water and cold, there should be frost and icicles and the mud under her feet should crunch like broken glass. Unless the cold is *inside* her, and that's why her breath doesn't fog, why the little streams fed by the walls of the tunnel wind and flow unhindered towards the place where the cavern begins. Chance hugs herself tight and follows them, shambles forward on numb feet like one of Victor Frankenstein's resurrected creations.

When she reaches the end of the tunnel, stands shaking and

teethchattering on a narrow, crumbling jut of rock, the last few feet of the tunnel's floor reaching out into the cavern beyond, she gazes across a fissure or chasm so vast, so deep, that she can't begin to see the other side. The other side might be miles and miles away, if the cavern doesn't go on forever, if there *is* another side to it, a place where the water works tunnel resumes and this abscess in the mountain ends. She looks up, looks up before she dares to look down, and instead of stalactites there seem to be stars, sapphire and diamond pinpricks in a moonless sky, and the weight of that sky on her shoulders presses down like the news of a death, the death of her own heart, like the loss of everything she's ever loved. Chance realizes that she's on her knees again, no memory of falling, but there she is on her hands and knees in the unfreezing mud, her tears dripping down to join the water gurgling over the edge of the precipice.

It's nothing you can know, *and when you've opened your eyes down* here, *it's nothing you'll ever be able to doubt again.*

The iron water pipes loom huge on her right before plunging towards the floor of the fissure and Chance lets her eyes follow them over the ledge, almost vertical descent along the steep wall of the cavern, fifty or sixty feet of rust and bolts before they disappear in a dense patch of the glowing fungi. Corpulent, living lanterns to illuminate the trunks and strangling vines of a forest that stretches away from the rock face, plants the unsightly color of buttermilk and semen that seem to strain towards the stars, their branches and leaves waving like the blind stalks and antennae of deep-sea animals. And farther away, over the pale, quivering canopy, she can see what might be a river, but what flows thick between its banks isn't water.

All these things in the instant before she sees what has come out of the forest and begun to drag itself along the pipes towards her, a thousand midnight and steelcable tendrils to haul itself slowly forward. And before Chance finally covers her eyes and backs away from the edge, she catches the dim hint of recognition in its faceted, sevensided irises, knows that it knows *her,* and she also sees the shriveled things caught in its quivering body like shreds of meat in the teeth of a dog; the bodies of Dancy and Elise, her grandmother and a dozen other faces she doesn't know, the decayed and hurting faces of corpses that can never die, that will never be permitted to fade into painless nothingness. Elise's eyes turn towards her, wide and pleading, and this *is* Elise, not some rough counterfeit or sleight of hand.

"Forget this, Chance," she whispers. "Forget this and don't look back," and then one of the tendrils slides quickly over her mouth and she's silent.

The constellations of subterranean stars begin to seep from the sky and fall in hot and icing streaks, and at the end, the only thing that Chance can hear is the way that they scream as they spiral down, one by one, to the blisterswollen surface of the distant river.

Chance's eyes open and not those alien stars, but the world crashing down on her, crashing back into place around her, and she's squeezed herself tight into a corner behind her desk; crouched behind two old produce crates full of fossil oysters and her teeth are still chattering, her skin still numb and cold. Her chest heaves, drawing greedy, urgent mouthfuls of the musty air, gasping like a woman drowned and coming suddenly, violently, back to life, hauled somehow back up through the same hole in a frozen river; the afternoon sun spills through the lab windows, gold across her face, welcomed fire across her skin, but her eyes burn and water like eyes that have never seen the day before this moment, eyes of a prisoner locked away from the sun half her life, and she blinks and wipes involuntary tears from her cheeks.

Both her hands are smudged with the dusty colors of the chalk from the bowl on top of the file cabinet, a pastel spectrum rubbed deep into her skin, and she glances past the crate, past her desk to the chalkboard. Crazy things scrawled there, Elise's name over and over again, the star and the heptagon obscured or almost wiped away entirely. And when the board was full, she must have begun writing on the walls, the white walls covered now with chalky pinks and blues, greens and yellows, handprints and a frantic scurry of numbers and geometry, and she's written *Dicranurus* a thousand times if she wrote it once. Some of the letters three feet tall and others so small she can hardly make them out from her refuge in the corner, and she lets her watering eyes wander up the walls to the low ceiling and there's the thing from the hematite again. Wiped off the chalkboard but restored up there, as wide as the room, and she has no memory of standing on the desks to do that, but she knows that's how it got there, doesn't need to see her boot prints on books and stacks of paper and daily planners to be certain that's exactly how it got there.

Something hot trickles from her nose, across her lips, and when Chance touches her face her fingertips come back dabbed red, crimson-wet stain to ruin the childish colors on her skin, or only another element in the painting, something intended all along.

If I start screaming now, I'll never, ever stop again, she thinks, imagines Alice Sprinkle finding her like this, the expression on Alice's face, and that's enough to get her up and moving. She wonders if she could find a bucket and a sponge, thinks there might be some cleaning stuff under the sink in the prep room, and then Chance remembers what she saw dragging itself up the water pipes towards her, remembers Elise's face, and she glances at the thing drawn so carefully above her head. A more perfect likeness of the fossil than she would have thought possible, the fossil and the eye of a nightmare, and Chance forgets about the mess and how pissed off Alice will be, and she grabs her grandmother's ledger and runs.

❰◈❱

Deacon is standing in the downstairs hall, has just set the telephone receiver back in its cradle, when he hears the squeal of spinning tires in the driveway. Like someone's doing fucking doughnuts out there and he heads for the front door, the door open but the screen closed to keep out bugs because Sadie's afraid of wasps. Through the screen wire he sees Chance's redorange Impala barreling towards the porch, cloud of dust and gravel spray and Chance behind the wheel, and he's wrestling with the latch when the car bounces across the lawn, crashes through the front steps and buries its front end deep in one corner of the porch. The impact knocks Deacon off his feet and he takes the coatrack down with him.

"What the hell was *that*?" Sadie yells from somewhere upstairs and Deacon pushes the brass coatrack off of him, a wonder one of the hooks didn't put out an eye or knock his goddamn teeth down his throat and "I think Chance is home, baby," he yells back at Sadie.

He stands up and pushes the screen door open, lets it bang shut behind him, and Deacon's immediately engulfed by a choking, thick fog of driveway grit and radiator steam. He coughs, pulls the front of his T-shirt up to cover his mouth and nose, and crosses the buckled porch boards to the place where the steps used to be. Nothing much there now but some shattered concrete blocks and a few broken slats, the steps sheared completely away; he sits on the edge and drops the five or six feet down to the ground. The Impala's taillights are flashing, like Chance is signaling that she wants to turns both ways at once, and Deacon walks around the rear of the car to the driver's side. Not much smoke on this side and he can see that Chance is slumped forward over the steering wheel.

"Jesus. Is she dead or what?" Sadie calls out from the porch, from someplace behind the settling, redgray fog, and he ignores her. Opens the car door and now he can see that there's blood on Chance's face, blood on the hard, plastic steering wheel, too; his heart races and his mouth is as dry as old bones.

"Don't move her, Deke! You're not supposed to move people in car wrecks," Sadie shouts. "I'm gonna call an ambulance!"

"You don't do *anything* but stay right where you are." He reaches for Chance's wrist, presses his finger to the soft spot where blue veins intersect. And Chance jerks her hand away, sits up in the seat and blinks at Deacon. He can see there's a nasty-looking cut above her eyebrows, probably where most of the blood is coming from, the spot where her head hit the steering wheel, he thinks, and if she'd been going any faster there'd probably be a big piece of it sticking out of her skull.

"Can you hear me?" he asks, ashamed that he sounds so scared when she's the one that's hurt, and Chance nods her head once. "Yeah," she says and more blood leaks from between her lips, dribbles down her chin. "Yeah, I can hear."

"Do you think you can move?"

"Don't move her, Deacon!" Sadie shouts from the porch. "Her neck might be broken!"

"Sadie, will you shut the hell up or go back inside?"

"My neck isn't broken," Chance says and she sits back, stares at her blood spattered on the inside of the Impala's busted windshield. "I just couldn't remember how to make it stop. I just kept going faster."

"Yeah, well, I'm gonna help you and we're gonna get you out of the car and into the house. I can't have you fucking bleeding to death in your own front yard," and then there's a sound from somewhere under the hood of the Impala, popping sound like a champagne cork, and Deacon jumps. "I think maybe we should hurry, Chance."

She nods again and reaches for something lying in the floorboard at her feet. Deacon sees that it's the ledger from the crate, and he puts one arm around her shoulders, the other under her legs, and lifts her carefully out of the car. Surprised that she seems so light, not half as heavy as he'd expected, but his back will still probably be giving him hell for this in a few hours. He moves as slowly, as deliberately, as he can, trying not to jostle her or trip or lose his balance, and his heart is pounding from fear and this unaccustomed exertion. He turns his back on the dying car, carries Chance to a shady place a few feet away, cool shadows cast by a shaggy oleander bush, and lays her on the grass. Deacon sits down next to her and looks back at the porch. Sadie's still standing there, hands on her hips and a scowl on her face, and he waves at her.

"It's okay," he says. "It's gonna be okay now."

Chance rolls over on her side and spits out a mouthful of blood and saliva, and then she looks up at him. And her eyes are so wide, so afraid, and he tells her again that she's going to be okay, the Impala's probably bought the farm, but he's pretty sure she's going to be fine. Chance coughs and he wipes the blood from her mouth with the tail of his T-shirt.

"No," she says and lies back down in the grass and dandelions, her face turned up to the wide summer sky above the mountain and "No," she says again. "I can see them, Deke. I can see monsters."

CHAPTER ELEVEN

The Forked and Shining Path

THE small hours of Monday morning, after the trip to the emergency room, seven stitches in Chance's forehead and a doctor who said no, she didn't have a concussion, but don't let her sleep for six hours and then wake her once every hour during the night. Deacon is sitting in the chair beside her bed, waiting for her to start talking again. Not like she's made any effort to hold back, more like she can only find the strength to speak for short intervals, five or ten minutes and then she closes her eyes and presses herself as tight as she can against the bedroom wall. As if there's only so much of it she can stand at a time and the powderblue Lortabs probably not helping much either. So Deacon knows *some* of it, what her grandmother wrote in the old ledger, fragments of whatever happened to Chance at the lab, but he suspects she's hardly scratched the surface and he can only sit, patient, pretend patience, and wait for her to open her eyes and begin again.

Sadie's downstairs, alone downstairs because that's the way she wants it. Angry at Deacon's playing nursemaid to his ex-lover and probably angrier that they're still not telling her everything that they might. Hours ago she brought up a cup of hot chamomile and peppermint tea and a big bowl of Campbell's chicken noodle, but the look in her eyes made Deacon wonder if he shouldn't check to see if the food was poisoned; no matter, because Chance only managed a couple of hesitant sips of the tea and ignored the soup altogether.

Deacon followed Sadie back to the top of the stairs, leaving

Chance alone longer than he wanted but afraid that Sadie was on the verge of walking back to Quinlan Castle by herself, hurt foot or no hurt foot, dog monsters or no dog monsters.

"Does she know what happened to Dancy?" Sadie asked. "That's all I want to know," and she peered resentfully over Deacon's shoulder towards the open door to Chance's room.

"Maybe. But listen, Sadie, I'm having a lot of trouble just trying to figure out how much of this *she* thinks is real and how much she thinks she imagined. I'm pretty sure Chance thinks she's losing her mind."

"Yeah, well. The way she plowed into the porch, I can see why," and Sadie crossed her arms and glared down at the toes of the hiking boots that Chance let her borrow Saturday night. Huge, silly things on Sadie's feet, at least two sizes too big for her.

"I understand it runs in the family."

Deacon wanted to hit her, one of those brittle moments when he knew that he needed to get as far away from her as fast as he could, and this time he didn't have the luxury.

"I'm going to *try* to pretend you didn't say that, because I know you're not one-half the bitch you like to *think* you are," almost whispering so Chance wouldn't hear, trying to find words to defuse the bomb ticking behind his bloodshot eyes. "If Chance knows what's happened to Dancy, she'll tell us. If not, well, I'm really fucking sorry about that."

"*Fine.* Whatever," and she clomped away back downstairs, limping in Chance's boots, and in a few minutes he could hear a movie blaring from the television set in the living room.

"I should have listened to her, Deke," Chance says and Deacon sees that she's opened her eyes, is staring out the raised window into the dark.

"You mean Dancy?" he asks and she nods her head, doesn't take her eyes off the window.

"Yeah," she says. "I thought I knew so much. I *always* thought I knew so much."

"Maybe we ought to talk about Dancy," and he looks down at one of the books he found inside the shredded remains of the duffel bag. A waterstained paperback copy of *Beowulf,* dog-eared pages and someone's underlined passages with a red ballpoint pen. There are notes written in the margins as well, and pictures drawn on the two or three blank pages at the back.

"I treated her the same way I treated you, Deacon, the same way

I've always treated everyone. Either measure up to my rationalist bullshit or fuck off."

Deacon picks the book up off the floor, holds it so that Chance can see the tattered cover, a cartoon-gaudy painting of the monster Grendel, the Geat warrior clutched in its scaly fist. "I assume you've read this," he says. "Even you scientific types have to read books, right?"

"Yes, Deacon. I've read *Beowulf*," and Chance touches her bruised and swollen face with the fingers of her right hand and winces. "I read *Beowulf* when I was in seventh grade."

"Well, good for you. You've got a bump on your head, but at least you ain't ignorant," and Deacon forces a weak smile and opens the book, starts flipping through the pages.

"What has this got to do with anything?" Chance asks and he sees that she's staring at the dark window again, flecks of fear and longing in her green eyes, and Deacon thinks about closing it, no idea if that would make things better or worse. He decides it's best to leave the window open and he goes back to flipping through *Beowulf*.

"I found this in Dancy's duffel bag, which I thought was pretty interesting in and of itself. It's not the sort of thing I'd have expected to find a homeless girl carrying around with her."

"Dancy wasn't *just* a homeless girl," Chance says, a hint of annoyance in her voice. *That's good,* he thinks, better than the shell-shock monotone and blank stares she's given him since he pulled her out of the wrecked Impala.

"No," Deacon says. "No, she wasn't."

"She tried to tell me. She *showed* me."

"Chance, just listen for a minute," and he opens the book, and Chance watches the bedroom window silently and waits.

"Last night, you asked me what I saw when I was at the tunnel. Well, one of the things that I saw was Dancy, and she said something that stuck in my head. I *knew* I'd heard it somewhere before and when I found this in her duffel bag I realized where. She's underlined passages all through here."

He coughs, his throat dry and there's half a can of Coke sitting on the dresser beside him; he looks at it for a moment, wishing it was a shot of Jack Daniel's or Wild Turkey, and then he turns back to the book, coughs again, and begins to read.

" 'The other wretched shape trod the tracks of exile in the form of a man, except that he was bigger than any other man. Land-

dwellers in the old days named him Grendel. They know of no father, whether in earlier times any was begotten for them among the
dark spirits,'" and he pauses for a moment and now Chance is
watching him instead of the window.

"'They hold to the secret land, the wolf-slopes, the windy head-
lands, the dangerous fen-paths where the mountain stream goes
down under the darkness of the hills, the flood under the earth.'"

For a moment neither of them says anything, and then Deacon
closes the book, lays it on the dresser beside the can of Coca-Cola.

"You saw a vision of Dancy reciting *Beowulf*?" and he can tell
that Chance is trying not to sound incredulous, not to sound skeptical, and maybe she could have managed it without the painkillers.

"Not just then, Chance. The night she showed us the finger, all
that talk about the Children of Cain. Grendel and his mother are
described as the kin of Cain. And that stuff about the dragon—"

"So you think she made all this up?"

"Not exactly. It's got to be a lot more complicated than that. But
I think *whatever's* happening, Dancy was using *Beowulf* to try and
make sense of things. The same way some people use the Bible—"

"Or science," Chance says, interrupting him, and she laughs a
weary, ironic laugh, and shuts her eyes.

"Well, yeah. Now that you mention it. It was part of her belief
system. Her paradigm."

"Jesus, Deke, this is so completely fucked up. I'm Scully and
you're Mulder, remember?"

"Yeah," Deacon says. "At least that's the way things used to
work." A sip from the can of Coke then, lukewarm and syrupsweet
but it's better than nothing at all, better than the dust bowl spreading itself out at the back of his tongue. "There's more, if you're up
to hearing it."

"Sure," she says, doesn't open her eyes but Chance rolls over
onto her left side, rolls towards Deacon and wraps both her arms
around her pillow, hugs it tightly, and "I'm listening," she whispers.

Sadie's staring at the television screen, *The Beginning of the End*
showing on AMC, but she isn't actually *watching* it, just staring at
the screen because it's someplace tangible to focus her eyes and her
anger. Something to look at besides the walls and the windows, the
night outside, and now if she could only stop thinking about
Chance and Deacon upstairs, trading their secrets and keeping her
in her place, creepydumb Sadie Jasper who can't deal with the truth.

I'm not the fucked-up bitch running cars into houses, she thinks and lights a cigarette, hopes that Chance can smell the smoke all the way upstairs, and her eyes drift from the TV screen to the old ledger lying on the coffee table.

Deacon almost couldn't get Chance to put the thing down, when he led her into the house after the trip to the hospital, and they had to use the back door and come through the kitchen because the front porch was too much trouble with all the steps gone. Him telling her that she should put it away for a while, that it would be okay, really, no one was going to steal it or anything, after she'd clutched the book the whole time they were waiting to see a doctor, didn't even turn it loose when they were sewing up the gash in her head.

And no one has told Sadie *not* to touch it, no explicit or implicit instructions that she was to leave the ledger alone. But she thinks it's probably like reading someone else's diary, that sort of unspoken understanding, and she should just stare at her movie and mind her own business.

But this is my own business, isn't it? she thinks. *If that book has anything to do with what happened at the apartment, or whatever's happened to Dancy, it's absolutely my goddamn business.*

And that makes sense on the surface, at least, which is about as much as anything is making sense. She reads the cover again, everything but the date meaningless to her and she hates that, feeling stupid just because she hasn't spent her life in college staring at rocks. Sadie sets her cigarette down on the edge of a china saucer, shifts about nervously on the sofa, half turns and glances towards the hallway, towards the staircase. Deacon and Chance's voices are faint, but she's sure she can hear them talking. Sharing their greedy confidences, so it's not very likely either of them will be coming downstairs any time soon.

This is what he's wanted all along, to be alone with her again. For her to need him again, and neither of them gives a rat's ass what happens to Dancy.

And she takes advantage of a fresh and disorienting surge of jealousy, the bitterhot flush across her cheeks, the cold knot in her belly, and Sadie picks the ledger up off the coffee table. The sort of thing she should have done a long time ago, she thinks, if they're so determined to keep her in the dark, if she's the only one who cares about Dancy. She holds the book in both hands and stares at the cover, stalling one last moment longer because even through the jealousy, she knows that a trust is being violated. Something that she'll never be able to take back, once it's done, regardless of her reasons or excuses or how well she plays the clueless innocent. And something else, too; a bright speck of dread somewhere behind her resentment. Maybe she *doesn't* want to know what's written in this book, self-doubt to muddle her resolve, and she thinks of Chance upstairs, the madness in her eyes, thinks of poor Dancy, and *Everything*, she thinks. *It could cost me everything.*

"Maybe it already has," Sadie Jasper says and she opens the ledger. And there's nothing on the first page that isn't anticlimax, scribbled cursive that she has to squint to read and what she can make out means about as much to her as the words written on the cover. Pages and pages about nothing but trilobites: collecting trilobites, the anatomy of trilobites, what trilobites are found where and in which rocks, how old the rocks are, and after she's scanned forty or fifty pages the anger and dread is beginning to fade and she just feels foolish, like the butt of someone's practical joke, like somebody that *deserves* to feel like a fool.

"Shit," she hisses, almost slams the book closed, then flips through fifty more pages or so, nothing left to lose now. The deed done whether she's learned anything or not, so she might as well. And about halfway through the ledger the notes and the drawings of trilobites end and something that seems even more baffling begins: a seven-sided figure and a lot of math and suddenly she wants to hurl the book across the room, throw it at the television and leave it lying there on the floor for Deacon and Chance to see whenever they get tired of each other's company and remember she's sitting down here waiting for them.

But then she notices what's written underneath the figure, not math and nothing that seems to have anything much to do with fucking trilobites. She holds the book closer to her face, scoots a little closer to the lamp, and reads the words out loud.

"*'I've been back to the water works tunnel, this last week with a man from the city. Looked more closely at the bricked-up section at about three hundred fifty m. near base of Srm.'*"

And Sadie stops, her heart beginning to beat faster again and her mouth gone dry and sour. Just the mention of the water works tunnel enough to get her attention, and she glances quickly at the stairs, the shadows there, before she turns back to the book and begins to read again.

"*'The masonry is still solid. Found several more cf.* Dicranurus *near that spot. Terrible smell too (rotten, like old cabbage) and the man from the city said he thought he heard things behind the wall sometimes. I can't* sleep *at night anymore. Can't stop thinking about the thing in the bottle and brick wall and polyhedrons. Our* drinking water *comes through that place'* "

And that's all. Nothing after that but more numbers and countless variations on the seven-sided figure, but Sadie reads the paragraph about the tunnel twice more, trying to squeeze more meaning from the words, the empty spaces between the words, and then she sits with the book open in her lap, alone with the implications of what she's read, and stares at the flickering television screen.

"Yeah, I still know someone on the force in Atlanta," Deacon says. He'd rather be talking about almost anything in the world, because of the promises that he made to himself years and years ago, that he was done with the cops forever. Done with letting them milk him for the bits and pieces of tragedy that he sees from time to time if he tries, and sometimes if he *doesn't* try. A malignant part of himself he can't cut out or ignore, but that doesn't mean he has to talk about it, has to acknowledge what it's done to him. Except that now that's *exactly* what it means, because of Chance and Sadie and the things he saw when he touched a piece of twine tied around the trunk of a dogwood tree.

Try to change what hasn't *happened yet,* Dancy said that night at the tunnel, only last night but it already feels like a hundred years ago.

"The detective that I used to work with sometimes," he says and Chance opens her eyes halfway, drugheavy lids and "You don't have to tell me about this stuff, Deke," she says.

"Yes I do, Chance. This time I do have to talk about it," but he doesn't say anything else for a few seconds, rubs his hands together and keeps his eyes on the floor. Like he'll lose his nerve if he looks directly at her too long, doing all of this *for* her so it doesn't make sense; the sight of her should make him stronger, should strengthen his resolve and keep him moving instead of frightening him even worse than he already is.

"I called him while you were at school. Actually, I'd just hung up the phone when you . . . you know," and he doesn't want to say *When you plowed your car into the house,* so he just jabs his left thumb over his shoulder at the bedroom window, in the general direction of the front porch.

"Right," Chance says. "I know."

"I haven't talked to that son of a bitch in for fuckin' ever. I thought he was gonna have a heart attack when he heard my voice."

"You called him about Dancy," Chance says and Deacon nods, keeps his eyes on the floor.

"I told him everything I thought I could, without him thinking I was totally whacked. It was that finger. Regardless of what she believed it was, regardless of what I felt when I touched it, I figured if she's really been killing people and hacking them up like that, then maybe somebody was looking for her. Maybe someone out there might know something that would help."

"You saw a monster, too, didn't you?" Chance asks him and the Lortab is making her slur; her eyes are closed again and "When you touched it," she says, "that's what you saw."

"Yeah, that's what I *saw*. But I learned a long time ago that some of the stuff I see when I touch these things, some of it can be influenced by other people who touched them before me, by what those people believed. If those beliefs are strong enough, Chance, it's like they can leave impressions behind, the same way that actual events can.

"So, when I found that marked-up copy of *Beowulf* and realized that's where she was getting all of this stuff, it started me thinking— maybe the things I saw when I touched the finger, and the things I saw at the tunnel, maybe they had as much to do with what Dancy *believed* was happening as what really has been happening."

"Yeah, well, what about the things *I* saw?" Chance asks him. "What about the things Sadie said *she* saw?"

"Like I said, this is complicated. I'm not saying you guys didn't see anything. At the very least, I know you *think* you saw something. But neither of you had these experiences until *after* you met Dancy, and maybe some of the things you saw, maybe you saw them because of what she said to you."

"You think we imagined it all."

"Chance, have you ever wondered why those folks who claim to have been abducted by space aliens all tell more or less the same story? Why their stories tend to have so much in common? I know you, so I know damned well you don't think it's because they've all been abducted by extraterrestrials with the same idea of how to go poking around inside people's butts," and she laughs, then, a clean, sane laugh, laughing just because she thinks something's funny. It's almost enough to lift some of the weight from Deacon's shoulders, from his mind, the simple sound of her laughing, and he can look at Chance again instead of the floor.

"The UFO nuts like to say it's impossible that *all* these people could have concocted such similar stories, that the similarities between the reports are proof that the stories must be accounts of real abductions. But you know that's bullshit, because all those people, I don't care if they're in fucking Kansas City or Kathmandu, *all* of them have been contaminated by everything from *Close Encounters* to supermarket tabloids to the stories they've heard other abductees tell on talk shows."

"And you think Dancy contaminated me and Sadie," Chance says. She rubs at her eyes like they're sore, rubs them like a sleepy child trying to stay awake just a little longer, and then glances back towards the open window. The nightwarm breeze ruffling the curtains smells faintly of kudzu and car exhaust.

"Maybe. And maybe me, too," he says. "She was trying, as hard as she could, to convince all three of us that she was telling us the truth. She *needed* to convince us, to reinforce her own beliefs. Personally, I think Dancy was a hell of a lot more afraid of her own doubt than she ever was of monsters."

"So, what did your detective friend have to say, anyway?"

Deacon sighs and rocks his chair back onto two legs, scuffs at the floor with the heel of one shoe.

"Some pretty wild shit. More than I expected, that's for sure. Dancy told me she was from Florida, down near Fort Walton somewhere, so Hammond called this guy he knows who's Florida State Patrol, and then he talked to the Feds in Tallahassee. And they told him that a sixteen-year-old albino girl named Dancy Flammarion escaped from a state mental hospital a few months ago."

He pauses, then, but Chance doesn't say anything, keeps her head turned towards the open window; she flares her nostrils slightly, once, twice, as if searching the breeze for some particular odor. An animal kind of a thing to do, almost like a dog, and that makes him think of things he'd just as soon not remember and he starts talking again.

"She'd been there about a year, ever since she was picked up last summer wandering along the highway near a place called Milligan. Turns out she was living somewhere back in the swamps with her mother and grandmother. The cops that found her knew who she was, but they couldn't get her to talk, so they just assumed she'd run away from home. But when they tried to take her back, turns out the cabin her family was living in had burned down to the ground. Her mother and her grandmother were both dead, and, as far as anyone in Milligan knew, she didn't have any other family. So Dancy became a ward of the state—"

"Since when do they put you in the nuthouse for that?"

"They don't. Hammond said he wasn't precisely clear on why she was committed, though she evidently gave the Milligan PD a hell of a lot of trouble before they shipped her off to Tallahassee.

"Anyway, when Dancy finally started talking, whatever she had to say to those shrinks must have sounded an awful lot like the sort of stuff she was telling us, because no one intended to let her out anytime soon. About a month before she escaped, she attacked another patient and an orderly and wound up in isolation, on some sort of high-security suicide watch."

"Jesus," Chance murmurs and Deacon leans forward and the front legs of his chair bump gently back down to earth again.

"No one seems to know exactly how she escaped, or if they do they wouldn't tell Hammond, or he wouldn't tell me, but in the process she assaulted another orderly. Some poor fucker that must have been trying to stop her and she bit off his finger, Chance, bit it *off* and took it *with* her. Since then, the police in Florida and Georgia have kinda been looking for her, but no one had seen hide nor hair, not until the day you saw her at the library."

"What does this mean, Deacon?" and she sits up slow, braces one hand against the headboard to steady herself. "Even if we know where the finger came from, it doesn't explain how she knew about my grandmother, or the water works tunnel, or Elise, or the trilobites—"

"There's a whole hell of a lot it doesn't explain, Chance. I know that. But it's a start. It's someplace to begin. And we have to start somewhere. We have to do something. Right now, I got you and Sadie both goin' fucking loony toons on me and I don't think I'm far behind you myself. This is the only thing that makes sense to me, figuring out what the hell was up with Dancy, because that's where this began, that day you met her at the library," and Deacon stops then, because he can hear the way he's starting to sound, scared and angry, desperate, everything that he doesn't want Chance to know he's feeling, everything that can only make it worse. He takes a deep breath and "I never said I had all the answers," he says and stands up.

"That's not where this began, Deacon," she says, "You *know* that's not where this began," looking up at him and her eyes are wet and bright, her green eyes and he'd almost forgotten how deep those eyes are, how there was a time when he could lose all the ugly parts of himself in them.

"What are you talking about?"

"The night we broke into the tunnel. Whatever happened to us that night, whatever happened to you and to mc and Elise. *That's* where this started. Elise knew. She tried to get me to talk, to remember, and I wouldn't because I was too scared and then it killed her. And it killed my grandmother, and Dancy, too. And all we do is talk and try to think of ways not to accept what's going on. I think maybe that's what it wants."

And then she's crying too hard to say anything else, and Deacon turns away, stares at a bookshelf on the other side of the room. Whatever miserly scrap of courage he has no match for her breaking down like this and he wants to tell her to stop it, stop it right now, wants to grab her and shake her until she shuts up. There are still too many things he has to do, too many questions left to answer if they're going to come out of this sane.

"I have to go to Florida, Chance," he says. "I've got to try to find out more about Dancy. Maybe then, maybe if I can understand how she fits into what's going on, I can make you see this isn't about monsters and it doesn't have anything to do with Elise's death—"

"Deacon, no, please, just once talk to me about that night. Sit down and tell me what you think happened to us in there."

But Deacon doesn't sit down, keeps his eyes fixed on Chance's bookshelf, the incongruous mix of children's picture books and natural history, *On Beyond Zebra* and Stephen Jay Gould. Neat and sensible rows of books to keep him from following Chance wherever she's gone, the black and devouring places he's spent his life running from, the places that his visions would have dragged him off to a long time ago if he'd let them.

"I've asked Soda to loan me his car for a day or two. I won't be gone any longer than that, I promise."

"*Please,*" she says, "if you *ever* gave a shit about me," and he shakes his head, only shakes his head no, because he can't do more, can't tell her that he's never given much of a shit about anything else *but* her.

"I'm not leaving until daylight and I won't be gone long," he says and starts to turn around, takes his eyes away from the sanctuary of the bookshelf, and there's Sadie standing in the doorway, watching them and holding the ledger.

A few awkward minutes and then Deacon went downstairs, left Sadie and Chance alone in the attic, and now Sadie's standing in the door, staring down the darkened stairs after him. She might still call him back, she thinks, if she tried, might even be able to talk him out of driving away to Florida on some bullshit wild-goose chase. But she doesn't. And she wonders if it's because of Chance or because she knows that he would try to stop her from going back to the tunnel to find Dancy.

"I'm sorry," Chance says, trying to stop crying, sounding more asleep than awake, and Sadie turns and looks at her.

"Why? What do you mean?"

"I'm sorry for getting you into this. I'm sorry for getting both of you into this mess. I know she only went to you to get to me," and that's just one more thing to make Sadie want to tell Chance how full of shit she is. But it's exactly the sort of thing she should have expected, too; that arrogance, the whole, wide world spinning around Chance Matthews, the whole universe and Sadie's only some dim, inconsequential satellite unfortunate enough to get caught up in her gravity.

"It's not your fault," Sadie says. "Really. None of this is your fault." And she walks over, sits down in the chair beside the bed, the chair still warm from Deacon sitting there before her.

"I wish I could believe that," Chance says. "Just for a little while," and she wipes at her eyes. Sadie looks around for a box of Kleenex, but there isn't any to be seen. She considers going downstairs and getting Chance some toilet paper, a little extra effort to seem more sincere, but Chance has already started talking again.

"I told him not to go, Sadie. He won't listen to me. Maybe if you asked him, maybe he'd listen to you."

"Maybe, but you know Deke. When he gets something in his head, there's not much anyone can do."

Chance leans back against the wall. "I'm so tired," she whispers and starts crying again. "I'm so goddamn tired."

"You need to lie down and try to get some rest. You've been through an awful lot today," and that's when Chance notices that Sadie's holding the ledger and she points at it.

"Oh yeah, you left it downstairs. I thought you might want it up here with you," and she lays it on the bed near Chance. "I know it's important to you."

Chance picks up the book and glares at it, kaleidoscope tumble of emotions across her teardamp eyes, anger and regret and confusion, something that Sadie thinks might be fear, and then Chance lays it down again and wipes her snotty nose with the palm of her right hand.

"I don't . . . I don't know what's important to me anymore. I should throw this goddamned thing out the window."

Sadie opens her mouth and quickly closes it again. *Tell me what it means,* she wants to say. *Tell me what's wrong with the tunnel,* the words almost out of her mouth and then she thinks it might be too soon, that Chance could get suspicious and she might not ever get a second opportunity.

"I don't know," Sadie says. "Usually, whenever I throw something away I wind up wishing that I hadn't later on."

And Chance looks up at her, a sudden, furious expression like Sadie has just told her to go to straight to hell, do not pass go, do not collect two hundred dollars, and Sadie instinctively scoots a couple of inches farther away from the edge of the bed.

"What was that supposed to mean?" Chance asks her and Sadie shakes her head.

"Nothing. It didn't mean nothing at all. Just that I think you shouldn't throw that book away, because it belonged to your grandmother and tomorrow you might wish you hadn't."

"You don't *know* about this book, Sadie," and now Chance is almost snarling, brandishes the ledger like a Baptist minister brandishing a Bible at a tent revival, something in her hands full of damnation and secrets and she can make a weapon of it if she wants. "You don't know what it *means,* this book, the things in here," and now Chance is stabbing at the cover with an index finger, stabbing the book as she speaks and a few drops of saliva and the tears that have run down her face to her mouth fly from her lips and speckle the front of Sadie's T-shirt.

"So *tell* me, Chance," and *There,* she thinks. *It's out. Whether this was the right time or not, it's out.* "I'm right here and you can talk to me. It's not like I haven't been going through all this right along with you. It's not like I'm not going to believe whatever you say."

"*I* don't even believe me," Chance says and she drops the ledger. It lands loudly on the floor and Sadie stares at it a moment, trying to find the words she can trust, the correct words, that can't be taken the wrong way or brushed aside.

"Chance, do you think Dancy is dead?"

"Why don't you go ask Deacon? These days he seems to be doing a better job of coming up with answers than me," and then Chance lies down, head towards the foot of the bed and she curls herself into a fetaltight ball, a smaller target for whatever Sadie's going to say next; she sniffles and buries her face in the patchwork squares of the quilt.

"Because," Sadie says and bends over, retrieves the ledger from the floor, "we both already know what Deacon thinks about Dancy, that she's some kind of psycho. That she's dead, or she's run off somewhere. But he doesn't think that she's in trouble."

"My head hurts, Sadie. Leave me alone now. My head hurts and I just want to go to sleep."

But Sadie has opened the ledger, flips through it until she finds the first page with the drawing of the star and the seven-sided figure inside the star and she turns the book towards Chance.

"Just answer one question for me, Chance. Just this one little question and then I'll go away and I won't bother you again. I fucking promise."

Chance is watching her or the book with one bloodshot, weary eye, just her right eye because the left is still buried in the quilt. The side of her face that struck the steering wheel and that eye is turning the purpleblackred of a ripe plum.

"Tell me what this is. This design that your grandmother drew over and over again. Tell me what it means and what it has to do with the water works tunnel."

"I don't know," Chance says so softly that Sadie can barely hear her. "I don't know what it is."

"Dancy *isn't* dead, Chance. I swear to god I know she isn't dead and I can find her, but someone has to help me. *You* have to help me, because Deacon won't."

Chance's bruised eyelid flutters and slips closed as slowly as a theater curtain coming down after a show. But she opens her mouth, her lips parting just far enough that Sadie can glimpse white teeth and her pink tongue, and the corner of her mouth stretches back into what that might be a smile, or something else entirely.

"*Please,* Chance. Just this one thing," Sadie whispers and downstairs Deacon's calling her, shouting her name from the kitchen or the living room, and she shuts the ledger and leans closer to Chance. Leaning close so there's no danger that Chance won't hear her.

"I know he still loves you. Help me and I'll leave you both alone, if that's what you want. But I can't let her die down there, not if there's any way to save her."

"What makes you think I want the bastard anymore," Chance says, flimsy ghost of her voice filtered through pain pills and half her mouth covered by the quilt. "Don't be so presumptuous, Sadie."

And Sadie is already getting up from the chair, ready to tell Chance to go screw herself and if she has to do this alone that's fine. She's spent most of her life figuring things out for herself, but Chance moves, then, reaches out and touches the back of Sadie's hand with her fingertips and "Wait," she says.

"Why? You don't know anything, remember? I'm wasting my time talking to you."

But now Chance is watching her with both eyes open, more alert than she's seemed since Deacon pulled her from the car, and Sadie sits down again.

◖◆◗

"Soda's car is a piece of shit," Sadie says and Deacon shrugs his shoulders and stares at the television.

"Beggars can't be choosers."

"I can just see you broken down in the boonies," but that's the last shred of anything like resistance or disapproval that she's willing to risk; just enough to make it all seem real, enough like herself so that he doesn't get curious and start asking questions. She glances across the room at the clock hanging on the wall, cheesy sunburst clock from the 1950s or '60s, and it's almost four in the morning. She fiddles nervously with the pocket of the button-down shirt that Chance gave her to wear before she came back downstairs, a big, crusty bloodstain on her T-shirt, blood from the cut on her foot; the shirt's the color of lime sherbet and Sadie thinks that it looks like something an old man would wear. First the clompy boots and now this shirt, and maybe it's like being assimilated by pod people, becoming Chance one piece at a time.

"Shouldn't you at least get some sleep?" she asks him and Deacon nods, but doesn't stop watching the television.

After what Chance said to her upstairs, what she said about the things that happened when she drew the design on the blackboard, the things that might have happened, Sadie's having trouble sitting still, trouble waiting. Hours to go before she'll be able to leave the house, before Deacon is on his way and no one will try to stop her. She realizes that she's tapping her fingers impatiently on the arm of the sofa, impatient *tap tap tap tappity tap,* and she makes herself stop.

"You know, maybe I should go home in the morning," she says, "just to make sure everything's okay. I didn't even shut the door when I left last night," because it's too damn quiet in the house, even with the television on and she has to say *something,* too anxious to just sit there watching Deacon watch television, watching the tacky old clock tick off the seconds, trying not to think about Dancy and the tunnel.

"No, baby. I'll have Soda go by and have a look. Anyway, Mrs. Schmidt probably shut the door. You know how she gets about doors. Don't worry about it."

"But my computer's in there, Deke. My book's in there."

Deacon turns his head towards her and the shifting, salt-and-pepper TV light makes him look older than he is, his eyes so tired, the stubble on his chin and cheeks, but he looks sober and she wonders how long since he's had a drink; for a second he's more important than Dancy, more important than being brave or strong, than anything else ever could be and even the thought of losing him is almost more than she can bear.

"I need you to stay here with Chance," he says. "Just in case she needs help. And I think maybe you're safer here. I'll be back as soon as I can."

"Right," she says. "Whatever you say," and there's just a hint of sullen in her voice, a realistic touch that isn't that hard if she thinks about how Deacon's probably a lot more worried about Chance than he is about her, how *in case she needs help* came before *you're safer here.* A sharp, little jab of reality to restore her perspective. Deacon turns away from her again, looks back at the television screen, and in a few minutes he closes his eyes and falls asleep sitting up on the sofa. Sadie waits until he begins to snore his ragged-loud Deacon snore, until she's certain that he's deep enough asleep that she isn't likely to wake him, and then she takes the piece of paper from the shirt pocket, the page she tore out of the ledger after Chance finally stopped talking, stopped crying, and dozed off.

She lays the folded, slightly crumpled piece of paper on her knee and smooths it flat with one hand, stares at the thing that Chance's grandmother drew there when Sadie Jasper was only twelve years old, sixth-grade Sadie still afraid of the branches scratching the window at night and the things that hid beneath her bed waiting for the light to go out, and "There's no such things as monsters, dear," her mother would say. "Even if there are, God would never let them eat little girls," and maybe her mother even believed those things. Her mother believed a lot of things, comforting, light-of-day things, but now Sadie knows better; the panting, gaunt apparition outside Quinlan Castle that wasn't a stray dog, that stopped her from helping Dancy, that and this piece of paper are all the testament she needs.

"When I shut my eyes," Chance said upstairs, "Every time I shut my eyes I see it again. I'll never be able to stop seeing it," and Sadie held her hand and said reassuring words she didn't mean.

"All of this, it's all about what we know," Chance said. "They don't *want* to be known, Sadie."

Sadie stares at the design while Deacon snores and the television talks to itself in too many voices to be sane. Later, when she begins to feel sleepy, she folds the paper carefully and puts it back into her pocket. She lies down on the sofa, her head in his bony lap, first dishwater light outside, watergray light leaking through the drapes, and Sadie tries to pretend that nothing has changed, and nothing ever will, until she falls asleep.

And when she opens her eyes he's gone and the sun is very bright outside. Bright morning sun and at first she can't remember where she is, only that Deacon was here a moment ago and now he's gone. Dreams she can't quite recall, dim and subterranean dreams, dripping water, and Sadie squints at the ugly clock until her eyes focus and she can see that it's almost noon.

She sits up, and *Chance's house*, she reminds herself. *I'm in Chance's house and I should have been up hours ago*. Too soon to let herself think about the tunnel, so she only thinks about how badly she needs to piss, how she's thirsty and needs to piss and wants a cigarette.

Walking as quietly as she can, the clumsy, too-big boots heavy against the squeaky, old hardwood floor, down the hall to the bathroom and she stops on the way, pauses to peer up the stairs towards Chance's attic bedroom. No sign that she's awake yet, or at least that's what Sadie hopes. Pretty sure that Chance isn't in any shape to try and stop her from leaving, but, all the same, she'd rather not have to find out.

The bathroom smells like Ivory Soap and Pine-Sol, a whiff of something more exotic, lavender or roses, maybe. Sadie flushes the toilet, watches the pee-colored water swirling away and "Our drinking water comes through that place," she says out loud. The words from the journal and not much point in trying not to remember, now that she's up and moving, now that she can't simply close her eyes and let the world slip mercifully away from her again.

She looks back at herself from the mirrored medicine cabinet door hanging over the sink; a few streaks of eyeliner smudged all the way down to her cheekbones, hardly any left on her eyelids at all, her black lipstick wiped away, and the cold, frostblue eyes that she's always been so proud of, a part of her she didn't have to *make* strange because they came that way, and if they truly are the windows to her soul then nothing could be more seemly, more appropriate. Like Dancy Flammarion's rabbitpink irises, her blue eyes faded almost white to mark her for life, *I'm not like the rest of them. See? Inside, I'm not like you at all,* and Sadie starts to wash her hands, remembers the words from the ledger again and so she settles for wiping them with a dry hand towel.

On her way out of the bathroom and headed for the kitchen, when she thinks to check her shirt pocket, just to be sure. And it's still there, the page she tore from the ledger still folded up safe until she needs it. The page she stole so she could get the design exactly right and now she wonders if she could possibly ever forget it; a hundred years and she would probably still remember. But always better to be safe than sorry, Deke would say. Better too much than not enough, every goddamn time.

Sadie finds a mostly empty pack of Marlboros on the kitchen counter, doesn't remember leaving them there so maybe Deacon did. There are still two cigarettes in the pack and she lights one off the stove, sits down and takes a deep drag, letting the nicotine fill her lungs and work its way into her bloodstream, waking her the rest of the way while she watches the smoke float lazily towards the ceiling. A cup of coffee would be nice, strong black coffee with lots of sugar, but she doesn't know how to use Chance's old-fashioned percolator, so the Marlboro will have to do.

"What are you doing, Sadie?" Dancy says, her voice as clear as the angry blue jay squawking somewhere in the backyard, *clearer* even because Dancy's voice is coming from right behind her. Sadie turns around quickly, but there's only the oven, the refrigerator and the fog of her own cigarette smoke.

"Dancy?" she whispers. "Was that you?" and Sadie's heart is beating like she's just run a marathon, sweat on her palms and upper lip, a sick feeling deep inside her belly; she waits a moment and calls Dancy again, speaking as quietly as her shaky, adrenaline-dabbed voice will allow because she's still afraid of waking Chance.

"Can you *hear* me?"

But no one answers, nothing but the traffic and the jaybird, the mechanical purr of the fridge, the distant sound of the living room clock ticking off the day. Sadie turns back around, takes another drag off her cigarette and stares across the kitchen table at the window; a dark stain on the glass, maroondark smear and she remembers the crow from Saturday morning. Her and Chance and Dancy having breakfast while Deacon finished being sick in the bathroom, and the crow crashed into the window. Bashed its fucking brains out on the windowpane and it scared her so badly she actually screamed. Probably the first time in her life that she ever screamed and it was over some idiot bird. She exhales, smoke spilling slow from her nostrils, and she sees that it's not just blood on the glass, but a couple of small, black feathers stuck there, too, and something white that it takes her a second to realize is a smear of bird shit.

"Don't look at it," Dancy says, and this time Sadie doesn't turn around, keeps her eyes on the window, ignores the prickling pins-and-needles sensation at the nape of her neck.

"Don't look at what, Dancy?" she asks.

"It's nothing like what you think," and this time Sadie notices a hollow, throaty ring in Dancy's voice, still perfectly clear, still right behind her, but Dancy sounds like someone speaking from the bottom of a well. *Or someone talking through pipes,* Sadie thinks, *water pipes,* and then those words again from the ledger, from the piece of paper hidden away in her pocket.

"Our drinking water comes through that place," Dancy says. "Whatever you're thinking, Sadie, it's nothing like that at all. It's nothing you can imagine—"

"Then what *is* it, Dancy? What the hell is it?"

"There are still giants in the earth," Dancy replies and now Sadie does turn to see, hard to pull her eyes away from the scabby windowpane but she turns towards the voice anyway. "Stop talking in goddamn *riddles*. Just answer the question," almost shouting and she doesn't care anymore if she wakes Chance or anyone else.

And she's still alone in the kitchen.

"I have to try to find you," she whispers. "I'll never be able to live with myself if I don't try." Sadie waits for an answer, anything that could pass for an answer, sits very still in her chair until the cigarette burns down to sear her fingers. She curses and drops it on the floor, not much left but the smoking filter and she crushes that out with the toe of Chance's boot, touches the tip of her tongue to blistered skin and closes her eyes, looking inside for whatever has brought her this far and still has to carry her the rest of the way to the water works tunnel.

Sadie finds all the things she'll need in the storage room at the back of Chance's house, the musty room where Dancy found the wooden crate. A small can of black enamel paint and a brush that smells faintly of turpentine, a flashlight that works, and what she thinks is a pair of lopping shears. Not the heavy-duty bolt cutters she hoped to find when she started searching through the tools, working from high-school memories of the janitors forcing open lockers suspected of harboring dope or liquor or stolen property. Nothing that formidable, but these two long, aluminum handles that end in a stout, tempered-steel beak, a robotic parrot's jaws, and she thinks they should do the trick just fine.

All these things and the page torn from the ledger, and Sadie follows the crooked, rootbuckled sidewalk down the mountain towards the park, walking beneath the scorching midday sun, blazing sun in a sky gone the palest blue to match her eyes. She's carrying the shears over her left shoulder like a rifle, and the paint, the brush, and the flashlight are all inside a brown paper bag she found under the kitchen sink. It isn't a long walk, three short blocks before the lawns and driveways end, and now there's shade below the sweet gums and water oaks, welcomed refuge from sunstroke and the indifferent gaze of the distant, cloudless sky. Not far, but far enough that her bandaged foot is getting stiff again and it's begun throbbing inside the borrowed boot.

Sadie crosses the road and there are weathered pineboard steps leading down from Sixteenth to the park, a steep and winding walkway to make a shortcut to Nineteenth Street and it ends at a dingy, little gazebo with a single picnic table. The park's deserted, but there's an old Taco Bell bag and a couple of Diet Pepsi cans that someone's left sitting on the table, someone too lazy to toss them at the green trash barrel with HELP KEEP BIRMINGHAM CLEAN—PUT LITTER IN ITS PLACE stenciled on the side in large, blocky letters. She sets her grocery bag and the lopping shears on the table, sits herself down on the picnic bench, and turns to face the entrance to the tunnel; the blockhouse is only twenty or thirty yards to her right now, back among the trees at the end of a trench in the mountainside. Red dirt and limestone rubble furrow leading right up to the opening, and she can see the rusty chain looped through the iron bars, the silver glint of a big padlock to make sure the chain stays put and the gate stays closed.

It isn't much cooler under the gazebo and Sadie wipes the sweat from her face with the palm of her hand.

"Where are you now, Deke?" she says out loud, the first thing she's said since the kitchen, since Dancy talked to her, and she pictures Deacon behind the wheel of Soda's old Chevy Nova, a small and homely car that looks like something that took a wrong turn and ended up in the middle of a demolition derby. No air conditioner and one headlight, the crumpled hood and fenders like a fucking dinosaur stepped on it because he got stoned and drove under a guardrail a year or two ago. "Jesus, Soda, it looks like Godzilla stepped on the damned thing," Deacon said, and she wishes he was here with her. Probably all the way to Florida by now, but it doesn't hurt to wish.

"Yeah. If wishes were horses," she says and wipes her sweaty face again, stares back at the blockhouse with its two tiny window frames like vacant eyes set too far apart. *It'll be plenty cool in there, I bet,* imagining shadows that never grow any longer or any shorter, all the places the withering Alabama summer sun will never touch. Sadie shuts her eyes, so hot and tired after the walk from Chance's house, and these thoughts to soothe her, to remind her that there's someplace to escape the heat, a hundred in the shade, a hundred and ten, and if she has to stay out here much longer her brains will start to bake.

"It's lying to you," Dancy says, her wellbottom voice even more hollow than before. "There's no comfort here. Everything burns down here."

Sadie doesn't open her eyes, has learned her lesson and maybe whatever's left of Dancy isn't something anyone can see, or she's speaking from somewhere much too far away.

"Oh, Dancy. I should have tried harder to *make* them listen—"

"Go *home,* Sadie. Please. There's still time. I'm not your responsibility. I never was—" and then a sound that's almost like radio static, not a sound from outside but coming from inside her head, radio static, white noise, and it *does* burn. Like ice crystals growing beneath her skin, blooming glass flowers to tear her apart, cell from frozen cell, and she gasps and opens her eyes. An instant when she'd swear that she's seeing her breath in the stifling air, less than an instant, before the static in her head fades away to the softest crackle and then to nothing at all.

And on the other side of the furrow, standing small in the useless shade of the trees, Dancy Flammarion bows her head and raises her left hand, sad and forgiving gesture like a plaster saint, and Sadie calls out to her. Screams her name, but suddenly there's a breeze blowing across the park, a wind that stinks of mold and stagnant water and it rustles the leaves of the trees, ruffles Dancy's clothes and hair and she dissolves as completely as a tear swallowed by an ocean.

The lopping shears left only a few, futile dents and scratches on the steel hasp of the padlock, its blades either too dull or Sadie too weak or both, and by the time she finishes painting the design onto the front of the blockhouse, blood and small pieces of flesh have been falling from the cloudless July sky for almost fifteen minutes. There's laughter coming from someplace just inside the tunnel, a low, guttural chuckle from something hiding behind the pipes. The laugh and the stickysick *plop plop plop* of blood and meat hitting the ground, and both these things only prove she's right, Sadie knows that. Cheap horror movie tricks to scare her away so she *must* be right.

She wipes the blood from her eyes and takes a couple of steps back from the blockhouse, slides in the mud and almost falls; the ground has turned the deepest red beneath her feet, a red that's almost black, and the mud is speckled with restless, white bodies, hungry maggots and grubs, and she lets the paintbrush fall from her slippery fingers. It lands in a small puddle, splashes her ankles with stringy clots and gristle, and Sadie stares up at the bold, black lines she's traced on the stones. The wall almost as bloody as the mud but the lines still plain enough to see, the star, the inner heptagon, and Sadie stands beneath the bleeding sky, the same wounded sky she invented two days before, and stares past the iron bars into the mouth of the water works tunnel.

Run, Sadie, run fast. It's not too late to run away, but that's not Dancy, clumsy lost girl impersonation, and it only wants her to run because she be might be fun to chase.

"Come on out, motherfucker. I'm getting tired of waiting for you," and the darkness crouched inside the tunnel laughs at her again, but she doesn't have to wait for very long.

CHAPTER TWELVE

Trollholm

Barely half past noon and already the heat is a demon stretching itself wide across the monotonous South Alabama landscape, a greedy, suffocating heat to lick at the pine sap and sandyred soil, at Deacon trapped inside the shitty little Chevy. Sweat drips from his hair, trickles down his skin into his eyes and he squints painfully through the bugspattered windshield at the burning day and licoriceblack strip of Highway 55, the watershimmer mirage rising off the blacktop to make him that much thirstier. He's been swigging lukewarm Gatorade for hours, but the orange liquid tastes vaguely like baby aspirin and, besides, it doesn't seem to do anything much for the thirst. The wind whipping through the open windows is hot and smells like melting asphalt and the dense forests crowding at the edges of the road, and it's easy for Deacon to imagine that the trees and brambles are pressing closer and closer on each side, taking back the highway, and the vanishing point up ahead is merely proof that they're succeeding.

Trying not to think about Chance or Sadie, about what he will or won't find in Milligan, and he glances at the odometer. One of the few things on the dashboard that seems to be working right, working at all, and he sees that he's driven almost two hundred miles since leaving Birmingham. Two hundred miles and most of it interstate, before he took the exit for Andalusia half an hour ago. It was better on the interstate, the breeze through the windows just the slightest bit cooler when he was driving fast. Now he's a lot more worried about cops, plenty of places for them to hide, waiting patiently, laying speed traps along the narrow highway and he's trying to stay under sixty. But it's all guesswork anyhow, since the speedometer is one of the things that doesn't work.

There's country music blaring from the radio, nothing but country and gospel stations this far south and so he's going with the lesser of two evils, a twangy stream of Garth Brooks and Trisha Yearwood, but at least it's something to keep him company. Something besides the sound of the wheels on the road, the unnerving assortment of noises that come from the Chevy's engine at irregular intervals. And every now and then there's a Johnny Cash or Patsy Cline song, like water holes in the wasteland, something small but genuine to keep him going.

A mile past Red Level, someplace that isn't actually any place at all, a crossroads and a gas station, two rusty house trailers and they both looked deserted, when he spots the hitchhiker standing by a faded Pepsi Cola billboard. A very tall man standing in the sun without a hat, an old, green knapsack on one shoulder and he's holding up a cardboard and crayon sign with ENTERPRISE printed neatly on it. He sees the Chevy coming and smiles, holds his sign a little higher so there's no chance that the driver won't see him. And *It might not be so bad, a little company,* Deacon thinks, better than the damned radio and maybe the guy doesn't look harmless, but then who does? He pulls over, raising a thick cloud of dust and sand, and a second later the hitchhiker leans in through the passenger-side window and smiles one of the widest smiles that Deacon's ever seen. Wide and nicotine-stained teeth the dingy color of old ivory or bone, and the man reaches inside and shakes Deacon's hand. He has eyes so brown they seem almost black, oildark eyes and long, black hair slicked down close to his scalp.

"I'm mighty grateful to you," the hitchhiker says. "Been standing there since dawn this morning and nobody's even slowed down to look twice. And old Mr. Sun up there's a bull-bitch on wheels, if you catch my meaning."

"I can only take you as far as Andalusia," Deacon says and the man's still pumping his arm up and down, up and down, like he expects quarters or a gush of cold spring water to come spilling from his lips. "I'm turning south there, for Florida."

"Yeah? Well, Andalusia will do just fine, then," the man says and finally releases Deacon's hand. He opens the car door, letting in more of the dust and Deacon coughs a dry cough into the palm of his hand and reaches for the half-empty Gatorade bottle tucked into the shadows beneath his seat. The man throws his knapsack into the back, lays the cardboard sign on top of it, and gets in, slams the door so hard it rattles the whole car.

"You got folks down in Florida?" the hitchhiker asks. "Or is it business?"

"Just business," Deacon says and unscrews the cap on the Gatorade bottle, takes a long swallow, washing dust and grit down his throat and trying to pretend it's an ice cold beer instead. The man keeps talking, watching the dust cloud start to settle on the hood of the car or whatever he can see farther down the highway.

"Florida ain't so bad, you know, except for all the goddamned tourists, all those goddamned, pasty-assed Yankee tourists trying to get away from the snow."

"Is that right?" Deacon asks, wipes his mouth on the back of his hand and briefly considers finishing off the Gatorade, only an inch or so left in the bottle anyway.

"Well, if you ask me, that's exactly right. But the deep-sea fishing's still good, Yankees or no Yankees."

Deacon wipes his mouth again and decides to save the rest of the baby aspirin–flavored Gatorade until later, much too easy to imagine Soda's car breaking down before he reaches the next town or convenience store, and he'd rather not think about being stuck out here with nothing at all to drink. He puts the cap back on the bottle and returns it to its place beneath the seat. The transmission makes an ugly, grinding sound when he shifts the stick back into drive, but Deacon ignores it, beginning to get used to the car's repertoire of complaints, and he pulls back out onto the highway.

"Where you coming from?" the hitchhiker asks and Deacon points out the window, points north, and "Birmingham," he says. "That's where I live."

"I've been lots of worse places," the man says and takes a deck of cards from the pocket of his shirt. Deacon switches off the radio and the knob comes away in his hand; he curses and tosses it out the window.

"Not exactly a goddamned Rolls-Royce, is it?" the man says and chuckles softly to himself, cuts the deck of cards once and shuffles them. "But listen to me, like I got a gold-plated chariot to haul my ass around in."

"It isn't even mine. I borrowed it from a friend."

"Well, it's sure as coon shit better than standing back there getting a sunstroke. Even if it ain't got an air conditioner, it's better than that."

"Oh, it *has* one," Deacon says, "but it only blows warm air," and the man laughs again, shuffles his deck of cards and turns the top card faceup.

"Well, look at that," the hitchhiker says and he whistles through his teeth. "Not exactly what I had in mind."

Deacon glances from the road to the cards and sees that they're not playing cards, a tattered, dog-eared pack of tarot cards instead, and the hitchhiker is holding The Tower between his left thumb and index finger. The lightning-struck tower perched on its rocky crag, fire from its windows and two figures plummeting towards the earth. "You see that there?" he asks and taps the card.

"What?" and so the man taps the card again.

"These drops of light here, falling down out of the clouds. The Hebrews call those things 'yods.' They sort of represent the descent of the life force into the material plane. Light falling out of the sky like rain."

"I've never picked up a hitchhiker who read the tarot before," Deacon says and the man smiles again, showing off his yellow-brown teeth and he places The Tower back on the top of the deck.

"I've been carrying this old deck of cards around with me since the war. I used to have a book to tell me what they all meant, but it got lost somewhere. I'd already memorized most of it, though."

"Which war?" Deacon asks him and the man shrugs his skinny shoulders and shakes his head.

"You think one's any different from the next? I mean, when it comes right down to brass tacks, people killing each other since they figured out how, that's all. Give them pretty names and numbers, but it's all the same to the worms. Worms can't count or read, and what's more, they got the good sense to stay down in the dark where the light don't come dripping out of the clouds onto their heads."

And Deacon's starting to think picking the hitchhiker up wasn't such a great idea after all, that perhaps he should have stuck with the road noise and honky-tonk music; already enough things in his head to give him the willies without this guy pulling out a deck of tarot cards and lecturing him about cabalism and worms.

"All the upheaval in the world in this card here," the man says. "The destruction of order and tradition, all your beliefs like a candle flickering in a hurricane. Enlightenment, but at a *cost,* you see."

"You're starting to sound like a preacher," Deacon says and he's trying to make a joke out of it, but the man nods his head and slips the card back into the deck.

"Yeah? Well that's one of the things I've been. That's one of the things I'll be again someday, I expect," and he turns over the second card. "The Queen of Pentacles, reversed," he says. But this time Deacon doesn't look at the card, keeps his eyes fixed straight ahead of him, the road and the pine trees and the unsheltering sky.

"Maybe this ain't where you're supposed to be today, this long, hot road going down to the sea. Maybe there's something else you're supposed to be doing, somewhere else. Neglected duties, and the Queen here, she says you've been thinking just that very thing all morning long."

"Does she now?" and he's trying to sound more skeptical than nervous, but his throat so dry it's almost sore and if he only had one goddamn beer, one stinking Bud or Sterling or PBR, maybe this fucker wouldn't be getting under his skin. "What else does she say?"

"Someone you don't trust, she says, someone you think ain't precisely what they been telling you," and he puts the Queen of Pentacles on the bottom of the deck and turns over another card. "The Eight of Staves. But, then, we already *know* you're on a journey. Question is, what's waiting for you at the end? What'll be left when you get back home?"

"Well, I suppose that's what you're going to show me next," Deacon says, glances at the man, and it's okay that there's an angry edge to his voice; if he can't fake disbelief he can at least make it clear that this whole shtick is beginning to piss him off and maybe the hitchhiker will take the hint and put the cards back into his shirt pocket.

"Dead dog," the man says, points at the windshield, and Deacon looks back at the road just in time to see the sunbloated corpse sprawled completely across his lane, the thick cloud of green-bottle flies and its body swollen big enough that it might as well be a deer as a dog; he cuts the wheel sharply to the left, but hits it anyway, plowing headlong through bone and rot and fur. The back tires squeal as the car fishtails and for a moment Deacon thinks he's lost control, a few more seconds and he'll be careening into the trees.

"Holy *shiiiit*, that was a ripe tomato," the hitchhiker cackles from the passenger seat, laughing like a madman, a high and delirious laugh.

"You just shut the fuck up!" Deacon growls at him. "We almost fuckin' *died* back there, for Christ's sake!" but the car has stopped swerving, is sailing along straight and smooth under the blue summer sky as if maybe it's decided to contradict him, angry about the radio knob and so it's decided to take the hitchhiker's side.

"Hey, *you're* the one ran over the son of a bitch," the man says and stops laughing, goes back to shuffling his tarot cards. "Don't be yelling at *me* 'cause you weren't looking at the road."

The cloying, sicksweet smell of roadkill so bad that Deacon's eyes are watering, and he swallows hard, trying not to taste it but tasting it anyway. He steals a quick peek in the rearview mirror and whatever's left of the dog is already too far behind them to see.

"You still got a long, long ways to go, Mr. Silvey, and you ain't never gonna make it at this rate."

Deacon starts to say something, ready to tell the man exactly where he can stick it, ready to pull over and let his smart-ass, spooky brains sizzle in his skull like a skillet full of scrapple and eggs, when he realizes that he hasn't told the hitchhiker his name. The tall man never asked and Deacon's pretty sure he didn't volunteer the information. He stares through the windshield at a ragged scrap of flesh caught on the hood of the Chevy, something dark and greasy that might be one of the dead dog's ears.

The hitchhiker shuffles his cards and sighs.

"Oh, I can tell you got some of the sight about you, so don't look *too* surprised. Just a glimmer, sure, not like that little albino bitch. That girl was a goddamn searchlight. She'd just as soon blind you as give you the time of day."

Not another car on the road as far as Deacon can see, not a house or a service station in sight, and it could easily go on like this for miles and miles. He licks his dry lips and puts more pressure on the gas pedal; if he's lucky there might be a highway patrolman with a radar gun somewhere up ahead.

"You been trying to keep your head down all your life, ain't you, Deke? You never did want any part of this hocus-pocus. Am I right or am I wrong?"

"I didn't ask for it, if that's what you mean," Deacon says. "But that really hasn't made a whole hell of lot of difference, has it?" The Chevy's accelerator is halfway to the floorboard now and the car races over a short bridge, a narrow, nameless creek fringed with bald cypress trees and Spanish moss. Deacon thinks he sees something moving about in the dark water, a shapeless mass gleaming wet in the sun, but then the creek's behind them and the man's talking again.

"No, I don't suppose it has at that. But sometimes a fellow's just got bad shit coming to him, whether he deserves it or not."

"Did Dancy deserve it?" he asks and the man clicks his tongue twice against the roof of his mouth and turns another tarot card.

"You better slow this junk heap down a bit, or you're gonna be spending the night in some cracker's piss-ant jail."

"That's sort of what I had in mind."

The hitchhiker clicks his tongue again, something cold and insectile in that sound, cold despite the heat of the day, and "This card," he says, "well, never you mind this card. You *know* you got a choice. You've always had a choice. All you have to do is forget about the albino and all the rest of this crazy shit, go back to that smart girl of yours in her great big ol' house and pretend like none of this ever happened. See that she does the same."

"Just like that," Deacon says and the Chevy has to be doing almost ninety by now, at *least* ninety, the way its front end has started to rattle and shimmy like it's ready to fly apart, and the steering wheel is beginning to shake in his hands. "Look the other way and I'm off the hook. It's that easy."

"I never said nothing about *easy*. Hell no, forgetting the messy truth of things ain't never been easy, but you and Chance might live a lot longer. It's your call, Deke. Your choice. You just don't look much like hero material to me. Let sleeping dogs lie, if you get my drift."

The man smiles, flashes all those sharp, yellow teeth, and then Deacon's coughing again, the air inside the Chevy suddenly so full of red dust that he can hardly see. He takes his foot off the gas and hits the brakes hard, and realizes that the car is already sitting perfectly, impossibly still as the engine sputters and stalls and is silent. The stereo's still blaring, the stereo and the rise and fall of the cicadas screaming in the trees, and he peers through the choking dust, through the windshield at the faded Pepsi billboard and he doesn't have to look twice to know that it's the *same* billboard, that he's no more than a mile past Red Level. There's nobody else in the car but him and no knapsack or homemade cardboard sign in the back, either. But there's a single tarot card on the seat beside him—The Tower—and Deacon sits and stares at it while the dust settles and the sun melts its way slowly towards the west. If there's no other mercy in the day ahead, at least the card has nothing more to show him than the gaudy, mystic's colors of its face.

Twenty long minutes waiting for the man that Vincent Hammond's sent him all the way to Florida to see, twenty minutes sitting on a bench in the lobby of the Milligan Courthouse, footstep echoes on the marble floors and occasional, suspicious stares from the people coming and going. The men and women dressed like they belong here, gray suits to remind him that he doesn't, and Deacon nods at each of them politely and smiles, spends the rest of the time reading a gold-framed reproduction of the Bill of Rights hanging on the wall. He's still reading it when someone calls his name and he looks up to see a pudgy black man with a gray mustache and an ugly yellow tie walking quickly towards him.

"Mr. Silvey?"

"Yes sir. That's me," and Deacon stands up, holds out a hand and the man shakes it.

"I'm Detective Toomey. You know, you're not exactly what I was expecting," the man says and tugs anxiously at his yellow tie. "The way Lieutenant Hammond talked, I thought you'd be a lot younger."

Deacon shrugs, uncertain what he should or shouldn't say to that, and then Detective Toomey rubs at his eyebrows like someone with a headache, eyebrows as gray as his mustache, and "Well, that's really neither here nor there, now is it? Why don't we step outside?" He motions towards the courthouse doors.

"Sure," Deacon says, "that sounds good to me," and he follows the policeman back out into the afternoon sun. There's another bench not far from the courthouse steps and they sit down there.

"Bet you it don't get this damn hot way up there in Birmingham," Detective Toomey says and Deacon glances up at the sun; it seems much closer than when he left Chance's house this morning, a spiteful, white thing sagging dangerously close to the ground.

"No sir. Not very often."

"When I retire, I'm gonna pick up and move all the way to Canada. I'm not gonna stop until there's snow so deep you need a bulldozer just to get from the front door to the mailbox," and Toomey wipes his face with a white handkerchief from a pants pocket.

"Right about now, that'd be fine by me," Deacon says, just wanting to get past the chitchat, get to the point, because he's never been any good at small talk, especially small talk with cops.

"Yeah. Snow and icicles long as my arm," and the detective stuffs the sweatstained handkerchief back into his pants. "So, tell me, Mr. Silvey, how can I help you today?"

"Hammond said you might be able to tell me something about a girl named Dancy Flammarion."

Toomey rubs at his eyebrows again and turns away from Deacon, gazes across the courthouse lawn towards a bronze statue of an Indian on a granite pedestal.

"Right, the albino girl. Fifteen years as a cop and you see some shit, Mr. Silvey, even way out here in the sticks, you do see some shit. But, well, there's the shit and then there's the depraved shit. And *then* there's things like Miss Flammarion. Jesus."

Deacon waits while the detective stares silently at the bronze Indian, wide, bronze shoulders streaked with verdigris and pigeon crap, and in a moment the man turns towards him again and smiles a tired, nervous smile like someone with something to hide, someone with secrets.

"That was my case. Not one of the ones I like to spend too much time thinking about, though. One of the ones I'd just as soon forget, to be perfectly honest. I was there the day Officer Weaver brought the girl in from the swamps. And let me tell you right now, just the time it took him to get her here from Eleanore Road, she'd already done a number on that poor man's head. Thought for a while he was gonna quit the force after that, and he *still* won't talk about it much."

"Eleanore Road?" Deacon asks and Toomey nods, points to the north, past the courthouse.

"Yeah, that's where Weaver found her. We'd been having some pretty bad forest fires that summer, what with all the dry weather. A bunch of volunteer firefighters down from Georgia had just spent two days out on Eleanore Road and Weaver was out there to be sure there weren't any hot spots left, you know. Well, about sunrise, he comes across Miss Dancy Flammarion walking right down the middle of the road, barefoot and dragging along this big ol' duffel bag, her clothes scorched to rags, like she walked straight through that fire. But there wasn't a burn, not so much as a blister, Mr. Silvey, anywhere on her. Or the damned duffel bag, for that matter.

"Well, sir, Weaver, he pulls over to see what's up, you know, and she takes one look at him and starts screaming bloody murder. Crazy shit about monsters and angels and lights in the sky. You name it, man. He finally had to handcuff the kid just to get her into the patrol car. And then she bit him," and the detective points to a spot just below his left temple.

"Took a plug out of the guy's cheek. Weaver was bleeding like a stuck pig when he brought her into the station."

"But you guys already knew who she was?"

Toomey leans back against the bench, tugs at his yellow tie and his eyebrows arch like excited caterpillars.

"Oh, yeah. Everyone in town knew about the Flammarions. There aren't too many bona-fide swamp folks left around these parts. And the Flammarions have been living out there in Shrove Wood since God was in diapers. I understand they gave the Feds a lot of trouble back during Prohibition, shooting at anyone who came near the place, and when alligators went on the endangered species list in the seventies, we almost had a civil war on our hands. Two of the old man's boys finally wound up in the state pen for poaching gators. Anyway, by the time this happened, this business with the albino girl, they'd all pretty much moved away or died or gone to jail. No one was left out there but the old woman and her daughter, Julia. That was the girl's mother, you know, Julia Flammarion. She went off to Pensacola at some point and got herself pregnant."

"So Dancy's illegitimate?" Deacon asks and Detective Toomey shakes his head and barks out a dry, thin laugh.

"Kind of adds insult to injury, wouldn't you say? But we're getting a little off the subject."

"Yeah," Deacon says and he looks down at his hands, the sweat standing out on his palms. "I guess we probably are. This Officer Weaver, was he the one that drove Dancy back home, the one that found the burned cabin?"

"Oh, hell no. After she bit him, Al Weaver swore he wasn't getting anywhere *near* that child. Said he'd resign before he ever got within spitting distance of her again. We had a doctor look the girl over, make sure she wasn't injured, and then Ned Morrison and someone from Child Welfare took her back, and they're the ones found the cabin and the bodies and all."

"And then you went out there yourself?"

"Yep, soon as they brought her back. And I don't mind telling you, Mr. Silvey, this job doesn't get much worse than having to deal with bodies that have been through a fire. Except maybe the floaters. You know, someone that's been in the water a good long while. Either way, the stink gets up your nose, into your sinuses, and it stays there for days."

"Yeah, I know," Deacon says, almost whispering, those smells too easy to remember, all the stink of death and decay that came along with the things he once did for Vincent Hammond, and Detective Toomey stares at him a moment without saying anything at all. No need to say anything out loud because the questions are all there in his eyes.

"Well, anyhow," the detective says, and he clears his throat, spits into the grass. "Like I was saying, after they brought the girl back, after Morrison called in the bodies, that's when this thing landed in *my* lap." And he stops, takes half a roll of peppermint Life Savers from his shirt pocket and offers one to Deacon before taking a piece of the candy for himself. "No thanks," Deacon says and Toomey shrugs, drops the roll back into his pocket and sucks thoughtfully for a moment on his Life Saver.

"We had to use dental records to get the official IDs on the two women. We all knew who they were, of course, but not by looking at what was left of them. At first, when I talked to Morrison on the radio, I assumed the forest fire got the cabin and for some reason they weren't able to get away."

"That's not what happened," Deacon says, not meaning to sound so certain, only meaning to ask, and he gets another long and wary look from Detective Toomey.

"You sure you need *me* to tell you what happened out there, Mr. Silvey?"

"I'm sorry," he says and the detective nods his head, uses his tongue to move the Life Saver from one side of his mouth to the other and back again.

"That fire never reached the Flammarion place. We found a couple of empty twelve-gallon gas cans at the edge of the woods. And there was plenty of residue from the expedient in the ash and timbers, *and* on the girl's hands and clothes. So we were pretty sure how the fire began, even if we didn't know why. Later on, after she was locked up in that hospital in Tallahassee, when she started talking again, Dancy denied the whole thing. Said it was a lightning strike started the fire."

"So she killed them?"

"Now, that's not what I said, is it?"

"But you're saying she started the fire," and a fat and stinging drop of sweat runs down Deacon's forehead, down the bridge of his nose, and into his left eye.

"The one thing does not necessarily lead straight to the other. Sure, that was the first thought popped into my head, until I actually saw the bodies and the coroner started working on them. Turns out, they both died *before* the fire even started. The old woman . . . well, we wrote her up as an animal attack. *Something* out there tried to tear her apart. We never did find one of her arms. The ME said maybe it was a bear or a panther. We still have a few of those around, so maybe that's all it was.

"And Dancy's mother, Julia, she drowned, Mr. Silvey, probably two or three days before the cabin burned. I don't think I would have believed that one if I hadn't been there myself when they opened up her chest and seen the water in her lungs. There's a place where Wampee Creek widens out, where it runs through an old sinkhole, not too far from the cabin. We figure that's probably where she died."

The detective pauses and spits out the half-dissolved Life Saver, makes a face and "Damn, I hate those things. But I'm trying to quit smoking, you know."

"So Dancy was only burning their bodies, like a funeral pyre."

The detective turns and glares at Deacon. "Listen, son. I'm about to tell you some stuff, and for the record, you absolutely did not hear any of this shit from me, and you didn't hear it from anyone else connected with me, you understand that? The only reason I'm doing this is because someone in the department owed someone in Atlanta a favor. If a single word of this turns up in the press or on the goddamn Internet—"

"That's not going to happen," Deacon says, still rubbing his sweatstung eye, still blinking, and "This is personal. I'm trying to help some friends, that's all. Some people that got a little too close to Dancy for their own good."

"Yeah, well, you just remember what I said."

The detective glances towards the bronze Indian statue again, takes out his roll of Life Savers and frowns at them. "Goddamn it, I need a cigarette for this," he says, and then Deacon listens quietly while he talks about the other things that were found in the ashes, the third body and the footprints in the swamp, and all the stories people tell their children to keep them far, far away from the old Flammarion place.

◊

North and then west of the city of Milligan, where the meandering Blackwater River wraps itself like a cottonmouth around the cypress swamps and pines, and Deacon hasn't passed another car since he turned onto Eleanore Road. More potholes than asphalt out here, and there have been stretches where he suspected there was nothing between the car and the sandy earth but a few shovels' worth of carelessly strewn gravel. The Chevy bounces and rattles as Deacon tries not to think about the flat spare tire in the trunk, watching for the turn-off and he should have come to it by now, wonders if maybe he's passed it, too worried about the car to pay attention. Just a dirt road, no name or sign, but Toomey said there was an old mailbox on a post, rusty, old mailbox full of holes from kids using it for target practice, but if you look hard enough, he said, you can still read FLAMMARION painted on the side.

Never mind that he's managed to spend his whole life without ever once leaving the South, the wooded desolation of this place is almost as alien to Deacon as the surface of the moon, the bottom of an ocean; always more comfortable lost in the brick and steel and glass mazes of cities, straight lines and right angles to keep the world in order, rats and pigeons and if he ever needed anything more exotic, there were always zoos. This wild place only makes him feel more alone, the loneliness that's followed him all the way from Birmingham and a growing, almost tangible, sense of genuine isolation, this city boy in a borrowed junkheap car wandering around out here alone, chasing ghosts as the day winds down and the sun throws treelong shadows across Eleanore Road.

After Toomey was finished talking, when Deacon was sure he was done so it didn't matter anymore whether or not the detective thought he was crazy, he took a deep breath and told him about what had happened in the car, a stretch of road he might have driven twice and the tall hitchhiker with the tarot cards. Just getting it off his chest, the dim hope that telling someone might effect an exorcism, at least take the edge off the creepiness; when he was finished, Toomey stared at him a while, tugged at his yellow tie one last time and "If I was you, son, I'd get back in that ugly, little car of yours and go home," he said. "Sometimes what we're looking for, it don't want to be found, and sometimes, we don't really want to find it." And then he shook Deacon's hand again, said good-bye and walked back up the marble steps into the courthouse.

A wide place in the road up ahead and now he's almost certain he's missed the turn somehow, is already slowing down to double back, when he sees the shotgun-peppered mailbox sitting on its post on the left side of the road, almost invisible in a clutching tangle of blackberry vines. And there's the dirt road, too, hardly even as wide as the Chevy, a weedy, rutted redbrown path leading away into the place that Toomey called Shrove Wood. As if this could be a place of absolution, as if the trees themselves, standing straight and tall and close together, have assembled to hear the paltry sins of man.

"This is it," Deacon says. "Last chance, buddy," but he knows that's a lie. That his last chance to avoid whatever's at the end of this dirt road was somewhere else, some*time* else entirely—before he and Sadie walked out of the laundromat Saturday night, perhaps, or maybe it's been inevitable since the moment he first saw Dancy Flammarion. Maybe it was always inevitable, but he knows damn well he isn't going to turn back now, even after all the things that Toomey said. Stupid or stubborn or just too afraid of what might happen to Chance and Sadie if he does chicken out, so he turns off Eleanore Road and the car bumps over a particularly deep pothole and stalls.

"It's more of a driveway than a road," what Toomey said when Deacon asked him directions to the burned cabin. "Hell, these days it's probably more like a deer trail." Sitting in the Chevy, staring down the narrow path winding through the trees and brush, Deacon wonders if even the deer would bother now. The forest is taking it back, has laid waist-high saplings and fallen branches, deep washouts he'd never get the car across, so he doesn't bother cranking the engine again. Through the pines, the sun is huge and red, and Deacon wishes he wore a watch, or that the car's clock worked, wishes he knew exactly how long he has before sunset. Not long enough, surely, an hour maybe, hour and a half if he's lucky, before it's pitch black out here.

What do you think you're gonna find at the end of this road, Deacon?

Aren't you getting thirsty?

Aren't you getting scared?

Questions that Chance asked him in a dream, the bright and dazzling dream where he wandered through these woods and watched impossible things through Dancy Flammarion's eyes, and it seems as if everything he's seen and heard since leaving Birmingham has only raised more questions; if there have been answers, they're certainly not the ones he came looking for, the ones to explain away, to ravel the mysteries and set the world on course again. Instead, only answers that cast as much shadow as light, answers to leave him jealous of lost ignorance. "Just get out of the car," he says. "Just get out the car and see whatever the hell there is to see."

Aren't you getting scared?

Deacon glances over at the glove compartment, a fat, silver piece of duct tape to keep it from coming open because the latch is broken, and maybe there's a flashlight in there, at least. He pulls back the tape and at first all he sees are two old copies of *Hustler* magazine crammed into the space, Soda's porn stash and a big, rubber dinosaur the color of a tangerine; he pulls the magazines out, lets them fall to the floorboard and the dinosaur lands feet-first on top of one of the glossy covers, hiding the smiling face of a woman with breasts almost as big as small watermelons. No flashlight, though, which figures, but at the very back of the glove compartment is something wrapped in an oily rag, most likely a baggie of marijuana or mushrooms, knowing Soda, and Deacon reaches in and takes it out.

It's surprisingly heavy, so probably not dope after all, and he unwraps the oily rag and then sits staring at the gun in his hand.

"Soda, you dumb-ass son of a bitch," he says, picturing what might have happened if some cop had pulled him over and found the thing. But they didn't and now there's no denying that the weight of it, the way it glints dull in the late afternoon sunlight, is a comfort; Deacon doesn't know shit about guns, has never touched anything but a BB rifle and that was when he was a kid, but he figures even he knows enough to point it and pull the trigger. He finds a small switch on the right side of the revolver, just above the grip, and pushes it; the cylinder swings open and there are five bullets inside and one empty chamber. He checks the glove compartment for extra ammo and finds nothing else but a map of Arkansas and four moldy Fritos.

"Just get out of the car," he says again and opens the door. "Just keep moving." And he takes a deep breath as he snaps the cylinder closed, locks all the Chevy's doors before he climbs out. Deacon tucks the gun into the waistband of his jeans, feels stupid doing it, like playing Dirty Harry or Charles Bronson out here in the middle of nowhere, and he wonders if anyone's ever blown their dick off carrying a gun around like that, if he'll be the first. In the trees there are crows and mockingbirds, and the incessant thrum of insects and frogs from every direction. Deacon wipes sweat from his forehead, looks at the car one more time, and then starts off down the trail.

Something more than déjà vu, standing in the clearing at the other end of the dirt road. The knowledge that he *has* stood here once before, and it doesn't matter if that first time wasn't real, only a vision, because this *is* the same place, exactly the same, only the ruin of the cabin and the blackberry and ferns reclaiming the clearing to make it any different at all. Dusk coming down on him instead of a scalding midday sun overhead, and that still doesn't change a thing. The hulks of rusting cars balanced on concrete-block crutches, bare wheels where there should be tires, and then the charred remains of the cabin. Deacon walks past a rose garden gone wild, two or three heavy, canary-yellow blooms among the thorns, a line of rocks whitewashed to mark what was once a path to the porch, something fallen over and shattered in the weeds and it takes him a moment to realize it used to be a cement birdbath.

The blackened bones of the cabin like a skeleton that has surrendered and collapsed in upon itself, roof timbers for the charcoal ribs of a defeated giant or dragon, and the tall chimney of soot- and smokestained limestone blocks and mortar rising defiantly above the wreckage. There are ferns and wildflowers growing among the bones, a carpet of new life in death, green and specks of brighter colors on a grave, and Deacon doesn't have to imagine what that last day was like, has seen enough himself to know.

Just past the birdbath and he finds a large rack of antlers still attached to a piece of deer skull, the points scorched and cracked from the heat and there's a big tenpenny nail still sticking out of the skull cap. He looks again and the antlers are everywhere, scattered across the ground and among the burnt wood, some burned almost beyond recognition, others untouched. Something else from his vision, and the dream of the vision, the antlers, and something else from Dancy's dog-eared copy of *Beowulf,* as well: the walls of King Hrothgar's hall, Hart Hall, Heorot, adorned with antlers, and whether this is coincidence or design, it's not a pleasant thought, something to send a shiver along Deacon's spine.

And he knows there's nothing important left here for him to see, just like Toomey said, everything carted away and buried or locked up tight where it might never be seen again. The bodies of Dancy's mother and grandmother and the heavy cast-iron disc found nailed to a nearby tree, metal engraved with a pentagram and a seven-sided figure set inside the star. Something that Toomey said gave him the heebies just to look at, that disc, and someone finally sent it away to an archeologist at the university in Gainseville. Deacon didn't tell him about the drawings from Esther Matthews' journal, the man already clearly fucked-up enough by the things he knows, the things he's seen, and Deacon saw no point in sharing fresher nightmares.

But the worst of it, the third body found in the ashes, and the police reports wrote that up, wrote it off, as the corpse of a black bear, the bear that must have killed Dancy's grandmother. Half its face blown off by a shotgun blast, but Toomey leaned close to him and "If *that* was a bear, Mr. Silvey, then I'm a goddamn Chinaman," he said and then flatly refused to say anything else about the beast.

Deacon bends over and his fingertips brush a scorched plank, what might once have been a step or part of a windowsill, door frame, and he half-expects the sudden smell of oranges, the pain behind his eyes, but there's nothing. No visions of the fire, of Dancy pouring gasoline or striking a match to hide whatever really happened here. Only the droning symphony of frogs and insects, the faintly spicy aroma of pine sap and ferns.

And Chance's voice again, the memory of the dream of her so strong and clear that he looks over his shoulder; *We both know what really happened that night. This doesn't change a thing.* There's nothing behind him but the watchful trees, the dwindling day, and "No," he says. "I guess it doesn't."

Deacon turns back to the cabin, the guardian chimney, and on the other side of the clearing, past a pile of scrap iron and rotting, moss-scabbed stumps, he sees the path that leads through the woods and down to Wampee Creek, to the deep pool where Dancy's mother drowned.

Or drowned herself, he thinks, remembering the story that Dancy told him about Pensacola, her mother and the ocean and the fishermen who rescued her. No idea whether that was the truth or the truth disguised, Dancy's way of dealing with how her mother really died, making it more distant and inventing a happy ending.

He can see from where he's standing that the path through the woods is overgrown, briars and saw grass up to his knees, up to his ass, and maybe this is as far as he should go. Maybe he's gone too far already, abandoning Chance and Sadie and driving two hundred and fifty miles just to listen to Toomey tell him spooky stories and poke through a burned-out cabin. He glances down at the butt of the pistol sticking out of his pants, feeling ridiculous and lost and scared, all those things at once.

The sound of wings overhead, then, mad flutter of a dozen or a hundred wings and he looks up, stares amazed at the flock of crows rising from the trees around the clearing. A storm of cawing, feather-black bodies to blot out the sky for a moment, frantic, living cloud moving in unison, responding to some signal too subtle for his dull, human senses to perceive.

Psychopomps, that word something lost for years in the dustier corners of his memory and the recollection triggered by the sight of these birds, something he read when he was in college, before he gave up trying to understand the things he saw. *Conductors of the souls of the dead,* blackbirds and crows and ravens especially, and the birdshadow is already breaking up, dissipating above the trees.

"What did you think you'd find?" she says and he isn't even surprised to see Dancy standing there by the chimney, standing in the ferns growing up through the charred and broken skeleton of the cabin floor. Her face is dirty, but she isn't sunburned the way she was that night outside the water works tunnel.

"The truth," he says and she smiles, sad smile that's more regret than anything else and she kicks at the ferns.

"Is that how you think this is all going to end, Deacon? Like in a book or a scary movie? You discover the truth and save us all?"

"I don't have a clue how this is going to end," he says, and the crows are already far away, just a distant commotion fading like the sun. "But that would be nice, don't you think, like an old *Scooby Doo* episode?" But from the way she looks at him he can tell she's never heard of *Scooby Doo,* no television out here, no Saturday-morning cartoons.

"Some stories don't have endings," she says. "In some stories, there aren't even answers."

"What are you trying to tell me, Dancy?"

"I've looked into their faces. Their *real* faces. The holes they have for eyes that go on forever, a longer forever than the stars, Deacon. You can stare at them until time ends and starts itself all over again, and you'll never know any more than when you began."

"Whose faces? What are you talking about?" and Deacon takes a step towards her and she takes a step back, a cautious, warning flash in her pinkred eyes and then it's gone and Deacon stays where he is.

"Land-dwellers in the old days named him Grendel."

"Grendel? Dancy, do you know what you've done to Chance and Sadie?"

"Yeah," she says and looks away from him, watches her feet down there somewhere among the fronds and rubble. "I should have stayed away from Sadie. But they would have found Chance, sooner or later. I just made it sooner, that's all."

"Because of what her grandmother knew, is that what you mean? The journal and that box full of rocks?"

"They are *afraid* of us, Deacon. They were already old when those rocks were mud and slime, and they are *terrible,* but they are as afraid of us as we are of dying. Sometimes we come too close—"

"Just tell me what I'm supposed to do, Dancy. Just tell me and I'll fuckin' do it," and at first he doesn't think she's going to answer him this time, the expression on her face like a teacher who's growing tired of lecturing a student too stupid to ever comprehend the basics. Her time wasted on him and then she holds out her left hand and there's something small and black crawling across her palm. Something alive that glistens wet and iridescent in the twilight, its needle spines and bulging, compound eyes, and she looks from the trilobite to Deacon and then back to the trilobite.

"You'll go to see the mere, because you've come this far. They're waiting for you down there, the ones that took my mother. That which has held the flood's tract a hundred half-years, ravenous for prey, grim and greedy—"

"You're just quoting fucking *Beowulf,*" he says, not wanting to sound angry, but sounding angry anyway. "I *know* that's what you're doing."

And she smiles again, but a different smile than before, a wider smile to show that he's beginning to see at last, a smile to show she's proud.

"Yeah, I am," she says. "Did you ever think there was more than one story? One's as good as the next. They're in all our stories, all the ones that matter. The path will lead you to the mere, Deacon. Stay on the path and don't believe the things they want you to believe and you might still be the hero in *this* story. Or, if Chance has to be the hero, you might keep her from falling. But there aren't any answers, and this will never make sense, not the way you want, so stop trying to force it to.

"Watch your step, Deacon. There are serpents in these woods, and hounds," and then she's gone, if she was ever there. Nothing left but the chimney and the rustling pine needles and all the patient, eternal voices of the forest.

Deacon pushes aside the last tangled veil of creeper and wild muscadine vines, and he's standing on a crumbling, chalksoft boulder at the edge of the pool. The noise of his shoes against the ground sends dozens of tiny frogs leaping from the rushes and bamboo thickets that line the water's edge, and they splash and vanish beneath the gently rippling surface of the pool. On his left, there's a small waterfall, the place where Wampee Creek leaves its bed and tumbles down a low, vertical outcrop of the yellowwhite limestone, the algae- and moss-slicked rocks, and if Chance were here she could tell him how old these rocks are, could put her scientific names to the imprints of ancient snails and clams that cover the stones at his feet.

The pool is wide, forty or fifty feet across, and the water so clear that he can see all the way to the bottom. The undulating forest of eel grass, flash and dart of silverfish shapes, and this late in the day there are strange shadows down there among the drowned logs and watchful turtle eyes. A sinkhole, Toomey said, and Deacon imagines this was once a small cave in the rock with the creek flowing over it, and one day its roof grew too thin, finally, too thin for the weight of the forest floor, the millennia of fallen leaves and pine straw. There must have been a violent, decisive moment when the earth opened up and the water rushed in to fill the void.

Deacon kneels on one knee at the edge of the pool, stares across it at the silent trees on the opposite shore, their snarled and crooked roots like lichengray knuckles, thirsty fingers abandoning the soil to gladly decay beneath the cool and crystal waters.

The mere . . . The stream down under the darkness of the hills, the flood under the earth.

There's a big snake over there, a copperhead, he thinks, stretched out to catch the last warmth of the day and keeping a mindful eye on him. Autumn-colored snake, viperchain of dusky browns and reds and golden scales and he nods at it respectfully, silently promising to keep his distance if the snake will exchange the favor.

"Don't you sweat it, Mr. Snake," he says. "I'll be out of here before you even know it," silly words to keep himself company because this is the loneliest place he's ever been, a loneliness that seems to rise out of the ground and drip down like syrup from the branches overhead. Not so much a *bad* place, a place where the things that people have done have left a stain or a bruise; he's seen more than his share of bad places, working for Hammond and just being the unlucky fuck he is, the houses and alleys and vacant lots that some people might call haunted. But this is different. This is worse, whether he could ever explain exactly why or not, and Deacon dips his fingers into the pool, breaking the surface, the transparent membrane between two worlds, and the water is as cold as ice.

And the pain carves its way through his head like a knife, bullets through his eyes and the back of his skull splattered across the ground. The acrid, bitter stink of dead fish and rotting oranges, and Deacon pulls his fingers back, pulls his hand away from the water, as if he doesn't know it's too late for that. His eyes squeezed shut tight, but that doesn't stop him from *seeing,* never has before and won't this time, either. The pool still right there in front of him, but the sun swallowed whole by a starveling night sky, midnight come to Shrove Wood in a single, timeless instant.

Somewhere very close he can hear a woman crying, close but this night so dark, just the faintest glimmers off the water, the dim forms of the trees and not much else. No moon, so no light but the glow from the distant, starspecked sky. And sometimes she's only screaming, not words, just the sound of being that afraid turned loose and pouring out of her, wild and inconsolable, and other times she's calling for her mother, *Momma, please, Momma make it stop now,* or she's calling Dancy, or she's praying. There's another voice, breathless, animal grunt past the impatient twigsnapping, vinetearing noises, something vast and heavy driving headlong through the dense underbrush, crushing anything that gets in its way.

Off towards the cabin, back the way he's come, Deacon can hear two more voices, Dancy and the old woman, both of them shouting frantically; "Julia, Julia where *are* you, child?" and "Momma! We're coming," and Deacon opens his eyes wide, the pain pressing at the backs of them like thumbs so it's a wonder they don't pop out and go rolling down his cheeks. He stares and stares into the dark, searching the velvet folds of the night for her.

"Julia Flammarion," he says, reaching for the revolver tucked into his jeans. "I can't see you. I can't see fucking shit," and there's a loud splash, then, somewhere off to his right, and struggling from the pool. The woman has stopped screaming, nothing from her now but a choking sputter, all the futile, strangling sounds that a drowning person makes.

"*No,* Grandmomma!" Dancy screams. "You might hit her instead," and Deacon turns away from the pool. Back there where the trail from the cabin makes one last turn and begins its gentle slope down to the water, there's a bobbing, yellow will-o'-the-wisp, a kerosene lantern gripped in Dancy's hands to light her face and the old woman's aiming the twin barrels of a shotgun straight at him.

"It's too late, Grandmomma! They're in the lake now," Dancy says. "It's too late," and Deacon slowly takes his hand off the butt of the pistol, turns towards the pool again. And now he *can* see something moving through the water, nothing he could ever put a name to, nothing he would ever want to try to name, those taut, ebony muscles and skin that glistens like oil, eyes that shine bluegreen fire, and the woman in its arms, still fighting as it drags her under.

And then the old woman squeezes the trigger and the big gun rips the Florida night apart, belching fire and gunpowder thunder, its killing load of buckshot, and Deacon braces himself for the blast. No way it can possibly miss him, except the night is dissolving, melting rapidly away in greasy strips to show the twilight that was waiting all along on the other side of his vision, this day that's ending instead of a night that was over a year and a half ago.

"Oh," he whispers as the last of the darkness leaks from the air. "Oh, god," and Deacon's on his hands and knees, vomiting all over the limestone boulder; there's nothing in his stomach to speak of and after the first hot rush of bile he's only dry heaving, cramping and his eyes full of tears, the pain in his head swelling. And maybe this time it'll just fucking kill him, he thinks. Maybe this is the last time and nobody's ever going to find his body, his bones gnawed clean and white, bleached by the sun until they crumble into dust and the merciful rain will wash him bit by bit into the welcoming, forgetful pool.

"Is *that* all you want, Mr. Silvey? A little trip down the Lethe," and Deacon looks up, blinking, and the hitchhiker is standing on the other side of the pool. He smiles his too-wide smile and squats down on the bank among the roots, slips his long fingers below the surface. "You should've just said somethin' before. Hell, I got all kinds of connections, you know."

Above him, the copperhead is draped across a low limb, dead snake bleeding from its crushed skull, venom and drops of blood, stickywet drops of life and death wasted on the water which is neither alive nor dead. The man stirs the pool with his hand and shakes his head.

"She told you there ain't no answers here, didn't she? I swear, that little whore has a mouth on her. Worse than her goddamn momma. Of course, that ain't nothing I hadn't already tried to tell you, if you'd half a mind to listen."

"You . . ." Deacon croaks, his throat raw and he gags again before he can say anything else. "You're the one, aren't you? The one that killed her mother."

The hitchhiker scratches thoughtfully at his chin, takes his other hand from the pool and holds it a few inches above the water, watches the crystal beads forming at the tips of his fingers and falling, one by one, back into the lake.

"No sir," he says. "That wasn't me. There are no answers here, Deke. No answers *anywhere*. That's what she said and she was right. No motherfucking answers."

Deacon's drawn the pistol and is pointing it at the man, but his hands are shaky and his eyes still watering so it's hard to see. He pulls the hammer back and "Maybe I'm losing interest in answers," he says.

"If I was you, I wouldn't go waving that thing at people unless you mean to go all the way," and the man stands and wipes his wet hand on his pants. "You're just not a killer. Not unless you count your own hopes and dreams, and maybe a pint bottle of Kentucky bourbon here and there."

Deacon stares down the pistol's stubby barrel and blinks, trying to clear his eyes, his mouth sour with the taste of vomit.

"Now, if it was the albino girl, if it was her pointing that thing at me, I *might* be worried. Say what you want about her, toys in the attic and all, but that little girl had the courage of her convictions. And you wanna know what else?"

"Shut up, fucker," Deacon says, because the tall man's voice is worse than his headache, full of edges sharp as steel and broken glass, twisting wormjawed voice digging its way into him and *All I have to do is pull the trigger*, he thinks. *All I have to do is pull the goddamn trigger*.

"You better use those five bullets you got wisely, Mr. Silvey, 'cause right now, out here, I ain't the only thing in these woods you got to worry about."

And now Deacon sees them, all the spindle legs and crimson eyes creeping out of the trees behind the man, separating themselves from the shadows, bones and twigs bundled together with barbed wire and string.

Serpents in these woods, and hounds.

"We like a little sport, now and again," the man says, smiles and this time his smile is as wide as the Cheshire Cat's, unreal, ear-to-ear grin and his teeth are huge and glint black like obsidian arrowheads.

"You start running now, Deacon Silvey, and we'll be along directly."

And Deacon lowers the pistol slow, because he doesn't need someone to tell him he's not a hero, and does exactly what the hitchhiker says, turns and runs back through the woods, down the path towards the cabin. The briars grab at his face and arms, thorns to scratch, to draw blood and stinging welts across his skin, and he makes it almost as far as the clearing before he hears them coming. The clumsy sounds they make moving through the trees, the dry rustle of leaves and *thump, thump, thump* of hard paws against the earth.

Past the clearing, the ruined cabin sinking swiftly into night and the fairy flicker of a hundred fireflies, and he's almost all the way to the Chevy before he stops and looks back. There's no sign of them, nothing but the darkening forest and the dirt road, no hitchhiker or ruby eyes slinking towards him through the gloom. Not even the pursuing noises they made. He's breathing so hard it's only a matter of time before he starts throwing up again, heart pounding and a stitch in his side and Deacon has no idea how long it's been since he's run, really *run*. Probably not since he was a kid, since before he took his first drink.

"There's nothing back there," he says, says it loud and angry to make himself brave, loud so the night slipping over Shrove Wood can hear him, so anything hiding in the night can hear. "Nothing at all," and he walks the last fifteen or twenty feet to the car. Deacon lays the pistol on the roof of the Chevy and reaches into his pocket for the keys, but he keeps his eyes on the dirt road, on the trees, because it's one thing to shout at the night and another thing altogether to believe a word of what he's said.

And the keys aren't in his pocket.

He bends over, squints through the driver's-side window and there they are, still dangling from the ignition switch. Too busy with the glove compartment and the gun, too worried about the time, to remember to put the goddamn keys in his pocket, and he swears and punches the glass hard, but it doesn't break. More likely he's broken his knuckles, broken his hand, and then he hears them again. Footsteps on the road and their eager, panting breath. He looks up and the hitchhiker is standing in front of the car, still standing on two feet but looking more like the twiggy dog things than any sort of man and he laughs a thin and hollow laugh.

"Is there a problem?" he asks, and Deacon thinks that it must be hard to talk through the knotted mess of wire and sticks that his face is becoming as the deceiving flesh peels back in dead and brittle ribbons to show what's underneath, what was always underneath. "Have we been careless again, Mr. Silvey?"

And right now what seems far more incredible to Deacon than anything he's seen, or imagined that he's seen, since turning onto Eleanore Road, since leaving Birmingham, is the calm and perfect clarity that washes over him as he stares into the hitchhiker's face. Clarity even through the smothering migraine, so maybe a stingy smidgen of strength locked away somewhere inside him after all, or this is simply how insanity feels. This detachment, and he reaches for the revolver lying on the top of the Chevy.

"I *told* you not to come here," the hitchhiker growls. "I showed you the cards and told you to get your ass back home," and then he can't say anything else because there's nothing left inside his mouth but bare bone and dog teeth, straw and copper wire. Deacon slams the butt of the pistol against the windshield, everything he has behind the blow, but the glass only cracks, concentric, spiderweb ring of a crack no bigger than a silver dollar. The hitchhiker's claws scrape loud against the hood of the car, as he clambers forward and leans towards Deacon, that skull loose and lolling on trashheap shoulders and for the second time Deacon cocks the pistol.

"I don't have *time* for this shit," he says, squeezes the trigger and the Chevy's window explodes, diamondshard shower of safety glass and the slug buries itself deep in the passenger seat. The shot louder than he ever would have thought from such a little gun, and the boom echoes and rolls away through Shrove Wood. Deacon unlocks the door and slides in behind the wheel, already turning the key in the ignition before he looks up at the hitchhiker again. But there's nothing out there now but the trees silhouetted against the indigo sky, a violetred rind of sunset above the forest, and he puts the Chevy into reverse and bounces backwards onto Eleanore Road.

CHAPTER THIRTEEN

In the Water Works

Dawn, and Chance sits alone on the floor of her attic bedroom in the big, white house that her great-grandfather built, sits with the loaded shotgun across her lap, a half-empty box of shells beside her, listens to the sounds still coming from the other side of the door. The restless, snuffling, animal noises from the narrow stairs that lead to the attic and the fainter, infrequent voices and less-recognizable commotions from downstairs. Outside, the sky is finally turning blue again, palest grayblue from first-light mauve, and the sun is beginning to dapple the leaves with a shifting wash of warmer colors, honey and amber against the summer greens; in the wide and cityclogged valley below the mountain, the sun glints bright off the distant windows of the downtown skyline, the high and sensible, unhaunted glass office buildings of another world.

Not like the zombie movies, surviving the night and now a clean, new day to drive away the monsters. Not like that at all. But she didn't expect it to be that way, because the voices have been telling her for hours that the sun makes no difference to them. Something that they'd rather avoid, but nothing that can stop them, and Chance has no reason to doubt the things they say. They told her that Sadie and Deacon wouldn't come back, that she was alone, and they were right about that, so why wouldn't they be right about the sun, as well? The slanted, yellow shaft of morning light through the bedroom window means nothing more than the time since Deacon left her here, at least twenty-four hours now, though she can't be sure exactly how long it's been. Deacon and Sadie both already gone when she woke up on Monday and she called Deacon's apartment and let the phone ring fourteen times before she finally hung up. Chance didn't bother calling again, because she knew there wasn't any point.

So all day Monday come and gone and nothing stranger than the persistent sense that she'd finally awakened from a long nightmare. She might even have been able to persuade herself that *was* the truth, every bit of this a bad dream, if not for the undeniable bits and pieces scattered around the house, all the inconveniently tangible remains: her ruined car, Dancy Flammarion's mangled duffel bag on the kitchen table and the marked-up copy of *Beowulf* on her chest of drawers, Sadie's bloodstained clothes in the bathroom, her grandmother's ledger. These grim souvenirs to give her madness form, to validate insanity, and finally the message that Alice Sprinkle left on her answering machine after she found the things Chance drew in colored chalk on the walls and ceiling of the lab.

"No, I won't call the police," she said. "I won't do that," but she would have the locks changed immediately and she left the name and phone number of a psychiatrist.

"Please get help, Chance. I'm sorry there wasn't more I could do for you."

And that's what Chance was thinking about when it started, when it started *again,* not long after midnight, sitting in the front porch swing drinking a Coke, sitting there in the dark, staring at the buckled place where her car was still jammed beneath the warped and broken boards: how quickly and completely her life had slipped away and how there was nothing she could ever do to get it back. Thinking about Alice's message and everything it meant, when she noticed the red eyes watching her from the edges of the yard. Eyes like hot, fireplace embers and at first she only stared back at them, not quite comprehending, too numb to feel the threat. And then, moving slow as stalking cats, cats stalking small and helpless animals, they began to come closer to the house and she could make out the rough shapes behind those eyes, but even then Chance didn't move, sat still and watched as they crept across the lawn towards her.

Come on, she thought, wondering if maybe they could hear the unspoken things inside her head. *Come on. You've already taken everything that matters to me anyway. Get it over with.*

Something like peace in that thought, something merciful in the simple, hopeless finality of it, but then they were near enough that she could clearly make out their faces, what they had instead of faces caught in the light of the living room windows, and Chance stood up and walked very slowly to the front door. Because it was plain enough to see these things had neither peace nor mercy to offer her, and she remembered Elise's face, Elise trapped in the writhing arms of something that would never die and would never let her die, either.

"It's only your memories keeping her there," one of the voices whispers from the other side of the bedroom door, a sexless, dog-throated voice like dry ice and burning straw. "Or don't you know that?" and Chance pumps the Winchester once and points it at the door, the door and the makeshift barricade of furniture.

"Your guilt," it says and downstairs, far away, there's laughter.

"Shut up," her finger on the trigger and she wants to shoot, but there would be a hole, then, a way in, a way for her to see out, and so she only stares at the door down the long, single barrel of the gun.

"If you truly want to help her, then you're pointing that shotgun in the wrong direction, little pig," the voice says; downstairs, the laughter is growing louder, getting hysterical, a lunatic's laughter working its way up through the floor and filling the bedroom like bad air.

"But all you have to do is turn it around. Open the door and we'll show you how. Open the door, Chance, and we'll do it *for* you."

And then something begins to scratch at the bottom of the door again, determined *scritch, scritch, scritch* of steelsharp claws against the old wood and without lowering the Winchester she scoots backwards, away from the sound, moving instinctively away from the door, towards the window and the brightening morning sun.

"It only hurts for an instant, and then nothing ever has to hurt again."

"*You* can die, too," she says to the voice, the scritching thing, and that's true. She knows that's true because she's already killed two of them downstairs. Just enough time for her to get to the gun before they found a way into the house, the gun and the box of shells from her grandfather's room, loading it as quickly as she could and when she looked up two of them were watching her from the hallway. The buckshot tore them apart, roared through the house and all these hours later her ears are still ringing.

A sound from the other side of the bedroom door like a deep, hitching breath or the wind pushed out before a summer storm, and downstairs the laughing ends as abruptly as it began. The scritching stops, too, but Chance doesn't lower the shotgun. Her arms are aching, her arms and shoulders, and the Winchester seems almost as heavy as if it were carved from stone, but she keeps it trained on the door, the white door and a chair stuck under the knob, the chest of drawers and the headboard of her bed.

"Little pig?" it whispers. "Can't you hear me, little pig? Aren't you listening?" and Chance slides a couple of feet farther away from the door, breaking the sunbeam now and it pours warm across her face, no idea how cold she was until that light touches her, no idea how tired, and she turns her head, lets the day wash pure and brilliant across her face. She shuts her eyes, drinking it in like medicine, strong and sobering medicine against madness.

That's what this is, isn't it? That's all this can be, she thinks, all of it too absurd to ever possibly be anything else. A crazy girl locked inside her house with a gun, locked up alone and hearing voices, seeing shit that isn't there. If she'd really fired the shots she remembers firing, someone would have heard, Mr. Eldridge next door would have heard and called the police. None of this anything but her life finally catching up with her, Elise the last straw and then Dancy just enough to push her over the edge. Just like Alice said, and hell, even Deacon didn't believe her.

"Little pig, little pig, let me come in," the voice whispers eagerly from behind the door. Chance opens her eyes and glances towards it, the muzzle of the shotgun dragging along the floor and she smiles, a weak, sick smile for her delusions, all the loss and hurt she's bottled up, hidden away, fucking *lived* through, and these sad and shabby horrors are the best that her mind can conjure.

"No," she says. "I *know* what you are now," and turns her face back to the sun.

And the staring, misshapen thing pressed against the attic window smiles back at her, a shadow clinging tightly to the roof by spider-thin legs or arms, and Chance screams and raises the Winchester. The clinging thing opens its jaws wide, a silent, straining yawn to mock her, and there are eyes inside that mouth, wild eyes, an albino's white rabbit eyes looking out at her. Chance pulls the trigger and the windowpane disintegrates in a deafening spray of buckshot and glass and stringy, black flesh.

Driving all night, drinking cup after scalding cup of sour, truckstop coffee to stay awake, bottles of Mountain Dew, and finally two foil packets of red ephedrine tablets that made his stomach hurt, made him feel like he was going to puke but kept his eyes wide open. Everything that might have already happened to Chance and Sadie to keep him moving and keep him from thinking too much about whatever he saw at the cabin, at the sinkhole, whatever chased him through Shrove Wood, all the way back to Eleanore Road. And then sunrise, and Birmingham, and Chance's house doesn't look any different than it did when he left.

He parks the Chevy halfway up the gravel driveway, cuts the engine, and sits there for a moment, gazing out at the house through the dirty windshield. Trying to see clearly past the adrenaline and cheap speed, the caffeine and fear, past jangling, strung-out nerves that want to color everything the same ruined shade of gray.

You just chill the fuck out, Deke. Get your goddamn head together before you go barging in there, scaring the shit out of them. And that's a good thought, Sadie and Chance safe and asleep in the musty sanctuary of that old house and *he's* the worst thing they have to fear, a very good thought, indeed, and he grabs hold of it like a drowning man clutching thin air and hangs on. He reaches beneath the seat and there's the pistol, still four bullets in the cylinder and it's not like he's going to need the damned thing, but a little insurance never hurt anyone, just in case. Deacon tucks it back into the front of his jeans and gets out of the car.

He makes it almost all the way to the front porch before Chance screams, has just enough time to look up before he hears the gunshot and the attic window explodes. Deacon ducks, covers his head with his arms, nothing but his own flesh to shield him from the jagged rain of glass and splinters, and one shard carves a long gash near his left elbow before it buries itself like a knife in the dewdamp grass at his feet. The blast echoes and fades as it rushes away from the house, escaping, losing itself at the speed of sound in the smoggy morning air, and Deacon stares down in surprise and shock at his own dark blood, blood to stain the glass that sliced his arm and the blood dripping steadily from his arm to the ground. A stickywet, crimson puddle of himself and the grass all around him littered with sparkling fragments of the window, and then Chance screams again.

Deacon forgets all about the blood and the pain, forgets the desperate, stupid fantasies that this house and those inside have somehow been spared, and he crosses the remaining distance to the porch in three or four long strides. No front steps, so he uses the wrecked Impala instead, clambers onto the trunk and from the trunk to the car's roof, rusty metal that pops loud and sags beneath his weight.

And that's when he sees all the ugly scrapes and gouges in the porch boards, and the front door busted in and hanging crooked and half off its hinges.

He calls out for Sadie, shouts her name twice at the top of his lungs, three times without a reply, before he draws the revolver, steps off the Impala onto the porch and the wood creaks underfoot. Behind him, the roof of the car pops back into shape and "Sadie!" he shouts again. "Goddamn it, somebody in there answer me!" but the morning is quiet and still, no birds or insects, not even the sound of cars down on Sixteenth to break the spell.

Deacon cocks the hammer and takes a step towards the door, another step and from here he can see that the gouges don't end at the threshold; the doorsill torn completely away and the scrape marks disappear into the house, as if someone's dragged the tines of a heavy, iron rake across the wood.

Or claws, he thinks. *Claws could do that,* remembering the marks the hitchhiker left on the hood of Soda's car. He holds the gun out in front of him, both hands around the butt of the pistol, cold steel and plastic slick against his sweaty palms, and he follows the marks into the house.

Chance sits with her back to the wall, squeezed into the corner where her bed used to be, before she pulled it apart to build the barricade. From here she can see the window and the bedroom door, so no more nasty surprises. No more misdirection, getting her to look the other way while something comes sneaking up from behind. There are a few tatters of flesh and gristle the greenblack of ripe avocado skin draped across the windowsill, a few oily spatters on her face and arms, but most of the thing went over the side. She has the box of 20-gauge Federal cartridges in her lap now and takes turns pointing the shotgun at the door and the shattered window, rests the barrel on her knee, trying to take a little of the weight off her arms.

The scratching and snuffling noises have stopped, nothing at all from the stairs since she pulled the trigger, so maybe they've gone. Maybe three's her lucky number and they have better things to do than getting picked off one by one. Or maybe she just can't hear them anymore, the ringing in her ears so loud now that she might be deaf for life. Her right arm and shoulder hurt like hell from the recoil and there's probably already a bruise, something in there dislocated or broken for all she knows.

"Listen to them, Chance, please," and Sadie is standing in the shadows on the other side of the room. Sadie just like the last time Chance saw her, the green shirt from her grandfather's closet, the borrowed boots too big for her feet, her black hair like it's never been introduced to a comb. And blood. Her skin and clothes slicked with dried and clotting blood like she's bathed in the stuff, like someone drowned in blood and come back, slaughterhouse Ophelia, and when she opens her mouth to speak it leaks from her lips and runs down her chin.

"They only want us not to think about them," she says and then a pause and she rubs at her left temple, rubs like she has a headache or is trying hard to remember something very important that she's almost forgotten. "Our thoughts make spirals in their world," she says.

"You're not Sadie Jasper," and Chance pumps the shotgun again, aiming at Sadie now instead of the door or the window. "I know they want me to think you're Sadie, but you're not her."

Sadie rubs at her head again, pain or a frantic concentration in that gesture, that maroonslick mask passing itself off as her face, grotesque parody of Sadie trying to remember something that's right there on the tip of her tongue. Something she must have known for certain only a second ago and she gazes at the floor for a moment and then looks back to Chance.

"I *told* them that I wouldn't be Sadie like this. Not like this. But they didn't give me a choice. Please, Chance. They won't let me go. They won't let *any* of us go, until no one knows about them anymore."

"I don't believe you," Chance says, knows that she's lying, but right now a lie that even she doesn't believe is better than the alternative, so she says it again. "I don't believe you're Sadie."

Sadie looks towards the ceiling and smiles, more blood spilling from her mouth, and she raises her arms as if she would worship the sky hidden beyond paint and plaster and shingles, her ghostblue eyes like someone who's waited a thousand years to be even this close to the sun again.

"Don't make me do this, Sadie," Chance says, realizes that she's crying now, hot tears streaking her face, salt to sting her eyes, and she slips her trembling index finger through the trigger guard. "Go back and tell them not to make me do this to you."

Sadie closes her eyes and her head droops to one side, but her face still turned towards the unseen morning sky. When she speaks, it's the deliberate speech of someone reciting a poem or a pledge, something memorized and care taken with each and every word.

"Where great things go on unceasingly . . . yet wholly different in kind . . . where immense and terrible personalities hurry by, intent on vast purposes . . . *vast* purposes, Chance."

And Chance is getting to her feet, back braced against the wall and the sudden swell and surge of anger to give her strength, despite the exhaustion and the fear, the ache in her shoulder.

"Are you really that *afraid* of me?" she screams at the barricaded door, screams through her tears, and something on the stairs begins to mutter excitedly to itself or something else. "You cowardly fuckers, you cowardly, fucking *shits*. You *are* afraid, aren't you? You *can't* do this yourself. You're too goddamn scared of dying to even *try*."

Sadie opens her eyes, raises her head, and she watches Chance. Like someone watching the world slipping away from them, and slowly she lowers her arms.

"You're *dead,* Sadie," Chance whispers, whispers like someone pleading with a drunk who wants to drive, a sleepy child who refuses to go to bed. And Sadie smiles again, smiles and shows teeth but not her teeth, crooked, needle teeth like a blind, abyssal fish, row upon row stained crimson and gums as black as coal.

"The division," she says and hugs herself, arms tight around her own shoulders like she's freezing, speaking from some white and polar place. "The division here is *so* thin that it leaks through somehow. Their *sound* . . . the humming of their region . . . It's *in* the willows. It's the willows themselves humming, because here the willows have been made symbols of the forces that are against us."

Chance raises the shotgun and aims it at Sadie's face, and the dead girl glares stubbornly back at her.

"Not the willows. I didn't mean to say that. It's the *trilobites,* Chance. The trilobites your grandmother found, and the thing in the bottle—"

"Please god, Sadie," Chance says, "I can't handle any more of this. I fucking swear I can't," and she takes a step towards Sadie, closing the distance between them because she knows she'll never be able to pull the trigger again if she misses the first time.

"You're not *listening* to me, Chance. Do you know how much this fucking *hurts* and you're not even listening," and now Sadie has changed, Sadie or the fabrication that only wants her to believe it's Sadie, if that makes any difference. Those blue eyes bright and furious and it moves so quickly that Chance doesn't have time to shoot, seems to slide across the bedroom floor like butter across a hot skillet, a thousand times smoother than that even: motion without the slightest effort, without the burden of time or distance. And Sadie has *grown*, no more of her than before but what there is stretched somehow, and now the shotgun's clutched in the twiggy fingers of her left hand, Chance's chin held painfully in her right.

"I'm not supposed to tell you *anything*, bitch," Sadie says, hisses angry past all those barbed and crooked teeth. "But you learn, over here."

Outside, something has started slamming itself repeatedly against the bedroom door, something hitting the door like a battering ram, *blam, blam, blam*, and already the wood has begun to warp and crack. Another minute and it'll be in the room with them.

"It's what the trilobites *mean*," Sadie says, Wonderland nightmare after the drink-me bottle, and so now she has to crouch down low to look Chance in the eyes. "Time, and what people find when they start looking in time. The willows, if they look in the tunnel. If they look behind the wall."

Sadie leans very close then, her lips pressed to Chance's ear, whispering, and her lips are cold but her voice is colder, the freezing words pouring out of her and "I don't give a shit about *you*," she says. "But Dancy's in here, and I won't have them getting Deacon, too."

And the other things she says, instructions before the door comes apart like it was made of paper and matchsticks, her flimsy barricade pushed aside easy as dollhouse furniture. Sadie dissolves, melts away to nothing as the long-legged thing pauses in the doorway, and it turns its wire and bleached-bone muzzle towards Chance and howls. An eternity of cheated, vengeful rage in that howl, in its hateful, scarlet eyes, and Chance doesn't stop to wonder how the shotgun got back into her hands before she pulls the trigger.

The gouges in the hardwood floorboards lead Deacon from the foyer down the hall to the staircase, and he stands staring up into the shadows and half-light waiting for him on the landing. Each of the steps as scarred as the porch, as the hallway, burnished and shoesmoothed pine damaged beyond repair, and there are wide, parallel grooves dug into the wall, too, the blue wallpaper torn and hanging down in ragged strips so he can see the ivorywhite plaster underneath. He glances back towards the front door, sunlight and the way back to the world, and calls Sadie's name again.

"I'm afraid Miss Jasper is occupied at the moment," and the hitchhiker steps out of the gloom at the top of the stairs. His dark eyes and oilslick hair, narrow, hatchet face and high, stubbled cheekbones, and he scowls down at Deacon.

"She's attending to a few loose ends for us, just now."

And Deacon doesn't wait for him to say anything else, fires the revolver and hits the hitchhiker in the right shoulder near his collarbone. There's a dark spray of blood as the man stumbles backwards, grabs the banister to keep from falling and now he's grinning the way he did back at the pool, that ear-to-ear Cheshire grin, those teeth like antique piano keys.

"*Damn*, Deke. That's some fancy goddamn shootin'," he says and steadies himself, lets go of the banister and gently touches the hole in his shoulder with two fingers, stares at the blood on his hand and shakes his head. "But how many bullets does that leave you now? Three?"

Deacon pulls back the hammer again and this time he aims more carefully, aims at the hitchhiker's face, the furrowed spot between his eyes, but Deacon's hands are shaking like an old man's. Palsied old man's tremble, drunkard's unsteady aim, and "How long *has* it been since you had a drink, Mr. Silvey?" the hitchhiker asks. "'Cause, personally, I'm thinking you're looking pretty dry. Couple of belts of something stiff and you might even have a chance. A little Jack, say, or maybe—"

Deacon squeezes the trigger again but this time the hammer clicks hollow and useless on an empty chamber.

"*Hey*. Now, I honestly can't say I saw *that* one coming," and the grinning hitchhiker is swaggering down the stairs towards him. "You gotta watch out for stuff like that, boy. Make sure all your ducks are in a row, if you get my meaning."

"You just keep right on coming, you smiling bastard," Deacon says, cocking the gun again, but then something is blocking the sunlight from the front door, eclipse at the edge of his vision to draw his attention away from the man on the stairs. Something like a dog that Deacon knows isn't really anything like a dog, familiar and monstrous silhouette, and "See there? That's just exactly the sort of shit I'm talking about," the hitchhiker says.

The thing coming down the hallway towards Deacon makes a parched and barren sound in its scarecrow throat, a thirsty sound, and now Deacon can see that there's another one of them right behind it. The whole house full of them, maybe, and he glances back at the hitchhiker, the tall man and his long, slicked-back hair, his wolf-friendly manners.

"The devil and the deep, blue sea, Mr. Silvey," he says. "That ol' Scylla and Charybdis dilemma. A rock and a hard goddamn place. But now it's *your* move, you and that little pop gun of yours. Or ain't you bothered to think that far ahead?"

Deacon looks at the things in the hall again, deadgray meat for tongues dangling dry and hungry from their jaws and the man is standing only three or four steps above him now.

"Call those motherfuckers off," he says. "Get the hell out of my way, or I'm going to put the next bullet through your ugly, fucking face."

The man takes one more step towards him and stops; he isn't smiling anymore, something on his face that's so much worse; whatever comes after the most exquisite extremes of spite, after the most studied malevolence. His slashthin lips like a wound, an unhealing, unhealable violation of flesh, and Deacon's heart is racing, trying to fight its way out of his chest. This man's face to steal away the last flimsy pretense of courage, and "Where the hell do you *get* this crap, Deke? Jesus, you know what you sound like? You sound like a goddamn nigger pimp, talkin' shit like that."

"Get out of my way," Deacon says again, each syllable punched out as slow and calm and hard as he can manage, but his voice quavering all the same. He's pointing the revolver at the hitchhiker's left eye and there's no way he could ever miss now, not even the way his hands are shaking.

But the man on the stairs shrugs his wide shoulders and "Checkmate," he says, opens his right hand and there are three shiny .38 cartridges in his palm. Fine blond hair on his palm and those three bullets and Deacon squeezes the trigger anyway, but there's only the dull click of the hammer falling on an empty chamber.

The hitchhiker's eyes glint as silver as new ball bearings and he lets the bullets roll out of his hand and bounce down the stairs to lie at Deacon's feet.

"Neat trick, huh? Wanna see another one?"

"Get out of the way, Deke," Chance says and Deacon sees her at the top of the stairs, sees the big shotgun in her arms, and then the hitchhiker turns around and he sees her, too.

"You tell them I'm coming," she says to the tall man, and Deacon falls to his knees as the shotgun tears the silent morning apart.

Chance behind the wheel of the old Chevy, driving too fast, ignoring stop signs, and Deacon's in the passenger seat with a damp washcloth pressed to his forehead and a full bottle of whiskey clamped between his knees. Still a steady trickle of blood down his forehead from where the buckshot grazed his scalp, his left ear, too, and it's a wonder she didn't blow *his* goddamn head off. His face is smeared with the hitchhiker's inkdark blood, his clothes soaked through with it, blood the color of India ink and it smells like soured milk and ammonia.

"*You're* gonna kill us if you don't slow the fuck down," he says, twists the cap off the whiskey with one hand, and Chance misses the rear bumper of a parked SUV by only an inch or two, maybe less. "Jesus, it's *over,* okay? All we have to do is find Sadie and—"

"She's dead," Chance says. "Sadie's dead, Deke," and she doesn't even take her eyes off the road, her face still as utterly unreadable as the moment he first saw her at the top of the stairs, that expression so intense and emotionless, both at once, and he looks away from her, stares at the plastic cap in his right hand.

The Chevy bounces violently over a speed bump, illegal shortcut across a convenience store parking lot. "I think she went to the tunnel after you left," Chance says. "There's a page missing from the ledger. I think she tried to get inside."

Deacon raises the bottle slowly to his lips and a few precious drops slosh out onto his hand; the bourbon smells almost like solace, like mercy. "How do you know she's dead?" he says.

"She told me," Chance replies, says it almost the same way someone might mention the weather or the time of day. Deacon takes a swig from the bottle, long and scorching swallow, burning swallow but nothing that can burn him deeply enough, burn the knot from his soul; he screws the cap back on the whiskey and stares out the window at Southside rushing by outside the car.

"I don't think I believe you," he says very quietly.

"I'm sorry," and Chance turns left. The tires screech like birds and she runs a red light.

"We have to go to the apartment," Deacon says, taking the cap off the bottle of whiskey again. "She might be waiting for me there."

"She's *dead*, Deacon. Just like Dancy's dead. Just like Elise."

"*No,*" he says, the violence coiled inside him close enough to the surface now that it shows, that he can hear it, and Chance slows down a little.

"There isn't *time* for this," she says. "It might be too late already."

"Too late for *what*, Chance? *It is over.* You shot the bastard," and Deacon points at the Winchester in the backseat. "You killed him and all the rest of them. They're lying back there in your house, dead, and I'm asking you to turn this goddamn car around and take me home. *Now.*"

Chance shakes her head and "It's not over," she says. "We're still alive, so it can't be over yet. It can't be over until there's no one left who knows what we found in that crate or what's written in the ledger or—"

"Chance, I'm not going to ask you again."

" 'Our thoughts make spirals in their world.' That's what she said, but I don't know what it means."

"Chance, you sound like a psycho, like a deranged lunatic, do you know that? Like you've lost your fucking mind," and she smiles, then, the way that crazy people in the movies smile sometimes. Secret, certain smile that scares him almost as bad as the hitchhiker and the dog things scared him.

"Sadie said you wouldn't believe me. She said I should ask you about the yods, and about meeting Dancy in the woods. That you might believe me then."

"The yods," he whispers, tiredsoft whisper, end of his rope whisper, and Deacon reaches for the door handle, the big bottle of Jim Beam tumbling to the floorboard between his feet, spilling across the tops of his shoes as he opens the car door. And he stares down at all that asphalt and concrete flying by, rough and unforgiving as time, as every moment of his life, leans out towards it, this stretch of road as good a place as any other to get it over with. Enough already, running on empty for years now, anyway, running on fumes, just the whiskey and beer to make it bearable.

Question is, what's waiting for you at the end?

What'll be left when you get back home?

But someone's hauling him back, Chance cursing and she's hauling him back into the car by his hair, one hand off the steering wheel and the Chevy swerves suddenly towards a telephone pole. "Oh no. Not yet you don't," she says. "I can't do this alone," and the door smacks into creosote-stained pine a second later, slams shut again and the window shatters in a crystalbright shower of glass.

"Not both of you," Chance says, pulling over to the curb, the brakes squealing as the Chevy rolls to a stop. "It doesn't get you *and* Elise, not unless it gets me, too."

Deacon stares at the glass in his lap, the crumpled door that'll probably never open again, at least not without a crowbar, and then he reaches down and picks up the whiskey bottle. Still a few good swallows left in there, three or four if he's lucky, and he wipes the mouth of the bottle clean with his palm.

"Just take me home first, Chance," he says and all the anger's gone now, nothing left to his voice but resignation and the thinnest rind of sadness around the edges. "Please. That's all. I just need to see that she isn't there, then we'll do whatever the hell you want."

"Yeah, okay," Chance says, sounding skeptical, breathless, and the fingers of her right hand still tangled in his hair, both her green eyes fixed on him. "If that's what it takes," and after a huge, pumpkin-yellow school bus rumbles past, she turns the car around and heads east, towards Quinlan Castle, driving into the morning sun.

The first time she's been in the castle since they split up, three months or more but everything exactly the same, the same squalid hallways, the same cloying stink of mildew and fried food, and she follows Deacon upstairs to the red door of his apartment.

First he knocks and they wait, and then he knocks again, but no one comes to the door. He tries the knob, turns antique brass painted the same unsightly shade of red as the door, but it's locked. "Do you even have your keys? Maybe Sadie had them," Chance says impatiently, as he digs about in the pockets of his pants; his keys are there, his *one* key, the one that opens this door hanging from a rubber Bullwinkle key ring. Something that she gave him for his birthday two years ago, because he likes those old cartoons, or at least he liked them then.

"Sadie said she left the door open. When she left Saturday night," he says. "She said she didn't even shut it," and he turns the key in the lock.

"Maybe it was the landlord . . ." Chance begins, but she stops herself, can see what he wants to believe, what he's *hoping*, that Sadie *has* been back, after all, that she's the one who locked the door and Chance is either lying or crazy or both. Full of shit, either way, and the door swings open, then, creaks loud on rustdry hinges, louder because the only other sound is a television blaring from the apartment directly across the hall. Chance remembers the old woman who lives there, the senile old woman and her greasy-looking little dog.

Deacon stands in the doorway for a moment, staring into the sunlit apartment. "Sadie? Are you here, baby?" When no one answers him, he steps across the threshold and looks over his shoulder at Chance.

"I had to know," he says. "I had to know for sure."

"I understand," and she does, but looks down at the floor because she doesn't want to see the emptiness in his eyes, the pain on his face so eager to fill it in.

"Well, come on," he says. "Let's see what there is to see," and he draws the revolver from his jeans, the stubby gun and the three bullets he picked up from the foot of the stairs. "We've come this far."

But there really isn't anything *to* see. Just Deacon's shabby apartment, his paperback books and Sadie's clothes, the posters for goth and black metal bands that weren't there before, so those must be Sadie's, too. But they walk through the whole place twice. And the second time around the bedroom Chance notices the squat, gray Macintosh computer sitting on the floor beside the bed. Even more decrepit than the donated LC II in the paleo' lab and it looks like someone's smashed in the screen with a hammer or the toe of their boot.

"Was it like that before?" she asks him, pointing at the Mac. Deacon shakes his head, slips the revolver back into his jeans, and steps past her, squats down next to the computer and picks something up off the carpet; a crushed handful of blue plastic and it takes Chance a moment to realize that it's what's left of a diskette.

"It was her novel," he says, laughs a hard, humorless laugh and lays the broken disk on top of the computer. "She was trying to write a novel. I made her keep this as a back-up." And then he sits down on the floor, leans back against the bed and stares up at the ceiling.

"She never let me read it."

"Sadie was like that," Chance says and immediately wishes that she hadn't, probably not her place to say anything at all, but Deacon nods, turns his face towards her, and "Yeah, I guess she was," he says.

"She always thought I hated her, didn't she?"

He's staring at the ceiling again, like there's something up there that she can't see. "I think Sadie thought you were evil incarnate," he says. "She was afraid of you."

"I never wanted it to be like that."

"Yeah, well, whatever. It sure as hell doesn't matter now, does it?" and Deacon closes his eyes.

Chance glances at the clock radio beside the bed, the red digital numbers there to remind her how much of the morning's slipped past already, how much time she's lost, and she wants to say *We can't stay here. It's not safe,* but that's so much like Dancy that it scares her. A little surprised that she can still be frightened, after what she's seen, what she's done, the shit in her head that will always be there now, no matter what happens next.

"Deacon, you said that you'd help me, if we came back here first," and he picks up the crushed diskette again, holds it a few inches from his face, trying to read Sadie's handwriting, the purple cursive scrawl on a crumpled Kinko's label.

"Yeah," he says. "I did, didn't I."

"I can't hold you to that promise. Not if this is as far as you can go." She pauses and now he's watching her, the hot threat of tears in his brown and bloodshot eyes. "Maybe this is something I was always supposed to do on my own. Maybe that's just the way it has to be."

"Not a chance," he says and almost smiles at the unintended pun, a fleeting quiver at the corners of his mouth, then he looks away, lays the disk gently on top of the computer again and turns his face away, towards the bedroom window. "You're the only thing I've got left now, whether you like it or not."

Chance sits down on the floor beside him, and for almost a minute neither of them says anything else, nothing but the babble from the old woman's television coming through the walls.

"So what's next, chief," he says and she takes his right hand in her left and holds it tight. Holds it the way she used to, when she loved him and the only monsters in her world came from the bottoms of his empty liquor bottles.

"There's some stuff I need from the lab, if I can still get in. And then we go back to the tunnel."

"The tunnel," he says, the tone in his voice to show there was never any doubt, only ever one possible answer to his question, and Chance doesn't have to see his face to know that he's started crying. "And what exactly do we do when we get there?"

"We're going to blow the fucker up," she says and Deacon laughs. "What good's that going to do?"

"I guess we'll see," Chance whispers, and they sit together on the floor for a few more minutes, listening to the traffic.

❖

Most of the morning behind them by the time Chance and Deacon make it back up the mountain to the tunnel. The sun beating down on them like it knows exactly what they're up to and maybe it doesn't approve, reproachful sunshine to bake the little park at the end of Nineteenth Street, but a few low, grayblue clouds gathering in the sky, too. Chance stops in the shade of a magnolia tree and gets out of the Chevy, and then Deacon climbs out after her, has to climb over the driver's seat because his door won't open, and he gazes up at that sun, that sky, the scattered clouds like bruised and wayward sheep. It could rain later on, late afternoon thunderstorms, lightning and a drenching downpour, and that wouldn't be so bad, he thinks. That wouldn't be so bad at all.

Chance has the trunk open, is already busy pulling everything out and setting it down on the white cement pavement at their feet. No trouble getting into the lab after all, and no one around to start asking questions, either; Chance's keys still good despite her concern.

"Maintenance is so damn slow it'll likely be at least another week before the locks are changed," she told him. "*If* Alice actually meant what she said."

He didn't bother asking what it was Alice had said, much more interested in why there were two cases of dynamite stored in the university's paleontology lab, so she explained quickly, while they gathered all the things on the list in her head. These two cases left over from a seismic survey project a year ago and "Just like sonar signals," she said. "Only we're looking through solid rock instead of water."

"And you know how to use this stuff?"

She nodded. "I picked up a few bucks that summer working on the survey. There's nothing to it, really," as she handed him a box of electric detonators. "It's almost as easy as jump-starting a car."

The very last thing out of the trunk is a slightly tattered, olive-drab canvas backpack, USMC stenciled across the flap and it's stuffed with a dozen or so of the brown sticks of dynamite. Chance slips a strap over one shoulder and closes the trunk.

"*Wear* this. I mean it," she says, handing him one of the two neon-orange hard hats. He puts it on his head, feels like he's in fifth grade again and all he needs now is a bright orange flag and vest to stop traffic so the younger kids can cross the street. "You actually think there's some possibility we're gonna live through this?" he says and she shrugs, puts on her own hard hat, adjusts the chin strap.

"Force of habit," and she frowns and glances back down the street, no way to be sure if anyone's watching them, far too many porches and windows, and "Don't forget the shotgun," she says. "And put some of those shells in your pockets."

When Chance is sure they have everything, that nothing has been forgotten, not the guns or the hacksaw or the flashlights, the bundle of copper wire and the big twelve-volt Eveready battery, her grandmother's ledger, they follow the winding path through the dogwoods towards the water works tunnel. Most of the twine that Dancy tied to the trees is still there and Deacon wishes someone had come along and torn it down.

"I shouldn't have gone," he says; Chance looks at him as if she doesn't know what he's talking about when he knows damn well she does.

"I should have stayed here with you and Sadie."

"I don't think it would have made much difference," she says. "They would have come for us anyway, sooner or later."

"But Sadie might still be alive if I'd stayed, if I'd done like you asked."

Chance sighs, a sound that's more weary than exasperated, and "Yeah," she says. "Sure, and if I'd listened to Dancy in the first place, if we'd all stayed together on Saturday afternoon, maybe *everything* would be different. We can play this game all day long, Deke. It's not going to change anything."

"No, but I should have talked when you asked me to. Hell, I should have done it a long time ago."

"What should you have talked about, Deacon?"

"About what happened that night we all broke into the tunnel, me and you and Elise," and now she stops and stares at him, shifts the heavy backpack from one shoulder to the other. Another one of those unfathomable expressions on her face, nothing he wants to see, and he turns away.

"No, you're right, Chance. It *doesn't* matter now, but I just wanted you to know I was wrong and I'm sorry. You were always the smart one," and he starts walking again, then, watching the dingy toes of his shoes and it's a moment before he hears her footsteps following behind him.

Around the last bend in the trail, past the last row of dogwood trees, and Chance whispers something, a curse or exclamation muttered under her breath, a word Deacon doesn't quite catch, but the tone of her voice enough that he looks up, and there's the blockhouse waiting for them, and the design Chance showed him from the ledger; the heptagon inside the star, sloppy black paint on the weathered stone wall and the gated entryway into the tunnel set right at its center.

"Sadie must have done that," Chance says.

"Why? What the fuck did she think she was doing?" and his eyes trace the crooked, intersecting lines, all the sides and angles and the whole that they add up to in the end. There are other things, as well, a brush and a small can of black paint tipped over on its side, a flashlight and a pair of long-handled shears, a crumpled paper bag, and Deacon leans down and picks up the flashlight. He flips the switch and the tiny bulb shines dimly in the sunlight.

"She was trying to get in," Chance says. "Trying to find Dancy. Jesus, she was calling them. I think this is my fault, Deacon."

"Why is this your fault? Did you *tell* her to do this?"

"No, I didn't, but she asked me about the design—"

"Bullshit," Deacon says and switches the flashlight off again, tosses it away, into a patch of poison ivy and honeysuckle growing near the blockhouse. "Sadie was a big girl, Chance. Whatever she did here, there's no one to blame but her. Let's just get this over with."

"Yeah," Chance says. "Sounds like a plan," but she doesn't take her eyes off the thing painted on the wall while Deacon takes the hacksaw to the padlock.

Past the entrance to the water works tunnel, the wider, anteroom half-light of the blockhouse where the enormous elbow bends of the two pipes turn downwards to burrow like giant and cast-iron worms into the moldering earth. The pipes so wide there's hardly enough space left to walk single file, Chance in the lead, Chance with her loaded shotgun and the dynamite and Deacon right behind her, the revolver in one hand and a flashlight in the other. Beneath their feet, the tunnel floor alternates between slick stone and ankle-deep mud, and Chance has almost fallen twice already.

"I don't remember it smelling this bad," Deacon says and his voice seems very big in the tunnel.

Chance shines her own flashlight up at the ceiling, ceiling so low that Deacon has to walk stooped over. There are small stalactites growing down from the limestone, uneven flowstone teeth glistening with groundwater. Below them are patches of travertine on the pipes themselves, calcite leached drop by drop from the rocks overhead and redeposited there.

"You were pretty baked," she says. "We all were," and hasn't that always been the explanation for whatever happened to them that night, Chance thinks. The times that Elise tried to get them to talk about it, and "We were stoned," Deke would say, or Chance would say it for him.

"I wasn't *that* stoned," Deacon says. "It smells like something died in here."

"It's just mold and bat guano, all this stagnant water," saying those things like she might actually believe they're the reason the tunnel stinks like rotting meat, charnel house reek that's making her eyes water, making her nauseous.

"I don't see any fucking bats in here," Deacon says.

"Trust me, Deke. They're around here somewhere. Probably hundreds of them," but she hasn't seen them either, the ubiquitous small brown bats that use almost all the mountain's abandoned mine shafts and natural caves for their colonies. But perhaps it's just that they're all a little farther in, not so close to the entrance, the noise from the street and the park to drive them back deeper than usual.

Chance's left arm brushes against one of the water pipes, brushes iron that feels dusty and dank at the same time, and she flinches, pulls back, something unwholesome in that juxtaposition of wet and dry.

"It can't be much farther," she says. "We have to be getting pretty close now," if her grandmother's notes are right, only twelve hundred feet or so from the blockhouse door, not far past the point where the Ordovician limestones change over to the redviolet sandstones and shales of the younger Red Mountain Formation.

So why didn't I notice it before? Why didn't I see a brick wall in April? and of course the always-handy answer that she was simply too high to notice, they were all too high. So high they managed to get lost walking in a straight line and wander around in here for hours before Deacon finally found the way out again. She stops to look back at him, looking back for a reassuring glimpse of sunlight, but the tunnel behind them is as perfectly dark as a night without the moon, without so much as city lights to trouble the blackness.

"It's started," she says and Deacon turns and looks back too. "We must have gone around a corner somewhere," he says and Chance shakes her head.

"No. It's a straight line, Deke. All the way from one end to the other."

"Then the pipes are getting in the way, that's all."

"You don't believe that any more than I do," she says, wishing that she'd brought a compass along, or some strong nylon cord to tie the two of them together.

"Just keep moving," he says. "That's all we can do now," and he gives her a little push, not hard, but hard enough, so Chance wrestles her feet free of the mud and starts walking again. *Just keep moving*, like he said and all the light she needs is right there in her hand, shining clean and white to show her the way.

"Talk to me, Chance," Deacon says. "Remind me what the hell it is we're looking for again," and she can tell that he's trying not to sound scared, but she knows him too well to be fooled, too well to fool herself.

"A wall. A brick wall. It's going to be on our right, I think, on the west side of the tunnel."

"A wall. A fucking brick wall on the right side of the tunnel," and he bumps into her, apologizes, and "So tell me about the rocks," he says. "How old are these rocks?"

Chance plays the beam of her flashlight across the roof of the tunnel again, relieved that he's changed the subject, because they're better off if she doesn't have to start talking about what might be on the other side of that brick wall, the things that Sadie whispered and her grandmother only hinted at, the things the workmen found down here more than a hundred years ago and built that wall against. The smallest part of it trapped inside a jar of alcohol, and so she concentrates instead on the maroon strata above them.

"Well, we're out of the Chickamauga Limestone now and coming into the Red Mountain. We're right at the bottom of the Silurian, so these beds are maybe four hundred and thirty million years old. The rocks will keep getting younger as we go, the way they're tilted." She has to stop and clear her throat, the meaty, rotten smell grown so strong that she can taste it, and Chance wishes she had a hand free to cover her mouth.

"And after the Silurian, then the rocks are Devonian age, right? You explained that to me once, remember?"

"Yeah," she says. "But I didn't think you would."

"Hey, I've still got a few brain cells left. The booze hasn't pickled them all—"

And then a sound, hollow, reverberating clang like someone's striking one of the pipes with a hammer, banging on it with a fucking sledgehammer. Noise so vast, so deep it rolls over them like an ocean wave, fills the tunnel from wall to wall, but no way to tell if it came from behind them or from somewhere up ahead.

"Don't think about it," Deacon says, but her head is still so full of the sound that he seems to be speaking from somewhere else far, far away. "Just keep talking to me, Chance. What comes next, after the Devonian?"

"The Mississippian. The Mississippian Period comes next, Deke," and she stops walking, then, stops so suddenly that he runs into her again, almost knocks her off her feet this time.

"The Mississippian," she says again. "The Maury and Fort Payne Chert formations," and that's all she has to say, because they've come to the wall, finally, unremarkable brick wall maybe four feet across, and Chance lays the shotgun down on one of the pipes, reaches out and runs the tips of her fingers gently across the damp masonry. Bricks laid here and mortar set in 1888, when her great-grandfathers were still young men and Birmingham was hardly more than a few dirt streets, a rough and coaldust cluster of steel mills and mining camps.

"Jesus, that's it," Deacon says, somewhere close behind her.

"Yeah, that's it," she replies. Her fingers still pressed against the bricks, and they're more than wet, more than cold, some sensation she doesn't have a word for because she's never even imagined it. *Waxy,* she thinks, trying to fill in the blank anyway, but waxy isn't even close to the way the wall feels.

"This is where it's coming from," she says, and slides the pack off her shoulder, sets it carefully down in the mud at the base of the wall, but doesn't take her hand away from the bricks.

"They found something down here, didn't they, Chance? When they were digging this damn tunnel, they woke something up. It's like the sinkhole by the cabin," and she doesn't ask him what sinkhole, what he's talking about, the time for all these questions come and gone and if there ever were such easy answers those are past, as well. Swallowed by the years, the decades, the way the tunnel has swallowed the light from the blockhouse gate.

"Can't you *feel* it?" she asks, and surely he can, surely Deacon Silvey of all people can feel it pouring out through this insubstantial barrier, leaking through the gaps between atoms as if these bricks were no more solid than screen wire. *Time, and what people find when they start looking in time,* Sadie said, and that's only a beginning, Chance thinks, one baby step towards comprehending what's hidden behind this wall. A thousand metaphors and she'd never come any closer, a seeping place where two worlds meet, where all worlds and all times meet, black hole, white hole, a *crossroads* and that's as good a way as any other of looking at it.

They used to bury suicides at crossroads, and "Shit," Deacon hisses and when she looks up he's holding the shotgun, pointing it at the dark, aiming back the way they came or the way they haven't gone yet. Impossible for her to be sure which is which, no point of reference anymore, nothing but this wall and two feeble beams of electric light.

"Christ, did you *hear* that?" he asks and she shakes her head no.

"I didn't hear anything, Deke."

She takes a deep, deep breath and pulls her fingers away from the wall, and she's surprised when it lets her do that, surprised when she isn't touching it anymore. *It didn't have to let me. It could have held me like that forever,* and behind her there's the sound of Deacon pumping the shotgun.

"If you're gonna do this, Chance, you better do it right fucking *now,*" he says. "We're not alone down here."

She kneels in the mud and undoes the straps on the backpack, folds open the canvas flap, but she's moving so slow, like running in a nightmare. All her effort, straining, and even these small movements almost more than she can manage.

"A slow sort of country," she says, pulling out a stick of dynamite and then another after it. "*Here,* you see, it takes all the running you can do to keep in the same place."

"You *had* to have heard it that time," Deacon says, a pause and then, "*There,* that's it. There's something on the goddamn pipes."

When Chance has taken six sticks of dynamite from the pack, embedded them in the mud like candles on a birthday cake, she reaches into a pocket of her jeans for the roll of green electrical tape.

The tape to bind the dynamite together and then she'll make another bundle from the last six sticks, just like she planned it hours ago, planned all of this out so deliberately, so precisely; the green tape to hold the dynamite together and then all she has to do is insert one of the brightly colored detonators into each of the bundles, the copper wire connected to the detonators, then, and the wire to the battery . . .

But that will take time, and if there is time here, if there's time like *that* here, she's losing track of it. Chance wraps the electrical tape around and around the first bundle of explosives, wraps it three times, charmed and magic number to keep away the bad things and "You're *dead,* asshole," Deacon says behind her. "You're *all* dead."

A minute or an hour later, no way to be certain with the seconds beginning to bleed together like this, one moment and the next no different from each other, and she reaches into the pack for the detonators. And the brick wall seems to shudder, gray and punky bits of mortar falling away, and she stops, stares directly at it while Deacon curses the noises she can't hear, sights that she can't see.

There's a trilobite, perfect bristly *Dicranurus* as big as a silver dollar, crawling slowly up the bricks, unexpected shimmer of phosphorescence at the tips of its long genal and pleural spines, the grotesquely retorted spines rising from the occipital rings like tiny horns, firefly specks of brilliance beneath its eyes; and she reaches out to touch it, reaching back across epochs, all the ages she named for Deacon recited the other way round. But the wall is crumbling now, shaking itself apart, and the trilobite sinks into it like a pebble dropped into a stream.

"Deacon, help me," she says, catching on too late, too slow or dull to see the strings until the show's almost over and it doesn't matter anymore. The wall shudders again and collapses, the disintegrating bricks sucked back into a night that the tunnel can only envy, darkness before there was even the premonition of light, still an hour before the birth of the universe in there, and she screams as eternity rushes out around her and Deacon pulls the trigger on the shotgun and the world slips away like a stain.

❖

Already twilight when Chance turns off Fourth Avenue into the parking lot of the Schooner Motel, this place probably a dump thirty years ago and nothing now but a cheap place to take hookers, somewhere for the crack whores and winos to hide out when they have the money to spare for a room. She has no idea why anyone would name a motel on the edge of downtown Birmingham something like that, *schooner*, more like a name for a motel in Panama City or Gulf Shores, some vacation city by the sea. She parks the Impala between a pick-up truck and a long, black Monte Carlo with a trash bag for its missing rear windshield, double-checks the number she scribbled on a Post-It note fifteen minutes ago, and then looks to be sure that the other three doors are locked before she gets out of the car.

The end of a stormy April day, tornadoes and she heard on the radio that seven people were killed in Mississippi. Nothing now but rain, and she forgot her umbrella, left it leaning against the coatrack by the door on her way out of the house. "Don't you go and forget your umbrella, Chance," her grandfather said, and "I won't," she promised him, but she forgot it anyway, her head too many places at once, too full, and so now she shivers in the cold drizzle and walks quickly across the parking lot towards the yellow cinderblock walls, the drab row of identical black doors. There are more cars and a narrow, stunted patch of deadbrown grass, a few hopeful clumps of clover and dandelions, before she reaches the doors.

"Number Seven," she says, but this is only number five, the room number painted directly onto the door in front of her, and so she walks down the row to seven and knocks. When no one answers, she knocks again, harder than before.

"Come *on*, Elise. I'm getting *cold* out here."

But no sign that anyone's even in the room except the lamp shining from the other side of the curtains and when she tries the knob it isn't locked, turns easy in her hand and Chance opens the door and steps inside out of the wind.

Two single beds and the wallpaper stamped with a faded bamboo pattern, gaudy wallpaper the swampy color of pea soup. Elise's purse is lying on the bed closest to Chance and she closes the door behind her and locks it.

"Elise? Where the hell are you?" but there's only the sound of water running in the bathroom for a reply. The bathroom door standing wide open and anyone could have come waltzing in here, anyone who pleased; Chance sighs and looks at the bed again, the familiar beaded purse lying there with everything spilled out of it, careless scatter of car keys and a pack of chewing gum, old movie ticket stubs and Elise's address book.

"I came as soon as I could," she says. "Are you decent in there

or what? You didn't even bother to lock the door," and Chance
walks past the bed to the bathroom where Elise Alden is sitting
naked on the toilet seat. The little bathtub filled almost to overflowing, steaming water almost all the way to the top, and Elise
looks up at Chance with puffy, red-rimmed eyes like she's been sitting here crying for hours. She opens her mouth to say something
but stops, and Chance sees the hesitant cuts on her left wrist, then,
the razor blade held between the fingers of her right hand and a
dark smear of crimson on the steel. The open and half-empty pre-
scription bottle sitting on the edge of the tub.

"I didn't think you were coming," Elise says, her voice hoarse,
hardly as loud as a whisper. "I didn't think that you would ever
really come."

Chance grabs one of the thin motel towels hanging from a rack
beside the sink, terry cloth that might once have been white, a long
time ago. "Give it to me," she says and when Elise doesn't move,
Chance takes the razor blade away from her, drops it into the tub
and wraps the towel tightly around her wrist to make a pressure
bandage. Then she glances at the amber pill bottle on the tub, the
orange-and-white capsules inside, Dreamsicle colors, and "How
much of this shit have you taken?" she asks.

Elise is sobbing something Chance doesn't understand, an apology or repentance, and Chance shakes her hard, shakes her until she
looks more angry than afraid. "How many of them did you take,
Elise?" she asks again.

"I don't *know*, okay? I can't fucking remember anymore," and
Chance doesn't wait for her to *try* to remember, takes the bottle and
runs to the telephone on the table between the beds, punches 911
and reads the label out loud to herself so she'll be ready when the
operator comes on the line, Pamelor, 75 milligrams each, and
"Don't you fucking *move*, Elise," she shouts back at the bathroom.

And that's when Chance notices the albino girl watching her
from the open motel room door, the girl and a sense of déjà vu so
strong and sudden that it makes her dizzy and she has to sit down
on the bed to keep from falling.

"I locked that door. How the hell did you get in here?"

"This isn't right," the girl says, her pink eyes bright as candy in
the garish light of the lamp and she takes a step towards Chance.
"This isn't where it really started."

"I don't know who you are," Chance growls back at the girl,
"and I don't know what you're talking about. But I want you to get

the hell out of this room right this minute." And then she's yelling into the telephone, yelling *at* the phone, because no one's picked up on the other end, five rings and still no one's answered.

"It was Sadie's idea," the albino girl says. "They're very, very old, Chance, and they *know* that you can hurt them. They all know now that we can hurt them, if we have to. But we don't have to. I was wrong—"

"Answer the goddamn phone!" Chance screams into the receiver and there's a splashing sound from the bathroom, and she thinks about the razor lying at the bottom of the tub.

"You can't save Elise from here. It's already too late here. You both already know what's under the mountain. You've already *seen* it." Then the girl with skin as white as flour, hair like strands of cornsilk, is standing next to her, standing right there in front of her, taking the phone from Chance's hand, prying it from her fingers.

"She's dying in there," Chance says, trying to think of words that will make the girl understand, tries to show her the bottle of Pamelor but she drops it and the capsules spill out and roll away from her across the bedspread.

"*Listen* to me, Chance. It can't be from *here*."

Chance reaches for the phone again and this time the albino girl slaps her, slaps her so hard that she tastes blood, so hard her head snaps back, and the motel room dissolves around her like a bad watercolor painting left out in the rain. . . .

. . . like liquid drops of fire from the sky, if there is a sky here, if there ever was or would ever be a sky here, anything that Chance would call a sky. And she stands someplace, sometime, everywhere and neverwhere, stands as the white stars fall around her.

"It's almost over now," someone whispers. "Don't be afraid," that voice soothing and so close, so familiar, but she knows she's never heard it before, voice from the day after she died or the day before she was born. And she turns her face up to see the lights streaming down on her from the abyss. They are the brightest and most beautiful things she's ever seen, beauty to break her heart because she knows that they're dying, all of them, and beauty to make her want to live again, because such things can be.

And the tall man steps from the black between the sparkling Roman-candle trails, and she does know *his* face, if she never remembers another she'll know his until the universe forgets itself. "I'm going to have to kill you," she says to him, except she might have done that already, his face erased when she pulled a trigger sometime else and "Oh, I knew that," the tall man says.

"You were going to hurt someone," and Chance tries to recall who, who the man was going to hurt, why she will have to kill him, and then it doesn't seem to matter anymore.

"Angels and devils," he says and smiles for her, not an unkind smile, but it's terrible, too, a smile like that. "Monsters and ghosts and gods," and he opens his hand so she can see the symbol burned into his palm. The shape that can't be, not without warping space, seven perfect sides and seven equal angles, and the darkness around him seems to flare and glimmer.

"Isn't it a marvelous thing to know?" he asks her. "Even if you forget it again in an instant, wasn't it worth it?"

"I'm half sick of shadows," she says to the man because it's the only thing left in her head, something borrowed from Elise's suicide note, high school Tennyson and a woman drifting towards her across the water.

"Aren't we all?" he says as the darkness around him flares again, supernova spinning backwards, the night opening its eyes, and she nods her head.

"You know the way, Chance Matthews. Hell, you *are* the way," and the man laughs like a dog laughing and she knows now or she knew or one day she'll know that the light is falling out of him, falling into him.

"Time is your cathedral. You *know* the present is only a pretty illusion in the minds of men. And I think you know that nothing has ever passed away, not entirely."

And the clock ticks, and worlds spin, and silt falls on the muddy floors of seas out of time where trilobites scuttle on jointed, feather legs, and she sees the tarot card in his hand, and opens herself . . .

. . . and Chance is lying on her back, then, staring up at the raindrops plunging towards her, kicked out of heaven and plunging helplessly towards the soggy earth where they began.

" 'Down, down, down,' " she says, and " 'I wonder how many miles I've fallen . . .' "

"You want to just leave her out here?" Elise asks, but Deacon is already hauling Chance to her feet. She shivers and leans against him, stealing the warmth off him, and kisses his stubbly chin, the arch of his long nose. "C'mon, girlie girl," he says. "Shake a leg," one arm around her tight as they step through the low, square archway leading into the tunnel. "It's time to go forth and explore the Stygian bowels of the world."

Chance laughs, but there was something strange and sad about the rain falling, something it means that she can't quite remember, can't forget either, so she doesn't start giggling again. Stops instead, stands with one hand tight around Deacon's arm, and "No," she says, trying to think through the haze of pot smoke in her head. "I don't want to do this, Deke. I don't want to do this again."

"Jesus, this was *your* dumb-ass idea," Elise says, taking another step towards the deeper gloom where the tunnel begins, where the two huge water pipes disappear beneath the mountain.

"Well, I think I've changed my mind," she says. "I'm cold and I think I'm going to be sick."

"Look," Deacon says, points at the iron chain lying on the floor of the blockhouse, rusty pile of chain like a snake coiled there. "We've already gone and committed a *crime* for you. This shit's breaking and entering, you know. And now you want to back out? I think you're just scared."

"Yeah," she says and pulls hard at his arm, pulls him an inch or so back towards the iron gate. "I am, Deacon. I'm *scared*. I'm just really fucking scared, all right?"

"Hey, okay, just a minute," and he's looking down at her, rain-water dripping from the end of his nose, his brown eyes hidden from her in the shadows.

"Please," she says. "It's not too late. Not yet."

He watches her for a second, watches her with those shadowed eyes, then Deacon Silvey nods his head, puts an arm around her and "Hey, Elise," he yells. "It fucking stinks in this place. Let's get the hell out of here."

Elise grumbles something rude from the darkness, pissed-off defiance, but then she's standing there beside them again anyway, marches past Chance and back into the rain. Deacon follows her, so Chance is the last one out of the blockhouse, last one out of that mustystale air that smells like mold and mud and the faintest hint of rot, faintest stink like an animal lying broken and dead on a scorching summer road. She pulls the heavy iron gate shut again and it clangs loud, the metal against metal sound of it echoing down the tunnel, and she stands there a moment, listening as the clanging noise grows fainter, listening until the only sound is the rain falling softly against the leaves overhead.

EPILOGUE

July

Two weeks after her grandfather died, and she wouldn't have ever come here alone, not without Deacon. Would never have come here at all, but the dreams have grown finally into something so real, so tangible, that they frighten her, the pale dream girl as real as anyone she has ever known awake. It doesn't matter that she doesn't believe in any of this psychic stuff, any more than the fact that Deacon does. Her therapist the one who finally sent her off to Florida, Dr. Miller who listens to her strange nightmares and makes notes on the pages of yellow legal pads.

"This isn't about what's factual, Chance," she said. "It's about what's *true*, what's true to you. You know that there's a difference, don't you?"

So now she's sitting here with Deke in this too-white, fluorescent-drenched room in a Tallahassee mental hospital. The ward where they keep the violent cases, all the patients who are a threat to themselves or someone else. Like something from a prison movie, she thinks, the cramped and shabby cubicles, the thick Plexiglas divider to keep the sane and insane apart and they can only talk through the big, black rotary telephones.

"You're absolutely sure you want to do this?" Deacon asks her, sounding worried and confused. "It isn't too late to back out."

"We've already driven all the way down here," she says.

"That doesn't matter. I wouldn't be angry."

But then it is too late, because a fat woman in a white uniform is leading the girl to the chair on the other side of the Plexiglas. The teenage girl dressed in blue jeans and a gaudybright Disney World T-shirt, Mickey Mouse and Pluto as if this wasn't already absurd enough. For a moment Chance can only sit silent and stare speechless at the girl, her hair and skin so white they're almost translucent. Her eyes like white rabbit eyes, shades of pink and scarlet, and she blinks uncertainly back at Chance from behind the protective plastic barrier, blinks her heavy lids that droop a little too much to be completely awake. *That's just from the medication,* Chance thinks. *Whatever they're giving her in here.*

Chance reaches for the telephone, but Deacon's already picked up the receiver for her, puts it in her unsteady hand, and the albino girl is watching her now the way a cat that isn't particularly hungry watches a careless bird. Then she lifts the telephone receiver on her side and "Hello," Chance says. "Hello there, Dancy. My name is Chance."

"Hello, Chance," the albino girl says and she's slurring a little. "You know my name."

"They told me. The nurses told me," and the girl nods her head once and glances back at the orderly standing guard behind her.

"They think they know everything," she says. "They think God comes down from Heaven every morning and reads them the newspaper."

Deacon's holding onto Chance's hand now, holding it tight, like he's almost as shaken as she is, and that makes her feel better. Maybe it shouldn't but it does, Deacon and all the weird things he tells her whenever he gets drunk enough, the stories about Atlanta and the things he's seen, the stories she's never really believed, but even he's unnerved that this girl is alive and breathing and sitting there looking back at them.

"I dream about you," Chance says. "For months now, I've been dreaming about you."

"Are they scary dreams?" the girl asks and she leans forward suddenly, moves quick and the orderly takes a cautious step towards her.

"Sometimes," Chance says, trying to think of the things she *needs* to say, the things she said over and over again on the drive down so that she wouldn't forget. She glances at Deacon, but his eyes are on the girl, staring at her like there's nothing else in the world and she might vanish in an instant.

"Sometimes, in my dreams, you're the one who's afraid, Dancy.

And I can't ever make you stop being afraid, no matter how hard I try."

"They give me these pills to make me not be afraid anymore," the albino girl says and looks back at the orderly again. "Sometimes I spit them out. They don't work, either."

"Dancy, I need you to tell me what you're afraid of, why I keep dreaming about you. Please, if you *know,* I need you to tell me." Chance is crying now, her eyes burning and tears rolling down her cheeks even though she swore to herself that she wouldn't.

"'There are things of which I may not speak,'" the girl says and then she rubs her hands together like they're cold. "I have done things, Chance. I have done so many things I can't remember anymore."

"No," Chance says and she leans forward now, too, places her left palm against the Plexiglas and this is the way she should have cried when her grandfather was buried, the night her grandmother killed herself, the way that she's never been able to cry her whole life.

"It's all right now, Dancy. I came here to tell you that. You can't seem to hear me in the dreams, so I'm telling you now, because I know we're awake and you can hear me."

"I try to *stay* awake," the girl says and now she's started crying, too. "But they give me these pills."

"It's okay to sleep, Dancy. I think that's what I'm supposed to tell you. I think that's why I dream about you. Whatever happened, whatever it is, you don't have to be afraid anymore."

And now there's a snarling, keening sound coming from the girl, like an animal trapped and dying, hurting and no way to know that eventually the pain will stop and she slams the telephone receiver against the divider so hard that one end of it shatters in a spray of jagged, black shards. Chance flinches, but she doesn't move her hand, her fingers that would reach through to the girl if she knew how.

"I am *not* afraid," the girl growls, hurls the words like stones or sharp knives, and pounds the broken phone against the Plexiglas again. Blood on her knuckles, blood smeared back and forth across the invisible divider to show it's there. "I am fire and metal wings," she says. "I am all the burning swords and I'm *trying* to forget you, Chance. I'm trying *hard* to forget you."

The orderly is on top of her then, dragging the albino girl back, fighting her, and in a moment there's another woman, a woman with a syringe and Chance wants to look away, wants to turn and run, as the needle pricks the girl's white skin. Then the nurse that led them in is standing behind Deacon and Chance. "You should both leave now, Miss Matthews," he says, his voice as soft as velveteen.

"I didn't mean for this to happen," Chance says. "You know that, Deke. You know I didn't ever want to hurt her."

Deacon takes her hand away from the Plexiglas, folds it up safe in his own.

"It isn't your fault," he says and puts his arms around her. "This sort of shit isn't anyone's fault, Chance," and in another moment the orderlies have taken Dancy Flammarion somewhere else and the nurse hurries them from the visiting room and down the long and sterile hallway that leads back to the day.

The End

GLOSSARY OF PALEONTOLOGICAL
AND GEOLOGICAL TERMS

(mya = million years ago)

actinistian   The coelocanths, one of the three major groups of lobe-finned fishes (or sarcopterygians), which first appeared in the Middle Devonian.

amphineuran   Primitive mollusks including the extant chitons.

brachiopod   Also known as "lamp shells"; marine invertebrates with two unequal valves.

bryozoan   Group of small, colonial, marine invertebrates, superficially resembling corals.

calcareous   Containing calcium carbonate ($CaCO_3$).

Carboniferous   Fifth subdivision of the Paleozoic Era, following the Devonian Period and preceding the Permian Period; 360 to 286 mya; in North America, the Carboniferous is subdivided into the Mississippian (lower Carboniferous) and Pennsylvanian (upper Carboniferous).

crinoid   Group of predominantly sessile echinoderms, common throughout the Paleozoic with some forms surviving to the present day. Crinoid stems are very common fossils and compose the bulk of many Carboniferous limestones.

Devonian   Fourth subdivision of the Paleozoic Era, following the Silurian Period and preceding the Mississippian Period; 410 to 360 mya.

eocrinoid   Among the earliest-known echinoderm groups, ranging from the Early Cambrian to the Silurian.

ferruginous   Term used by geologists to describe rocks with a high iron content, such as the Red Mountain Formation.

formation   In stratigraphy, the primary unit into which rocks are divided, based on distinctive features or combinations of distinctive lithic features (i.e., Pottsville Formation, Red Mountain Formation, etc.).

genal spine   In trilobites, elongated, paired, posteriorly directed processes from each side of the head (or cephalon).

geology   Science that studies the earth, including its history, physical composition, and the processes which have formed it.

hematite   A mineral, Fe^2O^3, the primary ore for iron.

horn corals   Solitary, conical corals (Subclass Rugosa) common during much of the Paleozoic.

Marsh pick   Double-headed pickax, named for American paleontologist O. C. Marsh (1831–1899), and commonly used by vertebrate paleontologists.

microfossil   Fossil remains of microscopic organisms, such as nannoplankton, forams, and pollen; the domain of micropaleontology, once crucial to the location of oil deposits.

Miraspidinae   Subfamily of spiny, Devonian trilobites, including the aptly named *Dicranurus monstrosus*.

Ordovician   Second subdivision of the Paleozoic Era, following the Cambrian Period and preceding the Silurian Period; 505 to 440 mya.

Paleontology   Branch of biology that deals with the history of life through the study of fossils.

Paleozoic   One of the eras of geologic time, occurring between the Precambrian and Mesozoic eras; 544 to 245 mya.

Pangea   The Pangean supercontinent comprised all the world's landmasses and formed during the Late Carboniferous, but began to break apart during the Early Mesozoic Era.

Pelmatozoa   Subphylum of echinoderms, most possessing jointed stems, including crinoids and eocrinoids.

pleural spine   In trilobites, paired processes of varied length arising from the body (thorax).

occipital ring   In trilobites, a portion near the rear of the head (or cephalon).

radula   Movable toothed or rasping structure found in the mouths of mollusks, used in feeding.

rhipidistian   Extinct group of predatory, freshwater lobe-finned fishes, dominant during the Late Paleozoic.

scale trees   Large members (some over thirty-five meters high) of the Lycophyta, the oldest extant group of vascular plants, forming a major component of Carboniferous forests.

siderite   A mineral, $FeCO^3$, which may also contain Mn and Mg; chalybite.

Silurian   Third subdivision of the Paleozoic Era, following the Ordovician Period and preceding the Devonian Period; 440 to 410 mya.

spicule   Small calcareous or siliceous structures, contained in the tissues of some invertebrates, including sponges.

temnospondyl   Very diverse and successful group of early amphibians, including giant, predatory forms reaching lengths of ten-plus meters. Common during the late Paleozoic, a few species survived as late as the Cretaceous Period (146–65 mya).

tetrapod   Literally, "four-footed." Sarcopterygian "fishes" possessing distinct digits at the ends of paired fins; fish- and amphibian-like vertebrates that first appear in the Late Devonian and eventually abandoned freshwater habitats for land, giving rise to amphibians, reptiles, birds, and mammals.

trilobite   Diverse group of marine arthropods with segmented shells and compound eyes, common worldwide throughout the Paleozoic. Divided into eight major orders, more than fifteen thousand species are currently known.